Praise for

LOYALTY

"*Loyalty*'s Fina Ludlow is my hero. If I were in a bad spot, I'd want her at my back. Don't miss it."

—Catherine Coulter, # 1 *New York Times*
bestselling author

"In her debut novel, Ingrid Thoft gives us Fina Ludlow, the newest private eye to prowl Boston's mean streets. Fina returns the female detective to the heart of the hard-boiled tradition: hard-drinking, hard-loving, moody. Writer Ingrid Thoft has given her a dysfunctional extended family that rivals the Ewings of *Dallas* fame, which adds a dimension not often seen in the PI novel."

—Sara Paretsky, *New York Times* bestselling author

"*Loyalty*, Ingrid Thoft's strong debut, is gripping, and Fina Ludlow, the black sheep of her male-dominated family of ambulance chasers, elevates it to a must-read. A seductive combination of sass and smarts, Fina reminds us just how hard it is for women in a male-dominated world without ever giving an inch. *Loyalty* reminds me just how great a PI novel can be. This is the start of something big."

—Ridley Pearson, *New York Times* bestselling author

LOYALTY

INGRID
THOFT

BERKLEY BOOKS | NEW YORK

THE BERKLEY PUBLISHING GROUP
Published by the Penguin Group
Penguin Group (USA) LLC
375 Hudson Street, New York, New York 10014

USA • Canada • UK • Ireland • Australia • New Zealand • India • South Africa • China

penguin.com

A Penguin Random House Company

LOYALTY

A Berkley Book / published by arrangement with the author

For information, address: The Berkley Publishing Group,
a division of Penguin Group (USA) LLC,
375 Hudson Street, New York, New York 10014.

ISBN: 978-0-425-26852-0

PUBLISHING HISTORY
G. P. Putnam's Sons hardcover edition / June 2013
Berkley premium edition / March 2014

PRINTED IN THE UNITED STATES OF AMERICA

10 9 8 7 6 5 4 3 2 1

Cover design by Richard Hasselberger.

ACKNOWLEDGMENTS

Lucky is the writer who has a team of supporters cheering her on this path. I am enormously grateful to those who have made *Loyalty* possible.

Davenie Susi Pereira has read every draft of just about everything I've ever written and offered keen observations, kind words, and graciously overlooked all the f-bombs. I would never have had the courage to say "I'm a writer" without the guidance and support of Catalina Arboleda. Erika Thoft-Brown and Chris Thoft-Brown were always eager readers, and their faith never faltered. Kirsten Thoft and Lisa Thoft rallied around me throughout this process.

Helen Brann took a chance on an unknown writer, and I will be forever in her debt. Ivan Held believed in me, and the teams at Putnam have been my greatest advocates from day one. Christine Pepe has been a wonderful guide on this journey, and I'm honored to have her as my editor and fellow pop culture aficionada.

My mother, Judith Stone Thoft, read countless drafts and provided insightful feedback every step of the way. Her love, humor, and grace are an example to me always, and, just so there is no confusion, she bears absolutely no resemblance to Elaine Ludlow.

Lastly, my husband, Doug Berrett, has been head cheerleader and my partner in crime for more than two decades. Quite simply, he is the best, and there would be no *Loyalty* without him.

1

~~~~~~~~~

This was her punishment. She was sure of that. There was no other explanation for the hell she was in. Being tied up and blindfolded had been bad enough. Then she'd heard the engines come to life and begun rocking against the walls of the small space.

That could only mean one thing: They were going somewhere, probably out to sea.

For days she had struggled to remain strong and optimistic, but now she gave in to her fear and sobbed uncontrollably. This was hard to do with tape over her mouth and a blindfold over her eyes, but every ounce of her energy was directed toward her outpouring of despair.

Minutes passed. She didn't know if it was six or sixty. The engine seemed to shift, and the boat slowed. A loud grinding sound prompted her to tighten her aching back muscles. The noise stopped after a minute, and she heard footsteps overhead.

When they pulled her out of the hole, she struggled to fight them, but it was useless. She was too weak, and they were too strong. Fresh air skipped across her skin, and she felt something like hope for a moment. But the hope died when the heavy, thick chain swung into her shins and around her calves. Hot urine trickled down her leg and raised goose bumps on her chilled skin.

Her arms and legs were cinched together tighter, and she was picked up off of her feet.

Then it was air.

Then water.

Then nothing.

"We can't find Melanie."

"What do you mean, you can't find her?" Fina asked.

"What I said. We can't find her."

Fina steered with her right hand and ate a hamburger with her left. She needed a third hand so she could flip the bird to the asshole who'd just cut her off on Storrow Drive.

"What do you want me to do about it? She's probably buried under a stack of clothes at Nordstrom."

"Just get over here," her father grumbled.

The elevator doors slid open to reveal the forty-eighth floor of the Pru, and Fina pushed through the glass doors etched with the words *Ludlow and Associates*. There were three receptionists behind the enormous granite counter, all thin, young, and pretty. Fina ignored them and followed the hallway through a series of turns. At the end, she found a blond woman she didn't recognize serving as the gatekeeper outside her father's door. Fina strode past her and walked into his office, where he was sitting behind his desk in a large swivel chair, his back to the view, a phone pressed to his ear. The blonde flapped into the room, and Carl shooed her away. He shot Fina an annoyed look and gestured to the phone. She shrugged and admired the view; Boston and Cambridge spread out before her, the Charles River a thick snake between the two. The grid of Back Bay looked orderly from this height, belying the disorderly Boston drivers darting through its narrow streets. It was the end of May, but they'd had a few days of heat that made the landscape appear fuzzy and blurred.

Carl Ludlow, Fina's father, was the king of personal injury lawsuits. He'd built an empire on attorney referrals, connecting the injured and wronged to the people who could squeeze the balls of every insurance company, doctor, and business owner across the land. He once told Fina—with relish—that one of his television ads ran somewhere in the United States every thirteen seconds. In the ads, he stared straight at the camera and proclaimed, "I'm Carl Ludlow, and I can make it better." Funny, that hadn't been Fina's experience growing up.

After a couple of minutes, her father put down the phone, and she plopped down in a leather chair in the sitting area of his office.

"Where are your manners, Fina?"

"I don't know. Ask my parents."

Carl was dressed as if he had a nontraditional awards show on the docket—the Grammys, maybe. He was wearing a beautifully cut silk suit in dark blue, which he'd paired with a slightly lighter blue shirt. His tie was a tonal match with his shirt, and bejeweled cuff links winked from his neatly pressed cuffs. His outfit was just this side of flashy, but stylish at the same time. Carl was handsome, in an alpha male kind of way: strong features, slicked-back dark gray hair, an even tan. You could tell from his broad shoulders and thick chest that he didn't slack off at the gym.

"You called, Father?"

"Melanie is MIA."

"Where's Rand?"

Rand, Melanie's husband, was Fina's brother and a partner in the firm along with their two other brothers, Scotty and Matthew.

"He's coming. Did you finish the Williams investigation?" Carl asked.

"Almost. I'll have the info to you by the end of the day."

A decade earlier, Fina had been slated to join the family business as an attorney, but flunking out of law school derailed that plan, for which she was eternally grateful. Carl punished her with a to-do list of menial tasks at the firm, but his strategy backfired when she got nosy and discovered that the most interesting work at Ludlow and Associates was being done by the lead investigator, Frank Gillis. Fina learned the trade from Frank and had taken over his role when he left the firm. Private investigation was an ideal fit for her: She could keep her own hours, roam the streets, and carry a gun.

Rand walked into the room, a phone glued to his ear. He was about five feet eleven, trim, with thick, wavy hair. He looked like a younger, slimmer version of Carl. He had full lips, a family trait, but rarely used them to smile.

"Okay, okay. I'll let you know." He tossed the phone onto the coffee table and lowered himself onto the couch. "Patty hasn't heard from her," he said, referring to their brother Scotty's wife. "Any ideas?" he asked Fina.

"Does she have a regular Thursday appointment?"

Rand shrugged. Fina waited and glanced between her father and brother.

"Look, Rand, I know your marriage has been dicey for a while," Carl snorted. "But she's still your wife." For Rand and Melanie, marital drama was like oxygen, and they had flirted with divorce on more than one occasion.

"Remind me why I'm still married to this woman?"

"Beats the hell out of me," Carl grumbled.

"You can file for divorce the moment she shows up," Fina said. "That should comfort you." Rand glared at her. "In the meantime, I need more info."

Carl leaned back in his chair and motioned for Rand to speak.

"Melanie didn't sleep at home last night, and she isn't answering her phone."

"When did you last see her?" Fina asked. She reached into her bag and pulled out a notebook and pen.

"Yesterday afternoon."

Fina made a beckoning motion with her hand.

"We had a meeting at Grahamson," Rand said. Grahamson was the pricey private school that their daughter, Fina's fifteen-year-old niece, attended.

"I assume the meeting was about Haley." Fina made a note. "Is she in trouble?"

"She's fine," Rand replied. "Then Melanie was going to have dinner with Risa."

Risa Paquette was Melanie's best friend and had a long history with the Ludlows. She'd grown up a couple doors down from the family and had attended school with Rand. Risa and Rand had lost some of their fondness for each other as they matured, but by that time, Risa and Melanie were as thick as thieves. Risa's connection to the family was solidified through their tight friendship, and Fina was used to seeing the Paquette family at most Ludlow celebrations and gatherings.

"Wait. Back up. Why were you at the school if everything is fine with Haley?"

Carl drummed his fingers on his desk. He was barely able to conceal his frustration when it came to Haley. The only kid in a family that would have benefited from more, Haley had been spoiled as a young child and had evolved into an entitled, impulsive adolescent. Fina had dragged her out of nightclubs and house parties on more than one occasion and knew that she dabbled in a variety of drugs and boys. Carl seemed to think that he could tame her if only given the chance, but Fina wasn't so sure. In her experience, teenagers were closer to wild animals than humans.

"There was a misunderstanding with her teacher. That's all." Rand and Melanie were the kind of parents who made teaching unbearable. They viewed Haley's private school education as a business transaction, one in which the customer was always right.

"So Melanie had dinner with Risa?" Fina asked.

"I don't know," Rand said, walking over to the window.

"You haven't checked with Risa?"

"You know I'm not her biggest fan, and the feeling's mutual. She's nosy and is always giving Melanie advice— bad advice. I'd rather keep her out of it."

Fina looked at her father and then Rand. "That's not going to be possible. I have to figure out who saw her last."

Rand started to protest, but was silenced by Carl. "Be discreet."

"Thanks for the tip, Dad. I assume you haven't con-tacted the police yet?"

"It's too early to file a report," Carl said.

"I realize that, but I could make some calls to see if anyone has heard anything."

"There's no point in involving the police unless they're actually going to do something. As soon as you tell them, it will leak to the press. We'll look like idiots when Mela-nie shows up."

Given their line of work, the Ludlows were disliked by entire populations in the city, including the police and blue-blooded Brahmins. Their wealth and the privileges it afforded were suspect to many, and Carl went to great lengths to avoid bad publicity. If he wasn't winning a huge settlement or making a donation to a worthy cause, he didn't want to read about the Ludlows in the *Globe* or the *Herald*.

"I don't want the police involved," Rand said.

"Fine," Fina acceded. "What makes you think she hasn't just taken off to the spa for a few days? She's done it before."

"I called her usual place. They haven't seen her," Rand said.

"She could be someplace new," Fina ventured.

"And if she is, you shouldn't have any trouble finding her," Carl said impatiently. "Do you want me to call Frank?"

"What? Dad, give me a chance to look before you decide I'm not up to the job."

"I thought you might want help, that's all."

"No, thank you. If I need help, I'll call Frank myself." Even though Frank had left the firm and was semiretired, sometimes he worked with Fina as a subcontractor. Fina loved working with Frank, but she resented her father's implication that she needed her mentor to get the job done. Frank had taught her well, and she managed just fine on her own.

"What about Haley? Has she seen Melanie?" Fina asked.

"I don't know. I haven't talked to her today," Rand said.

"Where is she now?"

"School?" he said.

Fina glanced at her watch. "It's four thirty. Isn't school out already?"

Rand shrugged. "So she's home."

Fina looked at Rand and blinked. "Rand, you don't know where your kid is?"

"Really? The spinster aunt is going to critique my child rearing?"

"You're right, of course. I have to squeeze a watermelon out of my lady parts before I can ask a child-related question."

Carl threw his hands up. "I don't want to hear about your lady parts!"

"Great! I don't want to talk about them. Did you see Melanie after the meeting?" Fina asked Rand.

"No. I was working late, and then when I got home, I worked in my office and crashed on the couch. I didn't realize she wasn't home until I went upstairs to shower this morning."

"Is her car in the garage?"

"Nope."

Fina tucked the notebook into her bag and pushed herself out of the chair. "I'll be in touch." She stopped at the door and turned to face her brother. "How are things with you two? Any worse than usual?"

Rand's face was blank. "Nothing to report."

Nobody said anything.

"Got it," Fina said, and left.

He couldn't bring himself to pack the junk drawer in the kitchen. Everybody has one—the drawer that holds batteries and extra keys, sunglass repair kits and Scotch tape. His also held a hospital ID, a Phillips-head screwdriver, and refrigerator magnets with pictures of sushi. It was all the stuff you always need and never need, but he couldn't foresee the day when he would wrap a present or bring a remote control back to life. He definitely wouldn't need the hospital ID. Even if they let him back, who would want to see him?

He left the junk drawer open and wandered into the now empty living room. He slid down the wall onto the floor and stared at the indentations left in the carpet by the furniture.

They had taken everything.

Bev congratulated herself every time she approached the condo. It was a stroke of genius buying a place smack-dab between two college campuses; no one questioned the young ladies who stopped by her place on a regular basis.

She climbed the broad staircase leading to the front door and slipped her key into the lock. Once inside, she followed the hallway toward the rear of the building and let herself into unit 1B. She glanced in the mirror hanging next to the front door and ran a hand through her silver hair. It was layered and fell to her collar, more short than long. Bev didn't think long hair was appropriate on women over fifty.

Satisfied with her appearance—that frosted apricot lipstick really was lovely—she proceeded into the condo. It was small, but the high ceilings and period details gave the space a sense of airiness despite its square footage. The living room area had a large fireplace and butter-colored walls. Yellow-and-white houndstooth fabric covered the club chairs and pillows on the white couch, and elaborate sconces flanked a large seascape painting on the wall. The bay window overlooked the parking area, but beyond, the green of the Esplanade peeked through. The galley kitchen led to a small bathroom and a bedroom that Bev had set up as an office. The only window in the office looked out on the alley, but Bev was glad for the privacy.

And the setting matched her high-end product: pleasure provided by beautiful, sophisticated women for discerning gentlemen. Bev would have been happy confining the business to the one enterprise and the one office, but these days, Prestige wasn't paying the bills. At least not the medical bills. Luckily all the new technology in the industry promised a wealth of opportunities, and Bev diversified and headquartered her new endeavors in a larger, cheaper space. She didn't involve herself in the details of the operation; no need to offend her delicate sensibilities. She knew what was going on in the basement of the main office—every good manager should know what their employees are up to—but she didn't dwell on it. Instead, she spent her time tweaking her business models and grooming the young ladies who worked for Prestige. She had no interest in the girls who worked for Gratify.

Except, that is, for one.

A couple years back, Nanny, Fina's paternal grandmother, sold her house in Natick and moved into Fina's parents' house in Newton with disastrous results. Fina wasn't surprised that an eight-thousand-square-foot house wasn't big enough for Nanny and her mother, Elaine, to peacefully coexist; Elaine was a challenging personality on her best days. Out of desperation, Carl bought a condo over-looking Boston Harbor and shipped Nanny to the big city. He even provided a high-powered telescope, and she spent most of her waking hours watching the boat traffic in and out of the harbor and the air traffic in and out of Logan. Her floor-to-ceiling windows were the modern-day equivalent of a front porch—minus the interaction with the neighbors—and her purview was more global than local; if British Airways flight 238 to London was running late on any given morning, Nanny knew it.

But Nanny had died six months ago, and Elaine hadn't packed up the condo. When Fina's lease ran out on her cramped, furnished apartment in Back Bay, she grabbed a duffel bag and some boxes and made the move.

After leaving Ludlow and Associates, Fina drove home and plopped down at Nanny's maple dining room table with her phone and her computer and started the search for Melanie. Everybody leaves a trail in their wake as they navigate the world on a daily basis. You fill up your car with gas, which leaves a receipt and maybe a brief interac-tion with the attendant. You drive through a toll booth, which captures your license plate and transponder num-ber. Maybe you stay home all day, but renew your library books online. It takes work to move through the world undetected.

Fina had an advantage in this search since Melanie wasn't a stranger. First she left a message for Haley and then called her sister-in-law Patty, who generated a list of Melanie's friends and their contact info. From those con-tacts, Fina identified her frequent haunts: the gym, nail salon, favorite stores and restaurants. She left a message for Frank Gillis asking him to keep his ear to the ground, and Rand's secretary provided credit card and banking information, car registration, and cell phone accounts. Some of this information Fina could track legally, and some required her to dip into the shady world that always operated under the surface of everyday life.

Just like there are people dying in the hospital while everyone else frets about losing those last ten pounds, there's a world of morally ambiguous and outright criminal activity that is always pulsing and known to few—just the criminals and the cops and attorneys who orbit their world. Over the years, Fina had built up a network of contacts, and she found it useful to tap into those contacts even if the missing person seemed far removed from that world. She'd learned the steps to a weird dance where she provided tips to shady characters and, in turn, they knocked loose helpful bits of information.

Her investigative tentacles unfurled, Fina stripped down to a sports bra and boy shorts and roamed around the living room waiting for her guest. Nanny had been a doting grandmother, and her love for her grandchildren was evident in the plethora of pictures that decorated the condo. There were baby pictures and graduation photos, shots from weddings and other celebrations. Fina didn't particularly like living under the watchful eyes of her siblings, but so far she'd been too lazy to do anything about it. She walked over to the sideboard and studied one photo in particular. A baby with shiny brown hair and dimples gazed back at her. Josie, Fina's sister and the firstborn, had died at the age of two and a half, before Fina was born. Fina had been named Josefina after her, and she was supposed to be her replacement, but that didn't exactly work out. Children were like NASA rockets: You poured money and time into them, but there was no guarantee they wouldn't veer off course seconds after blastoff.

A knock at the door brought Fina back. It was one of her regular visitors, someone special enough to be on the doorman's "send him up and don't bug the tenant" list.

Fina let her visitor in and spent ten minutes bending, walking, and contorting. Milloy, her masseur and best friend, assessed the situation, after which she hopped up on his massage table and he got to work.

The two had become fast friends during freshman year at Boston University while commiserating about their horrible roommates. Like soldiers in the trenches, they traded war stories of stolen breakfast cereal and hairballs in the sink (Milloy), and noisy couplings on the other side of the room (Fina). They had dated briefly, and now Milloy's ministrations occasionally concluded with a happy ending for both of them. But not always. Whatever happened, happened. Fina liked a friendship that was free of expectations and disappointment, and the arrangement suited Milloy just fine. He liked his life just the way it was.

An hour later, Fina rolled off the table like a wet noodle.

"You're a miracle worker. *Masseur* doesn't do you justice; it makes you sound like a gigolo," Fina called over her shoulder as she threw on some sweats and went to scrounge up some dinner.

Milloy collapsed the table. "Have you been talking to my mother?"

"Hah! One of these days she'll come to realize that you're a healer. I'm living proof."

In the kitchen, she washed the dirty dishes in the sink and doled out the leftovers she'd unearthed in the fridge. Fina didn't understand the point of washing dishes, putting them away only to take them out again. Why not wash dishes on an as-needed basis? She wouldn't have even bothered with dishes, but Elaine had ingrained in her that company called for fancy.

"This place is weird," Milloy commented when they sat down at the table and started to eat.

"What do you mean?"

"There's crap everywhere. An archaeologist could dig down through the layers. The first layer is old lady circa 1940, and the second layer is slob circa 2012." Fina took the same approach to home organization as she did dishes: Why put things away when you would need them again?

"Makes it easier to find things."

"How's that?" Milloy surveyed the scene. "It's a mess in here."

"Because I can see everything at once. Like there." She pointed at a small bundle of sheer fabric on the sideboard. "My thong is right there in plain sight."

"Why would your underwear be on the sideboard anyway?"

"Why wouldn't it?"

"You could keep your underwear in a drawer like most people do."

"Who has the time?"

"Everybody, apparently . . ."

While they ate, Fina filled Milloy in on Melanie's mysterious absence.

"You don't seem that worried," Milloy remarked.

"She's done this before, stomped off to Canyon Ranch in a fit of pique. If I lost sleep every time someone in my family had a hissy fit, I'd be exhausted." They continued eating and chatted about the Sox. A year in Boston could be marked by its sports teams.

Fina was happy to leave the dirty dishes in the sink, but Milloy insisted on stacking them in the dishwasher and wiping down the counters. He stretched out on Nanny's blue velvet couch, and Fina entered her notes into her laptop, keeping one eye on the baseball game. The only addition she'd made to the space, other than her clothes and general mess, was a fifty-one-inch TV with a paper-thin flat screen and a surround sound system that rivaled most movie theaters. There was no way she was going to watch sports on Nanny's old box.

Her phone rang.

"Any luck?" Carl asked.

"Not yet, but I'm on it."

Fina could hear ice clinking on the other end. "Just find her."

"Aye, aye, captain," Fina said to a dead line.

2

~~~~~~~~~~~~~~~~~~~~~~~

By Sunday, the Ludlows' irritation and mild concern had turned to alarm. There was no sign of Melanie—no withdrawals or charges from their joint accounts, no calls to friends. Melanie wasn't in any of the obvious places. E-mails appeared in her account at the usual rate, but nothing was sent from her outbox.

"I thought this was going to be wrapped up by now," Carl complained to Fina in his office that afternoon. There was no such thing as a weekend to Carl.

Fina looked at him.

"Well?" he asked. His jewel-tone tie was tucked into his shirt so as not to be spotted by the soy sauce accompanying his sushi.

"Well, what do you want me to say? If she were easily found, I would have found her."

"What the hell is going on, Fina?"

"I don't know, Dad."

"Any news on her car?"

Fina shook her head. Carl drummed his fingers on his desk.

"This doesn't mean we won't find her," Fina said. "It just means—"

"It means she isn't off somewhere getting her toenails painted."

"Exactly. We need to call the police."

Carl scowled.

"This is a legitimate missing persons case. We need to call them before they call us."

"Too late," Rand said as he walked into the office.

"What?" Fina asked.

"Risa reported Melanie missing to the cops, and they want to talk to me. They're starting to poke around."

"Goddamnit," Carl said.

Fina shrugged her shoulders. "It was bound to happen. I don't think the cops are a bad idea."

"Of course the cops are a bad idea," Rand exclaimed. "When has anything ever been improved by the cops?"

"They have resources, and from a PR perspective, you don't want to be seen as stonewalling the cops when your wife is missing. You know that."

"They don't give a shit about Melanie. They've just got a hard-on for me because of who I am. If I were some poor schmuck from Southie, they wouldn't hassle me about my missing wife."

Fina felt the color rise on her face. "Yeah, your missing wife. Don't forget about her."

"I'm sure she's fine," Rand said. "She's just doing this to make my life miserable."

"Right," Fina said. "Let me know what happens with the cops. In the meantime, I'm going to track down Risa. And Haley. I need to talk to Haley. She still hasn't called me back."

"Call her cell." Rand waved his hand dismissively and left the room.

A quick conversation with Risa's housekeeper revealed that Risa was out for her daily constitutional at the reservoir. Fina made the trip in her usual efficient driving style; speed limits were really just suggestions as far as she was concerned. Her 2008 Chevy Impala was a nondescript, forgettable car, which was completely the point. She couldn't tail people or run surveillance in a flashy car. As long as her vehicle performed (hence the custom V-8 engine), it didn't bother Fina if it was ugly. Elaine couldn't wrap her head around the idea that her car was a tool of her trade, not a reflection of Fina's worth. Her mother often urged Carl to buy Fina something better, like a luxury SUV with room for her imaginary grandchildren.

At the reservoir, she squeezed the Chevy into a barely legal parking space. She walked over the grassy embankment to the path that circled the water and searched in both directions. Three women who fit the bill—designer tracksuits and highlighted hair—were rounding the curve on her left. Fina sat down on a nearby bench and watched them approach. With their arms and jaws pumping, they called to mind a venue of vultures.

"Risa," Fina said when the women were about to pass her.

"Fina? What are you doing here?" She stopped walking and dropped her arms to her sides. "I suppose this is about Melanie."

"Could we talk?"

The other women were marching in place—interested in the gossip, but unwilling to fall below their optimal heart rate.

"Go ahead, girls. I'll call you later," Risa said.

After they had moved on, Risa spoke. "If your brother sent you to scold me, don't bother."

"I've been calling you for days. Since Thursday. Didn't you get my messages?"

Risa was silent. She tracked her companions as they climbed a set of stairs leading back to the street.

"I was calling about Melanie. Rand has been worried."

Risa snorted. "Really?"

"Yes, really."

"I find that hard to believe."

"Really?" Fina parroted. "Risa, we all know they've had some rough patches in the past, but he's genuinely concerned." In his own unique Rand way.

"I just find that hard to believe given what I witnessed at Grahamson."

"Why were you at Grahamson? There's no way Jordan's in trouble." Risa's children were polite and well behaved. She and her husband ran a tight ship.

"Of course not. I'm on the auction committee; we had a meeting."

"So what did you witness?"

"A fight."

"Between Rand and Melanie? What were they fighting about?"

"I don't know. I wasn't close enough to hear."

"So how do you know they were fighting?"

Risa wagged her finger at Fina. "You know better than to play lawyer with me. I was close enough to know that Melanie was upset. We were supposed to have dinner that night, but after Rand drove off, she told me she couldn't. Then she took off like a bat out of hell."

"Did she say where she was going?"

"Nope, but she was upset."

"And now you've contacted the police?"

"Yes, when I couldn't reach her, and when it became clear that Rand wasn't going to. I told them about the fight and her disappearance. Something's wrong, Fina."

"I know that now."

"And you can't be objective about this." Risa tugged on the waistband of her tracksuit jacket.

"Maybe not."

"You're not going to be able to investigate Melanie's disappearance if your brother's the main suspect."

"Who said anything about a suspect? I think you're jumping to conclusions."

"And I think you're kidding yourself. Think about it: His wife disappears, and he doesn't want to call the police? It's suspicious. If I disappeared, Marty would call the cops, pronto."

Fina watched two mothers walk by with babies strapped to their chests. "You've been watching too much *Dateline*, Risa."

It was true that Rand hadn't called the police, but that said as much about his personality and history as it did his alleged involvement in Melanie's disappearance. He hated the cops, not only because of a natural lawyerly distrust of them, but also because he'd skirted the law throughout his adolescence and adulthood. Carl had been kept busy cleaning up after Rand's "boys will be boys" transgressions, which included wrecked cars, drug possession, and rumored assaults. Rand was convinced the cops were out to get him and rarely factored his responsibility into the equation. He'd stayed out of trouble since joining the family firm—the only firm that would have him—but Fina doubted his feelings about the police would ever change.

"Will you let me know if you hear from her?" Fina asked. "If she wants to be left alone, that's fine, but we need to know that she's okay."

Risa studied her nails. They were buffed with clear polish. Unlike most of her chums, Risa was an avid cook and gardener and used her hands for more than just handing over her credit card. "Of course. I'll call."

"Thanks, Risa."

Fina watched her walk away.

"Josefina Ludlow. To what do I owe the pleasure?" Cristian Menendez asked as he climbed into her car. He'd agreed to meet her in a Dunkin' Donuts parking lot, a safe distance from his desk at the Boston Police headquarters. Cristian was a detective in Major Crimes, and he and Fina had swapped tips and bodily fluids over the years.

"I was in the neighborhood and couldn't resist visiting my favorite law enforcement officer."

"I bet you say that to all the cops."

"Only the handsome ones." Cristian was in his early thirties, with cinnamon skin and short, dark hair.

He adjusted in the seat so his gun wasn't digging into his side. "Broken any laws lately?"

Fina brushed a strand of hair away from her face. "You already know the answer, Cristian."

He grinned. "Yes, I do."

"So, you've probably heard that Rand's wife, Melanie, doesn't seem to be answering her phone."

"Is that how you describe a missing persons case?"

Fina shrugged.

"I've heard things. Which one is Melanie?"

"She's Haley's mom."

"Ahh. The niece," Cristian said. "The naughty niece."

"What have you heard?" Fina asked. Cristian looked at her blankly. "I'm not just asking for my brother. I'm trying to be a good citizen and help the police."

"This'll be good."

"You guys have resources, but you don't have much latitude when it comes to certain avenues of investigation. You can't break in somewhere, for instance."

"Neither can you, technically."

Fina waved her hand away. "I try not to get bogged down by technicalities."

"So I've noticed. What's your theory about Melanie?"

Fina looked into the window of Dunkin' Donuts. People really did eat doughnuts at all hours of the day. "My initial theory was that she and my brother had a fight, she got pissed, and was off having a hot stone massage and a juice cleanse in some small, artsy hamlet."

"And your current theory?"

"I don't know."

"And your brother?"

"What about him?"

"I hear he's meeting for a chat this afternoon."

"Cristian, he didn't do anything to her. He's an arrogant windbag, but they fight and make up all the time. She's probably just teaching him a lesson."

"Your family never does anything on a normal scale, do they? Like give one another the silent treatment for a day."

"Nope. We're from the 'play big or go home' school of thought."

"Sounds exhausting."

"It is. Speaking of wives, how are things with the ex?"

"She's busting my balls, as usual. I think going to court is her new hobby."

"I always pegged Marissa as the scrapbooking sort."

"I wish."

"Did that referral help at all?" Fina had set Cristian up with the meanest divorce lawyer in town.

"Oh yeah. He's a total prick."

"That's terrific. Just what you want in a divorce lawyer. Let me know if you need anything, and in the meantime . . ." She smiled at Cristian. "You'll keep me in the loop?"

"What's in it for me?"

"Sexual favors or doughnuts, your choice. I'll keep checking with people on my end."

Cristian tapped his knuckle against the window. "People like Mark Lamont? You still pal around with him?" Mark was an old friend from high school who made his living in various criminal enterprises. He successfully straddled the legal and illegal worlds, and he'd proven to be an invaluable source of information over the years.

"I don't pal around with him. We help each other."

Cristian leaned toward Fina like he was going to share a secret. "He's dangerous."

She leaned closer so their foreheads were practically touching. "I know."

Cristian opened the door and climbed out.

"Don't be a stranger!" Fina called after him.

He barely made it to the men's room in time. When he leaned over the toilet, his meager dinner came spilling out. He hadn't eaten much—half a pulled pork sandwich and a biscuit from the drive-thru, but it all came up with a slightly orange tinge, compliments of the orange juice he'd downed. He stayed doubled over, his palms resting on his knees, careful not to touch anything. The only thing worse than throwing up was throwing up in a filthy bathroom stall, like this one at the Cincinnati Airport. He wiped his face and damp brow with some toilet paper.

Maybe he could take a later flight. But doing that would presume he'd actually feel better later.

He needed to get to Boston. He needed to get to a room where he could close the door, lower the blinds, lie down on clean sheets, and forget.

Fina picked up a message from Carl ordering her to get down to the marina where the family kept their boats.

The Ludlows were a powerboat family, just another way they deviated from their more refined peers. Boston and its environs were sailboat country, and real mariners took pride in the cramped quarters and rustic charms of being under wind power. You weren't supposed to fire up the satellite TV and throw in a load of laundry while cruising out for a whale watch.

Carl's boats had gotten bigger as his practice became increasingly successful. He loved the material rewards of his work, but he got an even greater thrill from screwing the powers that be. He'd stumbled into medical malpractice and personal injury because of his daughter Josie's death—a strep misdiagnosis had led to massive organ failure and changed the course of the Ludlows' life—and it suited Carl to a tee. Every case was an opportunity for revenge, and you couldn't put a price on that.

Unlike Carl, Elaine had no interest in the water, so it was a way for Fina to have some family time with less drama. Her brothers started buying their own boats once they had the houses and fancy cars covered, and all of them were docked at the Boston Harborfront Marina across from Quincy Market.

Fina walked down the ramp leading to the slips and stopped at the stern of Rand's boat, *Guilty Pleasure*.

"Your father send you down, Ms. Ludlow?" It was Bob, the dockmaster. He'd been at the marina as long as Fina could remember and looked like Burt Dow, deep-water man, from the children's book. As far as Fina could tell, he'd been born seventy-five years old.

"Yeah, but he didn't give me any details."

"There were a couple of cops here earlier."

"What did they want?"

"Wanted to know when Mr. Ludlow, Rand, was last on his boat, and if I'd seen anything unusual."

"What did you tell them?"

"Said he was here a few days ago with the usual gear, some duffel bags and a cooler."

"Did they go on the boat?"

"Told them they'd need a warrant for that."

"My family's rubbing off on you," Fina said, and pulled two twenties out of her wallet. She folded them up and slipped them into Bob's hand. "If you see anyone else hanging around, give me a call." She held out her card between two fingers.

"Will do." Bob pocketed the card and started walking toward his office.

"And Bob? If anyone asks, I was here getting a sweatshirt that I left on my dad's boat."

Bob smiled.

Fina climbed onto the dive platform of Rand's boat. She found the key wedged between some life jackets under one of the seats in the stern and let herself into the cabin. She looked around the main space that housed the living room, dining area, and inside bridge, but nothing looked out of place. Downstairs, the beds in the staterooms were tightly made, and the bathrooms were spotless. Two duffel bags full of towels and sweatshirts sat on one of the beds, but Fina didn't see the cooler anywhere.

Back upstairs, she locked the cabin behind her and climbed the narrow stairs to the flybridge. The heavy canvas-and-plastic cover was snugly snapped in place, trapping the warm May sun. Downstairs, Fina edged between the cabin and the side railing and made her way to the bow. A slight breeze stirred her hair, and as she looked down toward the ripples on the water's surface, something caught her eye. Next to one of the cleats there was a small smear. Fina knelt down and looked closer.

Fuck.

She was unlocking her car when the cavalry arrived. Cristian and another cop got out of an unmarked Crown Victoria, and a second unmarked sedan arrived thirty seconds later. Cristian slammed his door and raised an eyebrow in the direction of the second car.

A short woman with frizzy, curly red hair got out of the passenger's seat and strode toward Fina.

"Fina," she said. "What're you doing at my crime scene, woman?"

Lieutenant Marcy Pitney stopped next to Fina and pulled a pack of gum out of her purse. It was Fruit Stripe gum with the colorful zebra on the pack. She unwrapped two brightly striped pieces and popped them into her mouth.

"Don't you need a crime for a crime scene?" Fina asked.

"I'm pretty sure I've got a crime." Pitney smiled. "And it couldn't have happened to a nicer guy. Actually, I would have been happy with any of the Ludlow men, but Rand's always been my least favorite."

"Not that you've rushed to judgment or anything."

"Of course not. I may be enthusiastic, but I follow the law." She was wearing an orange pantsuit that made her look like a habanero. Her boobs formed a shelf, and Fina wondered if she had to dig crumbs out of the chasm at the end of the day.

Fina didn't say anything. Carl had taught his kids that the worst clients were the ones who couldn't keep their mouths closed. When in the presence of the cops, shut up, shut up, shut up.

Pitney folded the gum wrappers and tucked them into her pocket. She looked at Fina and beamed. "I'm not going to have any trouble with you, right?"

"No more than you usually do, Lieutenant."

"And I know that you and Menendez have a special relationship, but there'd better not be any pillow talk," Pitney said, gesturing toward Cristian, who was talking to Bob outside the dockmaster's office. She leaned toward Fina. "Believe me, I get it. He's smoking hot."

"Isn't that sexual harassment?"

Pitney threw back her head and laughed. "Probably. I'm sure you can recommend a good attorney if he wants to sue."

3

Fina hightailed it over to Ludlow and Associates and paced outside her brother Scotty's office. Boisterous laughter was emanating from the room, and after a few minutes, four men exited the office, each looking identical to the one before.

"Come on in," Scotty said to Fina. "Michelle, can you tell everybody that we're ready?" he asked his assistant.

Scotty's office had the usual accoutrements of a successful litigator—glass desk, leather sofa, flat-screen TV, private bathroom—but it also boasted more personal touches, like a pinball machine. The lights on the Magic Genie were flashing, but the sound had been muted.

Scotty gave Fina a kiss on the cheek and directed her to the couch and chairs clustered around a coffee table. She sat down, leaned back against the couch cushions, put her feet up on the table, and looked at him. All of

Fina's brothers were handsome, and each of them looked slightly different from the others, like variations on a theme. Scotty was about five feet ten, with thick hair that was straighter and lighter than Rand's. He had a broad smile that lit up his face and a goofy laugh that Fina never tired of hearing. He looked like a brighter, happier version of Rand. And whereas Rand looked a couple of years older than his forty-three years, Scotty could easily pass for a couple of years younger than thirty-nine.

"What's up?" Scotty asked.

"I'd rather wait until everyone is here."

"Fine." He tossed a legal pad onto the coffee table and took a long drink from a mug. "You going to the Sox game on Wednesday?"

Fina stared at him. "You know, that kind of depends on whether or not our sister-in-law is still missing."

Scotty looked sheepish. "I don't mean to be insensitive, but the kids are excited, and I want to keep things as normal as possible for them."

Fina pulled out her phone and made a quick call to Mark Lamont. When the standard investigative channels don't net results, you have to dig deeper into the swamp of questionable activity. A lunch meeting with Mark was a good entrée to that world.

Carl walked into the room and took a seat behind Scotty's desk. Any office that Carl strode into was his. He was followed by Rand and Fina's other lawyer brother, Matthew. He looked like Rand and Scotty, but he was the most handsome of the Ludlow brothers. His wavy hair was a deep brown color, and when he smiled, a dimple emerged on his right cheek. At the age of thirty-six, he still looked boyish, and people sometimes thought he was younger than thirty-four-year-old Fina. This misperception never failed to annoy her.

Scotty grabbed a baseball off a credenza and began to toss it into the air. Matthew sat down on the couch next to Fina, and Rand leaned against the corner of the desk.

"Talk, Fina," Carl instructed.

"I haven't found any trace of Melanie, but the cops are at the marina executing a search warrant on *Guilty Pleasure*." None of the men looked surprised. "I had a quick look around before they showed up, and a couple of things are off."

Carl sat forward and laced his fingers together on the desktop.

Fina looked at Rand. "Where's the cooler that Bob saw you bring on the boat the other day? I searched the boat and didn't see it anywhere."

"I didn't leave it on the boat."

"Where is it?"

Rand shrugged. "I have no idea."

"You have no idea? What does that mean?"

"It means I don't know its current whereabouts."

Fina gave her father a pleading look.

"Rand, cut the shit," Carl said.

"It was old and smelly, so I left it outside Bob's office. I figured someone would want it."

"So you brought a large cooler to the boat, but now you can't produce it?" Fina asked.

"Asked and answered," Scotty offered.

"Don't get your panties in a twist over a cooler, Fina," Rand said.

"And the blood on the bow? How did that get there?"

To the average observer, the Ludlow men had no reaction, but Fina saw each register surprise in his own way. Scotty paused before tossing the ball into the air, Rand adjusted his butt against the desk, Matthew stole a glance at Carl, and Carl tugged on his shirt cuff.

"Are you sure it's blood?" Carl asked.

"It's blood. Not a lot, but it's there."

"Melanie cut her foot the last time we were out. She caught it on the cleat," Rand said.

"Did she see a doctor?" Matthew asked.

"No, it was a small cut."

Carl tapped his fingers on the desktop. "So what theory do we think the police are gonna concoct? That Rand carried Melanie onto the boat in the cooler, and when he dumped her, he left a bloodstain on deck?"

"That doesn't make sense," Scotty said. "If he threw her over in the cooler, why would there be blood on deck? Wouldn't it be contained in the cooler?"

"Unless some dripped out. Maybe the seal wasn't airtight," Matthew said.

"For Christ's sake!" Fina exclaimed. "We're talking about Melanie." Her family's ability to effectively sort through disturbing information was an asset in their work, but Fina found it discomfiting when the issue at hand was more personal.

"And I didn't kill her," Rand chimed in.

"Of course you didn't kill her," Carl said. "We don't even know if she's dead. We're just covering all the angles." Carl stared into space for a minute. His children knew better than to disturb him. "Scotty, get over to

Rand's house. They're probably executing a warrant as we speak. Matthew, call your contact at Channel Seven. I want Rand on the news tonight making an appeal. We've got to get ahead of this thing. Rand, you better talk to Dudley Prentiss, make him earn his fee. And you"—he pointed at Fina—"stick around."

The brothers filed out of the office and closed the door behind them.

Fina got off the couch and sat in one of the chairs across the desk from her father.

"This could all be cleared up real easy if you would find Melanie," Carl said.

"Yeah, I know, but like I've told you, she's off the radar. She hasn't accessed any of their joint accounts or used her Fast Lane transponder, and we can't get the records for her personal accounts without a court order. So far, no money, no Melanie."

"Whatever happens, I don't want this coming back to us. So from now on, update me before your brothers."

"Before Rand?"

"Especially before Rand."

"She's his wife."

"Is it so hard for you to do what I say?" Carl asked.

Fina ignored the question, just as she would probably ignore the directive. "Does Mom know what's going on?"

"She knows what she needs to know."

Fina stood and walked toward the door. "You know I don't have a problem breaking most laws, but if Rand did something to Melanie—"

"If Rand did something to Melanie—and that's a big *if*—our job is to support him."

In other families, *support* meant bringing a dish to Thanksgiving.

In the Ludlow family, it could mean all kinds of things.

The next morning Fina rolled out of bed, showered, ate a cold Pop-Tart, and perused the floor. She was blessed in the looks department, and she tried to make the most of it, particularly when meeting with certain contacts, like Mark Lamont. She opted for a snug T-shirt, jeans that made her ass look glorious but covered her business, and wedge sandals with three-inch heels. She took special care with her makeup—more than just the usual mascara and lip gloss—and studied her reflection. Carl and Elaine were both attractive and had passed good looks on to all their offspring. Fina had her mother's high cheekbones and her father's wide mouth and ample lips. Taken individually, Fina's features were imperfect, but together, they melded into a unique, beautiful face. Her skin was clear, and there was a faint smattering of freckles that emerged after time spent in the sun. The freckles, and the possibility of eventually looking like a saddlebag with eyes, prompted Fina's regular sunscreen use. She was also blessed with a great figure and the metabolism of a hummingbird. Fina knew she was lucky, but hey, her family was nuts; she deserved a consolation prize in the genetic lottery.

After working the phones for a few hours, Fina dropped her car with the valet at the Liberty Hotel rather than hoofing it from a nearby parking garage. The hotel was a former Boston city jail, which combined the original building with a new wing built for relaxation, not penance. She stepped onto the escalator and took a moment to appreciate Mark's choice of location, an overt "fuck you" to everyone who thought he belonged in jail, which, quite honestly, he did. The escalator carried her up to the lobby with its soaring ceiling and enormous wrought-iron chandeliers. The brick walls of the original jail contrasted with the modern reception desk and conversation clusters of leather furniture. Metal catwalks circled the walls, and former cells had been incorporated into the lobby-level restaurant.

Mark was easy to find; he exuded wealth and power, which may have been a function of the bodyguards who always lingered nearby or the impeccable tailoring of his suits. He was sitting on a black leather couch in the corner, and a waitress was leaning over him. Fina approached him and was swiftly met by the chest of one of his guards. Mark waved him aside, and she took a seat in the chair next to him.

"Have you eaten, Fina? The skirt steak is out of this world."

"Just water, thanks," she told the waitress, who was poured into a skintight black dress.

Mark leaned over and kissed Fina on the cheek. "You look gorgeous, as always."

Unlike Fina, Mark wasn't improving with age. He'd gained weight since she'd last seen him a couple of months before, and his hairline was receding. The sorta cute guy from high school was quickly becoming a distant memory. Mark was Scotty's age and was part of a clot of boys who frequented the Ludlow household during high school. Carl was always working, and Elaine was always oblivious, which made their home the ideal spot for teenagers looking for trouble. Like Risa, Mark had stayed in touch over the years, and just as the Ludlows' wealth and power increased, so had his. Mark's relationship to the law, however, was more fluid than the Ludlows'.

"You look prosperous," Fina said.

He grinned. "So." He settled back into the couch and pulled his jacket across his wide stomach. "What do you need?"

"I don't know if you've heard, but we can't locate Rand's wife, Melanie."

Mark cocked an eyebrow. "I hadn't."

"Well, she's dropped out of sight, and we're starting to worry."

"The Ludlows are worried about something?"

"Not worried exactly, but concerned. You know everything that goes on in this town. I thought if there's something to hear, you'd have heard it." Fina had yet to meet a man who didn't fall for this line, even the jaded, savvy ones. "Here's a picture," she said, and reached into her bag.

Mark laughed. "I know what she looks like, Fina."

"I know, but it might help jog your memory."

Mark took the picture and studied it for a moment. "Your brother never changes. None of them do. Never lose their hair or gain any weight."

"They all have weird alpha male eating disorders. Tons of protein, wheatgrass smoothies, hours on the rowing machine. Trust me, they're trim, but miserable."

Mark kept looking at it. "I haven't heard anything, but I could ask Vanessa. You know she can be discreet."

She has to be, Fina thought, *given that she's married to a criminal.*

The waitress returned with a full tray. She gracefully

dipped down to her knees, a move that smacked of strip club, and balanced the tray on the edge of the coffee table. She slid a large plate with a slab of steak, fingerling potatoes, and a bloodred tomato salad in front of Mark. Next to it, she placed a jar of ketchup and a cup of black coffee. Fina took the glass of water she was offered and cradled it between her hands. She waited for the waitress to leave.

"This may just be some tantrum on Melanie's part," Fina said.

"Sure, I understand." Mark cut a large piece of steak, and Fina watched the pale pink juices dribble onto the plate before he popped it into his mouth. "How about I let you know if I hear anything?"

"That would be great. I appreciate it." Fina sat back in her chair and sipped her drink. She didn't want to spend any more time schmoozing than she had to, but just like the business world, the world of crime and punishment has its rules of etiquette. "So how are Vanessa and the kids?" she inquired politely.

Thereby followed a fifteen-minute monologue about little Bobby's recent triumph on the soccer field, an exploit that a casual listener might have mistaken for a World Cup final given Mark's play-by-play description. Fina's eyes were just starting to glaze over when Mark took the last bite of tomato and wiped his hands with his napkin.

"It's always good to see you, Fina," he said, dismissing her.

"You too. Thanks for keeping your ear to the ground."

Fina drained her water and slipped the photo into her bag.

Mark covered her hand with his. "You need anything, you'll let me know?"

Sometimes, Mark seemed like such a caricature that Fina had trouble taking him seriously, but then she'd remember that he was rumored to be responsible for a few murders. There was nothing funny about him.

"Of course. I appreciate the offer. Give my love to Vanessa and the kids."

The bodyguards parted like the Red Sea, and she walked toward the escalator. She knew that Mark and his goons were examining her butt, so she added an extra little swing to give them a thrill.

The red-faced uakari monkey was the subject of this episode of *Mutual of Omaha's Wild Kingdom*. Bev smoothed the blanket over Chester, sat down in the recliner, and picked up a copy of *Southern Living* magazine. She took off her shoes and rotated her ankles, which were sore. The nurses had just changed shifts, and the replacement peeked in to check on Chester.

"He's fine," Bev said without looking up from her magazine. "I'll let you know if he needs anything."

The young woman went down the hall in the direction of the small bedroom that had become the base for all the home health care workers. Initially, Bev considered putting Chester's hospital bed there, but it would have left space for little else. Instead, she pushed back the furniture in the living room and that became his room. One of the muscular male nurses had moved a TV in and placed it on a side table. Bev wasn't a big fan of TV, but Chester seemed to enjoy the nature and history programs, and it was better than having him staring into space for hours on end.

She supposed they could move and get more space, maybe someplace out in the suburbs, but Bev loved their Beacon Hill condo. The white stone exterior and curlicue railings reminded her ever so slightly of her childhood in the South. Not the same as Mississippi, obviously, but it was the best she could do.

She also didn't want to move for fear of what that might signal to Chester. If they left their cramped, many-storied home in the heart of the city, it would be a sort of surrender, giving in to the massive stroke that had robbed Chester of his faculties. And Bev didn't care what the doctors said; he was in there, somewhere, garnering strength to reemerge. As long as they stayed on Beacon Hill, there was hope that he would improve, and one day they'd stroll hand-in-hand through the Public Garden.

A cell phone rang, and Bev dug into her large leather purse and checked the number. It was Janie, her office manager.

"Yes, dear? What can I do for you?"

"I'm sorry to bother you at home, Mrs. Duprey, but I thought I should call."

"Of course, it's no bother. Just let me scoot into the other room. I don't want to disturb Mr. Duprey." Bev held the phone against her chest and patted Chester's hand, which was thin and delicate like tissue paper. "I'll be right back, sugar."

"What is it, Janie?" She asked once she had closed the kitchen door.

"I have a client who wants to see Molly tonight, but she's not available. I tried to convince him to see someone else, but he's throwing a tantrum."

"Well, we don't like that, do we? No tantrums allowed."

"Nope, and normally I would tell him to be in touch when he could control himself, but I noticed that there's a flag in his file."

"What kind of flag?"

"Just a note that you should be contacted if anything out of the ordinary happens with him."

"What's his client number?" Bev looked at her reflection in the kitchen window. Her hair was looking a little more gray than silver. She'd have to see to that.

"Seven-four-six-eight."

Bev stopped running her hand through her hair. "You were right to call me. He's an unusual and important client. Give me Molly's number, would you, darling? I'm going to call her and see what I can arrange."

Bev called Molly and convinced her that one appointment at twice her usual rate was a fair trade for missing her favorite reality TV show.

"You take good care of him," Bev instructed.

"Yes, ma'am." Bev taught her girls Southern manners even if they had grown up in Alaska. Everything went more smoothly when there was a measure of civility.

Bev hung up and riffled through the cabinet. She pulled out a bag of chocolate chip cookies and popped a few in her mouth. She knew she shouldn't, but between Chester and the business, the stress was doing her in.

Fina spent the day pounding the pavement, trying to meet face-to-face with everyone in Melanie's life and ferret out where she might be. Melanie knew a lot of people, and

Fina's lower back was aching by the end of the day. She went home to Nanny's, soaked in a hot bath, and was drying off when her phone rang.

"Hi, Milloy."

"Sorry I'm a few minutes late. I'll be outside in five."

Fina paused and glanced around as if she might find some illuminating information on the bathroom walls.

Milloy sighed. "Don't tell me you forgot."

"Of course I didn't forget. I'm just finishing up getting ready. Where are we going again?" Fina dropped her towel, dashed into the bedroom, and began pulling clothes from the closet. "Hamersley's?"

"No, Davio's. It's my mom's favorite."

"Right, of course. I'll see you soon." Fina threw the phone onto the bed and pulled on a pencil skirt and a silk blouse, released her hair from its messy updo, swiped on some lipstick, and carried a purse, shoes, and some earrings with her into the elevator.

Milloy's parents visited a couple of times a year from Oakland, and during the more recent visits, Fina had done duty as his dinner companion. They didn't explicitly claim they were dating, but they didn't disabuse Milloy's mother, in particular, of the notion that they were romantically entangled. Fina suspected that his father was onto their ruse, but probably agreed that keeping his wife happy was worth the subterfuge. Milloy's mom was a Chinese immigrant who wanted her son to find a nice girl and start making babies. At least with a woman by his side, she could cling to the possibility. Fina was ideally suited to the job; she didn't have any trouble playacting, and she could hold her own in a fancy restaurant and make casual conversation. And she liked helping Milloy; he always did the same for her.

Two and a half hours later, stuffed with lobster bisque, duck confit risotto, tiramisu, and red wine, Fina and Milloy were back on Nanny's blue velvet couch.

"Are you up for a field trip?" Fina asked Milloy as he skipped through the channels.

"What do you have in mind?"

"It's a long shot, but I can't just sit around doing nothing. Let's poke around at Crystal," she said, naming a huge nightclub popular with a weird cross section of people, including rich kids looking for trouble, gangsters, and cougars on the prowl. She knew that Melanie had been there on a few boozy girls' nights out. Fina didn't think she frequented the place, but if you were looking for dirt, Crystal was a good place to start.

"There's nothing on. Sure, why not?"

Fina went into the bedroom and changed out of her more conservative dinner attire into a tight black dress that skimmed the top of her knees. She slutted it up a little with strappy high heels, smoky eye makeup, and a few strands of cheap necklaces. She liked to think that she could pass for midtwenties and shave ten years off her age with the proper clothes and dim lighting, but it may have been her own faltering eyesight that allowed her that illusion. She knew she looked good, but it wouldn't be too long before the dreaded suffix was added to that assessment: *for her age*.

Milloy was perfectly dressed in his well-fitted suit. He didn't have to fiddle with his age or degree of cheapness in order to get into the club; he exuded mystery. Milloy was very handsome, and his Chinese heritage always made people ask, "What are you?" a question that never failed to irritate him. "I'm human, man," was his standard response.

At the club, he turned his keys over to the valet, gave Fina his elbow, and they walked to the front of the line outside of Crystal. The bouncer was short and overmuscled, each thigh the size of a toddler. He looked them over, and when he hesitated, Fina pulled on Milloy's arm.

"This is a joke. Let's go to Club 100," she said.

The Neanderthal looked anxious for a moment. Milloy shrugged, and they turned away. The bouncer reached for the velvet rope and unhooked the clasp. They walked through the door. Nothing like seeming uninterested to make you interesting.

Crystal looked small from the outside, but actually stretched all the way from the street to the Mass Pike, which butted up behind it. The space had a low ceiling and was painted black, which contributed to the tunnel-like feel. It was dominated by the dance floor and anchored by the DJ's setup. A huge bar spanned the left side of the room, and tables littered the right side. There was a staircase near the entrance that led to the VIP section.

Milloy and Fina parted company so she could snoop and he could scoop. She made her way through the crush of bodies and found a bartender who wasn't completely besieged by underage girls ordering fruity drinks.

"Can I get a Sam Adams?" She held a twenty between two fingers, and the bartender reached behind the bar, pulled out a bottle, and popped off the top.

"Ten bucks," he yelled over the din.

"Jesus," Fina said. She laid the twenty on the bar. "Is Willie here tonight?" Willie Kendrick was one of Fina's go-to guys for reliable information of dubious provenance.

The bartender started mixing a drink for the young guy who had muscled in next to her. "Ask Dante." He looked up at the VIP section. "He's upstairs."

"Thanks. Keep the change."

Fina took her beer and ran the gauntlet through the crowd. At the top of the stairs, she asked for Dante and watched as a neckless bouncer walked over to the largest table in the corner and spoke to a young man seated there. She'd heard of Dante Trimonti, but hadn't had the pleasure of his acquaintance. He had a reputation as a businessman (read: pimp) on the rise who was ruthless, crazy, and in love with himself.

Dante was ensconced in the circular booth with two girls on either side, like a young Hugh Hefner. A discussion between him and the bouncer ensued, and long stares were leveled in Fina's direction. She nursed her beer, and after a few minutes, the bouncer came back and beckoned her into the VIP area. As she approached the table, the four young women slid out and scattered like birds. She sat down at the edge of the booth and looked at Dante. He was probably in his early twenties and was handsome, but in an oily way. His hair was slicked back and his T-shirt clung to his pecs. He raised his arms and spread them across the back of the booth, providing a glimpse of his abs, which were hair-free and sculpted. He grinned at her.

"You like what you see?"

"I bet you work out a lot."

"I don't get this way by sitting on my ass."

"Nope."

Dante leaned forward and rested his elbows on the table. "You're a little old for what I'm looking for."

"What are you looking for?"

"I mean, maybe you could do the naughty soccer mom thing, but . . ." He squinted at Fina. "You got a nice rack." He raised his glass in a toast to her boobs.

"Yeah, I'm actually not looking for a job."

Dante frowned slightly. "What are you looking for?"

"Willie."

"He's not here, sweetheart."

"Where is he?"

"None of your business."

"Hmmm."

"We're done," Dante said, and tipped his head toward a bouncer who began to approach the table.

"Hold on a sec," Fina said, waving away the bouncer. "How about her?" She pulled out the family photo of Rand, Melanie, and Haley and placed it on the table. She pointed at Melanie.

Dante looked at the picture. There was the briefest flicker of a question mark on his face, which quickly morphed into a scowl.

"This isn't the goddamn lost and found." He pushed the picture away dismissively and scanned the room.

"Dante—can I call you Dante?—I'm asking you because you're in the know. Everyone says that if something is going on, you know about it." The young, dumb ones were highly susceptible to flattery, too.

He straightened up at the compliment and then reached down and adjusted himself. "Maybe you're a cop."

"I'm not." Fina reached into her bag and pulled out her license. "I'm a private investigator." She handed it to him, and he studied it for a moment.

"Josefina Ludlow. You related to that lawyer?"

"I'm related to all of them."

"I know about your pops."

"Yeah, everybody does. I'm not looking to make trouble for you, and I don't care about your business." Fina straightened the picture on the table. "This woman is missing. People care about her and are looking for her."

Dante flicked the picture toward her with his fingernail. "Can't help, Josefina Ludlow."

Fina returned the picture to her bag. "Got it. If you see her . . ." She handed him her card.

He reached out and grabbed her wrist. "Now, why would I do that?"

"Because I know lots of people, and someday, I might be able to do you a favor."

"You'd do a favor for a guy like me?"

Fina shrugged, pulled her hand away, and slid out of the booth.

Downstairs, she did a cursory search for Milloy, and in the process was cornered by an overeager BU student. Ahmad from Saudi Arabia invited her back to his penthouse apartment at the Ritz, where she could snort some blow and give him a blow job. Tough offer to turn down, but Fina took a rain check and left without Milloy.

4

The next night, Fina sat in her car in front of Rand's house waiting for Milloy. It was nine P.M., and she'd spent the morning being deposed for a case she'd investigated and the afternoon tracking down the meager leads she had. Nobody had heard from Melanie—at least nobody would admit it. She had fallen off the grid, which wasn't easy to do as long as you were breathing.

A black BMW pulled up behind her, and Milloy got out.

"You gotta be kidding me," he said as they walked up the path to Rand's enormous colonial Tudor.

"You can see why I called you," Fina said. She knocked and opened the front door simultaneously. "I can't search this place on my own."

Milloy shook his head.

"I just want to take a look around, and I trust you. You're discreet and can be devious; my favorite combination."

Scotty greeted them. His tie was off, and he had a tumbler of scotch in one hand. The foyer was the size of a small apartment, with marble floors and a sweeping staircase.

"Dad said the cops were here yesterday," Fina said.

"And today," her brother commented.

"So what'd they take?" she asked.

"A couple of bags of clothes and some boxes of paperwork." He grabbed his suit coat off the stairs and shrugged into it.

"We're going to take a look around," Fina said. "Is Rand here?"

"At the office. Haley's upstairs, though, watching TV."

Scotty left, and Fina pointed Milloy in the direction of the living room, dining room, and guest bedrooms—the rooms that saw the least amount of traffic—and she went downstairs. The lower level of the house boasted a large family/media room, an outfitted exercise room, and Rand's office. Both the family room and his office featured French doors that opened to the backyard, which was dominated by a large in-ground swimming pool and Jacuzzi and beautiful landscaping, including a pristine lawn and a plethora of flowers and shrubs. Blue and purple hydrangea bushes bordered the grass, and another bed boasted rosebushes, their colors only hinted at by the tight buds. The rhododendrons had bloomed and their waxy green leaves were left behind. Undoubtedly the gardener had picked the flowers once they'd lost their beauty; Melanie cared how things looked.

Fina stood at the door of Rand's office. It was anchored by an oriental carpet, and the furniture was made from walnut. The desktop was empty except for a few desk accessories and a pad of legal paper. Fina took a seat in the executive leather chair and began to open the drawers and riffle through the file folders. Next, she moved on to the custom-made filing cabinets, the media cabinet, and the marble wet bar. An hour later, she had nothing to show for her search, except the news flash that her brother was outrageously rich and had a luxurious lifestyle, as evidenced by $40,000 monthly credit card statements for first-class airline tickets, restaurant tabs, and an account at Nordstrom.

Fina climbed two flights of stairs and found Milloy reaching into the depths of a linen closet. She padded down the carpeted hallway and went into the master bedroom. The walls were painted a faint mint green, and another large rug dominated the wood floor. Venetian glass dangled from the elaborate chandelier in the center of the room, and a marble fireplace stood opposite the bed. The wall was dotted with paintings in heavy gold frames, the themes of which seemed to favor boating parties and children frolicking. If their value could be measured in ugliness, then Fina imagined the paintings were priceless.

She looked through the drawers of the matching bed-side tables and found nothing to raise suspicion. The first dresser she searched was obviously Rand's—lots of black socks and boxers. Fina didn't like pawing through people's personal belongings, and there was something particularly creepy about searching through the underwear drawers belonging to her brother and sister-in-law. Melanie's stash was equally boring; pricey, neutral-colored French bras and panties were neatly laid out in the top drawer of the bureau. The other drawers held neat stacks of designer clothes. The walk-in closet was vast but, thankfully, organized, and if Melanie had packed a bag or hit the road with clothes, it certainly wasn't obvious. Not that it would be, given the size of her wardrobe.

Moving on to the master bath, Fina found Melanie's ridiculously large collection of firming lotions and moisturizers. There was a drawer of skin care samples from Neiman Marcus, which she pocketed before opening another drawer to continue the search. Beneath the standard over-the-counter pills, Fina found bottles of Xanax and Valium with Melanie's name on them, which she slipped in her bag. Was it her, or are parents just stupid? You have a teenage daughter with shoddy judgment, and you leave prescription drugs in your bathroom? Duh.

The sound of a TV drifted down from the loft on the third floor, so Fina slinked into Haley's room. It was straight out of a furniture catalog or a teen magazine. The walls were painted lavender, and filmy white curtains hung from the top of the large windows. The bedding on the queen-size bed was sky blue and lavender striped, and the shaggy rug stretching across the floor was light blue with large white polka dots. There were a dozen pillows of various sizes topping the bed. The surfaces of the white painted furniture were clear, with monogrammed fabric boxes neatly stacked on shelves. The floor was free of clothing, and when Fina opened the door of the large walk-in closet, she was greeted by a color-coded spectrum of neatly hanging clothes.

It reminded Fina of her own teenage room, a memory that never ceased to piss her off. Elaine had always insisted that Fina's room be neat and tidy, and she had no com-punction about barging in and rearranging things. First of all, Elaine had thousands of other square feet to rule, and secondly, whatever happened to having an outlet for a little self-expression? Teenagers have to get their ya-yas out somehow, and having a pigsty for a bedroom seemed to be a healthy way to do that. The alternatives—like banging the boys' lacrosse team—were undoubtedly more unsavory than an unmade bed.

The neatness of the room made Fina's search easy, but she paid special attention to the hiding places she'd employed as a teenager—zippered suitcase pockets, shoes, the underside of desk drawers. She did find a small stash in one of the hollowed-out compartments of the box spring, but decided to leave the dime bag and rolling papers. She didn't want Haley to know about her little search. When Fina was a teenager, she'd hidden a bag of revealing clothes in the deep recesses of her closet and would stuff it in her backpack and change after leaving the house. Given the current state of teenagers' clothing, this was no longer necessary; walking around buck naked was the only uncharted territory.

Fina climbed the stairs to the loft and found Haley sprawled on a leather sectional. Her niece was beautiful, with long, blond hair and a knockout figure. There was no question that her body was leaps and bounds more advanced than her brain. She was wearing gray sweat shorts, and her midriff was exposed in a clingy tank top. Fina sat on the arm of the couch and watched the TV for a moment. It was a reality show featuring buff guys and seemingly sex-crazed girls. *No wonder the rest of the world thinks Americans are idiots*, she thought.

"Don't even start the lecture," Haley said, looking up at Fina.

"What lecture?"

"The 'there's too much sex and too much drinking on these shows, blah, blah, blah' lecture."

Fina shrugged. "I don't care if you have bad taste in entertainment."

Haley snorted. "Thanks."

"I've been calling you for days."

"I've been busy."

"Doing what?" Fina asked incredulously.

"Just . . . stuff."

Fina sighed. "So I'm assuming you haven't heard from your mom."

"I haven't heard from my mom," Haley said in a monotone. "I wish everyone would stop asking me that."

Fina and Haley both watched the TV for a moment. A guy with enormous pecs was trying to convince a girl with equally large pecs that he loved her. Fina looked at her niece, but neither fear nor anxiety registered on her smooth skin. Nothing seemed to register there.

"So you don't have any idea where your mom might be?"

Haley rolled her eyes. "I don't know, Aunt Fina! The spa? Isn't that the last place she went MIA? I don't know why everyone's freaking out."

Fina knew that this time was different, but she didn't see the wisdom in telling Haley that. Not yet.

"Do you want me to hang out until your dad gets home?"

"I don't need a babysitter."

"I thought you might like company."

"I'm fine, Aunt Fina. Thanks, though."

On the way downstairs, Fina wondered if she would have been so blasé if Elaine had dropped out of sight when she was Haley's age, even if she'd done it before. Who was she kidding? She would have been elated.

Fina found Milloy in the kitchen; banks of ecru cabinets with brushed gold hardware ran down both sides of the large room. The island in the middle was topped with brown-and-gold-swirled granite, and a bowl of fruit sat near the sink. The bananas on top were brown. Fina reached into her pocket and passed the skin care samples to Milloy. "Merry Christmas."

She reached into the fridge and pulled out a bottle of water for each of them.

"You rock," Milloy said, and stuffed the samples in his pocket.

Fina walked over to the built-in desk and began pulling Melanie's cookbooks off a shelf.

"Find anything?" she asked Milloy.

"Melanie keeps a tidy house."

"You mean Fernanda keeps a tidy house." Fina held each cookbook up by its spine and fanned the pages open.

"I didn't find anything useful, but I only did a cursory search."

Fina grinned. "You worried I might sue you if something turns up later?"

"The thought did cross my mind."

Fina restacked the books on the shelf and examined a pile of invitations and flyers. She flipped open a wooden recipe box and pulled out half the stack of cards, which she handed to Milloy. She started sorting through the other half.

"What's this?" Milloy asked and handed Fina a card. It was a recipe card with no recipe, just a phone number.

Fina turned over the card, but the back was blank. "I don't know. Maybe she was cooking and had to write down a number before she forgot? I'll check it out."

She slipped it into her bag.

On the way home, Fina pulled into a grocery store in the South End and went in to get some batteries for her camera. She was contemplating the missing cooler and the nutritional value of packaged cupcakes as she walked out of the store and across the dark parking lot, which explains how she was suddenly sprawled across the pavement on her stomach, a large man on top of her.

"What the fuck!?" Fina struggled under his weight, but he pinned her down with his knee in her back. He twisted one of her arms behind her and pressed her cheek into the pavement. She could feel the rough surface tearing into her skin.

"Shut your mouth, bitch. Keep your nose out of other people's business." He pushed Fina harder, and she felt her lower back muscles contract with pain.

"Fuck you," she grunted.

He leaned down next to her face. She could smell his sour breath. "Shut the fuck up." He pushed her head harder into the pavement. "Back off. Got it?" He twisted her wrist.

Fina didn't respond.

He pulled on her hair.

"Got it! Got it!"

He stood up slowly and released her arm. She pulled herself to her knees and brushed the gravel and dirt off her face. She watched him walk away.

Fina didn't even think about it. She just ran up behind him and sucker punched him in the kidneys. He cried out, doubled over in pain. She followed with a jab to his face and a quick right hook to the side of his head.

Her fighting skills could be directly attributed to her brothers, a childhood trauma she'd opted to use to her advantage. When Fina was about ten, the boys devised a game called Sucka, which entailed punching one another within a complex system of rules and circumstances. Rand, Scotty, and Matthew saw no reason why their sister should be exempt from the game, and Carl and Elaine were clueless. The siege lasted about two weeks, until the day Carl came home from work and was greeted by a daughter with a huge shiner. Carl lined them up on the couch, Elaine pacing behind him with her cigarette, and screamed at his progeny until he was red in the face. If he caught them doing any more of this bullshit, they'd be out on their asses. His diatribe spooked them, but it was hardly the end of physical skirmishes amongst the Ludlow children. As Fina got older, Boston's criminal element paid the price.

Fina ran to her car and drove a circuitous route back to Newton, checking her rearview mirror frequently. Once parked outside Frank and Peg Gillis's house, she pulled down her visor mirror. There were scratches on her cheek and a small welt emerging on her forehead, but no other physical signs of the fight. He, on the other hand, probably had a black eye, an egg on the side of his head, and—fingers crossed—a bruised kidney.

Fina winced as she pulled open the metal door of the bulkhead and sidestepped down the narrow stairs into Frank and Peg's basement. She fumbled putting the key into the lock and was greeted by a wash of cool, dry air when she pushed the door open. Fully clothed, she dropped onto the bed facedown and folded the duvet cover over herself like a large human burrito. The pillowcase smelled like lavender, and she struggled to slow the surge of adrenaline coursing through her veins. She'd been tired before her skirmish, but now she was tired and wound up, not a great combination. Fina tried to picture a serene setting—any place her family wasn't—and finally dropped off to sleep from pure exhaustion.

Hours later, a gentle tug on her leg awakened her, and Fina rolled over to see Frank standing over the end of the bed. He smiled. "You're a sight for sore eyes."

"Really?" Fina asked. "Have you looked closely?"

Frank gestured for her to scoot over, and he took a seat at the edge of the bed. He took her chin in his hand and studied her face. "Ouch."

"Exactly."

Frank Gillis was the private investigator who used to work at Ludlow and Associates and was Fina's mentor and friend. He'd taught her the trade, and their relationship had evolved over time from strictly business to personal.

Frank and Peg were her parents' age, but unlike Carl and Elaine, they were principled and kind and normal, and Fina sought refuge with them on a regular basis. With Frank and Peg, Fina didn't question her competency, and she wasn't required to be perfect, either. In the Gillis home, she had nothing to prove.

"What time is it?" Fina asked.

"Five fifteen."

"Ugh. Why are you up so early?"

Frank patted his belly, which approximated the second trimester. "It's time for our daily constitutional. I wanted to check on you. Heard you come in last night and wanted to make sure everything was okay."

"I'm fine. I just didn't want to go home, and I needed some sleep before going to see my dad." A few years before, Frank had given her the key to the basement once he realized that Fina was essentially a nomad and incapable of creating a real home of her own, despite her glaring need for one. Those nights when she couldn't face her own place and wouldn't dream of going to her parents', she came here, to the tidy double bed in the basement of their modest Newton home.

"So who'd you piss off?" Frank gestured at her face.

"I'm not sure. I think it has something to do with Melanie. You got my message?"

Frank nodded. "Anything I can do to help?"

"Not yet, but there may be."

"Be safe. Don't get in over your head." Frank squeezed her arm. "Everybody can, even the best."

"I know. I'll call you before I let that happen." Fina

glanced toward the door leading to the hallway. "Is Peg already up?"

"Yup, and I better get up there. She's like a drill sergeant; doesn't like any dillydallying." He stood and walked to the door. "You better shake a leg or the cinnamon toast she made you is going to get cold."

Fina lay on her back, and the corners of her mouth crept up. "I'll be right there."

At Ludlow and Associates, Fina walked in the direction of Carl's office. Big law offices like the family firm never stop, and it was a hive of activity, even at six in the morning. Billable hours were the coin of the realm, and a second and third shift of paralegals and secretaries manned the office all through the night to provide support services, so the attorneys had no excuse for stopping.

Fina could hear voices from Carl's office, so she slowed as she approached it. Through the crack in the door, she could see Rand standing in front of her dad's desk.

"That's done, right?" Carl asked.

"Yes, Dad. Don't worry about it."

"I've heard that before, and then something comes back and bites us on the ass."

"It's done."

"I'm counting on you, Rand."

"I know."

The conversation switched to a client, and Fina knocked on the door.

"What?" Carl barked.

"Just me," Fina said and walked in. She made her way to the couch in the sitting area and lay down with her feet propped on the armrest. She shifted in an effort to ease the aching in her back. Fina closed her eyes and zoned out while they kept talking.

"What happened to you?" Carl asked a few minutes later. Fina opened her eyes to find him standing over her. She rolled onto her side.

"Apparently, I pissed someone off. Some asshole jumped me at Stop & Shop."

"You were grocery shopping?" Rand asked.

"No, and not really the point, Rand."

"Let me talk to your sister," Carl said, and sent Rand off with a flick of his hand.

Carl gripped her under the chin and examined her face. "You'll live. I assume it wasn't random?"

"No, it was personal. He warned me to stop nosing around, but I've been nosing around on a few fronts, so I'm not sure who sent him."

"I assume he looks worse."

"You got that right. I'm sore, but he might need dialysis."

"Well done. As your father, I'm duty-bound to tell you to be careful and all that business."

"That's heartwarming."

"Ehhh, you can take care of yourself."

"Well, it's progress, at least," Fina said. "I'm going to poke around some more. Maybe he'll make a return visit."

"He'd better. We're running out of options." Carl went back to his desk and dropped into his chair.

Fina walked to the door. "You're not keeping anything from me, are you?"

"Like what?" Carl studied the paperwork in front of him.

"Something about Rand that's going to have an impact on this investigation?"

He looked at her. "You shouldn't eavesdrop, Fina."

She held his gaze. "I can't do this if I don't know the whole story."

"You know everything you need to know to find Melanie."

"That's bullshit, and you know it."

"Just find your sister-in-law."

"I will, but don't tie my hands behind my back."

Carl peered at her. "You saying you're not up for the job?"

Fina exhaled loudly. "No, that's not what I'm saying."

"Aren't you supposed to testify in the Craig case today?"

"Yes, Father."

"Well, you look like crap. Go get cleaned up."

Carl picked up a pen and starting writing on a legal pad.

She had been dismissed.

5

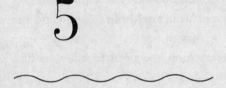

An ache radiated across Fina's back when she got out of bed the next morning. In the bathroom, she washed down four Advil and stood under a hot shower for ten minutes. Breakfast was peanut butter spread on Ritz Crackers accompanied by a diet soda. She left a message for her insider at the phone company requesting information on the number Milloy had found in Melanie's recipe box. Her contact was like a crooked government official; Fina had to hand over a lot of money and be satisfied with whatever she got, whenever she got it. The idea of waiting even a few hours for the information made her antsy, especially since the previous day had been eaten up by her court appearance, but she had no choice. In the meantime, she needed to figure out who had sent the goon.

Dante seemed like a good place to start—undisciplined enough to sic someone on her after a "friendly" conversation and green enough to hire someone who wasn't really up to the job. She worked the phones for the next hour and got an address for Dante. She looked at the clock. If he was home at eight thirty A.M., he was probably asleep and hungover, which suited Fina just fine.

She threw on some cargo pants, a T-shirt, and flats, grabbed her gun, and headed to Allston. Once there, Fina parked outside a two-family house and climbed the front stairs. That small exertion, coupled with the humidity, gave rise to beads of sweat that stung the scratches on her face. Paint was peeling off the porch, and there was a stack of Yellow Pages in shrink-wrap next to the front door. Inside, four mailboxes were nestled in the wall, and a milk crate overflowed with flyers and junk mail. Fina continued down the hall and tried the knob on the last door on the left. It didn't budge, so she pulled out her kit of lock picks and got to work.

Three minutes later, she was in, gun in hand. Cheap venetian blinds were lowered in all the windows of the living room, so she navigated with care through the dim room. Stacks of dirty dishes teetered on every surface in the small kitchen to the right, and beer bottles peeked out of the top of the trash can. The living room was equally messy—containers of Chinese food on the laminated wood coffee table oozed thick, brown liquid, and dirty clothes lay strewn along the back of the couch. A large flat-screen TV was pushed against the fireplace, flanked by enormous speakers. Fina peered into the bathroom and decided not to flip on the light. She didn't need to see any more.

That left the bedroom.

The door was ajar. Fina gently pushed it open with the gun and crept into the room. It took a moment for her eyes to adjust. A queen-size bed was pushed into one corner, and a large dresser sat against a wall across from it. There was nothing on the walls except for a Celtics poster and a pinup of a *Playboy* centerfold who was outfitted very practically in a cowboy hat, boots, and piece of straw. Fina tiptoed over to the dresser and leaned her butt against it. She studied the mass on the bed. Either Dante had grown or he wasn't alone.

"*This* is not at all what I expected," Fina proclaimed in a loud voice.

There was a flurry of activity under the duvet, and Dante's head emerged. He was momentarily tangled, and when he freed himself, his gyrations revealed a smooth ass in a thong lying next to him.

"Who the hell are you? What are you doing in my house?" Dante moved to get off the bed. He was naked except for a clingy pair of boxer briefs.

Fina held up the gun. She flicked on the light. "Get back in bed."

The girl had emerged from the covers. Her dyed blond hair was a mess, and her smoky eye makeup looked like smudged ashes.

"You need to go," Fina told her. She scampered off the bed and gathered her clothes before running out of the room.

"I'm disappointed in your living arrangement, Dante. I expected more from you." Fina pinched a pair of briefs between two fingers and dropped them on the floor.

"This does not match the up-and-coming pimp persona at all."

"You're that girl I met the other night," Dante said, sitting up straighter. He kicked off the rest of the covers and spread his legs, giving Fina too much information.

"I'm a woman, actually, and yes, we met the other night."

"What do you want?"

"I want to know why I was jumped by some thug less than twenty-four hours after I talked to you."

Dante curled his lip. "I don't know anything about that."

"I don't believe you. Have you ever been shot?"

"Believe me, bitch, if I sent someone to mess you up, you wouldn't be here talking to me."

"You didn't answer my question; have you ever been shot?"

Dante flared his nostrils. "You don't have the balls."

Fina reached into her purse and took out a silencer. She started to screw it on the end of the gun.

Dante's eyes bounced around the room nervously. "Are you fucking kidding me? I didn't order a beat down."

"I just don't . . . I just don't believe you." Fina gave the silencer a final twist and started to raise the gun.

"I didn't send anyone after you," Dante said.

"I'm not going to be happy leaving here empty-handed."

"You are one crazy bitch, you know that?"

"I'm not crazy; I'm extremely efficient. I could spend a lot of time following you and trying to convince you to cooperate, and that would be a colossal waste of time. Tell me what I want to know, and I'll leave you alone."

"You're going to pay for this," he sneered.

"Well, be that as it may . . ."

Dante breathed heavily.

"Really? You're going to make me count?" Fina asked. "Ten, nine, eight—"

"I don't know anything about some goon or that other lady."

"—seven, six, five—"

"But I know the girl," he blurted out.

Fina tilted her head and peered at him. "What girl?"

"The one in the picture."

Fina took a small step back. She reached into her purse and pulled out the photo of Rand, Melanie, and Haley. She held it up for Dante to see. "You mean this girl?"

Dante's eyes darted between Fina and the photo. "Yeah, her."

"How do you know her?"

"I don't really know her, but I've seen her around."

"Where?"

"I don't remember."

Fina pulled the trigger, and a confetti of feathers floated up from Dante's pillow.

Dante scuttled toward the foot of the bed. "I've seen her at Crystal and another club hanging out with some other girls. There's one named Brianna. Talk to her."

"Where do I find Brianna?"

"I don't know where she lives, but she's at the club most nights."

"You'd better not be jerking me around, and you'd

better keep your mouth shut about our little talk," Fina
said as she backed away from the bed. "And if you see the
girl in the picture, don't you lay a goddamn hand on her.
If you do, I will come back and shoot off your balls, one
at a time."

"You're a fucking charmer, you know that?" Dante
called out as she left the room.

"I know!" Fina hollered over her shoulder.

Connor rolled over and faced the wall. He stared at the
floral garlands snaking across the wallpaper. Seen from
across the room, the pattern was dizzying, but up close,
he could isolate each flower and vine. He reached out and
traced a rosebud with his finger. Footsteps passed by the
closed door, and he heard activity in the living room.
The view of the wall was preferable to the piles of medical
supplies on the bureau. He spent his life in hospitals, but
there was something about seeing supplies related to his
own parent that made him queasy.

When he'd arrived, having survived the flight from
Cincinnati with the help of two gin and tonics, he was
newly shocked by his father's condition. It wasn't any
different from his last visit, but seeing him in the bed,
shrunken and helpless, was a sight Connor would never
get used to. He braced himself each visit, and yet he always
felt rocked when he walked in the room. Where was his
dispassionate detachment when he needed it the most?

There was a rap on the door. Connor rolled onto his
back and stared up at the ceiling.

"Sugar? Are you awake?"

"Come on in, Mom."

The door opened and Bev stepped into the room. She was dressed in black pants, a floral blouse, and a yellow jacket with a round neckline and bracelet sleeves. Her hair was perfectly coiffed, and large pearl earrings were nestled in her lobes.

"Did you sleep okay, honey?" she asked, standing over him.

"I slept fine. How's Dad?"

"The same." Bev leaned down and straightened the duvet cover. "I made some breakfast, that creamy hash brown casserole you love."

Connor groaned. "Mom, you're going to give me heart disease."

She mussed his rumpled hair. "Oh, come on. Live a little."

"It's not good for you, either. When's the last time you had a physical?"

"I'm fit as a fiddle. Don't you worry about me. I can take care of myself and the rest of this family."

Connor knew that he should protest, that a grown man shouldn't expect his mother to take care of him, but he wasn't particularly interested in taking care of himself these days. The idea of letting his mom take charge had serious appeal. Connor closed his eyes and sighed deeply.

"You still tired, darling? Go back to sleep. I've got some business to take care of, but I'll be back this afternoon."

Connor burrowed under the covers, and Bev walked to the door.

"Thanks, Mom."

"I know you may not believe this, Connor, but things are going to get better. Just you wait."

She pulled the door closed behind her.

Fina's next stop was 326 Forest Road, the site of Mark Lamont's new house in Wellesley. Mark wasn't someone who liked drop-ins, but she didn't have the time to follow the usual protocol. Every hour that went by was another hour that Melanie was missing, another hour that Rand was under suspicion, and another hour that Fina's attacker was possibly planning his next move.

Forest Road wasn't a complete misnomer; there were actually trees swaying in the light breeze. Fina drove between two large stone pillars and pulled around the circular driveway to the front door. The house was set back enough from the street to provide some privacy, but still in full view so it could be admired by all. Fina supposed the enormous dwelling would be characterized as Nantucket-style, given its stone-and-shingle exterior, but it struck her as one of those made-up styles, generated by developers whose wives dressed them.

A crew of sweaty guys was laying sod in the front yard area. They checked her out as Fina bypassed the elaborate stone wall separating the front flagstone patio from the driveway, and she walked into one of the four open garage bays. At the door leading to the house, she grabbed a pair of protective booties from a box, pulled them on, and then walked through a succession of large, empty rooms with floors that shone like mirrors. She found Mark in the powder room just off the kitchen. He was arguing with a man about the walnut vanity.

"It's supposed to be a rooster," Mark said, gesturing at a bird painted on the vanity door.

"It *is* a rooster!" exclaimed the man in paint-splattered Dickies.

"It's a fucking hen!" Mark said. "For crying out loud, just make my wife happy. Whatever she wants. She wants a dick on the damn bird, paint one on!"

"Sorry to interrupt," Fina said, and studied the bird in question. *Rooster? Hen? What does fowl have to do with the powder room?* she thought.

"Fina, I didn't expect to see you." Mark squeezed past the painter and gave her a peck on the cheek.

"I'm really sorry to just show up, but I was wondering if you have a few minutes. I wouldn't ask if it weren't important."

"Of course. I need to take a look downstairs. Come with me." He glanced at her over his shoulder. "What happened to your face?"

Fina waved her hand. "It's fine. No biggie."

He led her to a staircase, and she followed him down.

The house was like Rand's in that the lower level was actually on the same level as the backyard. She could see a tennis court and pool out back, and a small army of men moving earth in the hot sun. Fina trailed behind Mark as he gave her the tour: a small kitchen, home gym, changing room, hair salon, meditation room, and family room. He took a seat in one of the large recliners in the screening room and gestured for her to sit next to him.

"Any word on Melanie?" he asked.

"Nope, but things are heating up for Rand. The police have searched his house and boat."

"Pain in the ass cops. I've been asking around, but nothing's come up."

"I've been asking around, too, and apparently I've pissed someone off." Fina touched her hand to her scratched face. "I was jumped the other night and told to mind my own business."

"That's what happened to your face," Mark stated rather than asked. "Are you hurt anywhere else?"

"Nah, I'm fine, but any guesses who might be responsible?"

Mark leaned back into the seat and put his arms on the armrests. He caressed the leather. "Italian leather. I had it flown in special from Milan."

"It's beautiful."

Mark gestured toward Fina's face. "Nobody comes to mind. Since we talked, I've put out some feelers, but I haven't heard anything. If my poking around set this in motion . . ." Mark gripped the armrests.

"I'm sure that's not what happened. I'm just trying to cover all the bases." Fina stood up and looked around the room. "Furnished basements bring back a lot of memories."

In high school, Fina, her brothers, and all their friends were a tribe of nomads moving from one rec room to another, drinking, getting high, and hooking up. They were like street peddlers: If a parent got wise to their activities, they just packed up and moved to the next location. Mark was often a part of these gatherings.

"Don't remind me. My kids better not do that." Mark stood up.

"Good luck with that," Fina said, and followed him out of the room.

He walked her out to her car and stood in the open door as she got in. "I'm going to talk to some more people," he said. "Hopefully, I'll be able to dig up some useful information."

"Thanks, Mark. I appreciate it."

Fina started her car. Before turning out of the driveway, she looked in her rearview mirror. Mark stood on the flagstone patio, his hands deep in his pockets, watching her leave.

Fina got chicken nuggets at a drive-thru and sat in the parking lot eating her lunch. She called Haley and left a message on her voice mail. Dante's claim about seeing her at the club was not good. Haley didn't do particularly well around booze and bad people; her impulse control and decision-making skills were poor to nonexistent under the best of circumstances. Fina needed to get a handle on the situation, pronto.

Milloy wasn't picking up, either, nor was Cristian. She was dialing Rand when her phone beeped. Her phone company contact had tracked down the mystery number from Melanie's kitchen, but it was going to cost her double. Did Fina still want it?

"Yes, I want it. Goddamnit, Shirley. I hate it when you screw me like this." Fina sucked on her diet soda.

"Oh honey, it's not me, it's the marketplace."

"Fine. What's the address?"

The number was a business listing in Framingham for

Zyxco, Inc. Fina popped the last nugget in her mouth, plugged the address into her GPS, and headed west.

It only took her fifteen minutes to find the right street, but another ten to find the actual office park. The low-slung buildings made of brick and concrete hugged the swell of the small hills on which they sat. There were intermittent signs that gave little hint to the business conducted inside; Sharwin Associates, TBK United, American Metrics. The building numbers weren't sequential, but after a few minutes of searching, Fina found herself in the parking lot farthest from the road in front of a building with the number matching Zyxco.

This building was two stories and seemed to have five separate entrances. A machine shop anchored one end of the complex, with large garage doors open to a two-story bay full of machinery and sweaty men. An outside area demarcated by a chain-link fence was crammed with an assortment of machines and parts.

Fina pulled her car into a space so she was facing the entrance. Her cell earpiece provided a good cover if anyone wondered why she was hanging around, and she pulled a map out of the glove compartment to complete the look. Fina scanned the numbers painted on the awnings. There was no sign for Zyxco under the awning matching the number; instead, the door with the correct number said MODE ACCESSORIES in black letters.

Fina trained her gaze on that door and sat and waited. Most people didn't realize that the average private investigator spends an inordinate amount of time sitting around, watching and waiting. You couldn't read or do a crossword or even talk on the phone when you were on surveillance. You had to focus on the absence of action and hope that something would relieve the boredom. Fina didn't plan to sit there all day, but she wanted to gather a little more information before she made a move.

The sum total of her two-hour surveillance: The machine shop was loud, and she needed to pee like a racehorse.

Fina had two accountants in her life: one handled her money, and the other, Hal Boyd, investigated other people's money on her behalf. On the drive back into the city, Fina called Hal and asked him to dig up everything he could on Zyxco and Mode Accessories. In addition to being a top-notch researcher highly adept at ferreting out obscure data in the public domain, Hal also favored a loose interpretation of the law. So really, every domain was Hal's domain.

After hanging up with Hal, Fina made a new round of phone calls to Risa and other friends of Melanie, but no one had heard a word from her. She dialed another number and waited for an answer.

"Menendez."

"How about I buy you a drink?" Fina asked.

"It's a little early, don't you think?"

"Well, I need to talk to you so I was trying to sweeten the deal."

"There are better ways to sweeten the deal."

"I agree, but I'm a little preoccupied right now. How about a rain check on that, and I'll buy you a beer in the meantime."

"I'll take the rain check and an ice-cream cone. Meet me at Scoops."

In the city, Fina wedged her car into a space on a side street near the Fenway and walked the few blocks to Scoops. Getting ice cream might seem like a distraction from the case, but those kinds of "distractions" were the bread and butter of any investigation. Fina had to court each person she met, and the courting took a variety of forms—a cup of coffee while admiring a clown statue collection, a nightcap in a hotel bar, a hand carrying in groceries. Expecting to get information without these interactions was like expecting to get lucky without buying a girl dinner. There were no guarantees either way, but shrimp cocktail and a steak increased the odds.

The streets were cluttered with young people carrying musical instruments and boxes bursting at the seams. It was that magical time in Boston—moving-out day, the mass exodus of students from the urban campuses. Some adults were thrown into the mix, hustling in their khakis and golf shirts, capris and sweater sets. The men's faces glistened with sweat as they hauled their kids' stuff, and the women guarded the cars. The labor of having kids never really ended.

Scoops was freezing inside; goose bumps rose on Fina's bare arms. Cristian was second in line wearing an untucked shirt that fell over his gun.

"What do you want?" he asked Fina when she stepped into line next to him.

"A cone with two scoops of salted caramel and jimmies."

Cristian studied the flavors on the chalkboard mounted

above their heads. "Nobody has normal ice cream anymore."

"That's not true." Fina pointed at the board. "There's chocolate chip and butter pecan. Pistachio."

"But those flavors are the minority. The rest is cardamom and honey lavender and rosemary Meyer lemon. They're trying to make my ice cream gourmet."

"You sound like an old man."

"I feel like an old man," Cristian grumbled, and gestured for Fina to give her order to the teenager behind the counter.

"What happened to your face?" he asked. They watched the skinny girl's biceps flex as she dug into the freezer.

"There was a thing."

"What kind of thing?"

"The kind of thing where I seemed to have pissed someone off."

"Hard to believe," Cristian said.

They took their cones outside and started down Mass Ave toward Commonwealth. On the grassy mall in the center of Commonwealth, they found a bench and sat.

"What do you want to know?" Cristian asked after taking a lick of pistachio.

"I'm looking for a girl named Brianna who hangs out at Crystal a lot."

"Oh, well, in that case . . . I thought you were going to ask me to find a guy named Michael who lives in Southie."

Fina punched his leg. "Oh, come on. It's not that bad." She licked a couple of jimmies from the web between her thumb and finger. "I'm going to Crystal tonight, but in the meantime, I thought it was worth a shot."

"Next you're going to tell me that I know everything that goes on in this town."

Fina grinned. "We both know that's a lie."

"Is this Brianna involved in anything in particular?"

"I don't know, but she knows Dante Trimonti, so prostitution is always an option."

"Why are you interested in her?"

"She may have some information."

Cristian gestured at an unkempt man shuffling toward them, pushing an empty baby stroller. "That homeless guy may have some information. Doesn't mean I'm going to spend a lot of time trying to get it."

Fina let some salt granules rest on her tongue for a moment. "Between you and me, she has a connection to Haley."

"Haley? And that has a connection to Melanie's disappearance?"

"I have no idea."

Cristian looked at her.

"Really, I have no idea. I'm just trying to figure it out and find Melanie. All I can do is follow the leads."

"And what happens if the leads lead back to Rand?"

"They won't."

The homeless man trudged by, mumbling to himself.

"I have a buddy in vice," Cristian said. "I'll ask, but if you're onto something, you need to let me know."

Fina bit into her cone and chewed.

"You're not talking because you're not going to tell me?"

"I don't know what I'm going to do, but I don't want to lie to you."

Cristian looked annoyed and tossed his balled-up napkins into the trash can next to the bench.

Fina shrugged. "Don't feel bad. I lie to everyone at some point."

Cristian stood up. "Even yourself, I'm betting."

Fina frowned and avoided his gaze. "I'll be in touch."

"See ya." Cristian walked away, and Fina followed his progress to the traffic light. He jaywalked and disappeared into the crowd.

6

Bev hated visiting the main office, but it couldn't be avoided. Before she gave her potential business partner a tour, she needed to make sure that everything was as it should be. In all her years of business, Bev's only partner had been Chester. If she needed capital, she got it from him and his enterprises, and he always offered sound strategic advice. That's the way she liked it; keep it in the family. Things were much less complicated that way, and you didn't have to suffer through the tedious process of courting and posturing, like a deb on her daddy's arm looking for the right suitor.

But with Chester incapacitated, Bev was running out of resources. An infusion of cash would enable her to expand the business and regain some stability. The Prospect, as she called him, had visited the Back Bay office, and they'd shared a couple of meals as they discussed terms. During the next meeting, he was going to see the real guts of the operation, and Bev had to be sure that he liked what he saw.

She pulled out a set of keys and opened a heavy steel door next to a dumpster. Inside, a long hallway loomed in both directions. Bev walked left and unlocked the second door with a different key. She was deposited in a stairwell that led both up and down.

Bev climbed the stairs slowly, slightly winded from the exertion. Connor was probably right; she wasn't taking very good care of herself. But really, if she needed to soothe herself with a sticky bun, that's just the way it was.

At the top of the stairs, she pushed through a heavy fire door. The buzz of activity stilled as she entered the room. After a moment, the eight women sitting at desks wearing headsets resumed their conversations, and Bev circled the space. Everything looked neat and tidy, including the girls. Nobody ever saw them, but Bev was a strong believer in the notion of dressing for success. Sloppy sweatpants and flip-flops fostered a level of insouciance that was subtly conveyed to the clients. Bev's standards were also a means of sifting out the unsuitable girls. If they balked at wearing pants that didn't have an elastic waistband, she knew they weren't right for her.

She paused behind one of the girls.

"I think you'll really enjoy Lydia. She has a degree in European history," the booker said. She listened for a moment. "That's right. Five feet eight and long hair."

Bev finished her lap of the room.

Two flights down, she pushed through another heavy door into the basement. The space was double the size of the upstairs since it spread under the office next door. Bev walked by two empty photo studios and another room that had video equipment. The rest was sectioned off into areas the size of small bedrooms and overlooked by a control room with windows. The "bedrooms" each had a queen-size bed made up with a satin duvet and pillows and a fake window with the curtains drawn. The third and fourth rooms were in use, with attractive young women on display. A blonde was wearing an X-rated cheerleader's outfit and brushing her hair. A brunette in the room next door was topless, wearing only a thong.

Bev stood in the darkened control room and listened as a woman conveyed instructions through a microphone to the two girls.

"He wants you to put your hair in pigtails," she told the blonde. Bev walked up to the glass and watched the girl part her long hair and begin to gather it into pigtails.

Bev closed her eyes and swallowed the bitter taste that was forming in her mouth. She knew that the girls of Prestige also did what their clients requested, but there was something undignified about taking orders from someone sitting in front of his computer at home. You never knew who was on the other end; it could be a horny twelve-year-old in Akron or a used-car salesman in Berlin. The equal opportunity of Gratify bothered Bev, but it was lucrative, so she tolerated it.

After conferring for a few minutes with the woman manning the mike, Bev climbed up the stairs and left the way she came in. The heat felt like a relief after the cold, recycled air in the building. She squinted in the sunlight before getting into her car, where she pulled a small bottle of hand sanitizer out of the glove compartment. She squirted the gel on both hands and rubbed vigorously.

Fina left another message for Haley, this one a mix of pleading and irritation, and tried to tamp down her anxiety regarding her niece. Even Fina didn't relish associating with people like Dante, and she had a gun and a hell of a lot more experience than Haley. The fifteen-year-old was at a decided disadvantage.

According to Rand's secretary, he was hunkered down at Carl and Elaine's house, so Fina made that her next stop. She entered through the kitchen door and grabbed a bottle of water from one of the two large Sub-Zero fridges. Fina needed to ease into family interactions, and the kitchen was always a good place to start.

She was shoveling a handful of corn chips into her mouth when Elaine and her newest slave came into the room.

"What are you doing here?" her mother said by way of greeting. "What are you eating?"

"Hi, Mom. Nice to see you, too." Fina leaned against the island. "I'm Fina. Elaine and Carl's daughter," she said to the Latina dressed in a maid's uniform. The woman smiled meekly and nodded.

"Don't distract her, Fina. She has work to do."

Fina snorted and washed her hands in the sink.

"What are you wearing?" Elaine asked, her eyes boring holes into Fina's outfit.

Fina sighed. "Pants, a shirt, shoes. I got everything at Nordstrom. You should be proud, Mom; it cost a fortune."

"You're a girl, Josefina. I cannot understand why you won't dress like one."

"What? This isn't *Little House on the Prairie*." She looked at her mother. "This is how women dress nowadays, even the ones who wore pink tutus when they were little."

Elaine pointed a finger at Fina. "Don't."

Mother and daughter glared at each other. The maid busied herself at the sink; she didn't need a strong command of the English language to understand this was not a happy moment.

"Is Rand here?" Fina asked, blinking to end the staring contest.

"He's in your father's office. Why haven't you found Melanie yet?"

"Oh, I don't know, Mom. I haven't been applying myself maybe?"

"The lip. It's always the lip with you."

"Well, it's a stupid question!"

"You're never going to find a husband if you keep this up."

"I don't want a husband, Mom," Fina said, and chugged the rest of the water.

"What are you saying?"

"What do you mean, what am I saying?"

"Is this your way of telling me you're a lesbian?"

"You'd love that. Just one more way I've disappointed you." Fina screwed the top on the empty water bottle and tossed it into the recycling bin.

Carl walked into the kitchen and eyed the two women. "Don't you two start."

"She says she's a lesbian," Elaine said, folding her arms across her chest.

"She's not a lesbian, Laney." Carl stared at Fina. "She's a pain in the ass. What are you doing here?"

"I need to talk to Rand."

"He's in my office."

Fina strode out of the kitchen and wandered through the downstairs of her parents' house. She knew where to find the kitchen, media room/family room, and Carl's office, but the rest was a blur. Carl and Elaine bought a new house every few years to reflect their ever-increasing wealth, and Fina had never lived in the current one. She knew her father's office was at the opposite end of the house from the kitchen where Elaine spent a lot of her time; he was no fool.

The office had a high coffered ceiling and a wall of windows that looked out on a pond and the woods beyond it. Carl's large glass desk faced the door, and two angular leather couches with stainless steel frames completed the U-shape. Over the desk hung a canvas splattered thick with yellow and black paint. Apparently, Carl was in a postmodernist phase.

Fina paused at the door and watched Rand. He was sitting on one of the couches, his cell phone in one hand. He rubbed his eyes with the other.

"How are you holding up?" she asked as she walked into the room.

"I feel like shit. Tell me you have good news."

"I'm making progress." Fina perched on the armrest of the couch. The stainless steel dug into her butt. "Do you know where Haley is?"

"No, why?"

"I don't get how you don't know where your kid is," Fina said.

"She's fifteen, Fina, not five!"

"That doesn't mean you shouldn't know her where-abouts."

Rand stood up and walked over to the windows over-looking the backyard. He faced Fina. "As soon as you have a kid, you can critique my parenting."

"I am so tired of that argument. You're right, I don't know what it's like to be a parent, but common sense would suggest that you should know where your daughter is spending her time."

"Why do you need to talk to her?"

"I just need to ask her a few questions."

"Tell me what they are, and I'll ask her."

"No, Rand." Fina shook her head. "That's not how this works."

"What difference does it make who asks the questions?"

"It makes a big difference, and as an attorney, you know that. If you hear from her, tell her I need to talk to her right away."

"I thought you were on my side."

Fina stood up and strode over to him. "I am on your side. I'm doing everything I can to find Melanie. Don't make it more difficult than it already is."

Rand glared at her, then looked back out the window. He leaned his forehead against the glass. "Sorry. This is making me crazy."

Fina squeezed his shoulder. "I know. That's why you have to trust me."

"Where the hell is she, Fina?" He looked at her.

"I'm going to find Melanie, but this laissez-faire parenting"—she held up a hand to silence him—"that you seem to think works, isn't working in this situation."

Rand punched a button on his phone and held it up to his ear. Fina heard ringing and then Haley in a singsong voice asking the caller to leave a message.

"Haley, it's Dad. You need to call Aunt Fina, ASAP. Seriously. No more screwing around. She's trying to find Mom, and we need to help her. Love you. Bye." He ended the call. "Happy?"

"Ecstatic."

Rand sat back down on the couch with his elbows resting on his knees.

"Are you familiar with a company called Zyxco?" Fina asked.

Rand was silent for a moment. "Doesn't ring a bell."

"How about Mode Accessories?"

He shrugged. "Nope."

"If you think of anything related to those names, let me know."

Rand nodded.

"Any word from the police?" she asked.

"Pitney is riding my ass, just barely staying on the right side of the law. She thinks I killed Melanie and dumped her over the side of the boat."

"What's your alleged motive?"

"Who knows? She can weave all kinds of stories—a potential divorce, money issues, an affair."

"Are you having an affair?"

"No, of course not."

Fina looked at him.

"I'm not having an affair! I'm no saint, but I don't have a girlfriend."

"All right, all right. I had to ask."

Fina left the room. She found her way to the front door and made her escape.

That night Fina recruited Milloy again to accompany her to Crystal. She worried that on her own she would appear cougarlike, an impression to be avoided at all costs. They parted company inside, and Fina marched straight upstairs to the VIP section. A beefy bodyguard stopped her, but not before her eyes met Dante's. His posture stiffened and he grimaced, but he recovered quickly. She smiled and mouthed *Brianna*.

Fina slipped her hand into her bag. She was trying to find her lipstick, but if Dante assumed she was fingering her gun, that wasn't her problem. He called over the bodyguard, and they had a whispered exchange. After more conversation with another man whose arms were the size of tree trunks, the first bodyguard came back and ushered Fina to an empty table.

"Dante says wait here."

"Sure. Get me a beer."

He squinted at her.

"I'm sorry," Fina said. "Get me a beer, *please*."

He stomped off, but she saw him yell something into a waitress's ear before he disappeared. Fina swiveled in her seat and looked down at the dance floor. It was like an amoeba, an undulating mass.

As the minutes passed, she tried to devise a plan B if Brianna didn't appear. She couldn't shoot Dante in public, and she was no match for his brawny compatriots. It would be hard to leave empty-handed and save face.

Luckily, her performance that morning had made quite an impression; after a couple of sips of beer, a young woman appeared in front of her.

"Brianna?" Fina asked.

"Yes."

Fina gestured toward an empty chair. "Have a seat."

Brianna glanced across the room at a man in his mid-forties wearing freshly pressed jeans and a pale green button-down. He stood at the bar, picking at the label of his beer bottle.

"You can invite your boyfriend to join us."

"He's not my boyfriend," Brianna said, and smiled at the man. She held her hand up to indicate five minutes, and he smiled back at her.

Brianna sat down. She was very thin, with long brown hair and big boobs. She wasn't pretty in the traditional sense, but her chiseled bone structure was arresting. Her eyes were carefully made up, and her lips glistened with gloss. Tight, skinny-leg jeans were topped by an equally tight tank top.

"I only have a couple of minutes. What do you want?" Brianna asked.

"I need information about a friend of mine. Dante told me you two hang out together."

"Okay."

Fina reached into her purse and pulled out the family photo. She pointed at Haley. "Has she been in recently?"

Brianna took the photo from Fina and studied it. Her nails were painted a deep cherry color.

"How do you know her?" Brianna asked.

"I'm a close friend, and I'm worried about her."

"Uh-huh."

"I need to find out what she's up to."

"Why don't you ask her?"

"Because I'm asking you."

"Are you her mother?" Brianna looked at the man at the bar. He checked his watch.

Fina grabbed the picture. "No, I'm not her mother! Do I look old enough to be her mother?"

Brianna shrugged. "Kinda."

"I'm her aunt."

"I knew you weren't just a friend." Brianna smirked. "Just because you're family doesn't mean you get to butt into her business."

"Ahh, actually, it does. She might be in trouble."

"Most of the girls who hang out here are trying to get away from home. Then Mommy and Daddy show up all concerned, and it turns out they used to beat her with a hairbrush."

"I promise you that nothing like that happens to Haley."

"That's what they all say," Brianna said. She looked over at her date. He was sharing a laugh with a curvy blonde. "I've got to go."

"Is it money? Do you want me to pay you for the information?"

Brianna curled her lip. "I do just fine, thanks. I'm not going to tell you anything."

"Suit yourself, but pissing me off is not a good plan," Fina said. "Ask Dante."

Brianna stood, walked over to the bar, and inserted herself between the man and the blonde. She planted a big kiss on his lips and looped her hand through his arm. She whispered in his ear, and his face broke into a huge grin.

At least somebody was going to get lucky tonight.

"What?" Fina grumbled into the phone. Her eyes were caked with sleepy seeds, and her teeth had a furry coating, a gross reminder of the previous night's sloppy bedtime routine.

"Sorry to wake you, Fina," Mark Lamont said, "but I thought you'd want to know."

"Know what?" She sat up, and her stomach cinched in on itself. She pulled a strand of hair away from her mouth.

"I talked to a guy yesterday, and I can't make any promises, but he knows a guy who might have seen Melanie."

"What guy?" Fina reached for a pen and a scrap of paper on her bedside table.

"The particulars don't matter, but the guy you should talk to is named Bob Webber. I have a project going in the North End, and he swears that he saw Melanie there last Wednesday."

"Has he told the police?"

"He doesn't want to get involved. He's got some child support issues he'd like to keep private."

"Got it. Where can I find him?"

"He's off today. Try him at home."

Fina showered, dressed, and ate a handful of Oreos while waiting for the clock to strike a more acceptable hour. She didn't have a problem rousing Dante before nine A.M., but it wasn't the best approach when you wanted to stay on someone's good side.

Fina rang the buzzer for unit 207 outside Bob Webber's two-story brick apartment complex in Braintree at 9:45 A.M. There was no answer, but Mark had given Fina a physical description, so she decided to hunker down in the parking lot until she came up with a better plan. She spent two hours doing tasks that required one eye and little brain power: She reset her radio station buttons, daydreamed about sex with the new attorney in the office next to Matthew's, and picked at her cuticles.

Finally, she was rewarded with the sight of a tall, thin man putting his key into the lock of the glass lobby door. Fina dashed out of the car and, before the front door could close, scooted in behind him. He looked at her, but either decided she wasn't dangerous (*How wrong you are, Bob*) or he was too polite to call her on her sneaky entrance. People would rather be robbed than be rude, and Fina took advantage of that on a regular basis.

Bob Webber stopped at the mailboxes, and she took the stairs to the second floor and found unit 207. All of the apartment doors were bordered with thick wooden molding and had large brass knockers in their centers as if to mimic the front door of a house. Hard to imagine those details really lulled the residents into a false impression of home ownership.

Fina pretended to be studying the wood grain of the molding when the door to the stairwell opened and Bob

Webber appeared. He was carrying a brown paper bag and glanced at her as he put his key in the lock.

"Are you Bob Webber?" she asked and smiled sweetly.

He looked around to see if Fina was speaking to someone else.

"Ah, yeah. Who are you?"

"My name's Fina Ludlow. Mark Lamont gave me your name."

At the mention of Mark's name, Bob straightened up and peered down the hall.

Fina looked in the same direction. "He's not here," she said.

"Right, sure."

Fina couldn't tell if it was relief or disappointment that passed over Bob's face.

"Do you have a few minutes? It's about my sister-in-law; she's missing. Mark said you might have seen her."

"Ah, sure. Come on in." He unlocked the door and motioned for Fina to go first. They entered into a small, dark hallway that led to a combo kitchen/living/dining room. The kitchen was on the right, with a counter separating it from the rest of the living space. To the left, Fina could see a bathroom on one side of a short hallway and a bedroom on the other side.

Bob pulled a six-pack out of the bag and put it on the kitchen counter. He looked at her blankly.

"You can sit down." He gestured toward the large, overstuffed couch in the living room area. It was way too big for the room, as were the oversize coffee table and recliner. The furniture sat opposite a TV and a shelving unit that held dozens of DVDs. Fina walked over and perused the collection. Bob had some of everything, but most of it was American action movies—the more explosions, the better. Fina had seen most of them thanks to Milloy, who dragged her to see every new release that promised fast cars, beautiful women, and maximum property damage.

"You're a movie buff?" she asked and sat on the couch.

"Yup." He pulled one of the beers from its cardboard sleeve and stuck the rest in the refrigerator. After popping the top, Bob walked around the counter into the living room area and took a long pull on his beer. Fina watched him.

He glanced at the bottle and then at her.

"You want one?" he asked.

"Thanks, but I'm fine; still have the toothpaste taste in my mouth." Fina suspected that Bob no more wanted to relinquish a beer than he wanted to pay child support.

He took a seat in the recliner, his lanky frame filling the length of the extended chair. Bob's thin hair was straggly at the ends, and he was wearing jeans and a blue T-shirt with an HVAC logo on the sleeve.

"So, I've always wondered," Fina said, gesturing to the DVDs, "do you watch things more than once?"

"All the time. I've seen some of my favorites more than thirty times."

"Wow." Too much free time. "Well, obviously, you're a busy man, so I'll get right to it," Fina said. "My sister-in-law is missing. Mark said you might have seen her last Wednesday."

Bob took another drink from the bottle. "I don't know for sure, but it looked like her. I mean, I saw something about her on the news, and I think it was her."

Fina reached into her purse and took out the photo. "Is this the woman you saw?" She handed it to him.

He screwed up his face in what Fina guessed was concentration. "I think so."

"Where did you see her?"

"The North End. I'm installing a bunch of HVAC systems in one of Mr. Lamont's buildings."

"What time?"

"Just after five. I had to stay late to finish up some wiring so the guys could install some drywall the next day."

"Was she doing anything in particular?"

Bob shrugged. "Nope, just standing there, looking out at the water."

"Did she seem upset?" Fina shifted her hand on the armrest and felt something hard and crunchy. Yuck. Hard and crunchy are never good in a stranger's house. She tried to surreptitiously brush her hand against her jeans.

"She wasn't smiling, but I just walked by her quick on the way to the truck." Bob drained the rest of the beer and launched himself off the recliner. He dropped the empty into a bag, where it clanked against other bottles, and opened the fridge, presumably for another.

"Mark said you didn't tell the police."

His head snapped up from behind the fridge door. "He said there wouldn't be any cops. I've got a bitch of an ex-wife, and I don't want her knocking on my door looking for a handout."

"Sure. I understand." Because women always do so well after a divorce.

Fina stood and felt her back muscles pinch in protest,

still feeling the effects of her parking lot tussle. "Do you remember what she was wearing?"

"Nah." He took a swig. "Except for the sunglasses. I don't get why those sunglasses are so popular. They make women look like big bugs."

"What sunglasses?"

"Those big-ass ones. She had them on."

"What exactly did they look like?"

"Black, with the bug eyes and some kind of jewel on the sides."

Fina was still except for her hands, which she squeezed into fists. "Was the jewel kind of yellowish brown? More like a stone than a jewel?"

Bob shrugged. "I guess. I thought they were ugly, but my girlfriend would probably like them."

Unless Bob won the lottery, those glasses were not in his future; they'd set him back about eight hundred dollars.

"Thanks, Bob," Fina said, and started toward the door.

"No cops, right?" he asked.

"No cops."

Fina let herself out and jogged down the stairs to her car. She turned the air on full blast and leaned her head back against the headrest. Bob's sighting was too vague to be definitive, but the description of the glasses was too specific to be discounted. It was something, and right now, it was all she had.

7

Fina raided Carl's minibar while she waited for him to return to his office. She pulled out a diet soda and a can of mixed nuts. The can made a satisfying sucking sound when she pulled off the airtight lid. Fina plopped down on the couch, inhaled the salty aroma, and tossed a handful into her mouth.

Scotty walked into the room and sat down in the chair next to her.

"Nuts?" She wiggled the can at him.

Scotty shook his head. "Full of fat."

"Where's Dad?"

"He's on his way. You seem upbeat. Good news?"

Fina licked salt off her fingers. "Maybe."

"Patty's freaking out."

"Since when does Patty freak out?"

"She doesn't really, but she's starting to show the strain."

"Well, if I really think about it, I feel like throwing up."

Scotty sighed. "At first I thought maybe Melanie was just taking a break, blowing off steam, but now . . ."

Fina held his gaze for a moment before turning and staring out the window.

"This is bad, isn't it?" Scotty asked.

"Are you asking me as your sister or as a PI?"

"Both."

Fina closed the can of nuts and wiped her greasy hands on her pants. "Yes. This is bad. Our sister-in-law is missing, Scotty. This is bad, even for us."

"He's not available!" Carl's gatekeeper said, rushing into the office on the heels of a small group of people. "Mr. Ludlow, I've tried to explain that your father isn't available," she said to Scotty.

"It's all right, Shari." Scotty waved her away, and Fina studied the group. There were two men in suits she didn't recognize accompanied by Lieutenant Pitney, who planted herself in front of Scotty and Fina.

"If it isn't the offspring!" she said. "Where's Pa and John-Boy?"

"Who?" Scotty asked.

"Your brother. The one with the missing wife," Pitney replied cheerfully. Today she was wearing a purple pantsuit and bright fuchsia lipstick. Her hair was in its usual unruly state, but pushed back from her face with tortoiseshell sunglasses that were serving as a headband.

"It's premature to call her missing. *Unavailable* is more accurate," Scotty corrected.

Pitney took a seat on the couch next to Fina. The suited men drifted away from the seating area and pretended to study Carl's photos and awards.

"You sure you want to wait?" Scotty asked.

"I'm sure," Pitney said.

"Why exactly are you here?" he asked.

"I told you. I want to see Carl and Rand."

"Why do you want to see them?"

"Are you their attorney?"

"One of them."

Pitney looked at Fina. "What about you? What have you been up to?"

"Oh, you know. A little of this, a little of that."

"Menendez is working on a different lead, FYI."

"Oookay," Fina said.

Pitney grinned. "I know you like to keep track of that hottie."

"Now what?" Carl asked as he stomped into the room. Rand and Matthew were behind him.

"We have something to show you," Pitney said, pulling a DVD out of her voluminous purse.

Matthew pulled open a pair of glossy cabinet doors to reveal a large flat-screen TV. One of the cops popped the DVD into the player, and everyone gathered around. Fina glanced at Rand. He was squeezing his hands open and closed.

The screen filled with static and then the traditional countdown from ten. No one spoke. A slightly fuzzy image of a convenience store checkout counter popped onto the screen. The only person visible was a dark-skinned man behind the register.

"This is fascinating," Carl said. "What is it supposed to be? An exposé on illegal immigration?" He started to walk toward his desk.

"Just wait," Pitney said. "We haven't gotten to the good part yet."

Fifteen more seconds passed, and then a woman stepped up to the counter. She put down a bottle of water and had a brief conversation with the clerk. He turned and pulled two packs of cigarettes off the display behind him. The quality of the footage wasn't great, but there was no mistaking that the woman was Melanie.

"When was this taken?" Rand asked.

"Last Wednesday at four-oh-three P.M.," Lieutenant Pitney said. She stared at him.

"Where?"

"The 7-Eleven on Broadway and Elm in Cambridge. We pulled her bank records, including her personal account"—Pitney smiled at Rand—"the one you weren't able to access, and this purchase showed up."

"So this was taken after Rand and Melanie were at Grahamson, correct?" Carl asked.

"Correct," Pitney said.

"So we're done here. Melanie was obviously alive and well after she left the school." Carl sat down at his desk. "It's been a pleasure, Lieutenant, as always, but we're rather busy trying to locate my daughter-in-law, something you and your colleagues have failed to do."

Pitney strode over to the desk and leaned on it with both hands. "The only thing this proves is that Melanie was seen after she left Grahamson, not that she and Rand didn't meet up later."

"This is ridiculous," Matthew said. "You can't prove a negative, and you don't even have a body." He, Rand, and Scotty moved toward Carl, and the two cops crowded around Pitney. Fina took a step back, away from the scrum.

"What was your wife doing in Cambridge, Rand?" Pitney asked.

"I have no idea."

"So she doesn't frequent that neighborhood?"

"I can't speak for Melanie."

"Of course you can't." She studied him. "You told us that your wife doesn't smoke."

"So?"

"So who was she buying cigarettes for?"

Rand studied a painting on the wall. "I have no idea."

Pitney reached up and fingered a curl. "Maybe she got them for herself. A lot of people fall off the wagon when they're stressed."

Rand thrust his hands into his pockets. "I have no idea."

"What did you and your wife fight about at Grahamson?"

"He already told you," Carl offered before Rand could answer. "It was a disagreement regarding which approach to take with the school. Rand wanted the teacher fired, and Melanie wanted disciplinary action taken."

"Right. I've spoken with the school, and they confirmed that the meeting was about your daughter's poor performance in math. You wanted a teacher fired because your daughter doesn't do her homework?" Lieutenant

Pitney looked at the other cops. "Shit. When I flunked a test in school, my parents grounded me for a week." The men smirked.

"So you have confirmation from the school that Rand is telling the truth," Carl said.

"I have confirmation from the school about the subject of the meeting. However, during the meeting, your wife was distracted, upset, and not the least bit interested in discussing math scores—so say the headmistress, school psychologist, math teacher, and chair of the math department." Pitney looked at Rand and shrugged. "Guess you'll have to have all of them fired, too. Being a pain in the ass is a full-time job."

Carl stood up from behind his desk. "Here are the facts: Melanie and Rand had an argument, after which Melanie went to Cambridge and bought a bottle of water and cigarettes. A purchase she made when she was irrefutably alive. This meeting is over." He picked up his phone and began to dial.

The lieutenant reached over and depressed the disconnect button with a coral-painted fingernail. "Your son and his wife had a terrible fight, not about Haley's math test. Melanie was seen crying in the parking lot and left hell-bent for leather after canceling dinner with her closest friend. Soon after, she was seen buying cigarettes in Cambridge, in a neighborhood she doesn't frequent. She was upset enough to take up a habit that her own husband claims she quit years ago."

Pitney and her men walked to the door, but she turned before leaving. "You know, I would love this cat-and-mouse game we have going, except for the fact that an innocent woman is missing."

Connor took a deep breath and helped the visiting nurse roll Chester onto his side. His mother had assured him that the nurse could manage on her own, but it seemed cowardly to step out of the room when his father was most vulnerable.

The nurse used quick, efficient motions to change the sheets, and Connor was reminded of his days as a med student. That was the last time he had assisted a patient like this. He didn't miss it. Connor generally liked the nurses he worked with and didn't envy them the bedpans and sponge baths.

But he didn't like this nurse.

"There he is," she cooed as they lowered him back onto the clean sheets. "Why don't I make him snug as a bug in a rug?"

Connor had spent a few shifts listening to Nurse Randall alternately treat his father like a toddler or an elderly Helen Keller. She was getting on his last nerve, as his mother would say.

"It's almost time for your medicine," she said directly into Chester's ear. "Won't that be good, to have your medicine?"

"Nurse Randall? May I speak to you in the kitchen, please?" Connor asked.

"Of course. We'll be right back, Chester." She followed Connor into the kitchen. He stood with his back to the counter, his hands gripping the edge.

"Nurse Randall, my father is infirm, but he's not retarded. Please don't speak to him like that."

The nurse's eyes widened. "Like what?"

Connor gripped the counter harder. "Like he's an infant. Don't patronize him."

Nurse Randall took a step back and raised her hands. "I'm sorry if you don't like the care I provide, Mr. Duprey, but—"

"That's another thing: He's *Mr.* Duprey, and I'm *Dr.* Duprey."

"Oh?" The nurse raised her eyebrow. "I thought you weren't a doctor anymore."

He stared at her, wishing he could slap the smug look off her face. "I am and will always be a doctor. If you don't feel you can meet the standards of care required by my father, I'm sure we can find another nurse who can."

Nurse Randall broke eye contact with him. Connor knew that his father qualified as an easy patient—no special instructions or abusive outbursts. Nurse Randall would be foolish to lose this gig.

"Of course, Doctor. Whatever you say." She retreated from the kitchen, and Connor heard the volume of the TV rise a few notches.

He turned on the faucet and filled a glass with cold water. He drank it down in a few large gulps and refilled it before sitting down at the kitchen table. The window overlooked the small garden in the back of the building, which the couple on the second floor had transformed into their personal Eden. A small table and chairs claimed the middle of the slate patio, but every other inch was covered by flowers and bushes. Connor imagined the space would be an explosion of color in another month.

Was he still a doctor? They couldn't take away his training. You didn't just unlearn the lunate and triquetral. He wouldn't easily forget the difference between a tricuspid atresia and truncus arteriosus. But without a license, what did it matter? And yes, he might get it back someday, but there was no time frame for restoring his reputation. He'd believed—foolishly, it turned out—that virtue and sense would prevail in the end. He'd believed that the system would do the right thing.

He was a fool. A smart, well-educated fool.

Fina sat in her car watching the unmarked police cruiser across the street. Two men walked over to it and climbed in. She didn't recognize them, but she was sure they were on the job; dark blue Crown Victoria, ill-fitting suits, and coffee cups in hand.

She slid down in her seat and kept an eye on them while eyeballing the buildings at Broadway and Elm. There was the 7-Eleven, a gas station, a Chinese restaurant, and a job training center. Each business anchored a row of large Victorian houses, most of which were probably broken up into apartments and offices. Her phone rang.

"Do you know what Melanie was doing in Cambridge?" Cristian asked.

"Beats the hell out of me. I was going to ask you the same thing," Fina said.

"Why do I have a feeling you're in Cambridge right now?"

Fina watched as the Crown Victoria pulled away from the curb and merged into traffic.

"I can't talk now. I'll call you later," Fina said, and hung up before Cristian could respond.

The next hour of canvassing was like a greatest hits tour for the worried well. Yoga, Pilates, massage, energy healing, and Rolfing specialists occupied space next to an optometrist, nutritionist, and a variety of MDs. You could have your aura checked, get your spine realigned, and have a colonoscopy, all without moving your car.

The first floor of a light blue Victorian with white shutters was devoted to a women's health clinic, and Fina wondered if Melanie's distress could be related. Was she pregnant? Was she having an affair? Rand and Melanie had planned on having more children, but were plagued by secondary infertility. Melanie had tried every imaginable procedure in a quest to get pregnant, a quest that always struck Fina as masochistic and slightly indulgent. Adoption was never seriously considered; Melanie and Rand weren't secure enough to raise a child that didn't look like them. They were more interested in reproducing than parenting. But if Melanie were pregnant, could Rand really be the father, given their reproductive history?

Ideally, Fina would walk into the clinic and ask if Melanie was a patient, but that approach rarely worked in medical settings, particularly women's health centers. Fina didn't like having to work harder to get information, but she respected this particular obstacle. She didn't want to

make it any easier for pro-lifers to harass patients. She'd
have to find a more discreet way to get answers.

The next building was painted a bright yellow, and the
tenant listing in the foyer indicated that its occupants
were therapists of one kind or another. Fina could tell
from the alphabet soup that there were psychologists,
social workers, and medical doctors, who she assumed
were psychiatrists. As far as she knew, Melanie didn't see
a shrink. Carl was biased against therapists; he thought
patient confidentiality was a farce, and he didn't think
you should air your problems outside of the family. Right.
Because the Ludlows were a wellspring of insight.

Fina studied the list of tenants and doubled back to
one that caught her eye. Dr. Gerald Murray. The name
was familiar, but she couldn't place it. She walked back
to her car and called Scotty.

"Do you know a guy named Gerald Murray?" she asked
when he got on the line.

"Gerry Murray?"

"I guess. He's a doctor."

"He belongs to the club. We've played golf a couple of
times."

"Does Patty know him?"

"Sure. We're friendly acquaintances. We've had lunch
on the patio with him and his wife."

"What about Rand and Melanie?"

"Same as us. A couple rounds of golf and a few lunches.
Why?"

"What kind of doctor is he?"

"Just leave them over there," Scotty said to someone

else in the room. "Sorry, um, he's a shrink. What does this have to do with Melanie?"

"I'm not sure yet, but I'll let you know."

"Does it have something to do with the video?"

"Maybe. Bye." Fina hung up.

Risa's house was a three-story Victorian in Newton with a deep front porch. It was enormous, but obviously not big enough for her family of five; a large addition mirroring the Victorian style had been added to the side of the house. Unlike the Victorians Fina had just seen in Cambridge, Risa's was decked out with all the elaborate gingerbread house painting that made it visually stunning and probably cost a fortune to maintain. There was no faded glory when it came to this building.

Risa's twelve-year-old answered the door and let Fina in after shouting her identity to his mom. Fina walked through the wide hallways to the back of the house and the kitchen, which had obviously been remodeled. It opened up to a family room and eating area complete with recessed lighting and ceiling speakers. The kitchen itself had a large granite island and a six-burner stove with an elaborate backsplash of earth-toned tiles. The walls were painted a light mossy green color, and the cabinets were white clapboard. The whole effect was New England meets Tuscany.

Risa was sitting on a stool at the counter facing the family room. She was sipping a glass of wine and flipping through a catalog.

"What are you making? That smells amazing," Fina said.

"Italian seafood stew," Risa said, and looked at her. "Chicken liver crostini and a white peach tart."

"Wow."

Risa took another sip of wine. "I cook when I'm stressed."

Fina nodded.

"Do you want some?" Risa asked and held up her glass.

"Actually, I would love some."

Risa slid off the stool and got a glass from an upper cabinet. She poured a generous amount of red wine into the goblet and handed it to Fina. Risa and the Ludlows were sewn into the tapestry of one another's lives due to proximity and history, but Fina genuinely liked Risa; she was smart and principled, but she didn't take herself too seriously. She was the rare childhood friend whom you actually wanted to know as an adult.

Fina took a sip. She didn't know anything about wine, except that this one felt rich and thick on her tongue.

"I have a couple of questions to ask you."

Risa sighed. "Go ahead."

"It's kind of delicate."

Risa snorted. "Fina, *delicate* is not a word I would ever associate with your family. If asking me a question will help find Melanie, then go ahead."

"Is there any chance Melanie was having an affair?"

Risa stopped her glass midway to her mouth. "No."

"You're sure?"

"I'm her best friend. I would know."

"So there was no one she was interested in, flirting with, anything like that?"

A timer went off and Risa went to the stove and took the top off of a heavy Dutch oven. Steam and a delicious aroma wafted across the kitchen.

"I know you're a smart girl, but I don't think you see the whole picture when it comes to your family," Risa said.

Fina put down her wineglass. It was exhausting, straddling the line between the Ludlows and the rest of the world. "Actually, I think I see a lot more than people give me credit for."

Risa dipped a wooden spoon into the pot and stirred it slowly. "So why on earth do you think any woman would cheat on one of your brothers?"

"Because they can be asses. Rand, especially. I thought we agreed on that point. And because people cheat."

"Anyone who crosses your family ends up crucified. The wives would be crazy if they thought they were exempt." She replaced the top on the pot and reached into the refrigerator for a wedge of brie. Risa put the cheese, a box of crackers, and a knife on a small wooden cutting board and set it down in front of Fina.

"If Melanie cheated on Rand she would lose everything," Risa said.

"Or she could take him to the cleaners."

Risa shook her head. "People don't want to mess with your family. Even if Melanie wanted another relationship, she never would have risked it."

"Because of the money? I'm sure she could find a sugar daddy someplace."

"Because of the money, and her friends, and Haley." Risa peered at her. "Your father and brothers would systematically dismantle her life. Stop being so naïve."

Fina topped a cracker with a slice of brie and chewed it slowly. "I know they're vultures, at least at work, but they're not always like that." Risa raised an eyebrow. "And anyway, I just can't imagine Melanie not leaving because of that."

"Of course you can't. You're a Ludlow. Nobody scares you." Risa poured herself more wine. "Are you still convinced that Rand had nothing to do with Melanie's disappearance?"

Fina took a sip. "I haven't found any evidence to suggest that he did."

Risa shook her head slowly. Fina swallowed the rest of her wine and brought her glass to the sink.

"Is there any chance Melanie was pregnant?"

Risa rolled her eyes. "We're getting a little old for that."

"Not too old, though. Could she have been?"

"Nothing would have made her happier. I don't think she could have kept it a secret from me or anyone else though. I sincerely doubt she was pregnant." She looked at Fina. "Do you think she was?"

"Not really, but I thought I should ask. You know, no stone unturned."

"She always wanted more, but the idea of a newborn? Kill me now."

Fina snorted and stood up. "Thanks for talking to me, Risa. I'll let you know if I hear anything."

"You better," Risa said, and gave her a pained smile.

Fina let herself out.

On the front lawn, Fina skirted around Risa's son and

his friends, who were engaged in a spirited game of soccer. She climbed into her car and closed the door firmly against their raucous cries.

Bev chose an upscale Italian restaurant in a suburb half an hour out of the city for the meeting. She didn't want to risk bumping into any acquaintances in the company of the two young ladies.

They were seated in a large booth at the back of the dining room with Bev facing the room and the girls facing her.

"I'm so glad you could join me," she purred in her Southern accent. Some people were annoyed by her honeyed tones, but young people and men were generally charmed. "I've heard such good things about the two of you."

The brunette was about twenty, with long, flowing hair and a knockout body. The blonde was younger, but Bev was sure with the right clothes and makeup, she could be aged a few years. She wasn't a bombshell, like the brunette, but she was pretty and curvy and fresh-faced.

"It's an honor, ma'am. I appreciate the invitation," the brunette said.

"Me too," added the blonde. Her gaze wavered between the two women. She was less confident about how to interact with Bev. Normally, Bev would find this annoying, but she would put up with it in service of her larger goal.

They were served a round of lemonade and made selections from the menu. Bev chose the fish, and the two girls opted for salads. Good. Bev had heard that some men liked a girl with a big appetite, but that hadn't been her experience. There was nothing alluring about watching a date slurp up a plate of spaghetti or gnaw at a rack of ribs before getting intimate.

"I wanted to talk to you about a new opportunity. I know that both of you have been working for the firm in a limited administrative capacity, but I think it's time to change that. You're both ready for additional responsibility."

The brunette beamed, and a sly smile crept across the blonde's face.

"You'll be interacting with important, powerful people, and of course, your earnings will reflect that." Bev took a sip of her drink. It was a poor substitute for Southern tea; the Yankees hadn't yet mastered her favorite thirst quencher.

"Doesn't that sound exciting?" she asked, and smiled sweetly.

"So, what's the update?" Frank asked as he leaned over and speared a hot dog with his fork. It was five forty-five P.M., and dinner was on at the Gillis house. Frank and Peg ate every night at five forty-five, which seemed ridiculously early to Fina, but she supposed if you got out of bed before six in the morning, you were more than ready for dinner before six in the evening. Peg passed a basket of rolls to Fina. She broke one off and slathered it with butter.

"Melanie was in Cambridge at four P.M. Wednesday afternoon. That was the last confirmed sighting, although I've got a witness who claims he saw her in the North End just after five."

"A reliable witness?" Frank asked as he scooped up a forkful of frank and beans.

"Are they ever?" Fina asked.

"How's everyone holding up?" Peg asked. She was wearing a tracksuit, which was her usual uniform outside of work. Peg was a middle school nurse in Newton and generally wore some kind of scrubs on the job. Lots of people assumed that being a middle school nurse was easy and that she spent her days handing out cough drops, but that wasn't the case. Nowadays, being a school nurse meant you dealt with all kinds of diagnoses—ADHD, celiac disease, diabetes—and their attendant medications, as well as the scourge of alcohol and drug abuse that was more rampant than ever. Not to mention sliced fingers in bio lab and concussions on the blacktop. Peg was tough but loving, a perfect combination for her job.

"They're fine. The usual. Vacillating between pretending everything is okay and imagining the worst-case scenario."

"What about Haley?" Peg was always most interested in the younger members of the Ludlow family.

"I haven't really seen her, but when I did she seemed okay." Peg opened her mouth to speak, but Fina held up her hand. "Trust me. I know there's no way she could be okay, given the circumstances, but I'm doing the best I can. She's impossible to track down, and that doesn't seem to bother my brother. When your boys were teenagers, you knew where they were, right?"

Frank took a drink of milk and wiped his mouth with his napkin. "I may have been the cop and the PI, but Peg was just as vigilant about their whereabouts." He sat back in his chair. "You don't want to suffocate them, but you know, their brains . . ."

". . . aren't fully developed," Peg finished. "They act so much older than they actually are, but they make terrible decisions."

"And her parents aren't exactly models of good decision making," Fina noted. "Haley's battling biology on two fronts."

"There's only so much you can do," Peg commented, squeezing Fina's hand.

"I know," Fina said, and smiled at Peg. "That's what worries me."

Fina had the first inkling on Route 9 near the mall. It was a black Toyota Camry, three cars behind her in the other lane. She couldn't get a good look at the driver, but was pretty sure it was a man. She changed lanes, and so did he, but that didn't mean anything. To be sure she had a new friend, she took the next exit into the residential streets of Chestnut Hill. The Camry rolled up two cars behind her at the bottom of the ramp. She did a circuit through the winding roads dotted with large lots and looming houses, and although he kept his distance, he stuck with her.

Fina got back on Route 9 and threaded her way through Newton. The Camry dropped back. Fina called Milloy.

"Where are you?" she asked.

"I just finished with a client in Back Bay."

"Fuck."

"What is it?"

"Some guy's following me. I wanted you to tail him."

"Where are you?"

Fina braked sharply as a motorcyclist pulled out in front of her. "Newton, heading toward the Pike."

"I don't think I can catch up with the traffic."

"All right."

"What are you going to do?" Milloy asked.

"I think I'll test his level of commitment. See what kind of a relationship he wants to have with me."

"That sounds like a bad idea. How about driving to a police station instead?"

"That's plan B, but he'll take off if I do that. I want to find out who he is."

"Be careful."

"Don't be such a worrywart. I'll be fine." Fina ended the call before Milloy could question her further.

Getting on the highway would give Fina and her tail more room. With some fancy maneuvering, she might even get behind him and get his tag info. She passed through the toll booth and settled into the middle lane. It was the end of rush hour, and for the first few miles, Fina and the Camry covered little distance at twenty miles per hour. At the second set of toll booths, though, traffic eased, and Fina sped up to seventy.

After ten minutes and a few lane changes, it was clear that their shared route wasn't coincidental. Fina dropped her speed. He dropped his speed, but they both stayed over forty-five miles per hour. The last thing she needed was to attract a statie for failing to maintain the minimum speed limit. She stole glances at the man in the Camry. She didn't recognize him—not that a glance in the rearview mirror at high speed is much to go on. He looked to be in his thirties or forties, thickset, with dark curly hair.

She sped up, and he grimaced and fiddled with something on the passenger seat. Fina reached into her purse and pulled out her gun. The speed limit would be the least of her problems if the guy started shooting at her on the highway, but instead of a gun, he brought a phone to his ear and engaged in an animated conversation. She slowed down again, as did he. After two minutes, he threw down the phone and gripped the wheel with both hands.

Fina maintained her speed, and they drove for ten more minutes. This wasn't going anywhere, except western Massachusetts, so she decided to cut her losses and get rid of him. She needed to dart off an exit when it was too late for him to follow, or even drive to a police station where she could act all damsel in distress. She was formulating her plan, but noticed that he was gaining in speed. The speedometer rose steadily, and the hairs on Fina's neck stood on end. The Camry was bearing down on her. Fina depressed the gas, her heartbeat picking up speed at the same time.

Maybe he wasn't tailing her after all.

Maybe he was trying to kill her.

8

It wasn't the first time Fina had found herself hanging upside down from her seat belt, glass fragments sparkling in her hair, but the last time she'd been knocked out for the event. Loss of consciousness was definitely the way to go, she thought, as the firefighters pulled her from her mangled car. She was relatively unscathed, despite the dramatic scene, but Carl was a big fan of documentation when it came to accidents and mishaps, so Fina didn't protest being loaded into an ambulance and driven to Mass General.

The next couple of hours were a mix of quiet alone time in a thin paper gown and bursts of noise and activity perpetrated by strangers in shades of blue and green. She was waiting for CAT scan results when Scotty arrived.

"What happened?" he asked.

"I was run off the road." She looked at her arms, which were scratched. Her left hand was bandaged.

"By?"

"I don't know. Can you find my clothes?"

"You're not supposed to go anywhere."

Fina pushed herself into a sitting position and groaned. Her back muscles felt sore and tight. "Fucking A, that hurts." She hobbled over to a metal closet and pulled open the doors. "You could help me, you know."

Scotty walked over to the storage cabinet and pulled out a stack of scrubs. "What size are you?"

"Let's try medium."

Fina leaned on Scotty as she pulled on a pair of the drawstring pants. "Where's my bra?"

"Don't look at me."

"All right. Turn around for a sec, but don't move."

Scotty put his back to her, and she leaned into him while stripping off the johnny and pulling on the top of the scrubs. She walked over to a mirror and was not pleased with what she saw. She had a bruise under her eye and a butterfly bandage near her hairline.

Carl walked in and stopped when he saw her in scrubs. "What? Now you want me to pay for medical school?"

"Ha," Fina said.

"Have you been released?"

"Not technically."

"Then get back in the goddamn bed." Carl pointed at her. "If they say you're fine, you can leave, but I don't need you taking off and dying from a clot or something."

"Although that would make a good lawsuit," Scotty offered, and Fina gave him the hairy eyeball. She climbed back onto the bed and pulled the thin blanket over her. She shivered.

"Get your sister a blanket," Carl told Scotty, who left the room. "What happened?"

"A guy was tailing me. I led him onto the Pike to try to deal with him, and he ran me off the road."

"Any idea who it was?"

"Nope."

Lieutenant Pitney burst through the swinging door of the exam room. "I see you're up for visitors." She was followed by her usual trailing police parade, like a law enforcement *Make Way for Ducklings*.

"He's not a visitor. He's family," Fina said.

"And counsel," Carl added.

"Why would you need counsel?" Pitney asked.

Scotty came back into the room and pushed his way past two other cops and Cristian, who was hovering in the corner of the room. Fina glanced at him as Scotty laid a blanket over her.

"I always feel better with my attorney present," Fina said.

"What happened?" Pitney asked. Cristian and the other two pulled out their notebooks.

"She was in a car accident on the Pike," Carl said. "Hardly warrants your expertise, Lieutenant."

"That's flattering, Carl. Really, it is." She smiled. "Do you know who hit you?"

"No."

"Did the car hit you on purpose?"

"Who's to say?" Carl asked, opening his hands to the ceiling. "Boston drivers are notoriously bad."

A tiny Asian woman in scrubs came through the door and walked to the side of the bed. "There are way too many people in here. Everybody needs to leave."

"Who are you?" Carl asked.

"I'm the attending, Dr. Wang. Who are you?"

Fina watched as Carl and the doctor had a staring contest.

"I think we can all agree that Ms. Ludlow's health is the number one priority, yes?" Dr. Wang asked the assembled group.

"Of course, Doctor. The police are only interested in apprehending the perpetrator," Pitney said.

Carl broke his gaze from the doctor. "We'll be outside, Fina." He opened the door leading to the hallway and beckoned to Pitney. She walked through, followed by Scotty, the two cops, and Dr. Wang. Cristian lingered in the corner.

"You okay?" he asked.

"I've been worse."

"Your car rolled four times. Pretty impressive."

"I look like I rolled four times."

"Don't worry. We can do it with the lights off," Cristian said, and grinned.

Fina held up her bandaged palm. "I think I'm on the DL for a little while."

Cristian walked over and put his hand on her arm. "You really don't know who did this?"

"I really don't."

He squeezed her shoulder gently and moved toward the door.

"But Cristian? It wasn't an accident."

"Of course it wasn't, Fina. There are no accidents when it comes to you."

The CAT scan was clear, and Fina went home, took a few Advil, and fell into bed. She slept deeply, except when she rolled over and her unhappy back muscles reasserted themselves. Shortly after the sun came up, she padded into the kitchen and got the OJ carton and a box of Pop-Tarts, which she took back to bed. She went back to sleep after two Pop-Tarts and a few chugs of juice.

The clock said 11:24 A.M. when she next woke. Two more Advil made a shower and dressing manageable, and then Fina got down to the garage before remembering that she'd totaled her car the night before. Luckily, Carl, in his quest for constant productivity, had left one of the Ludlow and Associates fleet cars in her space. Lack of transportation would not be an adequate excuse for failing to get the job done.

Driving was no easy task with her aches and pains; individually, some pulled muscles, a cut hand, and a constellation of scratches and bruises weren't too problematic, but put together, they made the job more taxing. Fina pulled up to the Whittaker Club twenty minutes later and sat in her car for a few moments, gathering her physical strength.

The Whittaker Club had been a part of the Ludlows' lives as long as Fina could remember. She'd grown up swimming in the pool, playing tennis on the courts, and stealing golf carts after hours to career around the back nine with boys who were up to no good. Family events were often celebrated at the club, including Rand and Melanie's wedding, and during the summer months, the Ludlows gathered there in various configurations for poolside meals. Fina didn't spend much time there given that she fit in like a nun at Mecca. Her contemporaries were generally stay-at-home moms with large broods or the occasional career woman who worked in medicine or law—corporate, not personal injury. Fina stopped by every few weeks to catch up with whichever family member was hanging out, but these forays were strictly political on her part. If Fina wanted to relax, she was better served by a trip to the shooting range.

She heard laughter and splashing as she walked around the tall hedges and entered the pool area. The pool deck was littered with chaise longues, and an attendant navigated through them, claiming the discarded towels. The eating area was on a flagstone patio off to the side, between the pool and the main clubhouse. Fina scanned the pool and saw Patty standing at the edge of the deep end. Fina noticed some stares and whispers as she walked the length of the pool.

"Hey, Patty," Fina said, and leaned in for a kiss on the cheek.

Patty wrinkled her nose. "Christ, you do not look good."

"Trust me, I don't feel good."

"I'm glad you're okay." She leaned toward Fina and asked in a quiet voice, "Any news?"

"Some leads, but nothing major. Scotty says you're freaking out about Melanie."

Patty spoke to a wet head bobbing in the water. "Out.

I mean it. Your lunch is almost ready." She looked at Fina. "Scotty is such a drama queen. I'm frantic, if you want to know the truth, but when have I ever freaked out?"

"That's what I said." Fina took a step back from the sopping child who had launched himself onto the pool deck. "Hey, Teddy."

"Hi, Aunt Fina," he said. "Cool black eye." He grabbed a towel from Patty's hand and ran over toward the eating area, where Fina could see her other nephews, Chandler and Ryan.

"Do you want something to eat? A drink?" Patty asked.

"Just some water and some information would be great."

They made their way over to the boys, who alternated between slouching down in their seats and perching on their knees like dogs anxious for a treat. A waitress brought out a large tray of food, and the boys dug in.

"You never feed them, do you?" Fina asked as she watched them scarf down French fries and chicken fingers.

"Never," Patty said. She cut into a salmon fillet.

Fina watched the waitress attend to the other tables. The club was probably a decent place to work, but there was something perverse about adults attending to young children, beyond the fulfillment of their basic needs, that is. Changing a diaper, bathing little kids—they couldn't do those things for themselves. But making a chocolate shake thicker or fetching a warm towel? Fina always felt uncomfortable with that degree of servitude.

"So what kind of information do you need?" Patty asked.

"Is it okay to talk about it with them here?" Fina asked

and nodded toward her nephews, who were chewing and telling jokes at the same time.

"Chew with your mouths closed, you monkeys," Patty said. "We can talk if we're quiet."

Fina scooted her chair a little closer to Patty's. "Do you think Melanie was seeing someone?" She fumbled with the straw wrapper until Patty came to her rescue.

"You mean 'seeing someone,' seeing someone?"

"Yeah."

Patty took a sip of her raspberry lime rickey. "I don't think so. Why? Do you think she was?"

"No, but I need to cover all the bases."

Patty sat back and thought for a moment. "Shit. What a mess."

"Mom!" Chandler exclaimed.

Patty waved him away. "I can't imagine she was having an affair, but who knows."

"Anyway, could she have been . . ." Fina made a gesture mimicking a protruding stomach.

"She would have been thrilled, but I think she would have told me."

"That's what Risa said."

"You asked Risa these questions?" Patty asked, her eyebrow cocked.

"Yes."

"Carl isn't going to like that."

Fina stirred the lime to the bottom of her water. "I can't find Melanie without asking questions. I'm not asking anything that the police aren't asking or going to ask."

"But you're not the police."

"I'll deal with Carl."

"Have you spoken to your mom about Melanie?"

"Just the usual: 'Why are you disappointing me? Why haven't you found her yet?' Blah, blah, blah."

"She's not that bad, Fina." Patty took a bite of salmon.

"Easy for you to say; she's not your mother."

"She hasn't had an easy life."

"You haven't had an easy life, Patty, and you're not a pain in the ass." Patty's father had died when she was a child, and her mother had succumbed after a long battle with breast cancer when Patty was in college.

"No, but I didn't lose a child, and that's a whole other kind of hell." Patty held up a hand to quiet Fina. "I'm not saying you can't understand because you're not a parent. I don't think anyone can fathom it. It's too horrible." She looked at Teddy as he licked honey mustard off his hand, thereby transferring it to his nose. "I'm just saying."

"Fine," Fina said, and had a sip of water.

Ryan was using a French fry as a plane, weaving it in the airspace over his plate. He did a barrel roll into the ketchup and then gained altitude to his mouth. Fina reached over and took a handful of fries from his plate.

"Hey!"

"Dude, you gotta share with your aunt." She nudged his foot under the table with her own. "Especially when she looks so gnarly."

He grinned. "Okay."

"Do you know a guy named Gerald Murray?" Fina asked Patty.

"Sure. He's a member here. He's a psychiatrist. Works at Harvard and sees patients."

"I need to talk to him."

Patty looked at her. "I assume you don't want an office appointment?"

"I'd prefer something a bit more informal."

"Well." Patty twisted around in her seat and scanned the pool area. "That's him, over there on the chaise."

Fina looked over at the man, who seemed to be in his sixties. A little girl in a striped two-piece bathing suit was standing next to his chair, talking and gesturing.

"Let me guess—his daughter?" Fina asked.

Patty smiled. "Actually, his granddaughter."

Dr. Murray had a small head covered in white hair, and his chin boasted a matching goatee. A woman about Fina's age with a swollen, pregnant belly wandered over to his chair and led the girl off by the hand.

"He's still on his first wife?" Fina asked.

"Yes," Patty said. "Amazing, isn't it? Around here, he's like an animal on the endangered species list. Do you want me to introduce you?"

"That would be great."

Fina and Patty tidied up the detritus from the meal, and the boys jumped back into the pool. They walked over to Dr. Murray's chaise.

"Hi, Gerry!" Patty said.

He put down his *New Yorker* and looked up at Patty. "Patty! Hello! Nice to see you." He struggled out of his supine position and gave Patty a kiss on the cheek. "Is Scotty here?"

"Working, of course, but I wanted to introduce you to Scotty's sister."

Fina offered her right hand and caught Dr. Murray glancing at her bandaged left. Up close, his eyes were a steel blue and were framed by slight wrinkles. He had straight, white teeth and an easy smile. Fina could imagine that patients would feel comfortable telling him their dirt.

"Josefina Ludlow," she said.

"It's a pleasure to meet you, Josefina."

"Most people call me Fina, actually."

"Fina it is." There was an awkward moment, but Dr. Murray quickly dove into it. "Are you here for a day of relaxation?"

"Oh," Patty exclaimed suddenly, remembering Fina's appearance. "She was in a car accident, Gerry. Hence, this." She made a sweeping gesture around Fina's face. "She doesn't have a boyfriend who beats her."

Fina glared at her.

"What? He probably can't go grocery shopping without everyone telling him their problems," Patty said.

"Actually, I'm here on a business matter," Fina said. "I'm a private investigator."

"If you'll excuse me," Patty said, "I think one of my children is drowning another." She walked briskly to the deep end and started reading the riot act to the only boy dumb enough to surface within earshot.

"That must be fascinating work," Dr. Murray commented.

"It is, except when I have to deal with family issues."

Dr. Murray stroked his goatee slowly. "Of course. Rand's wife is missing."

"She is, and actually, it seems that she was in your neighborhood the afternoon she disappeared."

"Oh, really?"

"I know you can't discuss your patients, but Melanie was seen at the 7-Eleven next to your office, and she was agitated and upset. I wondered if she had paid you a visit."

"Josefina—"

"Fina, really."

"Fina. You're right. I can't discuss my patients. It would be a breach of professional conduct."

"I know, and I don't mean to put you in a difficult position, but that was the last known sighting of her. She's been missing for more than a week. Time is not on our side."

Dr. Murray put his hands in his pockets and rocked back and forth on his Docksiders.

"Maybe you could just point me in the right direction. Could you confirm or deny that you saw her that day?" Fina asked.

"I assume you're working for your brother on this?"

"My brother and father asked me to find Melanie, but really, I'm working for Melanie." Fina studied him for a moment. "Why? Is there something you want to tell me that you don't want them to know?"

He sighed. "In my line of work, much like yours, I imagine, you learn that things are often not as they seem. Sometimes it's hard to know who's reliable."

"I realize you don't know me, but I just want to find Melanie. I'm not interested in protecting anyone except her. I'm working with the police on this." Lying to a shrink felt like lying to a priest, but he was probably used to it.

A woman Dr. Murray's age gestured to him from across the pool. She and the pregnant woman had taken seats at one of the tables. Dr. Murray held up his hand, indicating he'd be a moment. "Melanie wasn't my patient, so I suppose I'm not violating her trust. She stopped by my office on Wednesday afternoon. She was extremely agitated."

"About what?"

"I wouldn't tell you if I knew, but I don't know. She wouldn't say. Initially, she said she wanted my advice, but then she changed her mind and said she would take care of it herself. She only stayed a few minutes."

"Did she say where she was going?"

"No. I urged her to take my next available appointment so we could sort things out, but she didn't want to wait. I wish I could have done more, but I had nothing to go on."

"I understand. You've been extremely helpful, and I'll be discreet with the information." Fina looked toward the seating area. "Your granddaughter's really cute. And there's another one on the way?"

"In July. My wife and I can't wait." He beamed. Fina looked at her feet. Unadulterated family bliss made her uneasy.

"Congrats. It was nice meeting you," Fina said, and walked toward the deep end.

She zoned out for a moment, contemplating the possibilities. A shriek and a cannonball brought her back.

"I don't get it. I wasn't really hurt, but everything hurts anyway." Fina was lying on Milloy's massage table in her living room, again wearing boy shorts and a sports bra. "It's annoying." She'd spent the previous night at Crystal, on the lookout for Dante and Brianna—both conspicuously absent—and hadn't rolled into bed until well after midnight, which explains why she hadn't rolled out of bed until noon.

"I'm all for your action-filled life, but you're not a twenty-year-old, you know?" Milloy backed away from the table and put his hands on his hips. "The accident was traumatic for your body, and you can't expect it to bounce right back. One of these days, it's really going to catch up with you."

Fina struggled to sit up. "And when it does, it does."

Milloy reached out his hand and pulled her up. Fina lowered herself onto the sofa, and he went to the kitchen and returned with a bottle of pomegranate juice and an open can of diet soda, which he handed to her. He sat down next to her, and they drank in silence. Fina let her head fall back against the couch cushion and closed her eyes.

Her phone interrupted her trance.

"Yes?" she answered. She listened for a moment. "Send him up." She looked at Milloy. "Hal Boyd is on his way up."

"Your secret moneyman?"

"My secret moneyman." Fina grimaced as she scooted to the edge of the couch. "Give me a push, would you?"

Milloy placed his hands on her butt and pushed her up. She walked into the bedroom and traded her boy shorts and sports bra for a bra, T-shirt, and some cutoff shorts. She left her hair loose, the better to hide her injuries.

There was a knock on the door, and Fina heard murmurings from the other room. One last look in the mirror confirmed her suspicions: Her face was a lost cause.

She padded back into the living room. "Hal, please tell me you have some information," she said. Yikes. She sounded like a slightly more polite version of Carl.

Milloy and Hal were standing next to each other, two ends of a spectrum. Milloy was tall and handsome with chiseled bones and muscles. Even his bare feet were nice to look at, which was highly unusual in Fina's experience. Hal was short and obese, and his pants were cinched around his waist like a lanyard around a potato sack. He was sweating, with dark stains under his armpits and a shiny expanse where his hairline should have been. The two men had met before, and Fina was convinced that Hal had a man crush on Milloy. He didn't want to sleep with Milloy; he wanted to *be* Milloy. It was a common affliction.

"Fina!" Hal exclaimed. He seemed to recoil at the sight of her. "What happened to you?"

"Car accident."

"You look terrible."

Fina frowned at him, and he backpedaled. "I mean, you never look *terrible*. Even when you look bad, you look good." Milloy rolled his eyes. "It's just that—it looks like it hurts."

"It does, but I'll survive. You want to sit down?"

Hal walked over to Nanny's easy chair, sank into it, and rested his cheap briefcase across his lap.

"Did it happen, you know, in the line of duty?"

Fina had worked with Hal for years, and he was endlessly titillated by the seedy underbelly of her job. He had just as much contact with the criminal world as Fina, but his interaction was confined to data and spreadsheets, all behind the safety of his desk.

"You could say that."

"What happened?" If Hal could have leaned forward, he would have.

Fina sat down on the couch.

"She rolled four times," Milloy said. "*Four* times." He held four fingers up to emphasize his point.

Fina stared at him. "Thank you, Milloy." She looked back at Hal. "Someone ran me off the road. I rolled over. I'm fine. End of story."

"She gets tetchy when she's in pain," Milloy said, sitting down next to her.

"So. Zyxco and Mode Accessories," Fina said. "Any news?"

Hal pulled a handkerchief out of his pocket and mopped his brow. The air-conditioning was on full blast, but keeping cool was clearly a losing battle for Hal.

"I've got some info. Any way I could get a glass of water first?" he asked. "This heat is killing me. They're not kidding about global warming. It's not supposed to be like this at the end of May."

"Sure," Fina said. She looked at Milloy. "Do you mind?"

"I live to serve you. You know that." He walked into the kitchen.

"I'm assuming that Mode is a front for something?" Fina asked. She tugged on the gauze around her palm. She was supposed to keep the bandage on for a week, but that was never going to happen. It was itchy and drew attention to her injuries, which made her look vulnerable.

"That's my guess," Hal said as he took a glass of ice water from Milloy. He took a large gulp. "Thank you." He put the glass down on Nanny's 1930s coffee table. It was glass-topped, with wrought-iron legs. It was probably a vintage find and worth some bucks, but Fina thought it looked like fussy lawn furniture.

"So, here's the skinny," Hal said. Milloy and Fina tried not to smile at each other. "Zyxco is a legitimate company with a number of subsidiaries, one of which is Mode Accessories, the one that looks dicey. Mode Accessories, not surprisingly, is in the women's accessories business, and very successful. Have you been to their office?"

"Not inside."

"Does it look like a big operation?" Hal asked.

"No way to tell. It's in one of those office parks in Framingham." Fina picked up her sweating soda can and took a sip. "What makes you think there's more to it than just accessories?"

"The amount of merchandise they handle, as indicated by shipping and manufacturing costs, doesn't match their profits. There should be a lot more handbags in the pipeline with that kind of cash."

"What kind of business is Zyxco in?"

"They have two primary income streams: the manufacture of specialized metal parts and paper napkins." Hal took another sip of his water.

"What are specialized metal parts exactly?"

"Say a company is building a machine to be used in coal mines, and there's no coupling that fits. A company like Zyxco builds the piece to order."

"And napkins?" she asked.

Hal shrugged. "Everybody needs them. There used to be a lot of money to be made in the manufacture of everyday items."

"That's no longer true?" Fina asked.

"Nope. Not with overseas labor, cheaper manufacturing costs."

Next to her, Milloy tilted back his head and swallowed the last of his juice. His neck was smooth and tanned. Why wasn't she having sex with him?

"So how does Mode Accessories stay under the radar?" Fina asked, still picking at her gauze.

"There are different ways to do it. A separate set of books makes everything look legit, especially if you are actually running the front business as a business. If you keep your head down and bribe the right people, that's even better."

"Do you have a name for me? A point of contact?"

Hal blushed slightly and shook his head. "I'm still untangling the web. Sorry. It's one shell corporation after another."

"So what kind of person or business would have legitimate business to conduct with Mode Accessories?" she asked.

"An accessories buyer for a department store. Mode also seems to have contacts in the hospitality industry."

"How do handbags figure into restaurants?" Fina asked.

"They don't," Milloy said. "Probably gift shops at hotels and tourist attractions."

Hal nodded vigorously. "Exactly. Cruise ships even. Someone's got to provide that schlock you buy on the lido deck."

"But a private individual wouldn't contact them?"

"Probably not." Hal clicked open the tabs on his briefcase and pulled out a document. "Here are the details. Read it and shred it." He closed the case and struggled out of the easy chair, which proved none too easy.

"Thanks, Hal. Send me the bill," Fina said as she took the proffered report.

"Will do. Feel better." Milloy walked him to the door. He returned to find Fina holding the document and staring into space.

"Why would Melanie be contacting a handbag company?" she mused.

"Why would Melanie be contacting a *fake* handbag company?" Milloy asked.

"Good question. We can definitely rule out the idea that she was actually buying their goods. She wouldn't have been caught dead with anything you could charge to a shipboard account."

Fina winced at her poor choice of words.

There was no proof yet.

There was no proof of anything.

Milloy left, and Fina stepped into the shower. She was supposed to keep her bandages dry—so she took them off. The cuts on her palm were red and tender, and she didn't attempt anything more ambitious than wetting her body and hoping the dirt and sweat would wash off on their own. After dressing and struggling to pull her hair into a bun, Fina rummaged around in the medicine cabinet and found a roll of gauze, which she wound around her hand and secured with small strips of duct tape.

She needed to talk to Haley, who was still ignoring her

calls. Haley was typically bad at returning calls, and Fina had hoped the atypical circumstances might change that, but who was she kidding? Ludlows were born and bred to be strong and unemotional. You didn't moan or cry about things; you acted as if everything were going according to plan, even when it wasn't. Most teenagers weren't known for their communication skills, but Ludlow teenagers would have excelled in the CIA.

Before reaching for her cell phone, Fina grabbed Nanny's cordless phone and punched in her niece's number. Haley's curiosity might just get the better of her.

"Hello?" Haley answered after a few rings.

"Where are you?" Fina demanded. "I've been trying to reach you for days."

"What number is this?" Haley asked.

"That's not important. Where are you?"

"I'm at Neiman's," Haley said. Fina could hear voices in the background.

"Why?"

"I need some lip gloss."

Fina started to pace in front of the windows overlooking the harbor. A large oil tanker was creeping along with a tugboat on either end. "Haley, cut the shit. Your mother is missing. The police are dogging your father, and I was almost killed. It's time to put on your big-girl pants and get with the program."

"Why are you being so fucking mean to me?" Haley whined.

Fina held the phone away from her ear and took a deep breath. Teenagers were the best form of birth control.

"I have to talk to you. Now. The only question is where."

There was silence on the other end.

"Haley?"

"Okay, okay. I'll meet you at Pap and Gammy's house." The line went dead.

"Ugghh," Fina groaned, and threw the phone at the couch.

9

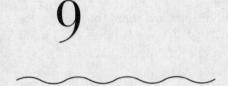

The first thing Fina did when she got to Newton was grab a beer from the refrigerator. She popped off the top and took a long pull. Technically, she wasn't supposed to mix alcohol and more than the recommended dose of pain relievers, but she imagined the warnings were just suggestions, not rules. Kind of like speed limits.

The maid came into the kitchen when Fina was halfway through her beer and pointed in the direction of the media/family room.

"Señora Elaine in there," she indicated.

"I don't want Señora Elaine. I want Señorita Haley."

"She there, too."

"Damn it." Fina didn't have enough meds on board to deal with Elaine, but she chugged her beer and then walked through the winding hallways to the family room.

It was a sunken room that overlooked the backyard,

like Carl's office. It featured an enormous sectional and a large flat-screen TV. One wall of the room was blanketed by built-in bookcases and shelves, which displayed various pieces of crystal and a smattering of family photos. Elaine and Haley were seated on the couch, their backs to Fina, with a selection of makeup spread out before them on the dark wood coffee table.

"This one is called Perilous," Haley said, while unscrewing the top of a tube of lip color.

"Ooh. That's pretty," Elaine said.

Fina stood in the doorway and glared at the back of her mother's head. She didn't know where to start. Breathing was probably a good idea.

"Hi," she said, and walked around the couch. She took a seat on the other side of the sectional. Haley looked morose, and Elaine's eyes widened.

"What happened to your face?"

"Huh? Mom, I was in a car accident. Didn't Dad tell you?"

"He didn't tell me about that," she said, pointing at Fina's eye. She shook her head in what translated to a physical *tsk*. Fina knew it well.

"I'm fine, in case you were worried."

Elaine shrugged. "I'm sure you are."

"I need to talk to Haley." Elaine didn't move. "Alone."

"Anything you need to say to her, you can say in front of me."

"Right. Please, Mom?"

Elaine glared at Fina.

"It's okay, Gammy," Haley said.

Elaine exhaled loudly. "You can show me the rest later,"

she said, and stood up from the couch. She scooted past Haley and galumphed up the deep-pile carpeted stairs.

Fina looked at Haley. Haley looked at a silver compact of eye shadow.

"Sorry I was bitchy before," Fina said. She really wasn't sorry, but she needed Haley to cooperate; generally, you do catch more flies with honey—unless you have a gun, of course.

"It's okay. I was kind of bitchy, too." Haley flopped back into the couch.

"How are you?" Fina asked. "I mean, obviously, you must be worried about your mom."

Haley nodded slowly, and her features sagged slightly.

"Haley, you can talk to me."

"What's there to say?" Her words came out in a rush. "Mom couldn't be bothered to stick around, and my dad is a douche who doesn't give a shit." Fina didn't respond. The silence in the room was punctured when Haley burst into tears.

"Oh, Haley, he does give a shit," Fina said, moving next to her on the sofa. "Why do you think I'm working so hard to find your mom? Your dad, Pap, and the rest of us, we're doing everything we can to figure this out."

Haley scrunched up her eyes, and her nose ran as tears rolled down her cheeks. Fina dug around in her bag and handed her niece a tissue. She'd been waiting for Haley to show some emotion, but now she felt helpless and inadequate in the face of her misery. Be careful what you wish for.

"I am doing everything I can to find her."

Haley sniffled. "Fine."

"And your parents' stuff has nothing to do with you."

Haley wiped under her eyes. "Fine. Could we please not talk about this anymore?"

Fina took a deep breath. "Fine. Let's talk about Brianna." The abrupt change of subject was the oldest trick in the book—because it worked. Fina felt a twinge of guilt for pushing her niece, but she couldn't worry too much about hurting her feelings if it kept her from finding Melanie.

Something flickered across Haley's face. A wave of recognition or surprise, maybe. "Who?" she asked as she fiddled with the strap of her tank top.

"Brianna. And I want the truth." Fina squeezed her shoulder. "Tell me the truth, Hale. Everybody is lying to me, and it's starting to make me nuts."

Haley examined her manicured nails. "How do *you* know Brianna?" she asked.

"I don't, not really. We've met, and we have some . . . mutual acquaintances."

"She's just a friend. We hang out sometimes."

"How old is she?"

Haley shrugged. "A little older than me, maybe."

"Where do you guys hang out?"

"Just . . . you know . . . places. Why are you checking up on me? My mom is the one in trouble."

"You think she's in trouble?"

Haley rolled her eyes. "She's missing, isn't she? Sounds like trouble to me."

"So where did you meet Brianna?"

"At Crystal."

"I suppose there's no point in my giving you the whole underage lecture."

Haley snorted. "No point whatsoever."

"Is she a hooker?"

"Huh?" Haley reached out and grabbed the eye shadow compact. She popped it open and studied the smooth, tiny cushions of color.

"Is Brianna a hooker?" Fina asked again.

"Oh my God, yeah right. That's likely." She curled her lip in derision.

Fina shrugged. "I think she is."

"Well, we all know that you're paranoid. Not that we don't still love you," Haley quipped.

"And Dante Trimonti? You know him from the club?"

"What? That sleazy, Italian Stallion wannabe?"

"That's the one."

"Everybody knows who he is, but I don't 'know him,' know him."

Fina looked down at the collection of makeup on the coffee table. She picked up a tube of lipstick and turned the bottom until a wedge of color emerged from the metal cylinder. "This one's nice."

"It's Cinnamon Fun Bun. It would look good on you. Try it," Haley urged.

Fina rolled the color over her lips and blotted them together. "Well?"

"You should keep it."

"Thanks." Fina capped the lipstick and dropped it into her bag. "Have you ever heard of a company called Zyxco?"

"No," Haley said as she smeared a line of sparkly blue eye shadow across the back of her hand.

"What about Mode Accessories?"

Haley shook her head and rubbed the shadow off her skin. "Don't know it."

"Okay." Fina reached over and gave her niece a hug. She stood up and walked over to the stairs. "Thanks, Haley. If you think of anything or need anything, call me. Okay?"

Haley turned so that her face was in profile. "I will."

Fina was still for a moment. From that angle, Haley's face was her mother's.

Cristian lived in a mid-rise brick apartment building, a few streets outside of Central Square. In the past ten years or so, the area had evolved from gritty to increasingly gentrified, and Fina wondered if, before too long, he would be priced out of the neighborhood, especially since he was paying for another household—that of his ex-wife and young son, Matteo.

Later that evening, Fina rang the bell next to MENENDEZ and listened for the static of the security system.

"Hello," he said.

"It's Fina. Can I come up?"

His answer was the buzz of the front door.

She climbed up to the third floor and found his door ajar. There was a large circular fan oscillating across the living room. Fina could see that the door to the tiny back porch was open, and she walked out to it via the kitchen. Cristian was sitting in a plastic folding chair, his feet propped on the railing, his chest bare, and a beer in his hand.

"Hola, chiquita," he said.

"Hola." Fina pulled a chair away from the railing and eased into it.

"How you feeling?" he asked.

"Sore. Cranky."

"Sorry to hear that."

She reached over and took a sip of his beer. Across the interior courtyard, there were what looked to be a couple of college students sitting on their little deck, smoking. "I hate heat," she said. "It's only May. I want my money back."

"Must be someone you can sue for the weather." Cristian grinned at her, took back the beer, and had another drink. "Any news today?"

"Yes. People are liars."

"That's news?"

Fina put her feet on the railing and tilted her chair back. "How come you never seem jaded?"

"What's the point? Lying is part of the human condition. People do it. It doesn't necessarily make them terrible people." Cristian shrugged. "Sometimes they can't help it. Sometimes they do it for the right reasons. You, for instance."

"Let's put me aside for a moment. I think we can agree that I'm a special case." Cristian arched an eyebrow. "I know everyone does it, but it bugs me, and it doesn't seem to bug you."

"What are my options? Be perpetually surprised and annoyed when people are meatheads? In that case, I better find a new line of work."

Cristian sipped his beer, and they sat in comfortable silence for a minute.

"Things the same with Marissa?"

"Yup." Cristian looked glum.

"Do you think Matteo would like *Disney on Ice*?"

"Are you kidding? He'd love it."

"I think I can get some tickets. Then you could be a bona fide Disneyland Dad."

"Yeah, 'cause that's how this feels, like the happiest place on earth."

Fina wiped her brow. The scabs forming on her arm were scratchy against her face. "I need to stand in front of that fan," she said, and got up.

"I've got a better idea," Cristian said. He stepped past her and put his beer bottle in the kitchen sink. He took her hand, grasped it loosely in his own, and led her down the hall to the bedroom. When he opened the door, a blast of cold air enveloped them.

"Ahh. Bliss," Fina said, and walked over to the bed. She stretched out on the duvet and closed her eyes. Cristian lay down next to her.

"This feels so good," Fina said with a sigh. "I don't even care if we screw around. You just go ahead and do what you need to do."

"That's super appealing," Cristian said. Fina listened to the hum of the AC and tried to ignore the myriad minor complaints from her body. She could feel the weight of Cristian next to her, but he didn't touch her.

They slept.

Hours later, the phone rang only once before Cristian grabbed it. Cops learn to sleep on the surface, rarely diving down deep into REM sleep.

"Menendez."

Fina shifted slightly on the bed.

He listened for a moment. "Yup, okay," he said, and hung up.

"Fina."

"What?"

"A body washed up near Logan."

She opened her eyes and looked at him.

Cristian touched her shoulder. "It's a woman."

Fina's mind jumped to the image of a runway and the flash of panic she always had when landing at Logan: *There's no ground, there's no ground, there's no ground.*

Fina gave Cristian a head start getting to the crime scene. Showing up with him or shortly after would only give credence to Pitney's theory about their special relationship. Instead, she jumped into his shower and washed off the layer of dried sweat she'd accumulated during the day.

At two thirty A.M., the humidity had subsided, and Fina rolled down her windows when she started her car. She grabbed her phone and hit the speed dial button that summoned her father.

"Fina?"

"A woman's body washed up near Logan."

"Is it her?"

"I don't know yet, but it doesn't look good."

"Are you there?"

"I'm heading there now." Fina glanced down the alley to her right. A large rat toddled by, sniffing around the base of a dumpster. "If it's her, Haley shouldn't find out from the news."

"I know. Call me when you know more." The line went dead.

Mass Ave was nearly deserted, but there were more signs of life once she crossed the river. She hopped on

Storrow Drive and sped down the winding road. The breeze from the open windows felt good, but nothing could ease the churning of her stomach.

It was a quick trip to the end of Harbor View Drive, and the scene was crawling with people. It took a cast of many to process the death of one. Detectives, police brass, crime scene investigators, medical examiners, district attorneys. And that didn't even include those indirectly involved: the press, the owner of the property where the body was found, the passersby who had to take an alternate route to work.

Fina pulled over to the side of the road behind a patrol car. There were no signs of news vans yet, but that might change depending upon the identity of the body. A homeless person would just be a "floater," but someone like Melanie would be a "victim." A uniformed cop held up his hand to hold her back as she approached the area cordoned off by crime scene tape.

"Crime scene, ma'am." He was young and as thin and tall as a reed. Fina could break him over her knee like a piece of kindling. And he called her *ma'am*, the polite notice that you have started the slide down the back of the hill.

"I know. I'm looking for Lieutenant Pitney."

"Your name?"

"Fina Ludlow."

The cop turned his back to her and mumbled into the radio affixed to his shoulder. It squawked back.

A few more incomprehensible sentences were exchanged, and then he held up the tape so Fina could duck under it. He directed her to an unmarked police car in the dusty, empty lot where a group of people were congregated. On the way, Fina was met by another officer, who asked her to sign the crime scene log. She scratched her signature and kept walking, trying to get a glimpse of the actual crime scene.

The harbor was about twenty yards away, and reflections from the city lights bobbed and danced like industrial phosphorescence. The lot sloped sharply to the water, but there was no clear path down. Huge boulders created a natural barrier between the water and land. A group of people in dark Windbreakers with various acronyms across their backs were wrestling floodlights into place.

At the car, Pitney was deep in conversation with a cluster of people, including Cristian. She stopped when she saw Fina.

"You're like a bad penny," she said, and glared at Cristian. "You just keep turning up."

"Do you have an ID yet?" Fina asked.

"Nope. Do you want to take a look?" Pitney asked, cocking her head to the side. She was wearing leggings and an oversize Red Sox T-shirt. Her hair was pulled into a ponytail near the top of her head. She looked like a cheerleader twenty years past her sell-by date.

"Sure," Fina said.

Cristian looked at her. He raised his eyebrow almost imperceptibly, and she returned his gaze. She generally didn't have a problem with bodies. Of course, it was different when it was family, but Fina wasn't going to lose a game of chicken with the cops.

A few miles away, Connor dipped a spoon into a dish of red velvet bread pudding. Looking at fatty tissue and blocked arteries during his medical training had gone a long way toward curing him of his taste for Southern cuisine. But proximity to his mother and her divine cooking had led to a regression in his eating habits.

Like this.

The color alone was enough to constrict arterial blood flow. The deep brownish-red color of the bread contrasted sharply with the bright white whipped cream that he had generously glopped on top. It was sweet and rich and smooth and creamy.

"You all right, darling?" his mom asked as she padded into the kitchen. Her hair was perfectly coiffed, and she was wearing a floral-patterned silk robe over a matching nightgown. Connor understood organic chemistry, but he still couldn't understand how his mother's hair stayed in place all the time.

"Couldn't sleep. I decided to have a snack."

Bev reached into a cabinet and pulled out a bowl in which she deposited a generous helping of the bread pudding and topped it with whipped cream. She sat down at the table and adjusted the belt on her robe.

"So, what are you worrying about?" she asked before taking a bite.

"Just the usual."

"Mmmmm. This is good."

"You haven't lost your touch, Mom."

"No, I have not. I just wish your daddy could eat some of this. I feel a little cruel cooking when he's in the next room eating through a tube."

"He wouldn't want you to stop cooking." Connor scraped a segment of the bowl clean with his spoon. He always approached his food in a tidy, methodical manner. As a child, he'd eaten all of one particular food on his plate before moving on to the next, or he divided a dish into quadrants that he emptied one at a time. "Are you doing okay, Mom?"

"What do you mean, sugar?"

"I know this is hard on you, Dad being sick and my stuff. I can't imagine business is great, given the economy. I worry about you sometimes."

Bev put her hand over Connor's. "You don't have to. I'd be lying if I said things hadn't been challenging this past year, but I've managed." She took a bite of bread pudding. "Actually, things are looking up. I'm in the final stages of entering a business partnership."

"I thought you hated the idea of having a partner— other than Dad, I mean."

"I did, as long as Dad was fully active in the business, but things have changed." Bev looked him in the eye. "One of the biggest mistakes you can make in life is refusing to acknowledge what's staring you in the face. Things change, and you have to change with them, or you'll be obsolete." She smiled. "Like the dinosaurs."

"I don't think the dinosaurs became extinct because they refused to change. I think it had something to do with a meteor and an ice age." Connor had finished his dessert. The spoon and bowl were so clean, they looked like they could be put right back in the cabinet.

"Well, whatever. You need to take stock and move forward." She stared at him. "You need to think about that, Connor."

"I know, Mom."

Bev held his gaze and seemed to make a decision to let the subject go. "So, I'll have a new partner, an influx of cash, and maybe the good Lord will see fit to heal your daddy."

Connor sighed. His mother didn't abide by her own advice when it came to Chester. From a medical standpoint, it was unlikely Chester would regain his capabilities. He was thirteen years older than Bev, and his body had been compromised. If his mother were truly taking stock and moving forward, she would acknowledge that his father would never be who he once was.

But most people, even those who claimed to face life head-on, veered off at some point, even Connor. His whole life, he'd studiously avoided learning about his parents' business enterprises. Sometimes, denial made life livable.

Fina got back in her car and wiped away the thin sheen of sweat that had sprouted on her brow. Her mouth tasted sour, even though she'd done an admirable job of not puking.

It was the worst possible outcome.

It was Melanie.

Obviously, she didn't look like she usually did, but if you could see beyond the bloat and the skin color, there were vestiges of her. Long hair, a short-sleeved cashmere sweater in a shade of purple Fina had once admired, and a pricey driving moccasin wedged onto one of her swollen feet. An official identification would be conducted by the medical examiner, but Fina was certain it would confirm her own conclusion.

She held her phone in her hand for a moment and then

dialed her father. It rang once. Carl picked up, but didn't say anything.

"It's her," Fina said. "It's not official, but I saw her."

Carl blew out some air. "Meet us at the office."

Fina hung up the phone. She cranked up the air conditioner and pointed the vent toward her face. She closed her eyes and leaned back against the headrest.

"Are you okay?" Cristian asked through her open window. He handed her a bottle of cold water.

"Yeah."

"Did you already call them?"

Fina opened her eyes. "Yeah. Why?"

"I'm sure Pitney wanted to be the bearer of bad news."

"Tough shit. That's the price you pay for an on-the-spot ID. I'm sure she'll have lots of chances to bear more bad news." Fina took a deep breath and tried to shake herself out of the inertia that had rolled over her like a wave. "I've gotta go. I'll call you later."

Cristian stepped away from the car, and she did a sharp U-turn and pulled back onto the road.

She sped through the Logan maze and into the Sumner Tunnel. After a few minutes of shaky hands and nausea, Fina took a deep breath and vowed to get a grip. There would be plenty of time to have a meltdown later. Right now, she had to focus on Rand and any role he might have had in Melanie's death. By morning, the Boston PD would be worked up into a gleeful frenzy, eager to put a Ludlow away for something.

She used a key card to get into the office parking garage and enable the elevator. One of the overnight receptionists buzzed her into Ludlow and Associates. Fina strode down the hallway and was aware of an undercurrent of murmuring left in her wake. She wasn't sure if it was her physical appearance that was causing the stir or if word about Melanie had already leaked out. Luckily, she was impervious to whispers and muttering; Carl had taught them at a young age that people would always talk about them because they were jealous. By the time Fina realized that wasn't exactly the reason, she was too old to care.

Carl, Rand, Scotty, and Matthew were in Carl's office. Carl sat behind the desk, and Matthew sat in one of the chairs facing him. Scotty was in a club chair, and Rand was on the couch, elbows on knees, head hanging. The conversation stalled when she came in the room.

Fina stopped and looked at them.

"It's Melanie," she said.

"Are you sure?" Rand asked.

"Yes. They still have to do a formal ID, but it's her. I'm so sorry, Rand."

He rubbed his forehead with his hands and closed his eyes.

"What the fuck am I going to do?" he asked, his voice tinged with desperation. Rand looked at their father with pleading eyes. In an instant, he was transformed into the little boy who'd left open the back gate through which the family dog escaped and was killed. He was equal parts anguish and dread. "This can't be happening."

Fina walked over to the minibar and pulled out a bottle of scotch and a glass. She brought them over to the coffee table and poured a generous amount for Rand, which he downed in one gulp. She poured him another. Then she took a large swig directly from the bottle.

"Gimme some of that," Scotty said, and she passed him the bottle. He drank and then handed it to Matthew, who took his turn and offered it to Carl.

Carl waved the bottle away. "Enough. We need to pull our shit together."

Fina took the bottle from Matthew and had another long pull. She poured a little more for Rand and then replaced the cap and set it on the table.

"You three," Carl said, gesturing at the boys. "Go eat something or pop a mint or something. The last thing we need is you smelling like booze when the cops show up. I need to talk to your sister."

"What about Haley?" Fina asked as her brothers rose to leave. "We need to tell her before she finds out some other way."

They all looked at Rand. He hung his head and exhaled loudly. "Fuck."

Fina exchanged glances with Scotty and Matthew; they wouldn't wish that conversation on anyone.

Her brothers shuffled out, and Fina looked at her father. Carl was nattily dressed as always—dark suit, shirt in a similar shade, and a bold tie—but his eyes looked tired.

"Josefina," he said, sighing. "Where are we with this? What do you have?"

"Well," she said as she sat down across from him, "Rand had a terrible fight with Melanie. She went to Cambridge, bought cigarettes, and had a brief conversation with a psychiatrist she knows socially."

Carl's eyes widened, and he started to speak.

"Wait," Fina said. "She disappears. The cops find blood

on Rand's boat, and his cooler is missing. I find a mystery phone number in Melanie's things, which turns out to belong to a dummy corporation in Framingham. I still don't know the connection between the company and Melanie. Haley is recognized by one of my contacts; she's been spending a lot of time hanging around Crystal with a dubious crowd. Specifically, one young woman whom I believe is a prostitute."

"Oh, for fuck's sake!" Carl exclaimed.

"Wait," Fina said again and held up her hand. "I'm jumped and then someone ran me off the road. And Melanie's body washes up next to Runway 4R/22L."

Carl thought for a moment and flicked his hand toward the scotch. Fina tipped back in her chair and grabbed the bottle and empty glass. She poured her father half a glass and watched as he threw it back.

"So much for getting our shit together," she mumbled.

"This is more shit than I imagined." He sat back in his chair. "Tell me about the psychiatrist."

Fina pulled on her bottom lip with her fingers. "First, you have to tell me something."

Carl raised an eyebrow.

"What were you and Rand talking about the other night when I overheard you?"

Carl drummed his fingers on his desk. "It's not important."

Fina gripped the armrests of her chair. "Dad, don't be stupid. Once I hear it from the police, it's too late."

Carl was silent.

"Seriously. We're getting into some scary shit here."

Carl splashed more scotch into the glass and sipped

it before answering. "This stays between us," he cautioned.

"Ugghh. Just tell me."

Carl fiddled with an expensive pen on his blotter. "Your brother was involved in a situation, and I assisted him."

Fina made a motion with her hand, urging him to continue.

"He got into some trouble, but I was able to keep it quiet."

"So you did damage control. What's new? What are we talking about? Drugs, sex, or money?"

"Sex."

"An affair? A love child?"

"No."

Fina stared at her father. "Did he hurt someone?"

"No!" Carl exclaimed. Fina tamped down her annoyance at her father's response. In college, there were rumors that Rand had forced himself on a girl who had the misfortune of attending a party at his fraternity. Nothing was ever proven, and Fina didn't want to believe that her brother was capable of that, but she wondered. Carl, more than anyone, knew what Rand was capable of, and he had no right to be offended by her question.

"Then what?"

"He was busted . . . for solicitation."

Fina stared at him. "Hookers." She leaned forward, grabbed the bottle, and took a drink. "Goddamn Rand. He isn't even creative in his deviancy. What happened exactly?"

"It was about a year ago. He called me after being picked up in a hotel room. Luckily, one of the vice guys was Sal Gisby's kid; you know, we helped them out with that med mal suit. I talked to Sal, and he talked to his kid, who was willing to pretend it didn't happen. Sal's got that huge house on the Cape—the one with the private beach and boat dock—because of us."

"So Rand just picked up some hooker off the street?"

"No, she was from a service."

Fina dropped her head back and stared at the ceiling. "Oh my God, that's even worse. That means he's in some system somewhere."

"Not necessarily."

"Of course he is, Dad. That's the management's insurance policy. You know that." She looked at Carl. "This doesn't help him."

"I know. That's why we were keeping it to ourselves."

"Did Melanie know?"

"I don't think so."

"But she might have?"

"I don't know, Fina. I have no way of knowing that."

"Maybe that's what they were fighting about outside Grahamson. Melanie would have been humiliated. It's worse than his having an affair."

Carl shrugged.

Fina knew that some of the men in their social circle thought paid company was the lesser of the two evils since it indicated a lack of emotional connection: Hey, it's only sex. Fina thought they should all work a little harder to keep their peckers in their pants.

"So, what do you want to do?" Fina asked.

Carl looked at her and gripped the pen firmly. "About what specifically?"

"About the escort. Do you want me to track her down? Are you going to tell the cops?"

"I haven't decided. We have to do something, though. We have to take action."

Ludlows were like sharks; if they didn't keep moving, they died.

Fina slept on the couch in Matthew's office for a couple of hours, but she didn't get any rest. Every fifteen minutes or so, she'd roll over, bleary-eyed and confused, until the knowledge of Melanie's death slammed into her consciousness. She didn't want to waste what precious time she had sleeping, but she didn't know what else to do, particularly at four in the morning. By first light, she damn well better have a plan.

"I need to talk to Rand," she said when Matthew came into the room a little after six. She sat up, and he handed her a cup of coffee and a sweet roll the size of a brick.

"He's not here. He went home to see Haley."

Fina blew across the surface of the coffee and took a small sip. It was hot and rich.

"Do you know when he'll be back?"

"Nope." Matthew sat in the club chair across from Fina. She put down the coffee and tore off a corner of the roll. Sugary icing clung to the folds of dough. Fina put a bite in her mouth and chewed slowly.

"This is so fucked up," Matthew said.

"Yup."

Matthew reached over to the coffee table and grabbed the large remote control. He pressed a button, and the

TV screen came to life. Fina pulled off another twist of sweet roll and watched the screen. Matthew bounced around the channels and finally settled on one of the local early bird newscasts.

The young blond anchor was describing the plight of a duck that had gotten his head stuck in a soccer net at a local elementary school. He was eventually freed, but not without a lot of angst on the part of the students and, undoubtedly, the duck.

"You could represent the duck," Fina commented. She sipped her coffee. "You could sue the school, the town, the net manufacturer, maybe some of the parents. There are deep pockets in that town."

Matthew gave her a dirty look. "You're seriously sleep deprived."

The newscaster turned toward a different camera with a flourish, and a serious expression dropped over her face.

"We have reports that a woman's body was found overnight in Boston Harbor near Logan Airport. The woman was discovered by a homeless man and has yet to be identified. The medical examiner will be conducting an autopsy this morning. There has been some speculation that the body is that of Melanie Ludlow, the wife of attorney Rand Ludlow. She has been missing for almost two weeks. We will update you as information becomes available."

Fina looked at Matthew. "Let the games begin."

10

~~~~~~~~~

Fina tracked down Mark Lamont at a diner in Brighton. Although his tastes ran to multi-million-dollar homes and luxury cars, he'd made his money in construction and real estate development and slipped easily into the world of blue-collar workers and greasy spoons.

Mark was sitting in a booth at the back of the diner across from a man wearing jeans and a dirt-caked T-shirt. Fina caught Mark's eye, and he did a small double take at her appearance. He beckoned her over. After a brief introduction, the other man left, and Fina slid into his spot on the vinyl banquette, which was sunken and warm.

"What happened now?" Mark asked.

"Car accident. I'm fine. Just sore."

"Is it true?" Mark asked as he flagged down the waitress.

Fina ordered a glass of orange juice and waited for the

waitress to leave before answering. "I think so, yeah. It's probably Melanie."

"Aww, Christ," Mark said, and rubbed his hand over his face. "That's horrible. I'm sorry."

"It hasn't been confirmed yet or made public, but that will probably happen in the next twenty-four hours."

"Do the cops know what happened?"

"I don't think so."

The waitress refilled Mark's coffee cup and plunked down Fina's juice in a dimpled plastic tumbler. She was wearing a dress and apron and thick-soled white shoes. She looked like a nurse from another decade.

"Do they have any suspects?"

"Other than Rand?" Fina asked.

Mark rotated his coffee cup in its saucer. "That's just like the cops. Go for the easy answer, not the right answer. Rand wouldn't hurt Melanie."

"*We* all know that, but they don't buy it. But that's why I'm here."

Mark picked up his coffee cup and looked at Fina over the brim.

"I spoke with Bob Webber," Fina said, "and he's pretty sure he saw Melanie in the North End on that Wednesday night, which is great. It opens up some new avenues of investigation, except he doesn't want me to say anything to the cops."

"Right, but I told you that when I gave you the tip," Mark said.

"I know, it's just that things are looking worse for Rand, and it would really help if we could point the cops in another direction."

"Ahh, Fina." Mark adjusted in his seat. "I don't know."

"It would help us figure out who actually killed Melanie."

"I understand. It's just complicated, you know? Bob is working on a big job for me right now. If he gets pulled, it'll be a mess, not to sound crass." Mark peered at her. "Not to mention I gave him my word. And you gave me yours."

Fina ran her finger through the trail of condensation that the cold orange juice had left on the table. "I know. I wouldn't ask if I weren't running out of options. I would owe you, big-time." She hated owing anyone anything, but sometimes it had to be done.

The waitress dropped the folded check onto the table. Fina didn't bother reaching for her bag; Mark was old-school and believed that as long as a man was present, he paid.

"Look, how about I talk to Bob and see if we can work something out," Mark said as he studied the check. He rocked forward and pulled his wallet out from his back pocket. He thumbed through some bills and put a crisp twenty on the table.

"That would be terrific. Thanks." Fina got up, and Mark followed her out to the parking lot.

"Any news on a funeral?" Mark asked as they stood next to Fina's car.

"Depends on when they release the body. I'll let you know."

"Give Rand my condolences. And the rest of the family."

"Will do. Thanks, Mark."

Fina pulled out of the diner parking lot and nosed into the morning traffic. She'd give Mark a little time to work on Bob Webber, but eventually, she'd take matters into her own hands. When it came to Mark versus her brother, there was no contest.

There were news trucks outside Rand's house, and local cops were parked at either end of the street. Fina identified herself and was waved through. It was cooler than the day before, but still, and she could hear the drone of a lawnmower somewhere down the street.

The front door was locked. Fina rang the bell and waited for a minute until there were muffled noises inside, and the door was pulled open.

"Risa?" Fina asked.

Risa hugged her and then pulled Fina through the door and closed it behind her.

"I'm surprised to see you here," Fina said.

Risa shook her head and smoothed her hands down the front of her white button-down shirt. She was wearing jeans and gold flats. "I'm here for Haley. And Elaine."

"Why does Elaine need you?" Fina asked, peering down the hall.

"She's devastated, obviously."

"Obviously."

Elaine got a lot of power and attention standing in Carl's spotlight, but oftentimes she resented his presence there. She took advantage of any opportunity to shine the spotlight on herself. No matter what was actually happening, it was happening to Elaine.

"How are you?" Fina asked.

"I'm . . . I'm numb. I can't believe this is really happening."

"I know."

"I guess there was a part of me that still believed she was going to show up. I'd yell at her for worrying me, but then we'd get over it and things would just go back to normal."

Fina nodded. One benefit of her job was that she never expected things to end well, and she was rarely disappointed in that regard. "How's Haley?"

Risa shook her head. "Oh, Fina. It was awful. She was so upset. She cried so hard she threw up. And she won't talk to anyone."

"This is a fucking nightmare."

Risa nodded and brushed a tear off her cheek.

"Is that Fina?" Elaine appeared in the hallway.

"Yes, Mom. It's me."

"Fina." She barreled toward the front door and grasped Fina in a tight hug. Elaine made sniffling noises. "It's just so terrible."

"It is." Fina patted her mother's back, more for Risa's benefit than Elaine's. She didn't want to appear as cold as she actually felt.

Elaine released Fina and stepped back. "Oh, Fina. If only you'd found her, none of this would be happening."

Fina made a show of looking at her watch. "That's quick. Even for you."

"I'm just saying—"

"I know what you're saying, and I don't want to hear it. Where's Haley?"

"Don't take that tone with me." Elaine stepped back and drew herself up.

"I need to talk to Haley. Can we agree that Haley is the most important thing right now?" Fina implored her mother. "Seriously, Mom."

"Of course," Elaine said. "Of course Haley is most important."

"Good. And I need to talk to Rand. If you think things are bad now, just wait 'til Rand gets arrested." Fina glanced at Risa. "Not that he deserves to, but it's quite possible."

"Arrested for what?" Elaine asked.

"Is she upstairs?" Fina asked Risa.

Risa nodded. "In her room."

"I'll be back." Fina trotted up the stairs two at a time and walked down the hallway to Haley's room. The door was pulled closed, so she knocked softly. There was no response; Fina slowly turned the handle and opened the door.

All of the shades were drawn, and the hum of the central AC made the room feel like a cool cave. Fina crept forward a few steps and peered down at the bed. Haley was curled up in a ball in a nest of pillows and blankets. She was wearing her usual uniform of a tank top and sweat shorts, and her hair was gathered back in a scrunchie. A few strands had escaped and were plastered to her forehead and cheek. She inhaled deeply and snorted softly as Fina studied her. Mr. Tux, a worn stuffed penguin, was in her arms. Melanie had bought it for her at the aquarium when she was a baby, and it had been well loved over the years.

Fina stared at her, and reality began to sink in.

Haley's mother was never coming back.

Rand was sitting outside at a table next to the pool. There was a plate of untouched eggs and bacon in front of him, and a half-empty coffee cup.

"Hey," Fina said.

"Hey." Rand stared at the pool. An automated vacuum was creeping across the bottom, presumably sucking up microscopic invaders.

Fina gestured toward his plate. "That looks pretty gross." The scrambled eggs were grayish and curdled, and the bacon was sitting in a small pool of grease.

"Mom made it."

"Ah. Next time, go with Risa. She's an amazing cook."

"Right. 'Cause that wouldn't piss Mom off."

Fina leaned back in the webbed chair. "Isn't it amazing? Everything else that's going on, and you're worried about pissing off Mom."

Rand shrugged. "It's just not worth the headache."

"How are you doing?"

"I'm hanging in there."

Fina planted the chair back on the patio and put her elbows on the table. "Dad told me about the thing with the prostitute."

Rand's shoulders drooped. "Why the hell did he do that?"

"So I can do something about it. I can't help you if I don't know what's going on. You guys should have told me as soon as Melanie went missing."

"The two things have nothing to do with each other."

"Right." Fina studied the backyard. It was early in the season, and when the rosebushes bloomed there would be an explosion of color that Melanie would never see. "Why don't you let me be the judge? Tell me about the escort service."

Rand took a sip of coffee and grimaced. "Even her coffee is toxic." He put the cup back down. "What do you want to know?"

Fina sighed. "Everything."

"All I do is call the number and put in my request. That's it. Nothing else to tell."

Fina swallowed hard at the mention of his "request." These were women, after all, not pizza toppings. "I know this is a terrible time, Rand, but my patience is wearing thin. I need names, numbers, locations. Please don't make me drag it out of you."

Rand sneered at her. "I certainly don't want to make your life difficult," he said sarcastically.

Fina slapped her hand on the table. "Rand! Stop being a fucking moron! I'm trying to save your ass."

"Right. Everyone always has to save Rand."

"Oh, here we go again. Here's an idea: If you don't want people saving you, stop fucking up." Fina looked at the pool. The vacuum was stuck in a corner of the deep end, running over the same small patch of tile over and over again. "Maybe I should just wash my hands of this and let you figure it out on your own."

Rand barked out a laugh. "And disappoint Dad? Two daughters who don't live up to his expectations?"

Fina gaped at him. "I don't think dying as a toddler

translates to falling short of expectations. I seriously don't think Dad sees it that way."

Rand waved his hand in the air. "You know what I mean. Disappointing him. You're not going to defy or disappoint him. That's never going to happen."

Fina was silent for a moment. "You're right. It probably isn't going to happen in this case, but not because of Dad. Haley's lost one parent. She doesn't need to lose the other. Although, sometimes, I have to wonder about your fitness as a parent."

Rand reached across the table and grabbed Fina's wrist. "Don't you ever question me that way." He glared at her, but released her hand after a moment.

Fina massaged her wrist. "I'm going to let that go since you're grief-stricken, but do it again and I will kick your ass. Or shoot you." She stood up. "I'll expect the details on your extracurricular activities by the end of the day." She started to leave the patio, but turned back toward Rand instead. "And a word to the wise: You might want to keep your temper in check. Pitney would be ecstatic if she got a glimpse of that."

Fina followed the slate path that wended its way around the side of the house and climbed the stairs to the front yard.

Some days, being an orphan had great appeal.

Normally, Fina didn't succumb to the pressures of a case. She was methodical, thought out every move, and made careful decisions, but Melanie's case was different. The family connection was fraying her nerves, and she found her thoughts ping-ponging around from one lead to another. She needed to regroup and make a plan.

She hadn't had a real meal in hours, so she pulled off Route 9 and into Kelly's parking lot. Inside, the excessive air-conditioning and garishly painted walls created an alternate reality. No matter what was going on outside, it was cool and cheerful inside.

Fina gave her order to the ponytailed teenager behind the counter and dropped into a booth to wait. She retrieved her food when her name was called and then sat back down and worked her way through a lobster roll, French fries, a side of fried clams, and a diet soda. It was enough fat and calories to sustain a sports team, but when she looked down at the collection of balled-up napkins on her plate, she felt calmer than she had in days.

Now.

A plan.

She couldn't wait around for Hal to do more digging on Mode Accessories. She'd have to do some digging of her own, and in order to do that, she had to be someone other than Fina Ludlow.

In her car in the parking lot, she fired up her laptop and fashioned a phony business card. She drove to a nearby copy shop, printed twenty copies of the card on fancy stock, and bought a leather folio. She called her computer go-to guy, who promised he'd post a corporate website place setter within the hour, and she rerecorded the message on her second phone to reflect her new job.

The trunk of her car yielded a black pantsuit in a no-wrinkle fabric, and a stop at Nordstrom Rack netted a silk blouse, some heels, and a high-end purse that was considerably discounted. It was the sort of thing Fina would never carry, with lots of buckles and snaps and chains, but she'd seen plenty of women around town weighted down with similar hardware. Haley would probably love it. Fina ducked into a restroom in the store, put on the suit and her purchases, and smoothed the flyaways that had escaped from her bun. Then she climbed into her car for the drive to Mode Accessories.

Fina sat for ten minutes and watched the front door. No one entered or exited. She pulled down her visor mirror and checked her face. Her bruises were creeping from one end of the spectrum to the other—purple to blue to yellow. Fina sighed. Disfigurement might actually work to her advantage; she looked pretty pitiful. She checked her wallet and made sure the business cards were nestled next to the fake driver's license confirming her identity as Amy Myers. One deep breath and she was in the bright sunshine, striding across the parking lot.

A plain woman—middle-aged and lumpy—manned the reception desk. The choice of receptionist said a lot about any business and generally confirmed Fina's theory that workplace discrimination was alive and well. Ludlow and Associates certainly subscribed to the practice, and this woman would never have made the cut; she was too homely.

"Hello. I'm wondering if you could help me," Fina said brightly, and smiled widely. "I'm interested in speaking with whoever's in charge."

The woman looked up from her computer screen and grimaced at Fina's bruises. "Do you have an appointment?"

"No." Fina tried to look pained. "Is that a problem? I wanted to speak with the manager about some potential business."

The receptionist's e-mail dinged, and she turned her attention to the screen. "You want Donald. Hold on. I'll see if he's available."

"Of course."

Fina waited while the woman clicked the mouse a few times and launched a video. She laughed at her screen—it was probably a cat rodeo or something equally inane—and after a minute she pushed back her chair and walked around the partition. Her backside was enveloped in tight black pants that did nothing to conceal the cottage cheese quality of her butt.

Fina dropped the smile. It was exhausting being nice.

The new shoes were digging into the sides of her feet, and she shifted her weight from one leg to the other. She didn't understand how or why women wore high heels all the time. Men would never put up with that shit.

After a moment, the receptionist returned to the front desk with a man in tow.

"I'm Donald Seymour. How can I help?" He extended his hand, and Fina shook with her right hand and held her left hand up in surrender.

"Please excuse my appearance. Car accident." She pouted slightly.

"Must have been a doozy," Donald said. "What can I do for you?"

"It's about your business, but I'm wondering . . ." She glanced at the receptionist, who had plopped back down into her seat. ". . . if we could talk privately."

"Of course, Miss . . ."

"Myers. Amy Myers."

Fina followed Donald through the office area, which held four standard-looking desks. Two equally nondescript women were working on computers, their desks crowded with piles of paper. Donald pushed open a door, which led to a small break room. He gestured for Fina to sit at the table that was wedged into the space.

"Can I get you some coffee or tea?" he asked, and swept some straws and sugar packets off the table and into the trash. Donald was probably in his forties, with brown hair and a mole on his right cheek. His teeth were straight, but slightly yellowed. He was wearing a tan polyester golf shirt and a brown pair of pants that were made from mixed fibers. His belt sat on his rather thick waist like an inflatable inner tube.

"I would love some water. This heat is killing me."

"I hear ya, but we shouldn't complain; it will be snowing before you know it." He put a cup of water down in front of her.

"You know, you're absolutely right," Fina said. "I should bite my tongue."

Donald poured himself a cup of coffee from the coffeemaker on the counter and took the seat next to her. Their knees were practically touching, but Donald didn't seem to mind; in fact, he seemed quite willing to overlook Fina's battered appearance in exchange for physical proximity to her.

"So how can I help you today, Miss Myers?"

"Call me Amy, please." Fina took a sip of water. "I

work in the retail industry, and I have a client who is very interested in your business."

"Really. Who's the client?"

"Actually, I'm not at liberty to say, but I can tell you that it's a small but prestigious entity in the hospitality arena. Their customers are willing to spend a great deal of money on the right goods, and my client is looking for a new supplier."

"How did you hear about Mode Accessories?"

"Are you familiar with John Smithson at Hagen International? You know, the parent company of Handbags Plus?"

Donald looked blank.

"I could have sworn he told me to contact Mode Accessories." Fina put on her best perplexed look. "I hope I didn't make a mistake. Let me check that I'm at the right place." She made a motion to reach into her purse.

Donald's eyes darted around the room. "No, no. I know John Smithson," he insisted, putting a hand on Fina's bag. "Sorry, I don't know where my head is." Bluffing Donald Seymour was child's play.

Fina dismissed his apology with a wave. "I forget things all the time." She leaned toward Donald. "I just wouldn't want to annoy John by contacting the wrong supplier. It's an important contract."

"No worries about that. You're in the right place."

Fina continued with her pitch, practically convincing herself that she represented a high-end cruise line that wanted purses for its onboard shops. She finished and sat back in her chair. She smiled at Donald and sipped her water.

"Why don't I tell you about our business?" Donald offered.

"That would be terrific."

So Donald talked for fifteen minutes about clutches and satchels and hobo bags. Leather and pleather and vinyl. Fina worked hard to stay focused, but worried that the combination of her meal and the conversation might send her into a deep food coma. She asked questions and took notes so as to stay awake and appear the interested potential client. Donald seemed satisfied by her performance.

"That's very helpful," Fina said. She pulled on the hem of her jacket. "I'm just wondering, is this an American-owned business?"

"Yes, ma'am. Stars and stripes all the way." Donald grinned at her.

"It's not that I or my bosses have anything against foreign companies, but we've had some bad experiences in the past. You know—sweatshops, that sort of thing."

"Well, I can't speak for our third-party suppliers, but I can assure you that Mode Accessories is owned by a born-and-bred American. Same as the parent company."

"Would it be possible to meet the owner? Just due diligence, you know how it is."

Donald squirmed in his seat and looked toward the bulletin board on the wall. Heimlich maneuver instructions were tacked to it—as if anyone had the time to read a poster when someone was choking. "I'm not sure that's going to be possible. With travel schedules and such."

"Oh." Fina turned her smile upside down. "That's a shame. I'll have to talk to my client about that."

"I'm not saying it's impossible, but I'll have to make some calls."

"I would really appreciate that," Fina said, and she started to push back from the table. "Is this your whole operation? It seems small for what you've described."

"We have another office, but we don't need much space."

Fina tried to look through the swinging door that led away from the front office. Donald beckoned her through the other door. "Do you have a card, Amy?"

"Of course." Fina pulled out her wallet. She took her time pulling a card out from the clear-paned slot next to Amy Myers's license. "I hope we can work something out."

"I'm sure we can." Donald pocketed her card and followed her to the door. "Stay cool."

"You too, Donald. Think snow!"

Fina pushed open the door and was hit by a wave of heat. She got back in her car and waved at Donald as she drove away. Half a mile down the road, she pulled into a mattress store parking lot where she stripped off Amy Myers and stuffed her into a shopping bag.

11

"How are you holding up?" Milloy asked Fina after she slid into a booth at Romy's Pizza.

"Eh. I'm okay."

Milloy had a Greek salad in front of him and was sipping a sparkling water. Fina reached over and took one of the large olives that glistened with oil and bits of feta.

"You can order something," Milloy told her.

"I don't want anything, other than your olive." She popped it in her mouth and savored the meatiness of it. She cleaned it to the pit, which she deposited on a napkin pulled from the silver tabletop dispenser.

The waiter brought her a glass of water, and she took a sip and looked around. A few of the other booths were occupied. Some teenage boys were digging into a large pepperoni pizza, and a couple of Newton cops were eating subs. "Why do you like this place so much?" she asked Milloy.

He chewed on a mouthful of lettuce. "Cheap, fast, and fresh."

"Ahh. The way you like your women."

Milloy raised an eyebrow and bit into a pepperoncini. The TV hanging in the corner took a break from the Red Sox game and a local update came on. The volume was low, but Fina recognized the area near the airport where the body had been found.

"I wish a celebrity would die or a politician would screw up," Fina mused. "Something."

Milloy craned his neck and watched the screen. "They'll grow tired of it soon."

"Not soon enough. So I did a little recon at Mode Accessories this afternoon."

"How'd that go?"

"I didn't get anything definitive, but I made a pitch and have put in my request to meet the owner."

"Did you figure out why Melanie contacted them?"

"No, but it's definitely a front for something. I thought maybe if I could get a name, then I could have Hal attack it from that angle."

"How'd you leave it?" Milloy asked.

"The delightful Donald Seymour is going to be in touch with Amy Myers."

"Good old Amy. Was she perky?"

"Always. However, I don't think Amy would ever look like she went a few rounds with Muhammad Ali." Fina pointed at her face.

"Yeah, the cops checked you out when you came in."

"Really?" Fina looked in their direction and smiled. "They probably think you beat me."

"Little do they know, you're the dangerous one." Milloy neatly laid his knife and fork across his plate. "So, any news from the family?"

"That reminds me. Hold on." Fina pulled out her phone and checked her messages. "One sec."

She dialed and waited as Rand's voice mail kicked in. "Hi, Rand," she said after the beep. "It's your sister. I'm still waiting for those details we discussed. Call me."

"What details?" Milloy asked after she'd hung up.

Fina pressed the paper wrapper from her straw onto the tabletop. "Turns out that Rand has been getting some paid action on the side."

Milloy shook his head. "Not smart. Was he busted?"

"He was, but Carl made it go away."

"You think it has something to do with Melanie?"

"I don't know, but it's a good place to look. And Haley seems to have befriended a hooker."

"Kids today."

"I know, really. If someone were to describe my family to me—if they weren't my family, of course—I'd never believe it. How many ways can you go off the rails?"

"Many, apparently."

Fina began pleating the wrapper, making it into a paper inchworm. "If I get the info I need from Rand, I'll need you to set up a date."

"With a hooker."

"An escort, and you don't need to actually sleep with her. I just want access."

"Of course you do."

Fina took a long drink. The cops were getting up from their table, adjusting their belts and holsters as they stood.

"Do you want to join me at Crystal?" Fina asked.

"Weren't you just there?"

"Yeah, but the people I was looking for weren't."

"What do you think you're going to get out of these people?"

"I have no idea, but I'm kind of running out of options here. I don't have many leads, so I need to work the ones I have."

"That's fine. I'll go."

"Thank you, and can you come to the funeral with me? It will keep my mother off my back."

Milloy had an equally hypnotizing effect on men and women of all ages. Elaine got giddy around him, and even Carl showed him a grudging respect. Fina chalked this up to the way Milloy carried himself; he didn't give a shit what anyone else thought, and his extreme self-confidence—not arrogance—was intoxicating.

"In the course of this conversation, you've asked me to make a date with a hooker—for conversation, not sex—accompany you to a nightclub to interview some punk-ass pimp, and be your date at your sister-in-law's funeral. Is that everything?"

"I think so. And you love our quality time together, so stop your bitching." Fina reached into her bag and put a ten on the table. "My treat. Pick me up around eleven P.M.?"

Milloy gave a little wave, and Fina pushed through the front door and stepped onto the sidewalk. A guy on a skateboard sped by her, close enough that he stirred up a slight breeze. Fina pegged him to be at least twenty-five years old. She was all for bucking convention, but there was something ridiculous about a grown man using a skateboard for transportation.

Back at Nanny's, Fina checked her messages again and wondered how much time she would give Rand before tattling to Carl. The way to get anyone to do anything was to get Carl to make it so. This was part of the Ludlow dance. Fina knew it was unhealthy and maybe even pathological, but it didn't seem like the time to alter her steps.

A cold beer and a lukewarm bath, with a couple of Advil, promised some relief from her nagging discomfort. She soaked for almost an hour, lying back in the tub, submerged up to her ears, only her face breaking the surface. She'd pulled off the gauze before getting in, and after a few minutes of stinging and throbbing, her hand adjusted to the water. The bath may have relaxed her body, but it did little for her brain. She kept thinking about Melanie.

When she was pruny, Fina got out, toweled off, and retrieved her phone from the coffee table in the living room. The envelope icon indicated a message, and she stood naked on the rug as she listened. Rand had left a message with the phone number for the service he used. She scribbled it on a receipt and then went back into her bedroom. Fina lay down on the bed and set her alarm for a couple hours. She'd need her beauty sleep to face the meat market that was Crystal.

Milloy drove up a few minutes after eleven, and Fina hopped in the passenger seat. All the windows were rolled down and the moonroof was open. A warm breeze offered a brief respite from the heat when the car moved. Fina asked Milloy to pull over at a convenience store, and she went in and bought two throwaway cell phones from the Korean man behind the counter. She handed one to Milloy when she got back in the car.

"So don't make a date, just get some general information." She pulled the phone number for the escort service out of her bag.

"We're doing this now?" Milloy asked.

"Why not?"

"Fine. What information do you want?"

"How it works, how much, locations, and if they take requests."

"What am I requesting?"

"Nothing, tonight, but if you got a name from a buddy, for example, could they set you up with the same girl?"

Milloy took the scrap of paper from Fina and dialed the number. She leaned over into his seat and pulled the phone closer to her ear.

"Do you mind?" Milloy asked.

"Nope."

After two rings, a woman answered. "Hello?"

"Hi there. I got your name from a friend."

"Is this your first time calling, sir?"

"Yes. That's right."

"Well, I don't know how much your friend has told you, but we are the most prestigious firm in the city, hence our name, Prestige. Our girls do this to complement their other endeavors." Fina scoffed, and Milloy slapped her lightly on the knee. "The rest of the time they are working in professional careers or studying for a degree."

"A degree in blowjobs," Fina whispered. Milloy glared at her.

"Our girls see only one gentleman per evening," the woman continued. Her voice was melodious and reassuring.

"That sounds good. I've never done this before."

Fina grabbed the phone and hit the mute button. "Oh my God! You sound like a twelve-year-old or a *Penthouse* letter!"

"That's all right, sir," the woman said. "You said a friend recommended us?"

Milloy wrested the phone back from Fina and unmuted it. "Yes, and discretion is essential."

"Of course. Our core values are discretion and service that exceeds your expectations," she cooed over the line.

"I was wondering: My friend talked about a particular girl. Would it be possible to see her?"

"I can certainly try to arrange that for you, sir."

"The only problem is, I don't remember her name," Milloy said.

"Perhaps you could ask your friend, or describe her? I want to make sure you get exactly what you're looking for."

"That's what I'll do. I'll ask him and call back. Thanks for your time." Milloy hung up and dropped the phone in the center console.

"We weren't done!" Fina exclaimed.

"I need a shower before I go any further."

"Like you've never been with a hooker before."

Milloy swiveled in his seat. "You think I have to pay for it?"

"Of course you don't have to pay for it, but I thought

it was some sordid rite of passage. Or, you know, if there was stuff you didn't want to ask your girlfriend for."

Milloy looked at her. "Just because your brother is a sleazy douche bag doesn't mean we all are."

Fina sat back in her seat. "Touché."

Milloy started the car and pulled into traffic.

Fina stared out the window. "Great. Now all I have to do is ask Rand for the name of his favorite hooker."

They left the car with the valet outside Crystal, and Milloy pulled aside one of the bouncers while Fina stood tapping her toe on the sidewalk. Tonight, she was wearing a strapless dress that fit more like an Ace bandage than an item of clothing. She'd stacked bangle bracelets on her arm in an attempt to distract from the scabs that were starting to pucker and peel, and her hair was loose, providing some distraction from her bruised face. Still, her appearance was no credit to the club.

The burly guy studied Fina's face while Milloy spoke into his ear. Whatever he said, it worked. The velvet rope was pulled back, and Milloy put his arm around Fina and led her into the club.

"Are you doing this solo or do you want a hand?" Milloy yelled in her ear. The music was blaring, and the floor shook from the bass.

"How about you stay close? My friend is in the VIP section, so there'll be lots of eye candy at least."

"After you," Milloy said, and gestured toward the stairs.

The VIP balcony was only half full, but still guarded

by another large bouncer. What did these guys do for work other than security? Their necks were the width of fire hydrants, their faces plastered with a permanent grimace. They'd look like escaped convicts in any other workplace.

"We're here to see Dante," Fina told the bouncer.

He held up a hand to keep her in her spot, and he gave Milloy the once-over before heading across the room. Dante was seated in the same booth as last time with a bevy of young ladies surrounding him. The bouncer leaned down and whispered in his ear, and a scowl eclipsed Dante's face.

Fina nudged Milloy with her elbow. "Did you see that? I can tell the exact moment when my name is mentioned; he got all angry-looking. Carl would be so proud."

The bouncer came back and motioned for Fina and Milloy to proceed to Dante's table. Dante glared at Fina when she reached them, and he chomped down on a mouthful of ice.

"Looks like you finally got what was coming," Dante said as he stared at her face. "Give me his name and I'll send him a thank-you note."

"Charming, isn't he, ladies?" she asked the girls.

"What do you want now?" Dante asked.

"I just want to talk. Why don't your girlfriends give us a little privacy," Fina said.

"We don't have anything to talk about," Dante said.

Fina shrugged. "Hey, if you don't mind talking about your erectile dysfunction in front of them, I don't mind."

Dante slammed his glass down on the table. "Make it quick." He nudged the two girls closest to him, and the group slid out of the booth and wandered over to the bar. "Who's he?" he asked while studying Milloy.

"He's my friend, but he really doesn't want to hear about your penis."

Milloy shook his head and wandered over to the bar. Fina sat down on the edge of the booth.

"You are the most fucking irritating woman I've ever met," Dante said. "If you were my bitch—"

"Oh, sweetie. That would never happen. Before we go too far, don't forget about my promise to shoot off your balls, one at a time. My offer still stands."

"What do you want?" Dante leaned his arms on the table.

"Is Brianna around?"

"How the fuck should I know?"

"Fine. Let me rephrase the question: Do you know who Brianna works for?"

Dante watched two girls dancing together, probably eager for them to break into a naked pillow fight. He was silent.

"Who has girls up here other than you?" Fina asked.

"None of your business," Dante said, and tipped his drink back. He bit down on an ice cube and rattled his empty glass in the direction of the bar. "I already told you, I don't know anything about your kid."

"She's not my kid," Fina growled.

"And I told you about Brianna. If she won't talk to you, that's your problem."

A waiter brought a drink over to the table, but before Dante could take it, Fina grabbed it and took a long pull. She moved her mouth into a moue. "What is this?"

"Coke and Morgan's."

"Dante, you have got to get with the program. Your apartment, your choice of cocktail, the outfit," she said, gesturing toward the shiny button-down shirt that revealed his hairless pecs. "You're supposed to dress for the job you want, not the one you have."

Dante grabbed his drink from her. It sloshed onto the table. "What will it take to get you out of my life?"

"Tell me what I want to know. Everything. Now."

Dante wiped his hands with a napkin and tossed it onto the table. He glanced in both directions and leaned toward Fina. "There are a couple of escort services that do business up here, and as long as they stay out of my way, I stay out of theirs. Mickey McKenna used to run some girls, but I put an end to that." He sat back and spread his arms across the back of the booth.

"There you go," Fina said. "Acting like the pimp in charge. Well done. So Brianna works for one of the services? What's the name of the service?"

"No idea. Now, are we done?"

"The next time Brianna shows up, you give me a ring." Fina pulled out her card and sent it sliding across the table.

"Why should I?"

"Because if you don't, I'll find out about it, and then I'll never leave you alone."

"Believe her, man," Milloy said. He was standing behind Fina with a beer in hand. "She's like a parasite, this one. You cannot get rid of her."

"No shit," Dante said, slipping the card into his pocket.

"Always a pleasure, Dante," Fina said as she stood up.

"Fuck you," he mumbled.

"Right back at ya," Fina said, and followed Milloy out of the VIP area.

Why couldn't people just do what she wanted without a lot of sass?

Milloy dropped her off outside her building, but he didn't pull away before seeing Cristian emerge from the shadows by the front door.

Milloy looked at her, but she waved him on. Milloy knew about Cristian, and Cristian knew about Milloy. They both knew as much as Fina knew: She had a thing for both of them and hooked up with each of them on occasion.

"How long have you been waiting?" she asked Cristian.

"Not long. Your doorman invited me to wait in there, but damn, he's a Chatty Cathy."

He followed Fina inside, where she waved at the man behind the desk, and they rode the elevator up to Nanny's.

"What have you been up to today?" Cristian asked once they were inside. Fina kicked off her heels and dropped down onto the couch.

"Who's asking? You or Pitney?"

"C'mon . . ."

"It's a reasonable question."

"Let's just say, people in the department are curious about your activities."

"Well, I went to see my niece and my brother. That was fun. I ate at Kelly's, did a little snooping, took a nap, and did some more snooping."

"Anything you can share?"

Fina reached down and massaged her feet. Between Amy Myers's heels and her Crystal footwear, they were throbbing. "Not yet."

Cristian exhaled loudly.

"Did Pitney really send you over here to get information? She must be desperate," Fina said.

"I'm trying to help you."

"That's what I've been telling everyone for the past eighteen hours." She switched to the other foot. "Okay, I can't give you details yet, but I may have found a witness who saw Melanie on Wednesday evening."

"Did this witness see someone other than Rand killing her?"

"No, but the tip may still be useful. At the very least it would help fill in the time line," Fina said sharply. "I'm working on it. As soon as I can tell you, I will."

A gentle hum filled the air, and Cristian tilted his head. "Why were you hanging at my place if you have central AC?"

Fina shrugged. "I can't stay away from you?"

"Is that a question or a statement?"

"Always the cop. Look, you're welcome to crash here if your place is too hot."

"Thanks, but I'll take a rain check. I think we need to be discreet."

"Any autopsy results yet?"

"Just preliminary."

"And?"

"Fina, I can't tell you that. You'll just turn around and tell Rand."

"What if I promise I won't?"

"I wouldn't believe you."

Fina slowly stood up and walked over to Cristian. "Fair enough. You sure you don't want to stay? No strings attached. Just for some company? I can nag you so it feels like the good old days with Marissa."

Cristian looked at her. "Tempting, but I'd better go."

Fina wrapped her hands around his waist and kissed him. Cristian had the best lips—soft but firm. He leaned into the kiss and grasped the back of her neck with one hand. He pushed her up against the wall, and Fina nudged her leg between his. She started to undo his belt, but Cristian gently pushed her hand away, his lips still firmly locked on hers. Fina ran her fingertips inside his shirt, up his bare back, and felt him shiver.

"You're sending me mixed signals," she said. She tugged on his earlobe gently with her teeth.

"I know." He kissed her more deeply. "I want to, but I don't."

"It's not that complicated." She reached down and grasped his perfect ass.

"Fuck," Cristian moaned softly.

"I'm trying."

"No, I mean, 'Fuck, we can't do this now,'" Cristian said, and he gently grasped Fina's wrists in his hands. "I want to, believe me, but we can't. Not with this case." He took a step back and straightened his shirt. Fina leaned back against the wall. "A rain check?" Cristian asked.

"Sure."

They walked to the door, and Fina gave him a kiss on the lips. "In the meantime, if you change your mind about those autopsy results . . ."

"I won't," he said, and kissed her back. "Give it a rest, Josefina."

He walked out, and she locked the door behind him. She moved to the windows and gazed out at the harbor and Logan.

When she had looked out the same window yesterday, was Melanie already down there? Snagged on the rocks like a piece of driftwood?

Fina flicked off the lights and went to bed.

The nurse was late, but Chester needed to be cleaned up now. Connor wouldn't allow his father to sit in his bodily fluids like a patient in a state hospital. Bev came into the room, and the two of them got to work. They avoided eye contact with each other and didn't speak except for the brief exchange of information necessary to get the job done. Although Connor was the doctor, Bev knew more about caring for Chester. Connor found himself in the unusual position of being the extra set of hands following directions.

Connor smoothed the sheet over his father, and his mother picked up the TV remote and flipped through the channels. The night nurse had been watching the early morning news show, but Chester didn't need to see that. She skipped up the channels, but stopped abruptly. Bev stepped toward the television and shushed Connor when he started to speak.

A body had washed up. They didn't know who it was yet, but there was conjecture. Connor stopped folding the afghan at his father's feet and froze. He looked at his mother and felt heat rising from his stomach to his head. She had a small smile on her face. Once the anchor had moved on to the weather, Bev looked at Connor, a benign, blank look settled across her features.

"Are you putting that over Daddy?" she asked mildly.

"Uhh . . . yeah," Connor said, and handed her one side. Together, they spread it over Chester.

"Perfect," Bev declared. "I'm famished. How about some peanut butter banana French toast?"

12

It was the Toyota Camry. Again.

Fina was driving west on the Mass Pike in Newton when she picked up the tail in her rearview mirror. Her scabs itched and served as a constant reminder of her previous interaction with the mystery man. Things would be different this time.

"Any chance you're in Newton?" she blurted out when Frank answered his phone.

"I am indeed. What's going on?"

"The same asshole, the one that ran me off the road last time, is back."

"What last time?" Frank asked, sounding more alert.

"Damn it. I forgot to tell you. I'll catch you up, but I'm trying to get a bead on this guy; he's making my life difficult. If I meet you at the police station could you pick up the tail? It's a black Toyota Camry."

"What case is this for?"

"I'm not sure. It may be related to Melanie." Fina glanced in her mirror and watched the Camry. As she slowed and exited the highway, the car tucked in behind another, but continued to follow her.

"See you in a few," Frank said, and clicked off.

Fina spent the next five minutes weaving in and out of traffic, one eye on the road, the other on her mirror. If this guy recognized her current car, he must have been keeping an eye on her. Not a comforting thought.

After five minutes, she pulled into the police station lot and climbed out of the car. Her tail parked across the street and watched.

There were a couple of cops talking in the parking lot, so Fina hurried over and asked for directions to the public library. She pointed in the direction of the Camry and was sure not to smile at the cops. Frank pulled over to the curb a couple of cars behind the Camry and seemed to be talking on the phone.

"So it's a right turn out of the parking lot?" Fina asked.

"No, you wanna take a left—here, let me show you," the nice, older cop said. He walked toward the street.

The tail fired up his engine and pulled into traffic. A moment later, Frank pulled out behind him.

"A left. Got it, Officer. Thanks so much," Fina said, and returned to her car.

She took a left out of the parking lot and made her way back to the highway. She punched the button for Frank on her phone.

"Are you on him?" she asked.

"Yup."

"Let me know where he ends up. It's time for us to be properly introduced."

Fina pulled into a drive-thru and ordered hotcakes and sausage. She also got a diet soda and sat in a parking space to refuel. Her adrenaline level was returning to normal, but she felt an underlying buzz that was familiar and welcome. If she could get some info out of the guy in the Camry, she could figure out who was so intent on putting her out of commission. That would bring her one step closer to figuring out who killed Melanie. It wasn't a smoking gun, but for the first time in a few days, she felt like she had an actual lead. But she had to wait until Frank called her, and since waiting wasn't Fina's forte, she decided to eat and come up with a plan.

She was dredging the maple syrup with a sausage link when her phone rang.

"What's up, Scotty?" she said through a mouthful.

"What are you eating?"

"That's what you called to ask me?"

"No, but I like to eat vicariously through you."

"Hotcakes and sausage."

"From a fast-food place?"

"Yup."

"Damn you and your fast metabolism."

"Why are you calling me?"

"Is Haley with you?"

"No. Why?"

Scotty sighed deeply. "She's MIA."

"Doesn't she have school?"

"There are only a few days left—special assemblies and field days—so Rand said she could bag it and hang out with Mom."

"Ahh, yes. The concerned grandmother."

"But Mom's no match for Haley. You of all people know that."

It was true. During Fina's adolescence, Elaine had tried to keep Fina on a tight rein, believing that because she was a girl, she would be easier to control than her brothers. She'd been sorely mistaken. Fina's high threshold for risk and her athleticism made her a master of escape and illusion. She could foil any curfew, lock, or alarm system that Elaine threw in her way. And the bigger the houses got, the easier it was to make a break for it. Eventually, Elaine pretended that she didn't care, that Fina snuck around with her implicit permission, but that was just her way of saving face.

"Did you try her friends?"

"Yeah, Patty's made some calls. No luck."

"Fuck. What does Rand say?"

"I haven't been able to reach him."

Fina picked at a cuticle. "I told him that his hands-off parenting isn't going to work right now. Fuck, fuck, fuck."

"Roger. I got that, but what about Haley?"

Fina sighed. "It's too early to panic, and we've got enough problems."

"Right. Okay. But let me know if you hear from her."

"Of course." Fina ended the call and stared at the entrance of the fast-food restaurant.

There really should be a licensing test for reproduction.

Fina found a coffee shop with Wi-Fi and started poking around Bob Webber's life. She hadn't heard from Mark, and she was loath to defy his "no cops" edict, but she needed to do something. Maybe there was some dirt on Bob Webber that she could use to compel him to come forward, or maybe someone else had seen Melanie in the North End that day. Once she got some background info on him, she would head back into the city and pick up some cannoli.

Fina picked up her phone and punched the speed dial button for Cristian.

"Menendez," he answered.

"Hi. It's me. You still mad at me?"

"I was never mad at you. I thought you were mad at me."

"Nah. I'm just frustrated. Sexually and professionally."

"Sorry I can't help."

"I know sex is off the table, but how about cause of death?" Fina asked.

The would-be novelist at the next table gave her a dirty look.

"I don't have anything to tell you."

"Which is not the same thing as not having information."

"What exactly do you want me to do, Fina? My hands are tied."

"I want you to tell me the cause of death. I'll hear about it soon enough anyway."

"Then why not just wait?"

"Because I hate being blindsided!" Fina exclaimed. Shakespeare glared at her. "And the sooner I get that info, the sooner I can get to work pursuing some leads."

Cristian exhaled loudly over the line. In the background, Fina could hear telephones ringing and furniture banging.

"Are you in the squad room?"

"No, I'm at the bridal sale at Filene's Basement. Yes, I'm in the squad room."

"Yikes. Easy, buddy."

"Wait a sec." The sound became muffled, and Fina waited for a minute. Cristian came back on the line with a hushed voice. "I can't tell you the cause of death, but I think Stacy D'Ambruzzi is on the team that did the PM."

"I thought she left the ME's office."

Her neighbor banged on his keyboard. "Do you mind?" he asked.

"If you want quiet, go to a fucking library," Fina hissed.

"Making friends, as usual," Cristian commented. "I don't know what the deal is, but Stacy's back. You didn't hear it from me."

"Thank you, Cristian. As soon as I can give you something, I promise, I will."

"Yeah. I'm not going to hold my breath on that one." He hung up.

The medical examiner's office was in a gray stone building in Chinatown. Fina pulled into a lot between two build-

ings with so little room, the cars were wedged in bumper-
to-bumper. She was usually wary about letting attendants
jockey her car, but she couldn't care less about the fleet
loaner.

The windows of the Chinese restaurants and shops
were packed with knickknacks and carcasses, and sometimes both. Fina walked by a display of featherless chick-
ens hanging by their feet, the dimpled skin whitish-blue.
She couldn't imagine carving up a body and then popping
next door for some Happy Family in a Nest. But if you're
carving up bodies in the first place, you probably have a
pretty strong stomach.

She stood across the street from the entrance to the
ME's building and evaluated her options. She didn't want
to go in and sign the visitor's log and risk bumping into
someone she knew—other than Stacy, that is. She was
watching the door when two women came through it and
sat down on the low stone wall that surrounded the
shrubs at the base of the building.

The older woman—who looked to be in her forties—
reached into her bag and pulled out a pack of cigarettes.
She lit one and handed it to the younger woman—barely
old enough to qualify as a woman—who was juggling a
baby on her hip. The child was drooling and grabbing
the mother's large hoop earrings. The older of the two
was overweight and kept tugging on the T-shirt that
strained across her boobs. She lit another cigarette for
herself and inhaled deeply.

After a couple of minutes, a security guard came out
and pointed to the sign forbidding smoking within thirty
feet of the building. There was some back-and-forth as

the women argued with the rent-a-cop, and Fina found herself siding with them. Come in and identify your dead relative, but first, put out that cigarette. Smoking kills, after all. The women ground out their smokes and walked back into the building.

At least that answered one question: Smoking wasn't allowed out front. If you were looking for someone who smoked—Stacy D'Ambruzzi, for example—you had to look for the smoking spot. Hospitals, police stations, government offices—in Fina's experience, the people who worked in these settings often smoked and drank to offset the stress of their jobs. They seemed to make a calculated risk when it came to those vices, and there was always a smoking spot close to the building. Since Stacy D'Ambruzzi couldn't smoke outside the front entrance, the spot must be somewhere else around the perimeter.

Fina crossed the street and walked down an alley bordering the side of the building. There was a set of heavy, dented double doors, but no one was hanging around, and the ground wasn't littered with cigarette butts, just ordinary urban trash—a discarded Dunkin' Donuts cup, a sodden receipt, and some gravel. She continued around to the back, where there was a chain-link garage door at the top of a ramp that sloped sharply beneath the building. This was the way in and out for the bodies. Fina kept walking toward a door where a young man was kneeling with his back against the wall, a cigarette in his hand.

"Hey," Fina said in greeting. "Is Stacy around?"

The guy didn't look much older than early twenties and was wearing scrubs and sneakers. He was Hispanic and wore a heavy gold cross around his neck. His hair was cut short, but the locks still waved gently over his scalp.

"She's inside." He gestured toward the door with his cigarette. "You should go around front."

"I'd actually rather not," Fina said, tracing a pattern on the pavement with her toe.

The guy studied her. "You're not a cop, right? I'd probably recognize you if you were a cop."

"Definitely not a cop. I need to talk to Stacy about something personal, and I'd rather not have to sign in, if you get my drift."

After a moment, his face brightened, and he nodded. "Are you the new girlfriend or the old girlfriend?"

"Neither. Just a friend. Would you let her know that Fina wants to talk to her?"

He pushed back against the wall and stood up. "You ladies, always with the drama." He grinned and shook his head.

"That's us," Fina agreed, and smiled.

He stood between Fina and an electronic panel, and he keyed in a numerical code. The door buzzed open, and he pulled it shut before ambling down the hallway. He hadn't agreed to deliver the message to Stacy, but he hadn't said no, either.

Fina decided to wait it out and was pleasantly surprised when, five minutes later, the door swung open and Stacy D'Ambruzzi stepped into the alley.

"Hey, hon," Stacy said, and hugged her.

"Hey, Stacy, how's it going?" Fina and Stacy's paths had crossed professionally over the years. Fina realized early on that Stacy was a kindred spirit, a woman in a largely male profession who didn't take shit from anyone.

"I'm back. The move to Portland didn't work out." Her shoulders sagged slightly. Stacy was in her midforties, thick around the middle, with hair shorn close to her skull. Tattoos peeked out from her scrubs, and her earlobes glittered with small hoops and stud earrings. Her face was lovely; smooth, clear skin and bright blue eyes. Stacy was the unexpected in human form.

"Sorry to hear that, but I'm sure they're glad you're back," Fina said, nodding toward the building. Stacy was a senior tech, competent and well respected.

"Well, they took me back, that's something. Mind if I smoke?" She reached into her waistband and pulled out a pack of cigarettes. A lighter was tucked into the soft pack.

"Be my guest."

Stacy lit up and inhaled deeply. "I assume you're here about your sister-in-law."

"Yup."

"You know I love you, Fina, but when you're around, trouble is never far behind."

Fina shrugged. "I can't deny it."

"What do you want to know?"

"Cause of death. Off the record, unofficially, all that."

Stacy cupped her cigarette in the palm of her hand. She blew out a long stream of smoke. "I do owe you."

Fina didn't say anything. A couple of years back, Stacy's brother was busted on a DUI. Recognizing the wisdom of having an ME employee in her debt, Fina convinced Carl that the firm should represent him. Ludlow and

Associates had taken the case pro bono and won her brother a favorable deal. It used to irritate her father when Fina bartered legal counsel for information, but the complex web of favors that she wove through town always ended up working to their advantage.

Stacy wiped her brow with the short sleeve of her top. "You didn't hear it from me."

Music to Fina's ears. "Of course not."

"The cause of death is drowning." Stacy took a last puff on the cigarette and tossed it to the pavement. She ground it out with the toe of her shoe and left it there with dozens of other butts.

"Any chance it was accidental?" Fina asked, knowing and dreading the answer.

"I don't think so. She had marks around her ankles and wrists." Stacy avoided Fina's gaze.

"She was tied up," Fina said.

"Yup."

"With what? Any idea?"

"Some kind of rope. We don't have all the info yet. And there was something around her waist. Something heavy."

Fina thought for a moment. "You mean a weight or a chain?"

Stacy looked at her. "Or both."

"Christ."

"I know. I'm sorry."

The heat suddenly felt oppressive, and beads of sweat trickled down between Fina's breasts. She had the urge to dive into cold water, but it passed just as quickly. Water meant Melanie.

"I've got to go," Stacy said. "We should have a drink sometime. Catch up."

"Sure. That would be great."

Stacy patted her on the shoulder and turned back to the door. She punched in the code and stepped inside.

Fina retraced her steps and was a block away from the ME's building when she bumped into Pitney.

"What are you doing down here?" Lieutenant Pitney asked her sharply. She was standing next to the passenger door of a Crown Victoria. One of her ducklings was climbing out of the driver's seat.

"I had a hankering for dim sum."

Pitney snorted. Today she was wearing a sheath dress that hung on her stout frame like a window blind. It was lemon yellow, and her hobo-style bag was eggplant-colored. The whole ensemble clashed with her bright red lips.

"If I find out you were at the ME's . . ."

"What?" Fina asked. "What are you going to do?"

"Arrest you for obstruction."

"Right. My father could take care of that in his sleep. I do have other cases, you know."

Pitney reached into her bag and pulled out a roll of breath mints. She unwrapped one and popped it in her mouth. "So what other case brought you to the medical examiner?" she asked.

Fina smiled. "I can't tell you that. That's between me and my attorney."

Pitney shook her head. "Maybe I should get your brother down here to identify the body."

Fina felt a current unleash in her body. "I already identified it." Christ. Melanie had become an *it*.

"I just want to do everything by the book."

"That's bullshit." Fina glared at her.

"You Ludlows are always the first to bitch and moan that the cops don't follow proper procedure. I'm trying to avoid that."

Fina threw up her hands. "Do whatever you want. My father and brothers will have a field day with this. I just didn't have you pegged as the cruel type."

"And I never realized you were such a softie, Fina."

"Right. Well, I like to keep you guessing." Fina looked out at the street. A city bus was inching its way along, trying to claim any real estate that opened in its path.

"Don't you have better things to do than stick up for your brother?" Pitney asked.

Fina stared at her. "He's my brother. What part of that don't you understand?" She jogged across the street and headed back toward her car.

A leggy long-haired blonde led Bev to a table at the hotel restaurant overlooking the Public Garden. Bev watched the young woman walk away, a slight swing in her hips, but nothing too obvious. Her earning potential was probably strong, if first impressions were to be trusted, but Bev never approached girls she didn't know. All of her employees came to her through personal recommendations. Anyone could judge a girl's physical beauty, but matters of class and discretion weren't always obvious until it was too late.

The waiter handed Bev a menu, and she ordered a dirty martini. She glanced at her watch. The Prospect, her future business partner, wasn't late—yet. A few more minutes, and he would be.

Bev was of two minds when it came to this particular businessman. On the one hand, he was extremely successful and well connected, both assets in a business relationship. On the other hand, his arrogance prompted him to take risks that Bev deemed unnecessary. Like many men, he made his way through the world under the presumption that everything would go his way. He didn't worry over the details or watch his step. Bev had met the occasional businesswoman who had the same approach, but generally, it was the men of her generation—white men— who believed their success was preordained, a foregone conclusion.

The waiter placed the martini in front of her, and she gingerly picked up the full glass and took a sip. It was delicious. She put the glass down and pinched the small plastic sword between two fingers before pulling an olive off it and sucking it into her mouth. Bev had almost finished chewing the gin-soaked olive when her phone rang.

It took her a moment to place the number, but then she recognized it as belonging to her most recent recruit, the young blonde whom she'd promoted.

"Hello, my dear. How are you?" Bev inquired cheerfully.

"I'm fine, Mrs. Duprey. How are you?"

The girl was still stiff, but at least she was falling into line.

"Very well. How can I help you?"

"I wanted to let you know that I'm ready. For the new project, I mean."

Bev sipped her drink. "That's wonderful news. Why don't we set up a time for you to come by the Back Bay office, and we'll get started."

There was a minute of back-and-forth, and they settled on a time later in the week.

"In the meantime, why don't you give some thought to your name."

"My name?" the girl asked.

"Yes, dear. The name you're going to use." Bev listened to the silence on the other end of the phone. "Are you all right?"

"Sure. I was just thinking."

"I make the final choice, of course, but I'd appreciate your input."

"Okay. I'll come with some ideas."

They exchanged good-byes, and Bev disconnected. Her employee didn't sound good. Bev's pet project might prove to be more time-consuming and labor-intensive than she had anticipated. She held a sip of the martini in her mouth. It didn't matter; she had the perseverance to see it through to the end.

The leggy blonde was returning to the table, the Prospect in tow. Bev watched as he admired the young woman's derriere. Men were so predictable.

13

Fina left a message for Haley on her cell and tried to tamp down the undercurrent of rising worry. Maybe she was freaking out about her mom, or maybe she was trying to get attention, or both. It was too soon to panic. There were still a few hours in the range of plausible explanation.

Carl and Rand were hunkered down with their criminal attorney, and Fina planned to join them, but first she wanted to swing by the North End to try to verify Bob Webber's tip.

Progress down Salem Street was slow. It was another hot day, and the sidewalks and stoops were thick with people visiting with neighbors and soaking up the atmosphere. Fina loved eating in the North End—she enjoyed the time-capsule feel of the place—but living there held no appeal. There was no place to park, the apartments were tiny, and everybody knew everybody else's business. But as she made her way toward the water, she got a glimpse of the new North End that was emerging. Old warehouses and office spaces were being converted to high-end housing, complete with water views and underground parking. These buildings offered proximity to great restaurants and Mike's Pastry without the headaches.

Fina drove to the approximate address where Bob claimed he saw Melanie and pulled over in a no-parking zone. There were two buildings under construction: One was sleek and made mostly of glass, and the other had a brick exterior, but jutted farther out into the harbor. She got out of her car and walked closer. Although Fina wanted to speak with some of Bob Webber's coworkers, she didn't want to bump into Bob Webber himself. Her presence would alert him that she wasn't going to let his information fade into the background.

After a couple minutes of searching, she saw a truck bearing the same logo as Bob's shirt the day she interviewed him. The van was parked next to the brick building with its back door open, the inside a jumble of wires, cords, and tools.

Fina walked back to her car and pulled her binoculars out of the trunk. She sat in the passenger seat and kept an eye trained on the general vicinity of the van. It was close to noon, and hopefully the guys would be breaking for lunch soon. Usually, construction workers carted their lunches to work sites and didn't stray from the group, but maybe someone would get a hankering for a cannoli or gelato and she'd have the opportunity for some one-on-one time.

Ten minutes later, a crew of men streamed out of the brick building with an assortment of small coolers, which they carried toward the only shady spot in the parking lot. Fina didn't see Bob Webber among them, but that didn't mean he wasn't on-site. The men perched on enormous spools of wire and a thick log that doubled as a parking barrier. They reached into the coolers and took out an impressive amount of food. One guy scarfed down two sandwiches, a bag of Fritos, two Hostess CupCakes, an orange, and an apple. He washed it down with a sixteen-ounce bottle of Mountain Dew. It was like watching another species, a hybrid of humans and vacuum cleaners.

They started to pack up their coolers and trash after fifteen minutes, and Fina's hopes sank, until one of the group stood and walked away from the others. He dashed across the street before Fina got out of the car, but luckily, he was easy to spot with his bright orange T-shirt. She dodged the traffic and dropped into step behind him.

After two blocks, he reached his destination and pulled open the glass door.

Of course.

Dunkin' Donuts.

Fina followed him into the store, and immediately felt goose bumps emerge on her arms. She hugged herself and cursed the overactive AC. The line was a few people long, and Fina stood behind the construction worker and listened as he ordered a Box O' Joe, the cardboard coffee urn that would keep the guys alert for the remainder of the day. The second cashier motioned to Fina, and she ordered a Boston Kreme doughnut. When she reached into her wallet to pay, she unzipped her change pocket and conveniently dropped a handful of coins at the construction worker's feet.

"Ugh. Sorry. Didn't realize it was unzipped," she said as she knelt down to retrieve the bait.

The construction worker knelt down beside her and collected a few coins with his dirt-caked hands.

"Here you go." He handed them to her as they both stood up. He glanced at her face a moment too long, and she was reminded that she wasn't batting 1000 in the looks department.

Fina dropped the coins back in her wallet and paid for her order. "Thanks. What a klutz."

"No biggie." He took his Box O' Joe from the cashier and held the door for Fina as she followed him back into the heat.

"Thanks." She started walking in the same direction as he was, back toward the building site.

"This heat sucks," he said, and slowed his pace.

"I know. I think I hate the humidity more."

"You're one of those people?" he asked, grinning. "Ever been to Arizona in the summer? Dry heat sucks, too."

"You're probably right. Hey, are you working on that new building next to the water?"

"Yeah. Been on it for six months."

"It looks really cool. When's it supposed to be finished?"

"We've got a couple more months." He stepped into the street when the sidewalk got too narrow for them to walk next to each other.

"I bet you know Bob Webber," Fina said, and smiled at him.

He smiled back. She couldn't peg his age, but he was handsome, medium height, and lean. His arms looked muscular, and the dirt on his face gave him a certain cowboy appeal.

"He's HVAC, right?" the man asked.

"Right. The last time I saw him, he mentioned the project. Is he around today?"

"I think he took off before lunch. Had another project he had to go work on."

"Damn. I needed to talk to him."

"Anything I can do for you?" he asked. Christ, men made it easy for pretty women.

"Actually, now that you mention it . . . Would you mind looking at a photo and telling me if you recognize someone? My friend's missing, and Bob saw her here the day she disappeared. I wanted to show him a different picture just to be sure." Fina reached into her bag and pulled out the family photo.

They'd reached the corner across from the construction site, and the man paused. "Are you a cop?"

"No, just trying to find a friend who's missing." Fina handed him the photo. He shifted the Box O' Joe to his other hand and took it from her. "That's the woman I'm looking for." She pointed at Melanie.

"I'm probably not the right guy to ask. I do a lot of the electrical work, so I spend most of my time inside." He gestured with his head toward the building. "You could ask some of the other guys."

Fina stepped closer to him. "I'd love to, but I don't want to interrupt their work."

He squinted his eyes, deep in thought. "Some nights, the guys go to Jordy's. It's a bar around the corner. You could stop by; let me buy you a drink." He smiled.

"Hmmm. Maybe I'll do that."

There was a break in the traffic, and the two of them jogged to the other side.

"Thanks for your help," Fina said.

"Seriously, stop by Jordy's. I'm Billy, by the way." He held out his hand, and she shook it.

"Josefina. Nice to meet you. I'll think about your offer." She walked to her car and climbed in. Once the air was blasting on full, she reached into the waxed bag and pulled out the doughnut. Her first bite was all doughy pastry, but the second revealed the thick, yellow crème filling. Fina ran her finger across the fudge topping and licked it.

A round of beers with construction workers? There were worse ways to spend her time.

"How's our friend in the Camry?" Fina asked Frank.

"Sitting tight."

Fina was back on the road, headed toward the meeting with Carl, Rand, and Rand's attorney. It promised to be a barrel of laughs.

"So you think that's his home?"

"Yeah. He hasn't moved for a few hours."

"Do you mind checking to make sure? Then you can leave."

"You want me to snoop through the mail? Just a little federal offense? Is that all you ask?"

"You could go the 'Sorry, I thought my buddy still lived here' routine. That one usually works. I learned it from the best."

"After I do that for you, maybe you could fit me into your busy schedule? Update me before I get any more involved?"

"Absolutely, but right now, I'm headed to the lion's den. Wish me luck."

The front door of Carl and Elaine's house was locked, which thwarted Fina's plan to sneak in and go directly to her father's office unobserved. Instead, she went in the side door and made a hasty retreat through the kitchen and down the hall. The office door was ajar, and Fina could hear voices murmuring within. She knocked lightly and pushed open the door.

Carl was sitting behind his desk. His tie was loosened around his neck, and his shirtsleeves were rolled up to his elbow. Rand was sitting on one of the couches, and across from him sat his criminal attorney.

"Fina, always a pleasure," Dudley Prentiss said, standing. He came over and gave her a peck on the cheek. "Good lord, what happened to you?"

"Car accident."

"Are you all right?"

"She's fine," Carl said.

Fina rolled her eyes. "It's nice to see you, Dudley." Fina sat down next to Rand, and Dudley reclaimed his spot on the other couch. He carefully placed one ankle over the opposite knee.

Dudley Prentiss was the epitome of male elegance. He was a tall, slim black man who had bone structure most models would die for. He was always impeccably dressed, although less flashy than Carl. If Carl looked like money, then Dudley was a platinum American Express card. His warm smile framed his perfect white teeth, and his hands were smooth with long fingers. If he had been closer to Fina's age—and not Carl's—she would have dated him.

"Do you have something to tell us?" Carl asked.

"Unofficially, I have the cause of death." Fina glanced at Rand. His eyes were bloodshot, but his expression was sullen. Fina couldn't tell if he was sad or pissed off.

"And?" Carl asked.

"She drowned."

Rand's head turned sharply, and he looked at her. "So it was accidental?"

"No. They think the manner of death is homicide. There were restraint marks on her ankles and wrists and around her waist."

"Any idea what the marks were from?" Dudley asked.

"Just guesses at this point." Fina glanced at her brother. "A rope or maybe a chain."

The room fell under a blanket of silence for a moment, everyone battling their own mental pictures.

"Well," Dudley said. "This isn't exactly a surprise. She was found in the harbor, after all."

"But this fits with the blood on the boat and the missing cooler," Fina commented.

"Jesus, Fina," Rand said.

"I'm just stating the obvious."

"Can it, the two of you," Carl said. "I need you to shore up your brother's alibi," he said to Fina.

"Which is?"

"He attended a meeting at Grahamson with Melanie, returned to the office, and then took work home," said Dudley.

"Did you make any stops?" Fina asked Rand.

"Nope."

"I need to know the exact route you took home. Maybe you were caught on some cameras. And were you on the computer at home? Logged in to the firm's extranet? Did you buy anything?" Fina really didn't want to know if Rand had been making any late-night purchases, but a sleazy alibi was better than no alibi.

"I was reading case files. I wasn't on my computer. And I took the usual route home."

Rand listed the streets he'd driven from the office to his house, and Fina jotted it down in her notebook.

"And Haley?"

"I didn't see her that night."

"Was she home?"

Rand shrugged. "Where else would she be?"

Fina didn't say anything. Any moment now, her head was going to explode.

"Does anyone know where Haley is now?" she asked.

Carl and Dudley looked at Rand.

"I talked to her this morning," Rand said.

"Well, Scotty can't find her. She isn't answering her cell. I'm starting to worry."

"Have you tried her friends?" Dudley asked.

"I haven't, but Patty has, and no one's seen her."

"Your mother could make some calls," Carl said.

"Dad, don't get Mom involved," Fina said.

"She's right, Dad," Rand said. "I'm sure Haley is just upset and hanging out with her friends."

"Patty can make more calls," Fina said.

Carl tapped his pointer finger on the desktop in a rapid staccato. "Fine. I'll call Scotty when we're through."

The men started batting around ideas about alternate theories of the crime, and Fina stole glances at Rand. He kept fiddling with his watch strap and contributed little to the conversation.

Fina glanced at her own watch and waited for a pause in the conversation. "I need to speak with Rand privately before I go."

Dudley glanced at Carl.

"Anything you two need to discuss, you can discuss in front of us," Carl insisted.

Fina glared at her father. "It's private and irrelevant."

Carl stared back at her. "Fine. I need to stretch my legs. Dudley," he said, and gestured for the attorney to accompany him out of the room. Dudley eyed the siblings and followed Carl out.

"I need to know who you hooked up with through the escort service," Fina said.

"Why?"

"Because I need to tie up that loose end."

Rand swallowed and looked at the floor.

"I'm not going to judge you, Rand."

"Of course you are. You already have."

Fina tilted her head back against the couch and closed her eyes. "You're right. I already have, so what's the harm in giving me more information?"

"Molly. Her name's Molly."

"Did you always see the same girl?"

"At first I saw a few different ones, but I liked her best."

"Can you describe her?"

"Why?"

"Because I need to meet her, and I want as much info about her as possible."

"You're going to hire a hooker?"

"Don't worry about the specifics."

"She was thin with long, blond hair."

"Did she have a specialty?" Fina swallowed. Some conversations should never happen.

"I don't want to talk about this with you," Rand said, and looked at her. His eyes looked wet.

"I don't want to talk about it, either, but I don't want you going to jail. Just tell me, and then I'll go."

Rand stood up and walked to the window. He stood there with his back to Fina, and she began to wonder if he was done talking.

"She didn't do anything special, but she would dress up. Young, like a schoolgirl or a cheerleader."

"How old is this girl?"

"Of age."

"But she looks young?" Fina asked.

Rand nodded. Fina slipped her notebook into her bag and left the room.

How long would it take Elaine to notice if Fina puked in one of her decorative urns?

"Any luck?" Fina asked Frank when she slid into the booth across from him at Dunkin' Donuts. Frank was sipping a cup of coffee and nibbling on a cruller. "Peg better not catch you eating that."

"I trust you to keep my secret." He winked at her. "I

think his name is Joe Winthrop, and he lives in the apartment in Southie."

"You spoke to him?"

"Yup. Joe was on the mail, and he answered to Joe when I gave the spiel about my buddy, Joe, who had moved. Our Joe has only lived there about a month, as luck would have it, so I think he bought it."

"Got it. Thank you. I think I'll pay our Joe a visit."

"Want some company?"

Fina pulled off a piece of the cruller and popped it in her mouth. "Not yet. I'll let you know."

"So is Joe Winthrop responsible for that?" Frank gestured to the bandage on her left hand.

"I think so, but I don't know what the deal is. I've stirred up some stuff, and I have to figure out which stuff he's connected to."

"I'm sorry about Melanie. That's a damn shame."

Fina ripped off another morsel of dough.

"Would you like me to buy you one?" Frank asked.

"No, I'm good." She grinned briefly, but it was short-lived, as her thoughts returned to Melanie. "I think a lot of shit is about to hit the fan: I've pissed someone off; the cause of death is going to be released; Rand has been up to no good."

"There's a surprise."

"I know, but his timing is extremely inconvenient."

"Which of the seven deadly sins are we talking about?"

Fina ticked through the list in her head. "Lust, and I would have you help me out with that, but Peg would never forgive me, plus it might send your heart rate into dangerously high territory."

Frank smiled and blotted his lips with a napkin. "I'll leave that to you young kids."

"I'm on it."

"Okeydoke, but don't be a stranger, Fina." While mentoring Fina, Frank had rightly surmised that she didn't have much experience collaborating with peers and, at times, he had to gently remind her that asking for help or advice wasn't a sign of weakness.

"I won't. Girl Scout's honor."

"That's reassuring from the girl who was booted as a Brownie."

"You worry too much, Frank," Fina said, and she slid out of the booth.

An hour later she was climbing into Milloy's car at the Chestnut Hill Reservoir. Milloy's BMW was cool and smelled like leather. It was immaculate—the only evidence that it belonged on the road and not in the showroom was the bottle of seltzer and the unopened can of diet soda in the drink holders.

"For me?" Fina asked as she picked up the soda. It was cold.

"Thought you'd want one."

"What I want is a shot of whiskey, but my day is young and I need to stay sharp."

"Elaine?"

"Rand." Fina popped open the drink, and it bubbled toward the opening. She quickly covered it with her mouth and sucked down the overflow.

"What's up with Rand?"

"I went over to my parents' house to update the gang. I heard from my ME source that Melanie drowned."

Milloy didn't say anything, just nodded.

"But it definitely wasn't accidental," Fina said. "She had restraint marks."

"That sucks."

"Yes, it does." Fina had more of her drink and then placed the cold can against her eye socket.

"Still hurt?" Milloy asked.

"A little achy."

Milloy reached over and massaged her constricted shoulder muscle with his hand. "You need so much work," he said.

"No shit, Sherlock. I'll let you know when my schedule opens up." She rotated in her seat so that Milloy could reach the other shoulder. "I asked Rand the name of his escort."

"How was that?"

"Fan-fucking-tastic."

"I'll bet. And?"

"Molly. She's thin and blond and young-looking."

"How young-looking?"

"I didn't ask for an age range, but when you call, you should request that she wear a cheerleading outfit or schoolgirl uniform."

Milloy stopped rubbing her shoulder. "Seriously?"

"Seriously. Trust me. When I think about it, I throw up in my mouth a little bit."

"So when do you want this date to happen?"

"Not sure. Do you mind having her come to your place?"

He looked at her. "Yes, I mind."

"All right. Don't get your knickers in a twist. I'll get a hotel room."

"Do you want me to call now?"

"No. I can only stomach so much," Fina said, and drained her soda.

She went home and took a nap. Fina felt exhausted and was starting to understand the phrase *bone tired*. Any one thing—the fight, the car accident, Melanie's death, Rand's revelations, the general family tension—would be trying, but the combination of events was a heavy load. Sleep seemed like a reasonable temporary escape.

After a shower and half a pint of Cinnamon Buns ice cream, Fina threw on a pair of black pants and a black T-shirt. She put her hair in a ponytail and grabbed a baseball cap. Her bag was loaded with the usual goodies, including her gun and set of lock picks.

South Boston was still busy with families pushing strollers in the twilight and teenagers hanging out on street corners. Fina pulled into a public parking lot. People around here were notoriously eagle-eyed when it came to their neighborhoods and their on-street parking spaces. During snowstorms, spaces were demarcated by the private citizens who shoveled them out, and the mayor had poked a hornet's nest when he threatened to ticket the self-appointed parking police.

She waited until the sun had set and the sky no longer glowed, then got out of the car and pulled a plastic shopping bag out of the trunk. It contained a couple of old newspapers, some empty coffee cups, and a roll of toilet paper on top. It was easier to blend in if you were toting the accoutrements of everyday living. She walked one block to Joe Winthrop's apartment and scoured the streets for the Camry. It was parked a few doors down. His apartment was the third-floor unit in a white triple-decker with red shutters. The house loomed over the sidewalk; there was barely room for the two concrete steps leading to the front door. Fina walked to the door—neither too slow nor too fast—and put down the shopping bag while she reached into her purse for her lock picks.

The door was locked, but it was a cheap lock that she opened in less than a minute. She grabbed her bag, stepped into the small entrance hall, and closed the door behind her. There were three unsecured mailboxes in the space, and a door with a crooked #1 directly to the left. Fina craned her neck and looked up the staircase in front of her. The coast was clear, and she started to climb. A TV was blaring in #2. She continued up to #3. TV sounds emanated from behind that door also. Fina listened for a moment to make sure there were no live conversations that would indicate company.

The lock took her a couple minutes to bypass, but she wondered at the poor security that Joe Winthrop had in place. He must be stupid or arrogant; either worked to her advantage. Inside, she carefully closed the door and assessed the scene. She was in a small hallway with four doors. She assumed the first was the TV room given the play-by-play drifting out from it. Through the second door, Fina glimpsed a counter and an oven hood. The third and fourth most likely led to the bedroom and bathroom.

The tricky part was surprising Joe. If his back was to her, it would be easy, but if he were facing the door, she'd have to hope his reflexes were a little slow. Fina pulled out her gun and crept across the hallway. Despite its apparent age, the floor didn't creak, a typical byproduct of New England breaking and entering. PIs in younger cities definitely have an advantage.

Fina stepped into the door and exhaled when she was faced with a huge screen and a major league pitcher adjusting himself. She tiptoed up behind the recliner that dominated the small room and peeked over it. Joe was sitting with a beer in his hand, his legs propped up on the recliner's footrest.

"Don't move," Fina said, pressing the gun against Joe's skull. He made a small motion toward his right side. "Seriously, don't move."

Fina walked around to face him, keeping the gun trained on him. She glanced to his right and saw a gun sitting on the ring-stained side table. She grabbed it and tucked it into the back of her waistband.

"Any more I should know about?"

He scowled and shook his head.

"Good. Now stand up slowly and put your hands behind your back."

He followed her directions. He wasn't especially tall, but he was meaty. His dark hair was curly, and his nose was slightly misshapen, almost like corrective lenses would make it look right.

Fina pulled a pair of handcuffs out of her bag and snapped them on his wrists behind him. Then she pushed him back into the recliner, where he settled with a grunt.

"At least you're not chatty. That's something." She walked over to the TV and pushed off the power button.

"Well, I'm here. What do you want?" she asked.

"I don't want anything." He looked at the floor. "I don't know who the fuck you are."

"Really? You've been following me. Ran me off the road. If you want a date, there are easier ways to ask."

"I don't have nothing to do with you."

"I find that hard to believe." Fina stood in front of him. She studied him. "I don't think you jumped me at the supermarket. You're a little too short."

He didn't say anything, but stared at her.

"Let's make this simple. You tell me who your boss is, and I leave you alone."

"I don't know anything, and even if I did, I was just following orders."

"Joe, Joe, Joe. The Nuremberg defense didn't work then, and it won't work now. Who hired you?"

Joe squirmed in his seat. "These are killing me. Maybe you could take 'em off and we could talk."

"Stop being such a pussy," Fina said. She wandered around the room without taking the gun off Joe.

A table pushed against one of the walls held paper wrappings from a sub. A bag of barbecue potato chips was nearly empty. DVDs were stacked in piles on the floor in front of the TV, and two cardboard boxes held books and some sports paraphernalia. Next to the only other chair in the room, a small box held a stuffed animal—a purple elephant—and a few kids' books.

Joe followed her gaze to the elephant. He had started to sweat. "I can't tell you anything. I'll be in deep shit."

"I know I seem really nice, but I'm not, and you definitely should have figured out that I'm resourceful. You can be afraid of your boss or afraid of me. Your choice." Fina nudged the small box with her toe. "Who's the elephant belong to?"

Joe's face tightened.

"Your kid?"

"Leave her out of this."

"I'd love to." Fina picked up the stuffed animal and stroked its ear. "Here's what we'll do. I'm going to give you some time to think about the situation, and I'll be in touch. In the meantime, if you try to hurt me again . . ." She looked at the stuffed animal. "I'm sure I'll think of something."

Fina dropped the elephant back into the box, pulled the handcuff key out of her bag, and went over to the window. She showed him the key, leaned out, and tossed it into the neighbor's shrubs. Joe growled.

"That should keep you busy." She walked toward the hallway. "I'm going to hold on to your gun. Think about what I said, Joe. I just want everyone to be safe and sound."

Fina grabbed her shopping bag and slipped her hand into her purse, gun firmly gripped. Outside, she casually walked to her car, got in, and pulled out of the lot. Her hands were sweaty on the wheel.

This case was bringing out the worst in everyone.

"This phone call better get you off my ass," Dante said. The music in the background was so loud, Fina could barely hear him.

"It's a start."

"Your friend Brianna is here."

"Oh, good." She started to hang up the phone.

"And there's someone else you might be interested in seeing."

Fina let up on the gas. "Who?"

"You'll see when you get here." He hung up.

Fina ditched her plan to go home and change. A mystery guest couldn't be good, and she didn't want to waste any time. She'd take her chances looking like an overage, under-made-up Goth and try to get into Crystal on the sheer force of her personality.

She paid too much to leave the car in a lot a few blocks down from the club, locked Joe's gun in the trunk, and then argued with the bouncer for a couple of minutes. He had trouble believing she was a friend of Dante's, probably because her parts weren't on display, and she looked like a boxer who'd gone a couple rounds. Luckily, some chump waiting in line decided to start a fight, and Fina snuck in while the bouncers were distracted.

Upstairs, Dante was ensconced in his usual booth, and he motioned for the bouncer to grant Fina access. He pointed toward a corner table where Brianna and a man were sitting close and whispering. Fina scanned the room, but didn't see anyone she recognized. She'd deal with Brianna first, then the mystery guest.

"I need to borrow your girlfriend for a few minutes," Fina said, pulling a chair over from an empty table. Brianna was wearing a tight red dress that barely covered the good family china. Her hair was pulled back in a high ponytail, and her lips were painted deep red.

The man looked askance. Brianna looked blank, and then recognition flooded her face.

"You need to leave," she whispered at Fina.

"I just need to talk to you for a few minutes. Promise."

The man glanced at Brianna and straightened up in his seat. He was in his thirties, extremely thin and tall. He was exactly the kind of man Fina wasn't attracted to; one of her rules was that her date had to have a bigger ass than she did.

"I don't mean to be rude," he ventured, "but Brianna's not available right now. We're on a date."

"Oh, I know you are," Fina said.

"So perhaps you could call Brianna later and discuss whatever it is that's so important."

Brianna glanced at the man with a mixture of appreciation and pity.

He cleared his throat. "Do you have a card?" he asked.

"Listen, junior, I'm not trying to ruin your night," Fina said as she grabbed a card from her bag and threw it on the table. "I need to talk—"

"You've got bigger problems," Brianna interjected. Fina followed her gaze to the bar and saw a man struggling with a girl. He was holding her by the wrists, and she was trying to wriggle out of his grasp.

Fina crossed the room in two seconds. She kneed the man in the balls. "Get your fucking hands off her!"

The man doubled over, and bouncers materialized from nowhere. Fina grabbed Haley and put her arm around her. She started to pull her out of the VIP area.

"I don't wanna go! What . . . fuck . . . I don't . . ." Haley's eyelids opened and closed slowly, like her blink function was on delay.

"I don't think she wants to leave with you." A huge, bald bouncer stood in front of Fina.

"You sure about that? I'm her aunt, she's underage, and I have a gun," Fina said. He stepped aside, and she dragged Haley down the stairs and out the front door. Walking to the car was like walking with a toddler; Haley was both easily distracted and obstinate.

In the car, Fina rummaged around in the backseat and found a bottle of water. She forced Haley to drink some.

"How much did you drink?"

Haley mumbled.

"Haley, how much?" Fina nudged her shoulder.

"I don't know, all right! Leave me the fuck alone!"

"Are you going to throw up?"

"No."

"Are you sure?"

"No."

"No, you're not sure, or no, you're not going to throw up?"

Haley turned her head and looked at Fina. "What was the question?"

Fina got out and popped open the trunk. She emptied the contents of her decoy shopping bag and walked around to the passenger side and opened the door.

"If you think you're going to—" She jumped out of the way.

Haley puked onto the concrete. Fina got some paper towels from the trunk and doused them with water. She wiped Haley's mouth and gave her a clean towel to apply to her forehead. Haley took a sip of water and rinsed out her mouth.

"As I was saying: If you think you're going to throw up, use this bag," Fina said, and handed her the bag. She helped Haley rotate in the seat and buckled her in before closing the passenger door.

Fina sprinted across the parking lot and dumped the soiled paper towels in a trash can. She ran back and started the car. It was hot still, but she rolled down the windows anyway in the hope that fresh air would help revive her niece. Haley leaned her head against the door frame, and they were both silent as Fina merged onto the Pike.

Fina kept her eyes on the road and tried to clear her mind of everything but getting Haley home safely. She was watching the lights of the car in front of her when a motion jumped into her peripheral vision. Haley's body was heaving, her head dipped down toward her chest. At first, there was no sound, but then a sob escaped her mouth that was so loud and guttural, it startled Fina.

"Oh, Haley," she said, and she veered sharply to the right to exit the highway. She pulled over just off the exit ramp and put the car in park. Fina undid her seat belt and put her arms around her niece.

"I'm sorry. I'm so, so sorry," Fina said, and Haley released her weight onto Fina, shaking and gasping. Fina stroked her hair and her back.

There was a lump in Fina's throat, but sadness wasn't its primary source.

It was anger that was making it hard for her to swallow.

Overwhelming, red-hot anger.

14

Haley needed her mom, but since that wasn't a possibility, Fina opted for the next best thing. Once Haley had cried herself into an exhausted, limp mess, Fina got back on the road and drove to Scotty and Patty's place. Most of the house was cloaked in darkness when they pulled up to the curb, but the path lights illuminated their slow progress up the front stone walkway. Fina rang the bell and gave Scotty a warning look when he answered the door: *Act normal,* it said.

"Is Patty still up?" Fina asked as Scotty took hold of Haley's other arm.

"Yeah. Let's go upstairs."

There was always room in Scotty and Patty's house, and the use of it came without strings attached, unlike a stay at Elaine's. Patty was the best kind of hostess—

hospitable, but not nosy. She knew that sometimes support and space were required in equal measures.

Fina and Scotty left Haley and Patty in the guest bathroom and went downstairs to Scotty's home office. Unlike the gentlemen's club feel of Rand's office or Carl's contemporary showpiece, Scotty's home office seemed real, not staged. He had a curved desk, one segment of which was cluttered with papers and file folders, the other, a staging ground for a LEGO Star Wars battle. Kids' books were scattered in front of the couch, and a small heap of Transformers robots were entangled on the coffee table. Fina sat down on the couch. She felt a lump under her butt and reached under to pull out a piece of fabric approximately the size of a hand towel. It was faded blue and pilly.

"What is this?" she asked as she held it between two fingers.

"Bubby! We looked everywhere for it. Ryan will be so happy." Scotty held out his hand and grabbed the blankie from Fina.

"That's disgusting."

"Don't disparage the Bubby. This smelly rag is more powerful than you can imagine."

"That's why I brought Haley over here. You guys understand this whole parenting thing."

"And Rand doesn't?" Scotty asked. He sat down next to Fina and put his feet up on the coffee table after nudging the Transformers to the side.

"I know it sounds sexist, but she needed a mom."

"Don't we all." Scotty pulled a small robot from between the cushions and began fiddling with it. "Where did you find her?"

"At Crystal. That club near Fenway. I think she's in some deep shit."

Scotty shrugged. "She got drunk. She's a teenager. It's gonna happen."

"I don't mean standard teenage shit. I mean deep shit."

"Like what?"

"I don't know yet." She rested her feet on the edge of the coffee table. "There's a name you should know: Joe Winthrop."

"Who's that?"

"He's the one who's been trying to kill me. Do you have a piece of paper?"

Scotty put the robot on the arm of the couch and grabbed paper and a pen from his desk. He handed it to Fina.

"Here's his name and address. Frank knows about him. I visited him tonight and put the squeeze on him. I'm trying to figure out who hired him."

"What do you want from me?"

"I just want you to know about him."

"In case . . ."

"Just in case."

Scotty's face pinched with worry. Fina's phone rang.

"It's Dad," she told Scotty as she answered. "I was just about to call you," she said into the phone. "I found Haley."

"Is she okay?"

"She's drunk and upset, but Patty's taking care of her. Will you tell Rand we found her?"

"I'll let him know."

"I need to hire some backup, Dad."

"For what?"

Fina sighed. "Can you just . . . I'm exhausted."

"Then come in tomorrow and make your case. Any-time after eleven. The DA is having a press conference then. They're going to identify Melanie."

"And Rand? What's the deal with the police?"

"Dudley says it could go either way." Ice tinkled in a glass. "Your mother's working on the funeral."

"When's it going to be?"

"Day after tomorrow."

"Okay."

There was a long silence. Fina could hear Carl breathing.

"You don't have anything for me?" he finally asked.

"Yes, I do. That's why I need more resources. Dealing with Rand's extracurricular activities is just one more thing on my to-do list." Scotty's eyebrow arched. "I'm making progress, but I can't do everything myself."

"You always want more money," Carl grumbled.

"Yeah, well, it helps solve cases. Name one case I've screwed up."

"Let me know when you have something," Carl said, and disconnected.

Fina pushed the off button and dropped the phone into her bag.

"Couldn't come up with a case, could he?" Scotty said.

"Of course not, so he took his ball and went home."

"What's up with Rand?"

"You didn't hear it from me, but he's been screwing around on the side."

"He has a mistress?" Scotty asked.

Fina looked at him. "A hooker."

Scotty shook his head. "You'd think that at some point, he'd stop fucking up."

"Why would he? He always gets bailed out. By us."

"I know," he conceded. "One of these days, we've got to do something about this 'us.'"

"Yeah, I'll get right on that." Fina took her feet off the table edge and stretched her arms to the ceiling. "I've gotta go. You'll keep an eye on Haley?"

"We'll do our best."

"That's all I can ask," Fina said, standing up.

Once in the car, she rolled down all the windows to try to dissipate the booze and barf aroma. At home, she dropped her clothes on the floor, took a long shower, and curled up in bed. The prospect of a new day wasn't reassuring.

Fina got up early and transformed into Amy Myers. She wore a different blouse and jewelry from last time, but the other elements were the same: tasteful makeup, heels, and bag, hair pulled back in a bun. Her bruises were fading, and she looked more like a businesswoman than a victim of domestic abuse, which was always a bonus when trying to convey power and confidence. Three peanut butter cookies and a can of diet soda served as breakfast, and Fina pulled into the parking lot of Mode Accessories a few minutes after nine.

The receptionist gave her the same lackluster greeting and disappeared behind the gray, felted partition to fetch Donald Seymour.

"He's on the phone. He might be a while," Fina was told when she reappeared.

"I'm happy to wait. I really need to speak with him in person," she said with a bright smile.

The receptionist disappeared again, returned after a few minutes, and gestured toward the plastic seats in front of her desk. Fina sat and picked up a copy of *Accessories Today*, a quarterly publication for the women's accessories industry. She tried to appear fascinated for the sake of her cover, but the minutia of zippers was enough to put her in a coma.

"Miss Myers?" Donald Seymour asked when he appeared twenty minutes later. "Sorry to keep you waiting."

"No problem. Just catching up on industry news," Fina said, and she followed him back to the break room. "I'm sorry I didn't call before dropping by."

"Coffee?" Donald asked. Fina shook her head. She sat down while Donald poured himself a cup.

"I was in the neighborhood and thought I'd follow up on our conversation."

"No need to apologize. Sure you don't want any coffee?"

Fina held her hand up. "Just gets me overheated in this weather. Water would be great, though."

Donald filled a plastic cup and handed it to her before squeezing into the seat next to her, their knees grazing. He sipped his coffee and sat back with his hands on his stomach. "Your bruises look better."

Fina sighed. "I suppose I don't look quite as ugly as before."

"You could never look ugly," Donald said, and looked down at the table.

"You're so sweet, and I'm sure you're swamped, so let's talk turkey, shall we?" Fina tried to conjure up a perky smile. "I wondered if you'd had any luck setting up a meeting with the owner. My clients are anxious to move forward."

Donald frowned. "I understand that, and I appreciate their due diligence. However, there is a tiny problem."

Fina frowned. "Oh no. Really?"

"Our owner has been traveling all over the world—that's how we get the best inventory, you know—and he just isn't available to meet."

Fina frowned. "I'm sorry to hear that."

"But that should reassure your client. If the business weren't a success, he wouldn't be on the road so much."

"I suppose. But surely, someone is running the company in his absence."

"Of course," Donald replied with a touch of impatience.

Fina sipped her water. "Sooo . . . maybe I could meet with that person. The one who's in charge?"

Donald shifted in his chair. "Well, I've spoken with our acting president, and she'd like some more information about your client before scheduling a meeting."

"Hmmm." Fina let her shoulders sag.

"Is that going to be a problem?"

Poor Donald probably didn't know what was really going on at the company. He was just trying to make a living selling baguette bags and found himself in a pickle. If he wasted his boss's time he was in trouble, and if he lost a potentially lucrative account he was in trouble. Fina wasn't unsympathetic, but she couldn't waste any more of her time.

"I see that you're in a terrible spot, Donald, but I sincerely doubt that my client would be willing to reveal more at this point. The fact is, lots of companies would love to do business with him." Fina smiled. "It probably makes sense for us to move on. We gave it our best shot, though, didn't we?"

"Well, wait. There has to be something we can do."

Fina picked up her purse and pretended to fiddle with her phone. "Donald, it's okay." She patted his hand. "It's just business. Sometimes things don't work out, but that doesn't mean we won't have common interests in the future." She stood up and smoothed her skirt down. "Thank you for seeing me without an appointment."

Donald looked flustered and stood rooted to the spot. When Fina stepped forward, he rushed ahead to open the door leading back to the office. Fina strode to the entrance and pulled an Amy Myers business card out of her wallet. She handed it to Donald. "It's been a pleasure."

"Wait. Let me give you mine. In case you're in the neighborhood. We could grab lunch." He pulled a card out of his wallet and smiled shyly. The poor guy thought romance was an actual possibility. Some people really do see the glass half-full.

"Give me a call if something changes," he said as he handed Fina the card.

"You, too." They shook hands, and Fina pushed the glass door open and walked to her car.

Inside, with the air on high and her heels slipped off, Fina rested her forehead against the steering wheel. A few minutes of contemplation netted no insights or mental relief, so she put the car in gear and got back on the road.

Fina drove home, changed, and turned on the TV to see Pitney having her big moment. She didn't make the actual announcement, but stood behind the DA with an appropriately solemn look on her face. Rand was identified as a "person of interest," which everyone knew was just another name for suspect. Fina looked at the assembled group; not surprisingly, Pitney was surrounded by men. Under different circumstances, Fina and Pitney might have been friendly acquaintances. Both women were smart and accomplished, always competing with the big boys, but Fina's family and Pitney's profession made that impossible. They were like the Capulets and the Montagues. Or maybe that was Fina and Cristian.

Fina wandered into the kitchen for a glass of water, and when she got back, the news had been replaced by a talk show, the host promising exciting news about peptides in the coming hour. Whoopee.

Fina left a message for Milloy and then punched in Cristian's number.

"How about lunch? I'm buying," Fina told him.

"No time."

"Cristian, I have to talk to you."

"Don't whine. It's unattractive."

"So sorry. Forgive my lapse in decorum."

"You're forgiven. I still don't have time for lunch."

"Are you punishing me?"

"For what?"

"I don't know. Withholding information?"

"Are you withholding information?"

"Call me when your schedule opens up," Fina said, and clicked off the phone.

Fina walked into Carl's office, which was empty, and sat down on his couch. His young blond assistant stalked in after her.

"You know, you can't just walk in here," she said, glaring at Fina.

"The door was open. I assumed that meant he was available."

"You have to check with me first."

Fina put her feet up on the coffee table and settled into the leather cushions. "Shari, I appreciate that you need to mark your territory and all that, but don't bother. With me, it's a waste of time."

The two women stared at each other.

"Fine," the assistant huffed, and left the room.

Fina leaned her head back and closed her eyes. She dozed off.

"Wake up," Carl commanded. He was easing into his chair behind the desk and glancing at the screen of his cell phone. "I'm not paying you to nap."

"You're not paying me to sleep, either, which is why I was up all hours last night rescuing your drunken granddaughter from a nightclub."

Carl stared at her. He drummed his fingers on his desktop. "You know, you think your grandkids are going to be different from your kids."

"Why would you think that? They're being raised by your kids." Fina pulled a section of her hair forward and examined the ends. "We're not that bad."

Carl considered that for a moment. Just as quickly, the moment of reflection passed. "Your progress report?"

Fina ticked things off on her fingers. "I've made contact with the guy who ran me off the road. I'm following up on the lead that Mark Lamont gave me. I'm investigating Rand's extracurricular activities. I can't imagine the escort service wants to go public any more than he does." Fina looked at her father. "I don't know who killed Melanie yet, but I'm making progress."

"What do you need?"

"More bodies. Frank did the ID on the guy who ran me off the road, but I don't want him sitting around on surveillance in case I need him for something else, so I want to pull in Dennis Kozlowski. I need to maintain surveillance. I'm sure this guy will meet up with his employer in the near future."

"Which will tell you what?"

"Who it is that doesn't want me digging around, which will lead me to who killed Melanie."

"Fine, but wrap this up."

Fina rolled her eyes.

"And don't roll your eyes at me."

"I'm not sitting around twiddling my thumbs, Dad."

"Maybe not, but you haven't figured it out, either."

"So until I've succeeded, I've failed?"

Carl shrugged slightly.

"Right." Fina got up and went to the door. "Gotta go. I have a drinking date with a construction crew."

But Carl had already dismissed her and was dialing his phone. Carl's mind worked like whale baleen: If it wasn't relevant, it was flushed right out.

"Do you have some free time?" Fina asked Matthew as she entered his office.

"No, never."

"Okay, I need to talk some stuff over, and you seem like a good person for the job."

"I don't know if that's a compliment or the booby prize."

"Take it how you will. Can we order some lunch?"

Matthew depressed an intercom button and summoned his secretary. They weren't called secretaries anymore, but that's what they were. The assistants at Ludlow and Associates were mostly young and pretty and did a whole range of tasks that related to their bosses' personal lives. Gifts for the wife, scheduling parent/teacher conferences, dry cleaning pickup. They were extremely well trained—for the 1960s.

Cynthia brought in a binder stocked with takeout menus, and Fina and Matthew made selections from the local sushi bar. Then she fetched drinks from the minibar and promised their lunch in two shakes of a lamb's tail.

"Where do you find these women?" Fina asked. "A time capsule?"

"She's great. I'm never letting her leave." They sat down on the couch. "You have that look," Matthew said.

"What look?"

"The annoyed, exasperated look that is always generated by a conversation with Dad."

"I can't help it," Fina admitted. "It's like an allergic
reaction. I tell myself not to react, but my nervous system
always overrides my brain."

Matthew looked at her sympathetically. They both
knew there was no cure for that affliction.

"But that isn't what you wanted to talk about," he
ventured. "What's up?"

"Who do you think killed Melanie?"

"Why are you asking me?"

"Because I know *you* didn't kill her, and I think you
can be objective."

Matthew puffed out his cheeks as he exhaled. "Did
you ask Scotty?"

"I can't ask Scotty. He's a softie."

Matthew gave her a questioning look.

"Maybe not in here," Fina said, gesturing to the office,
"but he still believes that people are basically decent, and
he actually spent a little time outside of the family bubble,
so he should know." After law school, Scotty went to work
at a large firm in the city with no ties to Ludlow and
Associates. He wanted to see what the real world was like,
but it didn't take long for him to decide that independence
was overrated. Pulling all-nighters on boring cases for a
shot at the partner track was exhausting and degrading,
so he'd slipped back into the fold where he was greeted
with a corner office, his pick of cases, and guaranteed
advancement. And even though Carl was often difficult,
Scotty loved working with his brothers. They challenged
and protected one another in equal measure.

"Unlike us."

"Unlike us. We believe that people are thoughtless idiots."

Matthew leaned back and laced his hands together behind his head. "I can't imagine that Melanie has any enemies. She was a nice, friendly person. And she didn't really do much, anyway; where would she have made an enemy? On the breast cancer research walk?"

"Right . . . however . . ."

"However, Rand has lots of enemies," Matthew finished her thought.

"But then why not just hurt Rand?"

"Because hurting Melanie would be worse?"

"Would it? Their relationship never seemed like wedded bliss, even to outsiders, and Rand doesn't emit that warm and fuzzy family vibe."

"True, and if he did give off that vibe, why not go straight for the jugular and go after Haley? Kids are generally their parents' Achilles' heel."

"Right." Fina thought for a moment. "But let's pretend someone did go after Melanie. Rand does piss off a lot of people. What about a client or someone he crushed in court?"

"It's possible, but it seems pretty extreme. Usually people just key our cars or throw eggs at us on the courthouse steps."

There was a tap on the door, and Cynthia came in with a lacquered bento box in each hand. She gently set them down on the coffee table and left the room, pulling the door closed behind her.

Fina examined the different compartments of the box. There was edamame, a few pieces of sushi, some teriyaki chicken, vegetable tempura, and blanched spinach with sesame sauce.

"This looks so healthy," she commented.

"I know. Don't let it scare you, though," Matthew said as he slipped a pair of lacquered chopsticks from a little silk bag and pinched a piece of chicken.

"I need to know what Melanie was so upset about the afternoon she disappeared," she said.

"Have you asked Rand?"

"Yes. He's not interested in sharing. But I'm going to ask him again."

"It may not have anything to do with Melanie's death."

"I hope not. Is he around?"

"He should be in his office."

As they ate, Matthew told Fina about his cases, cases she'd probably be working on if not for Melanie's disappearance and death. It had been two weeks since Melanie had gone missing, but it felt like forever. It was similar to having a bad flu: You feel like shit and can't imagine there will come a time when you won't. What she wouldn't give for a run-of-the-mill med mal case or a wrongful death suit.

"Why don't you just pick it up and lick it?" Matthew asked as Fina ran her finger around the teriyaki chicken compartment of her bento box.

"'Cause that would be gross."

"Right."

Girl Friday poked her head in the office and reminded Matthew that he had an appointment in five minutes. She cleared away the boxes and left the room.

"She's nicer than Dad's girl."

"Of course she is. She works for me," Matthew said, and stepped into his private bathroom to wash his hands.

"I'm going to find Rand, and then I'm going drinking with a construction crew," Fina said, pausing at the office door.

"All right. See ya."

Jesus.

Did nobody give a shit?

"Hey," Fina said as she stood in the doorway of Rand's office. He was sitting in his chair, not slumped exactly, but there was a distinct lack of vigor in his posture.

"Hey."

"Do you have a minute?"

"Sure." He beckoned her into the room. "Thanks for last night, for helping with Haley."

"Of course. Is she okay?"

Rand shrugged and dropped his hands into his lap. "She's okay."

"We'll all help her," Fina said, and took a seat in the chair facing his desk. "Whatever she needs."

He exhaled loudly and pressed his palms onto his leather desk blotter. "She'll be okay. She's a tough kid."

Fina squirmed in the leather chair and looked at Rand. "I know you don't want to talk about this, but I need to know what you and Melanie fought about the day she disappeared."

"I already told you. It was Haley and math or some other equally unremarkable topic."

"I know you think it was unremarkable, but it may not be. Let me be the judge."

Rand stood up and walked to the window behind his desk. He gazed out the glass, the sun beaming down on the rooftops below. "What does it matter? She's gone."

Fina took a deep breath. "I need to know so I can help you."

"I don't need help as much as everyone seems to think," he said with a trace of annoyance.

Fina gripped the arms of the chair. "Fine. Who hates you enough to kill Melanie?"

Rand turned and stared at her. "What?"

"Who wants to hurt you so much they would kill your wife? Actually, I bet a fair number of people would like to see you suffer. Who has the balls to actually do it?"

"I don't know."

"You're gonna have to do better than that."

"For Christ's sake."

Fina threw her hands up in exasperation, got up, and walked to the door.

"I need to see your case files."

"Those are privileged."

"Then you or one of your . . . comrades needs to go through them and give me some names. I need to know who'd want to wreck your life by killing Melanie."

"You think whoever killed Melanie was trying to get to me?"

"I have no fucking idea, Rand, but unlike you, I'm trying to figure out a solution, not throw a goddamn pity party."

She stomped out.

15

Jordy's was dark and smelled like smoke even though smoking had been banned in Boston bars years ago. Fina walked in, and the half dozen patrons looked at her before returning to their own business. There was a small cluster of drinkers in a booth toward the back and two men at the bar. One of the guys was old, with gray stubble and flabby jowls. The other was young, with greasy hair and pitted skin. Apparently, the beautiful people hadn't yet arrived.

Fina climbed onto a stool and ordered a beer in a bottle. She sipped it and watched the TV hanging in the corner. It was tuned to a local cable channel where two hulking professional athletes were debating the off-season exercise regimens of various Patriots players.

"That guy sucks, man," offered the younger guy at the

bar, referring to one of the players in question. "He's such a pussy. I could play better than him."

Fina, the old guy, and the bartender all swiveled their heads to assess the validity of the claim.

"Is that right, Benny?" The bartender chuckled and hitched his foot up on a case of vodka sitting on the floor. "I don't know." He squeezed his eyes as if making mental calculations. "I think you're a little small."

The old man worked his jaw as if he were chewing something. When he spoke, Fina realized he'd been warming up the muscles that made speech possible. "They wouldn't take you in Pop Warner, Benny. You're small, and you're ugly!"

Fina snorted and sucked some beer into her nasal cavity.

"What are you laughing at?" Benny asked with a sneer.

"That was funny. Come on, you have to admit it was funny."

"What are you even doing here?" Benny asked.

"Waiting for some friends," Fina said, and sipped her beer.

"Everyone's welcome here, Benny," the bartender said, "especially the good-looking ones." He winked at Fina and uncapped a second beer, which he placed in front of her. "This one's on Benny."

"Thanks, Benny," Fina said, raising her beer in his direction. He scowled, but returned his attention to the TV screen.

Fina was nearing the end of the second beer and her patience when the door swung open and a crowd of orange-shirted, hard hat–toting men filed into the dark space. They crowded around the bar, and within seconds, Billy appeared at her elbow, a wide grin on his face.

"Josefina, right?" Billy asked as he leaned on the bar. He was grubby, but still handsome. He smelled like dirt and sweat, a surprisingly appealing combination.

"I hope your offer was genuine, 'cause here I am," Fina said.

Billy insisted on buying her another beer, which she nursed. She was working, after all, and needed to stay, if not sharp, than at least somewhat alert. He introduced her to the other guys, and Fina was treated to one story after another, most of which featured Billy as the protagonist. It was actually sweet to watch the other guys act as his wingmen and make Billy look good. Maybe *they* wouldn't get laid tonight, but somebody would if they had any say.

After the construction crew was appropriately lubricated by booze and flirting, but wasn't too far in the bag, Fina pulled out the picture of Melanie and passed it around. No one remembered seeing Melanie around the work site, but that didn't mean she hadn't been there. It was hard to keep track with all the pretty women in the neighborhood, and most recently, the guys had been working inside the building. Fina showed them a picture of Melanie's sunglasses; one of the plumbers thought they looked familiar, but he couldn't be sure.

Fina bought a round of drinks for the guys—courtesy of Carl, of course—and waited an appropriate interval before slipping off her stool and heading for the door. Billy followed her outside, and she leaned against the brick exterior of the building.

"How about we go out for a real date?" he said. "No guys, no photos, someplace nice?"

Fina looked at him. "Sounds good. Things are pretty hectic right now, but I'll give you a call in a couple of weeks." She pulled out her phone and waited for his number.

"Right," Billy said, and stared down the street. "Just forget it." He turned and started to walk back to the door. Fina grabbed hold of his elbow and turned him toward her. She leaned in and gave him a long kiss.

"Does that seem like a blow-off?" she asked.

Billy looked at her and then kissed her back. "Not really."

"Then give me your number."

He recited it, and Fina typed it into her phone. She slipped her phone into her bag before kissing him again.

She had every intention of calling Billy, but if things got dicey, at least he got something for his troubles.

The sun came up hours after Fina had abandoned any hope of sleeping. As she lay in bed, her thoughts ricocheted between images of Melanie sinking in the ocean, chains weighing her down, and Haley, dressed provocatively, hanging around with Brianna. The image of Melanie was obviously more disturbing, but at least it was over. The danger had passed; Melanie was gone. But Haley was an open question. She was safe for now, but what about tomorrow? If this was what being a parent was like, tubal ligation was becoming an appealing option.

She watched TV for a couple of hours, then showered

and dressed in a black sheath dress and black pumps. She pulled her hair back into a chignon and transferred her gun, wallet, and sunglasses to a smaller black bag. In the kitchen, Fina leaned over the sink to eat four Mallomars and swigged down a small bottle of diet iced tea. Milloy called and interrupted her living room pacing to say he was waiting downstairs.

She moved through the over-air-conditioned lobby into Milloy's car. After pulling her door shut, Fina depressed the button to close the moonroof.

"I'm trying to avoid the bedhead look this morning."

"You look very *Breakfast at Tiffany's*," Milloy said, and rolled up the windows before cranking up the air-conditioning. "You've got chocolate on your cheek." He reached over to touch her.

"That's a bruise," Fina said, batting his hand away.

"That's chocolate, genius," Milloy replied, and rubbed his hand over her cheek. "Breakfast?"

"Yup."

They didn't speak as Milloy navigated through the morning traffic. Fina loved to drive, but occasionally, she liked someone else to take the wheel. It couldn't be just anyone, though; it had to be someone who was equally skilled and aggressive, and Milloy satisfied both criteria.

Fina pulled out her phone and dialed Dennis Kozlowski's number. The night before she'd put him on Joe Winthrop surveillance.

"How's Joe?" she asked.

According to Dennis, Joe had been lying low since her visit. He'd stayed in his apartment except for a couple of runs to the convenience store on the corner. Fina instructed Dennis to maintain the surveillance and let her know if Joe made any moves.

"No luck?" Milloy asked when she hung up.

"Nope. He seems to be sticking close to home."

"What's the plan?"

"Another visit, if he doesn't give me something soon. Can you come with me?"

Milloy glanced at her. "Sure, but wouldn't you prefer Frank?"

"Frank doesn't possess your biceps or pecs. Sometimes that's more persuasive than a gun."

"You know what you're going to do when you get there?"

Fina pulled down the visor and examined her reflection in the mirror. "Nope. I'll figure it out."

Outside the church, the street was swarming with news crews and uniformed police trying to keep things orderly. The Ludlows weren't dutiful churchgoers, but they did donate to the local Episcopalian church on a regular basis, which afforded certain privileges. When occasions called for some degree of pomp and circumstance and respectability, they had a place to go.

Inside, Fina and Milloy were directed to the parish hall, where the rest of the family was milling around. Scotty's boys raced around the space, jumping off the stage at one end of the room and then climbing the stairs to do it again and again. The men were huddled off to one side, Dudley Prentiss among them, and Elaine was sitting on a couch, a small cluster of women in her orbit.

"You're late," Elaine informed Fina when she and Milloy joined their group.

"No, I'm not," Fina said, and turned to hug Patty. "Thanks," she whispered into Patty's hair. Patty gave her a squeeze and looked in the direction of a metal door propped open to the outside. Fina followed her gaze and saw Haley sitting on the stoop. Fina and Patty exchanged a look.

"You look lovely, Mrs. Ludlow," Milloy said as he bent over to kiss Elaine's leathery cheek.

"You look so handsome, Milloy. Doesn't he look handsome?" Elaine asked the assembled group. They murmured their agreement while Fina rolled her eyes.

"You're too kind, Mrs. Ludlow," he said.

"You're such a good boy, Milloy," Elaine said. "How will you find a girl to marry if you spend all your time with her?" She nodded at Fina.

Fina scowled and broke off from the group. She started across the room to the men, but changed course and stepped outside into the bright sun.

Haley was wearing a black dress and black heels.

"You're going to roast out here in this sun," Fina said. She lowered herself down next to her niece.

"It feels good," Haley said, her eyes closed and her faced tilted toward the sun.

"You and your mom, the hotter the better."

They sat next to each other in silence. Fina felt a bead of sweat roll down her back.

"Are you feeling better?" she asked.

"Yeah. Nothing like puking your guts out multiple times," Haley commented.

Fina wanted to return to the relative cool of the parish hall, but she didn't want to leave Haley to bake by herself. Elaine had always been more concerned with her own comfort than her children's needs, and it was something that Fina couldn't forgive. When Fina got sick as a child, it was always the au pair who would spend the night rubbing her back and urging her to sip ginger ale. Elaine couldn't possibly do it; she needed to be fresh the next morning for tennis and her mani/pedi. Nanny had told Fina that her mother wasn't always that way; it seemed that Elaine's nurturing spirit died with Josie.

So Fina sat in the heat and felt the beads of sweat slicken her skin while she kept Haley company. She was saved by Scotty five minutes later.

"It's time to go," he told them, and offered each a hand as they struggled to standing positions.

Fina grabbed a napkin from a dispenser in the parish hall kitchen and dabbed at her neck and face. She watched as Rand looked around for his daughter. Haley floated toward him, but when he tried to put his arm around her, she shrugged him off and drifted toward Patty. Fina balled up the napkin and tossed it into a trash barrel. Then she fell into step with the rest of the group and prayed to a god she didn't believe in that she'd survive the next hour.

Bev fussed with Connor's tie.

"Mom, it's fine. You don't need to come up with me."

They were standing in the lobby of a skyscraper in the financial district, the top three floors of which were occupied by one of the city's most prestigious law firms. Bev didn't want to see another lawyer as long as she lived, but that was a luxury she didn't have. As far as she was concerned, the last team had failed Connor. He needed some fresh blood—out for blood—moving forward.

"I won't go up if you don't want me to, but there's no shame if it would make you feel better."

"I'm a grown man, and you're my mother."

"That's right. I'm your mom, and that's what moms do. They take care of their kids, no matter how old they are."

The lobby of the building was an atrium that soared up a dozen stories. High-heeled shoes click-clacked across the marble floor as smartly dressed women walked to the elevator banks. People were scattered along the leather benches, and small tables ringed the open-air coffee shop. One corner of the lobby had been fashioned as a pseudo jungle; thirty-foot trees and a wall of water softened the view toward the building next door.

Connor glanced at his watch. "Do you want some coffee? I've got time."

"Tea and a scone, please," Bev said, and watched him walk to the end of the line. It was clichéd but true: They were still your babies, even when they weren't babies anymore. And when someone wronged them, it stung just as much as childhood transgressions did. When did being a parent get easier? That's what she wanted to know.

Bev walked over to an empty table near the water feature and brushed the crumbs off the surface. She sat and watched the steady flow of people ingested and coughed out by the revolving doors. Connor came over with a tray and carefully transferred a cup of tea, a coffee, and a plated scone to the table. He propped the tray against the table leg after emptying it of napkins, sugar packets, butter, and a knife.

"You going to share this with me?" Bev asked as she cut into the scone and nestled a pat of butter into the seam.

"I'm not hungry."

"Just like your daddy; lose your appetite when you're stressed. Wish I had that problem," she said, and bit off the corner of the warm scone.

Bev prattled on about a show she'd watched with Chester the night before. Apparently, there's a small tribe of people called the Sentinelese who live on a tiny island in the Bay of Bengal. They're a "lost tribe" and have rejected all contact with the developed world. They even kill people who fish in their waters. Hard to believe that such pockets still existed in the world.

"I wonder if they're happy," Bev mused.

"They probably don't share our definition of happiness," Connor said, and glanced at his watch. "Time to go. You sure you want to hang around? I know you have things to do."

"But unlike the Sentinelese, I have my cell phone and can attend to business while I wait. I'll be here."

Connor started to pile the trash on the tray, but she shooed him away. She watched him walk toward the elevators and mentally urged him to stand up straighter. Those people who looked like they didn't need help were, more often than not, the ones who got it. Desperation was like a strong odor; people steered clear.

Bev's phone rang. She looked at the screen and recognized the number of one of her favorite girls.

"Hello, dear. How are you?"

"I'm well, Mrs. Duprey. How are you managing in this heat?"

"Reminds me of home, sweetheart, which is never a bad thing. What can I do for you?"

"I'm wondering if you have time to meet later today. There's a situation that I'd like to discuss with you."

Bev flattened a crumb on the table with her fingertip. "Is there a problem with one of the clients?"

"No, no."

"One of the other girls?"

"I'm not sure. It may not even be a problem, but you always tell us to let you know if something doesn't seem quite right."

"I do indeed. Can it wait until tomorrow? My day is packed tighter than a can of sardines."

"Sure. It's not an emergency."

"All right, sugar. Why don't you come to the Back Bay office tomorrow, and I'll take you out for a nice lunch."

"That would be lovely. What time?"

"Let's say noon."

"Thank you, Mrs. Duprey. I'll see you tomorrow."

Bev ended the call and sat with her phone in her hand. It could be anything. Maybe one of the girls was being indiscreet or forgetting to shave her legs. She'd just have to wait until tomorrow. She was doing a lot of that these days, waiting.

Fina saw a host of familiar faces during the service, including Frank and Peg, and caught a glimpse of Pitney and her merry band of men at the back of the church. Afterward, they milled around outside and followed the procession to the cemetery, but had the good sense to keep a fair distance during the actual interment.

Fina and Milloy were walking to his car when Pitney stepped out from behind an obelisk and stood in Fina's path.

"I'm sorry for your loss," Pitney said. She was wearing an electric blue pantsuit, which Fina supposed qualified as understated and muted in Pitney's sartorial book.

"Really?" Fina walked around her and waited for Milloy to unlock the car.

"I'm not heartless, Fina."

"Ah . . . okay. Thanks? What do you want? Undying appreciation for your sensitivity?"

"Do you really want a killer to go free? Even if that killer is your brother? Wouldn't that make family gatherings a little awkward?"

Fina snorted. "Trust me. You can't begin to fathom our family gatherings."

"I'm sure I can't. Making any progress on the case?"

"Yes." Milloy started the car, and its low purr hummed in the background.

"We could join forces, work together."

Fina shook her head in disbelief.

"Think about it," Pitney said, and walked away.

Fina grabbed the door handle and then paused. The mourners had left Melanie's freshly dug grave, but two people stood nearby, their heads bowed. She took her hand off the door and motioned for Milloy to wait. She walked toward the couple and watched as her mother bent and placed a bouquet of pink roses on Josie's grave. Elaine always said that Josie's favorite color was pink, but thirty months of life didn't give you much to go on. Fina leaned her hip against a large statue as Carl put his arm around Elaine, who was dabbing at her face with a tissue. Every once in a while, Fina pondered a world with Josie in it, but the thought was always fleeting. At this moment, it was replaced with a wash of sympathy for her parents.

Everyone reconvened at Carl and Elaine's, and Fina newly appreciated her parents' sprawling house. With a crowd this size, if she kept moving, she could avoid Elaine all day. Carl and Dudley huddled in Carl's office, and Haley took her cousins to the family room, where they zoned out in front of the TV. Fina cut two large slices of a six-layer chocolate caramel cake and wandered back to the solarium, where Milloy stood next to Risa. Milloy was looking at Risa and leaning in, his head tipped as if his ear couldn't get close enough. That was why the ladies loved Milloy; he listened, or did a damn good job pretending to.

Fina walked to a large rattan sofa and put the plates down on the glass coffee table. Frank and Peg walked over to where Fina was standing. He was holding a coffee cup and saucer and looked longingly at the slices of cake. Peg gave him a sweet smile, and Fina recognized the shorthand that long-standing couples share: *I'd love that cake; that cake will kill you; I won't have that cake; I love you for not having that cake.*

"How are you holding up, hon?" Peg asked as she embraced Fina.

"Okay."

Frank gave her a one-armed hug so as not to spill his coffee.

"It was a lovely service," Peg said.

Fina held her hands open in a question. "If you say so. How are you guys?"

"We're good," Frank said, and sipped his coffee. "What's our guy been up to?"

"Joe Winthrop? Nothing. I've got Dennis sitting on him, but so far he's been a colossal disappointment."

"What else are you working on?"

Peg didn't seem to be listening, but Fina knew this was one of her secret talents, perfected by years of working with adolescents. She could appear completely uninterested, but at the same time catch every word that you said.

"I followed up on a tip from Mark Lamont," Fina said. She saw Peg squint at the mention of his name. "I think I told you that one of his guys saw Melanie in the North End after she'd been in Cambridge. I checked it out, but couldn't come up with anything definitive. And I'm working that other lead we discussed. Milloy's helping me out with that one."

"I'm sure he's very unhappy about that," Frank chortled.

"Actually, he is kind of unhappy about it."

"I'm guessing this lead has something to do with young, beautiful women?" Peg asked.

"And you're the detective in the family?" Fina teased Frank.

"Let's go find Rand and pay our respects," Peg said to her husband. She gave Fina a peck on the cheek. "Come for dinner soon. We always love to see you."

"Thanks," Fina said. "I love seeing you guys, too." She gave Frank a kiss and watched them leave the solarium.

She noticed Mark Lamont across the room, gazing out at the pond. He saw her at the same moment and walked over.

"Fina," he said. He gave her a big hug and then stood back to look at her. "How are you?"

"Eh. I've been better. Thanks for coming."

"Of course. Melanie was practically family."

Fina gestured to Mark, and he sat down next to her on the sofa. She reached for her cake and took a bite. "Do you want some? I'm in serious need of a sugar fix."

Mark patted his round belly. "Trying to cut back, and I don't want Vanessa to catch me."

"Did you happen to talk to Bob Webber?" Fina asked.

"He's been tough to track down, but I'm seeing him later today."

Fina swallowed her irritation with a forkful of chocolate cake and creamy caramel. "I don't mean to be pushy, but it's important."

Mark held his hands up in surrender. "You're not being pushy. You're being a good sister. But you know how it is; people can be hard to get ahold of."

"Sure."

"Either way, if he hasn't contacted the police by noon tomorrow, you should go ahead."

"That's great, thanks." Fina smooshed a dab of frosting with her fork and watched it balloon over the tines. "I'm wondering, though, why wait? Couldn't I just do it now?"

"A few more hours and I might be able to help him

out with his child support issue. You know, make going to the cops a more appealing option."

"I understand. It's good of you to even consider it."

"I got to go. Watching you eat that cake is too much for me." Mark stood up and tugged on the cuffs of his shirt. "So we'll talk tomorrow?"

"Yes. Thanks, Mark. I appreciate it."

Fina finished her slice of cake. Then she put down the empty plate and started on Milloy's slice.

"You know what would be a perfect end to the day?" Fina asked Milloy. They were sprawled on her couch, each with a glass of wine. She was still in her black dress, but her hair was loose from its chignon, and Milloy had tossed aside his jacket and tie. The day had been consumed by the funeral and reception, and although Fina was tired, she also felt restless.

Milloy looked at her and raised an eyebrow.

"Yes, that," Fina said, nudging him with her bare foot, "but I was thinking of something else."

"I didn't bring my table. I can work on you, but it won't be my best work."

"That's also very appealing, but wrong again. I think we need a date with a hooker."

"That was going to be my next guess," Milloy said, and drained his wine. He massaged her bare foot. "Do we have to? I'm kinda worn out."

"Remember what I said? You don't have to have sex with her. Just get her here. Or there."

"Where's there?"

"I'll get a room. See if Molly can meet you at eleven P.M. at the Solstice."

Milloy reached into his pocket and pulled out his phone. He scrolled through his call log and selected the entry for Prestige. "You owe me."

"Indeed."

Fina padded into the kitchen and opened another bottle of wine. She brought it back to the couch and refilled Milloy's glass.

"That's right. Molly. Uh-huh," Milloy said into the phone. He avoided eye contact with Fina. "Tonight would be great. I'll be at the Solstice." He listened. "I don't have my room number yet . . ." He made a *hurry up* gesture to Fina. She grabbed her cell phone and dialed her contact at the hotel. Luckily, Prestige required a lot of information from first-time clients; Milloy was still nodding and listening two minutes later when Fina mouthed the room number to him.

"I actually just checked," Milloy said, "and I'll be in room five fourteen."

After a few more nods and yeses, Milloy finished the call and looked at Fina.

"Eleven P.M. with Molly. What exactly are you going to do with her?"

"I just want to ask her some questions. Determine if she's a threat to Rand."

"If they're as discreet as they claim, she might not tell you anything."

"Might not, but people tend to change their tunes when money or fifteen minutes of fame is involved."

"What? You don't believe in loyalty among prostitutes?" Milloy asked.

"As much as I believe in honor among thieves."

The Solstice was the newest boutique hotel in the city and had the aura of hip wealth. The lobby was a wash of grays with eggplant and fuchsia popping out of pillows and extravagant flower arrangements. The textiles were sumptuous—velvet, fur, and brocade—and though busy, the lobby was hushed. Loud cell phone conversations were gently discouraged, and there were private salons if a call couldn't wait. The restaurant was known for tiny helpings of exquisite food, although Fina didn't think that foam qualified as food. She'd eaten there once and had stopped at Kelly's afterward so she wouldn't go to bed hungry.

They left the car with the valet, and Fina checked with her friend in security. He gave her the room key, and she provided a description of Molly. Upscale hotels use a lot of security measures that fade into the background, many of which are specifically designed to deter working girls. The hotels have a thin line to walk: They don't want to be known as the kind of establishment where hookers loiter, but they want their guests to have a good stay, whatever extracurricular activities they might enjoy. Fina knew that some hookers dressed as businesswomen, a disguise that worked given the number of legitimate businesswomen who traveled regularly for work. Ah, the benefits of the feminist movement.

Room 514 boasted a king-size bed backed by a cognac-colored leather headboard. The pillows were stacked three high. The rest of the furniture in the room was large with curved edges. There were touches of stainless steel and glass thrown in, but the cold minimalism that passed for modern these days was missing.

Fina launched herself onto the bed and rolled over to look at the ceiling.

"Hey, don't mess things up," Milloy said.

"Dude, she's a hooker. She doesn't care about your linens." She stretched her arms and legs in opposite directions. "I could sleep here for hours."

"So what's the plan?"

"You always want a plan."

Milloy sat down on the bed. "What can I say? Plans make me feel safe."

Fina sat up and scanned the room for the minibar. She grabbed a king-size bag of M&M's and plopped back down on the bed. "I'll be in the bathroom when she gets here. You let her in, talk for a minute, and then I'll come out and see what happens. She's probably going to check in with her handler when she first gets here, so I won't come out before then."

"Okay." Milloy flipped on the Red Sox game, and Fina occupied herself reading the room service menu. At 10:55 P.M., she slid off the bed and went into the bathroom. She left the lights off and kept the door ajar. She didn't want the poor girl to think she was being ambushed—even though she was.

"This is weird," Milloy called out after a couple of minutes.

"It's actually weirder for me," Fina said. "I'm standing in the shower stall, fully clothed, in the dark. We have to be quiet; we don't want her to hear us."

Thirty seconds later, there was a knock on the door. Fina could hear the announcer's voice fade and Milloy walking across the room.

"Mr. Smith?" a young woman asked.

"Call me Joe," Milloy said. "You must be Molly. Come on in."

Fina listened to five minutes of inane chitchat, and then Molly called the office and let them know that she was with Mr. Smith and everything was copacetic. It was like listening to tweens after they've been dropped off at the mall. They sounded like a couple of virgins.

"Hi," Fina said, and held up her hand in a friendly gesture when she came out of the bathroom. Molly looked startled and abruptly stood up from the velvet-covered club chair.

"Wait a second." She scanned between Milloy and Fina. "No one said anything about a threesome."

"Just relax. I'm *so* not interested in a threesome," Fina said.

"Ever?" Milloy asked, looking at her.

Fina glared at him. "We're not cops, and we're not going to get you in any trouble. We just have a couple of questions." She sat down on the bed to try to reassure the girl she wasn't going to make any sudden movements. It also gave Fina a chance to assess her and be appropriately appalled.

Molly looked barely eighteen. She had long, glossy blond hair pulled into two braids. Her makeup was subtle, except for the bubblegum pink lip gloss that covered her lips. She was wearing a tight, short-sleeved, white blouse that showed ample cleavage and a tiny plaid kilt that barely covered her ass. Kneesocks and loafers completed the look. Fina saw a trench coat and briefcase sitting on the bench at the foot of the bed. Presumably she hadn't traipsed through the lobby looking like a Catholic school-girl or a music video extra.

"I'm not going to talk to you," Molly said, and reached for her coat. "This is seriously uncool."

"We're still going to pay you," Fina insisted.

"You bet your ass you're going to pay me," she snapped.

"Look, I know your company is all about discretion, but I think its security might be threatened in the not-too-distant future."

"Maybe I should call my boss."

"Why don't you? I'd love to talk to your boss," Fina said.

Milloy poured a glass of champagne from the bottle he'd opened and offered it to Molly.

"No, thank you."

He handed it to Fina and poured one for himself.

"Are you really over eighteen?" Fina asked.

"Of course, and escort services are legal."

"Right. Right up until the moment you start swapping bodily fluids."

"That's gross," Molly said, and wrinkled her nose.

"I thought you were going to call your boss?"

"I changed my mind. Can I have my money now?" she asked Milloy. "Or maybe she should go," Molly looked at Fina, "and I'll finish the job."

"Not tonight, sweetie," Milloy said. "You're beautiful, but the only thing people should be buying from you is Girl Scout Cookies."

"Thanks." Molly sniffed. She looked hurt.

Fina reached into her pocket and pulled out a thick stack of hundred-dollar bills and her card. "I'll throw in some extra if you'd consider introducing me to your boss. I'm serious about the business being at risk."

Molly buttoned up her trench coat and cinched the belt around her waist. She tugged the elastics off her braids and pulled her hair into a low, sleek ponytail. "I'll think about it." She took the wad of money and card and put them in her pocket.

Milloy walked her to the door, and she left.

"Wow," Milloy said. He sat down on the bed next to Fina. "I'm never going to look at your brother the same way again."

Fina shook her head. "You and me both."

16

~~~~~~~~~~~~~~~~~~

Fina awoke in a tangle of sheets. When she opened her eyes, it took her a moment to figure out what she was looking at. Ahh. It was the landscape of Milloy's sculpted pectoral muscles. She watched his chest rise and fall as he sighed deeply in his sleep. Fina burrowed her naked body closer to him and closed her eyes. Molly, a bath, room service, Milloy. The night had definitely ended better than it had started.

She slipped out of bed and went into the bathroom. The shower had a rain forest showerhead, and she stood under it for ten minutes and let the water sluice over her skin. She massaged a generous squirt of lemon-sage shampoo into her hair and followed with the conditioner. Once she was dry, Fina slathered the complimentary lemon-sage body lotion over her skin and slipped into a robe.

Milloy was splayed on the bed, his eyes closed. Fina

pulled her phone out of her bag and scrolled through her messages.

"You smell like a muffin," Milloy mumbled, and rolled over.

"I didn't mean to wake you."

"What time is it?"

Fina glanced at the clock. "Nine thirty. Do you have appointments this morning?"

"Not until noon." He threw back the covers and walked into the bathroom. Fina admired his spectacular backside.

"I know you're looking," Milloy called from the bathroom before closing the door.

Fina smiled and looked at her call log. Carl had called, as had Matthew and Risa. She didn't feel like calling anyone back. Ever.

Instead, she climbed onto the bed with the room service menu and clicked on the TV. She bypassed the morning news shows and settled on a cable show that chronicled the birth of a baby. It was one of her favorite shows. It was like birth control in a tidy half-hour package that didn't mess with your mood or give you chin hair. Most of the women seemed normal and clearheaded, but there was a segment of expectant moms who weren't yet sleep-deprived, yet they were completely deluded. No matter what your body is telling you, the baby isn't really craving General Tso's chicken, two orders of lo mein, shrimp with cashews, and egg foo yung. That's just your inner fat girl finally getting her way.

When Milloy emerged from the bathroom, it was time to push. He perched on the edge of the bed, a towel wrapped around his chiseled torso, and watched. The woman's legs were spread, knees up by her ears, her lady parts a blurry blob.

"Who wants this to be filmed, let alone broadcast on national television?" Milloy asked, shaking his head.

"I have no idea, but thank God they do. What would we watch otherwise?"

Milloy tilted his head. "I think that's the head," he said.

"How can you tell? I think her bits are just shifting." Fina's phone rang. "Shit." She looked at the caller ID. "I've got to take this."

She went into the bathroom, put down the toilet lid, and sat before pressing the connect button.

"What's going on?" she asked Carl.

"Why didn't you call me back? And why is your phone off? It should never be off."

"I was just about to call you, Dad."

"Right. I need you to talk to your police contact, find out if your brother is being arrested today."

"What makes you think that he is?"

Carl ignored her question. "We need to control this thing. Find out and call me back."

"I'll see what I can find out, but they're probably keeping a lid on it."

"Just find out, Fina."

"Fine," she said, but her father had already hung up.

She looked at the small clock on the marble bathroom counter. It was 9:48 A.M. If she was going to get any information, she better have something to trade. She dialed Mark's number and picked at her toenail while it rang. Her toenails were bare and short. Occasionally, she toyed with the idea of getting a pedicure, but something about it made her uneasy. Patty had told her that the ancient Egyptians had pedicures, so it was really an ancient art form, not a modern luxury. But the ancient Egyptians also put their genitals in separate containers after death. Was this really a culture we wanted to emulate?

Mark's voice mail kicked in, and Fina hung up. Mark would see that she called, but she didn't want to leave a message and risk irritating him. You had to be careful with Mark; he was easygoing, until he wasn't.

Next, she dialed Cristian's number.

"Menendez," he answered.

"Hi. It's me."

"Hey. Sorry about yesterday."

"You have nothing to be sorry for."

"Pitney was kind of a bitch at the funeral."

"Eh. She was just doing her job. Before I forget, I got those *Disney on Ice* tickets."

"That's awesome. Matteo is going to be so excited. You're going with us, right?"

"Oh, was that part of the deal?"

"Who will make fun of those beloved storybook characters if you aren't there?"

"But I'll spend the whole time worrying about safety issues; that Beast looks very top-heavy."

"Come on . . ."

"All right, all right, I'll go. That's not the reason I called, though. I think I have something else for you, something related to Melanie."

There was a squeaking noise on the other end. Fina

imagined him leaning back in his desk chair, waiting to take in the information.

"I'm all ears," Cristian said.

"Have you heard from a guy named Bob Webber?" Fina asked.

"How does asking me questions equate with you having information for me? And don't think that *Disney on Ice* tickets get you a free pass."

"Ouch. The tickets are a gift, Cristian, and I'm only trying to figure out what you know and what you don't know."

"Why don't you just assume that I don't know and go from there?"

"Fine. There's this guy named Bob Webber, and he claims that he saw Melanie the afternoon she disappeared."

"I'm listening."

"He's a construction worker, and he saw her near a building site in the North End, after she was in Cambridge."

"He's sure?"

"He's sure. He gave me a really good description, including her hideous sunglasses."

"Anyone else see her?" Cristian asked.

"I haven't found anyone else yet, but presumably, you guys know where her body went in the water. Does a sighting in that area fit with the tide and current info?"

"We only have preliminary info about that."

Fina sighed. "I don't have the resources to check this out, not like you do. If you guys canvass the area, you might get another sighting."

"When did you say you talked to this guy?"

"I didn't say. Uh . . . last Friday."

Cristian was quiet on the other end. "Why didn't you tell me this when you talked to him?"

Fina stood up and looked in the mirror. There was a small magnified mirror hanging to the side of the large one. She peered into it. "Oh God, that's horrible."

"What?" Cristian asked.

"Nothing. Sorry. You know those magnified mirrors in hotel rooms? I think their sole purpose is to horrify women. Do men ever look at their pores like this?"

"Why are you in a hotel room?"

Fina pushed the mirror back on its hinged arm and turned her back to the larger mirror. "I had to do some surveillance. Totally unrelated."

"You still haven't answered my question."

"Which was?"

"Why didn't you tell me about Bob Webber from the beginning?"

"I got the info from a source, and I couldn't compromise the source. And Bob has some problems of his own."

"What? A warrant?"

"He owes a lot of child support."

"So you're protecting a deadbeat dad?"

"It's a little more complicated than that." Fina could hear Cristian breathing. "One other thing: You can't chase it down for a couple of hours."

"Why not?"

"Because I promised my source. He's trying to get the child support thing sorted out. You've waited this long. What are a couple more hours?"

"Sounds like a wild-goose chase to me."

"It's a legitimate lead, Cristian."

"Are you listening to yourself? You're giving me a lead that's a week old, and you're forbidding me from following it until your sleazebag source can work his magic. I might as well wear a blindfold and tie my hands behind my back."

"Well, then you really wouldn't get anything done," Fina said. She fiddled with the tie on her bathrobe. "I'm doing the best I can. I'm being pulled in every direction."

"Really? I have no idea what that's like."

"Hey, is Rand going to be arrested this afternoon?"

"I have no comment on that."

"You have nothing to say? Nothing at all?"

"Nope."

Fina waited a moment. "Okay. I'll talk to you later."

Cristian's chair squeaked. "Fine. Just don't call me at five P.M. I'll be busy," he said, and hung up.

Fina stared at the phone. "Fuck me!" she groaned.

"Again?" Milloy called from the other room.

"I wasn't talking to you, stud." Fina dialed Carl.

"What?"

"It's happening at five P.M."

"Fuck!"

"That's what I said."

"Don't turn off your phone. It pisses me off when I can't reach you." Carl hung up.

Fina left the bathroom and tossed her phone on the bed. Milloy was lying naked, a cup of black coffee on the bedside table. Fina climbed up next to him.

"What'd I miss?" she asked. Onscreen, a tiny baby was pawing at the air, her hands tucked into the long sleeves of a onesie. She was like a boxer, sparring with the strength of a wet noodle.

"They named her Nevaeh," Milloy said. "It's *heaven* spelled backward." He looked at her. "What's up?"

"Rand is going to be arrested this afternoon."

"That sucks." Milloy reached for the tie on her bathrobe and pulled it open. "Let me help."

"I shouldn't do this now. Everything is going to hell in a handbasket."

"That's exactly why you should do it now." Milloy traced a line with his fingers from her collarbone to her belly button. "We'll be quick."

Fina closed her eyes. "Ahh. Music to every woman's ears."

"Just shut up," he said as his breath tickled her neck.

Bev sat back in her seat and let out a huge sigh of relief. It was right there in black and white. Six figures in the account balance column. She and the Prospect had finalized their agreement last night, and he'd made good on his promise of the influx of cash. For months, she'd felt close to the edge—with her bank account, Chester's health, Connor's disaster—and finally, she was able to take a big step back from the precipice. Things were still more bad than good, but it was a start.

With this transfusion, she could make some key investments in the business. The technology they were using needed to be upgraded, and she'd consider giving the girls bonuses. Sometimes she got nice bags or makeup for them, but at the end of the day, everybody wanted cold, hard cash. There were also some improvements she wanted to make in Chester's equipment; certainly he was better cared for than most patients, but she wanted nothing but the best for her Chester.

She stood up and wandered into the small kitchen of the Back Bay office. She put on the kettle and pulled a teacup and tea bag out of the cabinet. While the water boiled, Bev walked over to the window and looked out toward the Esplanade. There was always a steady stream of walkers and runners and people pushing strollers. She could understand the appeal of a walk in the sunshine, but running—especially in this heat—made no sense to her. Who wanted to sweat? Why get dirty if you didn't have to? Connor was always urging her to get more exercise, and she did take walks a few days a week, but it seemed especially cruel to work on her own body when Chester's was so compromised.

There was one other place the influx of cash would be most helpful, but her partner didn't need to know about it. Connor's new lawyer was the best that money could buy, and it took a lot of money to buy her. Eight hundred dollars per hour; you'd think she provided actual oral pleasure at that price. The new money would help the business, and as business got better, Bev would have the funds to pay the lawyer. Anybody who said all you needed to succeed in this country was hard work was deluded. You needed cash, and lots of it.

The teapot started to sing, and Bev went to the kitchen and poured the hot liquid over the tea bag. The water changed from clear to amber-colored as steam rose off the surface. She transferred the dripping bag to the trash and stirred in a heaping spoonful of sugar and a generous splash of milk. The cinnamon cream brioche in the bakery window had been extremely tempting this morning, but she had decided to be good and splurge during her lunch date instead. Maybe she'd order the warm chocolate bread pudding with peanut butter ice cream. She'd worked hard. She deserved a treat.

Fina and Milloy parted company, and she drove to Dudley's house in Wellesley. On the way, she called Dennis to check on the stakeout at Joe Winthrop's apartment. Ideally, Fina would make a return visit to Joe to press her point, but it would have to wait. She could have cut her morning with Milloy short, but hooking up with Milloy was like putting on her own oxygen mask first; before she could help anyone else, she had to help herself.

Fina was ushered into Dudley's home by a uniformed maid and asked to wait in the entry hall. The center entrance colonial was immense, and everything looked shiny and new. The house could almost pass for something built in the 1600s, but the young landscaping on the vast grounds, and the Italian stucco behemoth next door, suggested otherwise.

"They're in the library," the maid said. She led Fina down a hallway to a large room, where Dudley, Rand, Carl, Scotty, and an unfamiliar man were scattered around the space. Floor-to-ceiling bookcases flanked a wall that featured an enormous photo collage. A hefty ceramic vase sat on the cast-bronze coffee table, and large sculptures dotted the room—a torso here, a tower of stacked boxes there. Couches covered in cream-colored velvet sat at right angles to one another, and antique Chinese lanterns hung from the ceiling. If anyone with less taste had put the room together, it might have looked like a high-end yard sale, but Dudley's design sensibilities had resulted in an elegant, comfortable room.

Dudley greeted Fina with a kiss on the cheek, and she sank down onto the sofa next to Rand. Carl and Scotty were both on their phones, pacing around the room, and the mystery man tapped furiously on the laptop in front of him on the coffee table.

Fina didn't doubt that her father and brothers loathed the current situation, but she recognized a familiar glint in their eyes: The wheels of the legal system had started to turn. The posturing, the strategy, the sparring. They lived for all of it. Yes, the stakes were exceedingly high and personal, and it was a criminal case, not a civil case, but the Ludlows were in their element.

"You've met Arthur Drummond, haven't you? From Wilson Bellows Public Relations," Dudley asked, gesturing to the man.

He looked faintly familiar when Fina looked right at him. "I think so, but I can't remember where exactly. Nice to see you, Arthur," Fina said, and nodded. She knew that, just like the world needed defense lawyers, it also needed PR hacks, but she'd yet to meet one she liked. Yes, Carl and the boys spun information to suit their needs, but at least they were bound by some laws. Facts figured somewhere into the equation. But the PR people were all about the spin.

"I remember our last meeting quite well, Ms. Ludlow." Arthur looked at her with a pained smile. "It was about the Drake case. I believe you told me, and I quote, 'Don't pee on my leg and tell me it's raining,' end quote."

"That sounds about right," Rand said, trying to suppress a smile.

"Did I?" Fina asked. She shrugged. "It seems like you got over it."

She looked at Rand. He was wearing jeans and a crisp button-down shirt. He looked better rested than the last time she'd seen him. Maybe he was sleeping some now that the funeral was past.

"Hey," Rand said. "How are you?"

"Good. How are you? How's Haley?"

"Hanging in there."

"Good. At some point, I want to talk to you about her," Fina said, and glanced at Arthur. "Who she's hanging out with. That sort of thing."

"We will. At some point. But you know, being a teenager, it's different now than it was for us."

"Uh-huh." Fina reached toward the table and grabbed a couple of mini mushroom tartlets. Only the Ludlows had their crises catered. "So, what's going on?"

"Dudley's working his magic. I'm going to surrender tonight, cut them off at the knees," Rand said. He sipped coffee from a china cup that was striped with bands of platinum.

"That sucks," Fina said.

"It's an inconvenience, that's all." Rand waved his hand as if swatting at a fly. "And when everything is said and done, I'm going to sue the City of Boston for all it's worth."

"This is going to make your brother a rock star," Arthur interjected.

"How so?" Fina asked. Arthur was bald, and the Chinese lanterns reflected off his head. It was distracting.

"He'll be relatable. He'll have been screwed by the system, just like his clients."

It was official; Arthur was a fuckwit.

Fina's phone rang. She saw that it was Cristian, so she stood up and walked over to a window that overlooked a full-size basketball court.

"What's up?"

"Any idea where your friend Bob Webber might be?" Cristian asked.

"He's not at home?"

"Nope. Not at his current job site, either. He didn't show up this morning."

"I don't know. Maybe he's at a bar. When I spoke to him, he was really putting them away before noon."

"I don't like this," Cristian said. "You're not screwing with me, are you?"

"No, Cristian." Fina brought the phone closer to her mouth so no one could overhear. "I wouldn't do that. I know I withhold information sometimes, but I would never give you a crap lead to chase down."

"All right. Talk to you later."

Fina sat down and dropped her phone into her bag. Her stomach growled, so she grabbed a couple of mini spring rolls and pushed Bob Webber to the back of her mind.

If there was one thing that Bev couldn't abide, it was tardiness. There was no excuse for it. Fifteen minutes ago she had placed her belongings in her calfskin briefcase, washed her cup and saucer, left them to dry on the drying rack, and powdered her face. She was ready, and she hated waiting. Chester had always teased her that she was the most impatient person he knew, but her business was built on punctuality. Plus, it was just good manners. Of course, there were some legitimate excuses—illness or being mugged—but even traffic didn't qualify. There was always traffic in big cities; one should plan accordingly.

Her stomach was starting to growl, so she left a message for her lunch date to meet her at the restaurant. Bev had been looking forward to the meal all morning, and she wasn't going to let someone else's thoughtlessness spoil it for her. She locked the office behind her and stepped into the heat. A cold sweet tea; that might restore her mood.

Dudley had negotiated for Rand to surrender at seven P.M. via the back entrance of police headquarters. The six P.M. newscasts missed the show, but they had plenty of time to put a piece together for the late broadcasts. Later that night, Fina lay on the couch at Nanny's, the AC turned to high, her bare feet tucked under an afghan that Nanny had presumably knit in her youth. The newscast featured the latest press conference held by the DA on the steps of police headquarters. According to the DA, there was blood, the missing cooler, tidal charts, a nasty fight, and other pieces of evidence he couldn't yet disclose. He was righteous and fierce. Fina sipped a glass of red wine and watched her father command the screen. The blood could be explained, the cooler was irrelevant, the tidal charts didn't prove anything, and what long-married couple didn't occasionally fight? He was measured and calm.

Fina drained her glass and turned off the TV. She walked into the bedroom, stripped off her clothes, and climbed under the duvet.

17

Her phone awakened her the next morning at six thirty. She held it up to her ear and pulled the covers up to her chin.

"It's early," she told Cristian.

"Where are you?" Cristian asked.

"I'm in bed."

"You need to come down to the station."

"Why?" Fina rolled onto her back and looked at the ceiling. "Something with Rand? You should be calling Dudley."

"It's not Rand. It's something else."

"What?"

"Stop being a pain in the ass and come down here, all right?"

Fina kicked the covers off and put her feet on the floor. "I'd be less annoying if you were less cryptic."

"This is a courtesy call, Fina. Pitney wants you down here, now."

"Fine. I'm on my way."

"Bye."

"Cristian, wait. Do I need a lawyer?"

"You're a Ludlow; you always need a lawyer."

Forty-five minutes later, Fina was deposited in an interview room by a Boston cop who was packing an extra fifty pounds around his waist and thighs. How did he find his penis in there? She watched him leave the room, a sharp contrast to the treat that had been Milloy's departure just the day before.

"Don't you guys have to pass a physical to be on the force?" Fina asked when Pitney and Cristian walked into the room an hour later. She was wearing an orange batik print skirt, a purple shirt, and a shiny purple jacket.

"Ah. I see you're in fine form this morning, Fina," Pitney said, and sat in the chair across from her that was bolted to the floor.

"It's a legitimate question."

Cristian rolled his eyes and sat down. Two other detectives leaned against the walls with the coiled nonchalance that so many cops share. They looked casual, but one sudden move and they'd pounce.

"I'm not answering any questions until my attorney gets here," Fina said, and sat back in her chair.

"You don't even know what this is about," Pitney said, tugging on one of her curls. "Who says you need an attorney?" She shot Cristian a look.

Fina looked at her. There was a long pause.

"Fine. You don't have to answer anything. You can just listen. Earlier this morning, the body of a young woman was found near Fenway," Pitney said.

Fina sat up and shot a pleading look at Cristian. "Is it—?"

"It's not Haley," Cristian said. Pitney glared at him. "What?"

"As I was saying, a young woman was found murdered near Fenway." She looked at Fina.

Fina was dying to ask a question, but stayed silent. Her outburst had been fueled by emotion, and she wouldn't let that happen again. Carl would disown her if he found out that she couldn't keep her mouth shut. Every good client knew: Silence is your friend. She looked at Pitney and then started to examine her nails.

"You really are good," Pitney said. "You're not even a little bit curious?"

"She's a Ludlow. She's not going to talk," Cristian said. He was wearing suit pants and a dress shirt. His tie was loosened around his neck, and his cuffs were rolled up, showing off his strong forearms and bronze skin.

"Your card was in the dead girl's purse," Pitney said. She opened a file folder in front of her on the table. She pulled out a photo and pushed it across the table to Fina. "Why?"

Fina straightened the photo on the table and studied it. She didn't speak or change her expression, merely looked at the picture as if it were a vacation photo. It only showed the victim from the chest up, but it was clear she was lying on pavement. Her eyes were closed, her hair fanned out behind her. She was wearing a lacy red bra and only one earring. Her neck was swollen, a kaleidoscope of bruises.

She was almost unrecognizable.

It was all arranged. Bev slipped her phone into her bag and sat back in her desk chair. Her young blond employee, the one she'd recently given more responsibility, would have her first official date that night. The gentleman was a longtime customer known for his impeccable manners. The girl's introduction to the business would be a positive one, and if she made a good impression on the client, it would be the start of a fruitful relationship for all involved. Bev had called her to offer some encouraging words, and she'd also spoken directly to the client. She didn't usually take such a personal interest in breaking in a new recruit, but this girl was too important to hand off to her underlings. At the end of the night, the girl had to want to do it again and again and again. Bev had a good feeling about it.

She had a decidedly bad feeling about her more experienced employee who had stood her up the day before. Bev had fumed during her meal; even the warm chocolate bread pudding with peanut butter ice cream hadn't made her feel better. But the annoyance she'd felt yesterday was slowly giving way to concern. Her employee was a good girl—reliable and conscientious. Missing their appointment was out of character. Bev had left a few messages on her voice mail, but hadn't heard back. She hadn't been with a client last night, and the other girls hadn't heard from her.

Where was she?

"So, do you recognize her?" Pitney touched the corner of the photo with her fingernail, which was painted bright purple.

"What's the name of that color?" Fina asked, pointing at Pitney's nails. "I'm thinking maybe I need to mix things up a bit. Add a little color to my life."

Pitney glared at her, and Fina saw the trace of a smile pass over Cristian's face. There was a quick tap on the door, and Scotty walked into the room and slid into the seat next to Fina.

"Hi, guys. Sorry I'm late." He put his briefcase on the floor next to his chair and smoothed down his tie. "So, what are we talking about?" He looked around the table, his face open and eager like a golden retriever's.

"Your sister's not talking about anything," Pitney said.

"That's my girl," Scotty said, and squeezed Fina around the shoulders.

"Oww."

"That still hurts?" Scotty asked.

"It's only been a little over a week. Did I show you the bruise on my shoulder?" Fina started to wiggle out of her jacket.

"Speaking of bruises," Pitney interjected. She pushed the photo in Scotty's direction.

"Christ," Scotty said. "That's awful."

"I'd like to know if your sister knows the victim."

Fina leaned over and whispered in Scotty's ear. He thought for a moment and then whispered in her ear.

"What makes you think my sister knows this woman?" Scotty asked.

"Because her business card was found in the victim's pocket."

Scotty tipped his head from side to side. "Interesting, interesting." The siblings conferred once more. Pitney tapped her purple nails on the tabletop.

Fina straightened up in her chair. "I didn't really know her, but I did meet her a couple of times."

"Where?" Pitney asked as Cristian poised a pen over his notebook.

"At Crystal. The nightclub."

"Under what circumstances?"

Fina whispered in Scotty's ear and then looked at Pitney. "I was at the club, and my friend thought she was cute. He wanted me to introduce him." Cristian's head bobbed up, and he looked at Fina. "I was just trying to be a matchmaker. Make a love connection for a friend."

"The friend's name?" Cristian asked.

"Milloy Danielson."

"And what did the victim tell you her name was?" Pitney asked.

"Brianna. No last name."

"What else did you learn about her?"

Fina studied the blank wall behind Pitney and Cristian. It was painted light gray, its only features a video camera mounted near the ceiling and a large clock encased in wire. These rooms were designed to make you anxious. You were supposed to feel claustrophobic and unsettled. A cop once told Fina that a suspect's behavior in the interview room was a pretty good indicator of guilt. The innocent people freaked out, but the guilty often napped. Even Fina, who'd had experience in the interview room, found it mildly unnerving.

"I don't know anything else about her."

"We were told you two were arguing."

"Who told you that?"

Cristian and Pitney exchanged glances.

Fina grinned. "Let me guess. Dante Trimonti told you that Brianna and I were at each other's throats. Pulling hair and scratching. Sounds like a fantasy he might have."

"So you weren't fighting?"

"Nope. I may have been passionate, trying to convince her to talk to my friend, but she wasn't interested in him."

"Really," Cristian said.

"I know—hard to believe. Milloy's yummy."

Cristian frowned and scribbled something in his notebook.

"Enough with the lover's tiff," Pitney said.

Scotty looked surprised. "Is that true? Are you two dating?"

"Can I go?" Fina asked. "I'm sorry about Brianna, but I don't have anything to add."

Pitney reclaimed the picture of Brianna and slipped it into the manila folder. "Just don't go far." She stood up and marched out of the room with Cristian in her wake. The two detectives pushed off from the wall and left.

"You ready?" Scotty asked as he swiveled out of his bolted chair.

"Yup." Fina stood up and put her bag over her shoulder.

Scotty and Fina climbed into his car, and he turned the key. The engine was so quiet, the only indication the car was on was the blast of air that came out of the vents.

"Who is she?"

"She's a hooker who hangs out at Crystal. Haley knows her."

"Huh?" Scotty looked at her, his features slack.

"When Melanie first went missing, I showed her picture around, and one of the regulars at Crystal recognized Haley, not Melanie." Fina leaned forward and adjusted the air-conditioning vent so it pointed at her face. "This guy told me that Haley hung around with a hooker named Brianna. The dead girl."

"So you talked to her?"

"A couple of times. I was trying to figure out what Haley was mixed up in, but Brianna claimed they were just friends."

"How do you know Brianna was a hooker?"

Fina gave Scotty a look. "Trust me. I know."

"What does this have to do with Melanie?"

"I don't know, but in any case, Haley shouldn't be BFFs with a hooker."

"Agreed." Scotty tipped his vents in Fina's direction. "You gave her your card?"

"Yup. The same night I brought Haley over to your house."

"Is that when you two argued?"

"It was more a discussion than an argument. I wanted to know who she worked for."

"Did she tell you?"

"Nope." They sat in silence for a moment. "It's going to be a problem if Pitney tries to jam me up for this."

"Trust me, it's a nonstarter. Don't give it another thought."

"Is Rand out?"

"Last night," Scotty said, nodding.

"I've got to talk to some people." Fina reached for the door handle.

"Good luck," Scotty said, and drove away after she slammed the door shut.

She watched him leave. She could feel a headache creeping across her skull, and she knew it would only get worse. That little fucker Dante Trimonti was due a visit.

"Your guy's on the move," Dennis told Fina when her cell rang an hour later.

"Where's he headed?"

"South toward Quincy."

"All right. Keep in touch."

Fina went back to Nanny's, took a long shower, changed her clothes, and got back on the road. Inertia was the enemy of any investigation. Doing nothing was never an option, even when Fina didn't know exactly what to do, which is why she was heading back to Mode Accessories. Maybe it would be a dead end, but Melanie had that phone number for a reason, and more importantly, Fina didn't have any better ideas. When she crossed the juncture of the Pike and 128, she dialed Donald Seymour and crossed her fingers that he worked on Saturdays. He answered on the third ring.

"Hi, Donald. It's Amy Myers." There was a pause, and Fina heard papers being shuffled in the background. "Don't tell me you've already forgotten about me," she teased. "I represent that big accessories client."

"Of course, Miss Myers. There's no forgetting you."

"Well, I just happen to be in the neighborhood and wondered if you were serious about that lunch offer."

"Sure, sure," Donald squeaked and then cleared his throat. "You mean today?"

"If you're available."

"That would be great. Do you have any place in mind?"

They settled on a chain restaurant close to the Mode Accessories office and planned on meeting in half an hour. Fina had some business to attend to before Donald showed up. First, she called Scotty and told him to call her cell in fifty minutes. He said he was too busy, but his assistant would do the honors. Once at the restaurant, she had a word with the hostess, who was only too happy to be of assistance in exchange for twenty bucks.

With ten minutes to spare, Fina took a seat on the bench that wrapped around the restaurant foyer and waited for Donald. He was seven minutes early.

Fina thrust out her hand and shook his hand firmly in an effort to reinforce the business nature of their relationship. She would do a lot of things for work, but she wouldn't sleep with strangers. Well, at least not ugly strangers.

"I was surprised to hear from you," Donald said once

they were seated in a high-backed booth with oversize menus spread open before them.

"Just because things didn't work out this time doesn't mean we shouldn't keep in touch," Fina said. "A good network is essential to business success, don't you agree?"

The waiter looked to be in his midtwenties and affectless; Fina wanted to suggest a course of antidepressants. He took their orders and returned a few minutes later with their drinks—a soda for Donald and a diet soda for Fina that was so large, she had to pee just looking at it.

Fina steered the conversation away from work and asked Donald a few questions about where he lived and how he spent his free time. It didn't take long for the floodgates to open, thereby unleashing a monologue about the joys of home brewing. Fina liked beer as much as the next person, but she had never understood the appeal of home brewing. Why go to all that trouble for something she could easily buy? And the level of enthusiasm and commitment required? Clearly she was missing the zealous hobbyist gene.

But the conversation made Donald happy, which was the point. Their bacon cheeseburgers arrived, and the next few minutes were devoted to salt shaking, ketchup squeezing, and the like.

Fina's phone chirped, and she made a face. "I just need to look," she said, and she peeked at the screen. She saw that it was Scotty's office and muted the ringer. Fina made a show of pressing a few buttons with exaggerated force. "This phone is making me crazy. Are you happy with your phone?" She put hers down and picked up the oversize, dripping burger.

"I love it," Donald said between mouthfuls, and set down his burger. He wiped his fingers on a napkin and reached into his pocket.

"Oooh. You have one of those fancy ones," Fina said admiringly when he pulled out one of the newest smartphones. "Do you mind if I take a look? I'm thinking of biting the bullet and getting one of these."

"Be my guest," Donald said, and keyed in the PIN. He handed the phone to her across the table. "It's fantastic."

Fina cooed appropriately and let him show off a few features. She was starting to tire of the charade when the hostess approached their table.

"Excuse me, Mr. Seymour?"

"Yes," Donald said, popping a French fry into his mouth.

"There's a phone call for you at the hostess stand."

"There is?" Donald looked perplexed.

"Donald Seymour?" The hostess glanced at Fina.

"That's me. I just don't know who would be calling me here."

"Did you tell the secretary where you would be?" Fina asked, praying the answer was yes.

"Yes, but I don't know why she wouldn't just call me on my cell." He looked at his phone and started to reach for it. Fina held on to it and smiled. "Do you mind if I keep looking while you take that call? I want to try out the Web access."

"Sure, sure," Donald said, and pushed himself out of the booth.

Fina watched him walk away. Then she got to work.

She reached into her bag and pulled out a memory card that was compatible with Donald's phone. She popped the phone open, pulled out his card, and slipped the fresh one into the slot. Fina peeked around the edge of the booth. She could see Donald and the hostess conferring. She selected his contacts list and downloaded it to the card. She'd made it through the letter *U* when she caught sight of Donald walking back across the restaurant. It would have to do. She swapped the cards back, slipped hers into her bag, and tapped on the Web icon on the screen.

"That was strange," Donald said as he sat down.

"What's that?" Fina asked, looking up from his phone.

"There was no one there. I called the office, and Jean claimed no one had called me."

"That is strange. Tell me, do you work on commission for this cell company? I'm ready to sign up for one of these." Fina giggled and handed the phone back to him.

"It's great, isn't it? I have access to so much info, wherever I am."

"It's amazing," Fina agreed, and took another bite of her burger. The cheese was starting to congeal. She picked up a couple of French fries and dipped them in ketchup. "So does that help you with your brewing?" she asked, knowing that the combination of home brewing and a gadget might give Donald a hard-on right there at the table.

"Yes," he said excitedly. "I have this app that . . ."

Blah, blah, blah, blah.

But after an hour and a $22.53 lunch tab, Fina had the *A*'s through the *U*'s.

She just had to hope that the president of Zyxco hadn't named the company after himself.

18

"He went to Best Buy and the grocery store," Dennis reported to Fina. She was sitting on the couch at Nanny's wrapped in a towel, her hair still wet from the shower.

"That's it?"

"And he stopped at an industrial park in Quincy. He popped inside for about ten minutes, then came back out and drove home."

"What's that all about? Do you know the place?"

"Nope, and there were no names on any of the vehicles. I did write down a few tag numbers. There was a gravel supplier just up the road, and the helpful secretary told me she knows the place as Ridleys."

"Ridleys. Okay. Give me the tag numbers, and I'll check them out."

Dennis read off the numbers. "Do you want me to maintain surveillance?"

"Yup. Just send me the bill."

Dennis chuckled. "Carl must be loving this."

"Oh, he is," Fina said.

She called her contact at the Registry of Motor Vehicles and put in a request for info on the license plate numbers that Dennis had provided. Her request was countered with a request for tickets to the Pats–Jets game in October. In Boston, sports tickets were the real ticket to information. The Ludlows had corporate boxes at all of the city's professional sports arenas, but it was rare that any family members attended a game. She promised her contact tickets and hung up.

Fina heard a knock on the door, got up, and secured the towel around her naked body. She glimpsed through the peephole and saw a young woman with a brunette bob, a pale pink boatneck sweater, and pearls.

"Emma," Fina said as she opened the door. "You look so Republican, as always."

"And you look so naked," the young woman commented as she stepped into the condo.

Emma Kirwan was ten years younger than Fina chronologically, but easily ten years older in terms of maturity and carriage. To the uninitiated, Emma looked like an upper-middle-class stay-at-home mom who favored shopping at conservative mall stores. She wore slacks and sweaters and pearls and loafers and probably cut the crusts off her grilled cheese sandwiches.

To the initiated, Emma was one of the top computer hackers on the East Coast, and despite her appearance, had no qualms about breaking the law. She was a peculiar mix; she regularly engaged in illegal activities, but would wrinkle her nose at *The Birth of Venus*. Her boob was showing, after all.

"Thanks for getting here so quickly," Fina said. She'd left Emma a message before hopping in the shower.

"That's why you pay me the big bucks."

"Do you want something to drink?" Fina asked.

Emma looked at her. "I'd be more comfortable if you'd put some clothes on."

"Oh for Pete's sake, how does a felon get to be such a prude?"

"Those charges were dismissed," Emma said, and strode into the living room. She ran her hand over the dining room table, apparently evaluating its cleanliness, and when she deemed it satisfactory, sat down and unpacked her laptop and a couple of phones. She pulled out a pair of horn-rimmed glasses and polished them with her sweater before putting them on. Everyone expected computer whizzes to be tattooed and grungy, but given younger generations' general facility with technology, they were coming on the scene in all shapes and sizes.

"Fine. Wait a sec." Fina went to the bedroom and pulled on a thong, bra, cutoff shorts, and a T-shirt. She pulled her hair into a loose bun and walked back into the living room. "I'm wearing a thong. Is that too scandalous for you?"

"It's too much information." Emma pushed her glasses up her nose. "What have you got?"

Fina handed the memory card to Emma. "I've copied a list of contacts from another phone. I didn't get the whole thing, but I want you to download it and see if anybody looks interesting."

"Interesting? You mean the usual?"

"Yup. Arrests, debts, deaths, any names you recognize. I'm trying to find a business owner's name. The list is from an employee's phone."

Fina got on her other phone and left a message for Hal, her secret moneyman. She gave him the address of Ridleys and asked him to see what he could come up with. Despite the brief interludes of violence, a lot of Fina's work consisted of sorting through information and waiting for some piece to rise up and take on new meaning. It was like looking at op art; it was usually when you were on the brink of giving up that the image revealed itself.

Fina went to the kitchen and stared at the inside of the fridge, searching for a snack. Emma interrupted her reverie. "Fina! Someone's at the door."

She closed the fridge door and grabbed a bag of Nutter Butters from the pantry. "Hi," she said midmunch when she opened the front door to Cristian.

"Hey. Do you have a few minutes?" he asked.

"Sure." She led him in and introduced him to Emma. Cristian said hello and raised an eyebrow to Fina.

"Can we go in the other room?" Cristian asked and gestured toward the bedroom.

Fina walked into the room and tossed her wet towel onto the floor. She kicked the duvet toward the foot of the bed and propped a pillow behind her back. Cristian sat down next to her.

"That AC feels really good," he said.

"I told you that you're welcome to crash here if your place gets too hot."

Cristian grabbed the front of his shirt and pulled on

it to generate some circulation. "We can't find Bob Webber."

Fina closed her eyes and inhaled deeply. "Fuck."

"He's not at home or at work. We checked his local hangout and some places in the neighborhood."

"Have you checked his cards and his phone?"

"No. Pitney won't go for it."

"He's a potential witness." Fina tipped the bag of cookies toward Cristian. He shook his head. She put another in her mouth.

"To what? He may have seen your sister-in-law. So what?"

"So don't you guys worry when a potential witness disappears?"

"It's too early for it to be construed as a disappearance. He's an adult. He can go wherever he wants."

Fina rubbed her temples with her thumbs. "Fine."

"If he had something to give us, we'll just have to find it another way."

"We?"

"We, as in the cops. We're going to find out who killed Melanie. It's just a matter of when."

Fina shifted on the bed. "We both know that murders go unsolved all the time."

Cristian ignored her comment and tipped his head toward the living room. "What's Lois the Librarian working on out there? Something illegal?" he asked.

Fina smirked and ignored his second question. "Another lead. Despite appearances, I'm actually making progress."

"Any new threats?"

"You mean other than the ones from your boss?"

"She didn't threaten you," Cristian said.

"Oh, come on. She dragged me in for questioning because my card was in Brianna's pocket. Are you also checking Brianna's dry cleaner and her manicurist?"

"Right—'cause you fall into the same category."

Fina pulled another cookie out of the bag, then folded it closed and tossed it onto the floor. "No. No other threats."

Cristian leaned forward and put his elbows on his knees. "I know we're usually on opposite sides, but this feels worse somehow."

"Because it's personal this time."

"I don't like it."

"Neither do I." Fina picked a hair off the sheet and dropped it onto the floor next to the bed. "It's going to be over at some point. We just have to keep going."

Cristian cracked his knuckles.

"Stop worrying," Fina said. "Everything is going to be okay." She smiled at him.

He looked at her. "Maybe . . ."

Cristian was proof that the most basic human urge was to believe in the possibility of a positive outcome. He knew better than most people that, oftentimes, things don't turn out okay. But even he was willing to accept a blanket reassurance when he needed it.

Cristian squeezed her knee, stood up, and she walked him to the front door. "I'll let you know if Bob Webber turns up," he said.

"And I'll let you know . . ." Fina's eyes drifted to the windows. ". . . anything I can," she said, and gave him a kiss on the cheek. She closed the door behind him, went into the bedroom, and changed into a blue sheath dress and high-heeled cork sandals.

Emma packed up to finish the job at her office, and Fina hopped in her car. It was time to shake some trees.

At Joe Winthrop's apartment, Fina rang the bell and then walked back to her car, which was parked across the street. She leaned against the driver's-side door and waited for Joe to peek out his window. When his face appeared a minute later, she smiled and waved and hung around for fifteen more minutes. Fina didn't want him to know about his tail, which was sitting a few parking spaces down, but she did want him to know that he was still on her shit list.

Carl called when she was back on the road and told her to stop by the pool club. She could tell by the tightness of his voice he was in no mood to negotiate, so she got off the Pike and wound through the suburban streets. She parked near the garage that housed the golf carts.

The polo-shirted pool attendant waved her in, and she spotted Patty drying off Ryan near the shallow end. The other two boys were horsing around near the ladder. First, Teddy would hoist himself up one rung and then launch himself backward into the water. Chandler did it next and accompanied his dismount with a high-pitched holler.

"Out, you two," Patty said, releasing Ryan from the towel. "Pap and Gammy are waiting."

The boys climbed out, dried off, and gave Fina quick high fives before following their younger brother to the patio, where Elaine and Carl were sitting.

"You were summoned?" Patty asked as she hugged Fina.

"I should have known. A Ludlow show of strength."

It made sense that Carl would summon the family to a high-profile gathering spot; one of the Ludlow family tenets was that you never backed down. You never hid in shame or kept a low profile regardless of what people were saying about you. Other people might stay at home when one of their family members had been arrested for murder, but not Carl's family. This approach had been a source of embarrassment at various times during Fina's youth; it was hard not to feel under fire when your father's picture was splayed across the *Globe* for getting off a baby-shaking nanny in a civil trial, but there was an upside to Carl's approach. If you go into hiding, eventually you have to come out. It's easier to stay in plain sight.

Fina and Patty walked toward the patio, but were waylaid by Dr. Murray, who struggled up out of his lounge chair. He held his place in the newest John Irving book with one hand and extended the other to shake hands and say hello. A yelp from the Ludlow table prompted Patty to make a hasty retreat, and Fina and Dr. Murray were left looking at each other.

"I was very sorry to hear about your sister-in-law," Dr. Murray said, and smiled a gentle smile, which made the corners of his eyes crinkle.

"Thank you. I appreciate that."

"Any progress in your investigation?"

Fina fiddled with a small, silver linked bracelet that tickled her wrist. "Some, but it's been frustrating. Right up until the moment you solve a case, progress can be slow and hard to measure."

"Ah. I think I know something about that," Dr. Murray said.

"Except you never really solve things in your line of work, do you?"

"It's more a matter of coming up with strategies and solutions, which is actually different from solving something."

Fina looked over at her family. Carl was conversing with his grandsons while Elaine looked off into space. "Food for thought." She smiled and nodded at Dr. Murray. "It's nice to see you."

"And you. Take care."

Fina walked to the table and sat down. Scotty was at work, but Matthew was there, sipping a beer and ignoring Elaine's needling about his romantic life.

"What were you and the good doctor discussing?" Carl asked. He rattled the ice cubes in his drink.

"Nothing in particular. Just exchanging pleasantries." Fina met Carl's gaze and held it until he looked away.

"I ordered you a salad," Elaine informed Fina.

Fina looked at her mother with wonderment. "I don't like salads. You know that."

"We can share," Matthew offered. "I got a burger."

"She doesn't need a burger," Elaine said, and she sipped her cocktail.

Sometimes, Fina had to fight the urge to reach into her purse and pull out her gun. She didn't actually want to shoot her mother, but she wondered if the threat of violence would make Elaine back off and let her adult daughter, at the very least, order her own food.

"Where's Haley?" Fina asked.

"She's at her friend Sydney's house," Patty said as she took a large sip from her white wine.

"She really should be here with us," Elaine said.

"She needs to be with her friends right now, Mom," Patty said. "Just let her be a teenager." Elaine sniffed, but was silent. Fina was in awe of Patty's ability to manage her mother. She chalked it up to distance and the fact that Elaine hadn't raised her. Patty was a good daughter-in-law: She made Scotty happy, produced babies, and followed the family rules. What was it like, Fina sometimes wondered, to not be a perpetual disappointment? Fina was also amazed that Patty would choose to call Elaine "Mom." She *was* Fina's mom, and Fina didn't like to call her that.

"How about Rand?" Fina asked.

"The office," Carl said. The adults were silent.

The food arrived, and Fina and Matthew exchanged plates. Everyone focused on the boys, illustrating the real reason people have children: to distract from the dysfunctional relationships amongst the older generations. Fina drained her drink, ate half the burger and all of her French fries before pushing back her chair and standing.

"I've got to go." She looked at Carl. "Work."

Carl nodded, which defused any objection Elaine might have raised. Fina bid everyone good-bye, but asked Matthew to walk her to her car. He got up and grabbed his beer bottle from the table. They walked, both noticing whispers and stares that punctuated their progress around the pool. Fina felt grateful, not for the first time, that she had siblings. Being Carl's kid was a heavy load, even as an adult, but it was easier to bear with someone by her side. This was part of the reason that she and her brothers had stuck close to home as adults, even though that meant staying close to their difficult parents. They were like war

buddies, comforted by the bond born out of their shared
trauma. She couldn't imagine what life was like for Haley
these days without someone to share the burden of being
Melanie and Rand's kid.

"I asked Rand for access to his files," Fina said after
she'd ducked into the car to start it and turn on the AC.
She stood sandwiched between the door and the car.

"He can't do that."

"I know. So I suggested that one of you guys take a pass
and let me know if there's anyone I should be looking at."

"That's a ton of work."

"Yup, but haven't the police asked you to do that
already?"

"Sure, but we've been stalling."

"Well, it needs to be done."

Matthew sighed. "Okay. I'll let you know if I find
anything."

Fina found a coffee shop and took advantage of their Wi-Fi
and air-conditioning for the next few hours. She bought
an iced latte and set to work updating her invoices and
time sheets. She treated Ludlow and Associates like any
other employer and always provided a detailed breakdown
of her investigations to the firm. She had a handy portable
receipt scanner that enabled her to make a copy of all her
receipts, which she then attached to an electronic invoice.

Although most of her cases were provided by the family
firm, Fina was still the owner of her own business and
was meticulous about record keeping. It made life much
easier in terms of testifying in court or filing taxes if she

could back up her claims with documentation, and it came
naturally to her. Ludlow family life was practically lived
in fifteen-minute increments.

When she was first learning the business, it seemed
wrong to take the time to fill out an invoice or track her
hours when she was investigating grave injuries like sev-
ered limbs and severely disabled children. But she'd
learned from Frank that the only way to stay on top of
the paperwork was to do it regularly, regardless of the
status of an investigation.

Satisfied that her files were in good shape, Fina checked
her e-mail and found that Emma had been in touch. She'd
attached a file of the names from Donald Seymour's
phone and promised to follow with a more in-depth dos-
sier in the next twenty-four hours. Fina clicked open the
file and scanned the names. Nothing jumped out at her.

It was dark by the time she packed up and called Rand
to see if he was available. At his house, she let herself in
and went downstairs to find him in his office. He was
wearing jeans and a Red Sox T-shirt and had his bare feet
propped up on his desk. There was a manila file folder
open on his lap.

"How was it? Were you in your own cell?" Fina asked.

"It was disgusting, but I managed."

"I've asked Matthew to review the case files and let me
know if anyone raises a red flag."

"Fine."

The rest of the house was silent and mostly dark. "Is
Haley here?"

"In her room. I think she was going to go to bed
early."

"I'm just going to pop up and say hi. I won't wake her if she's already asleep."

"Sure," Rand said, and looked back at the file.

Fina climbed two stories and came to Haley's bedroom door. She leaned toward it, but didn't hear a sound. She knocked softly. When there was no response, she carefully grasped the doorknob and started to turn it. It was locked. Fina tried once more to be sure it wasn't just stuck, but it didn't budge.

"Why is Haley's door locked?" she asked Rand when she got back to the lower level.

He shrugged. "I don't know. Privacy."

"You let her keep her door locked when she's sleeping? That doesn't seem safe."

"You didn't lock your door when you were her age?"

"Ah, no. Have you forgotten about Doorgate?"

Doorgate was yet another memorable episode in the Ludlow family history. At the age of fourteen, Scotty had decided that he needed more privacy, more to keep his nosy siblings at bay than his parents. He started locking his bedroom door, which Carl took as a personal affront. He paid for everything in that house, he often reminded them, every door, screw, nut, and bolt. He would have access to every corner of it, 24/7. Scotty defied this edict a couple of times, until the day he came home and found his door off its hinges, leaning against his bedroom wall. That was that.

"I'm not Dad," Rand said.

"Clearly. I just don't get what she's doing in there that would require a locked door. Are you sure she's even in there?"

"Of course I'm sure. Her room is three floors up from the ground. She's not as crazy as you were, Fina."

She leaned on the door frame. "Okay. Well, if you see her, tell her I stopped by."

"I will give her the message when I see her."

"Thanks." Fina put her bag over her shoulder. "I'm glad you're home in one piece."

Rand sighed deeply. "Me too."

Fina nodded and climbed the stairs. Mail was piled on the side table in the front hall. A T-shirt was thrown over the banister, and a heap of socks was strewn on one of the lower steps. Melanie may not have done the manual labor around the place, but she kept their lives on track. It wouldn't take long for Rand and Haley to go off the rails.

Fina decided to swing by Dante's apartment in Allston before heading to Crystal. Even though it was ten thirty P.M., it was still early for club-goers. Fina parked and could see light peeking out from the edges of Dante's venetian blinds. She tread carefully on the porch and opened the front door. As she started down the hallway, Fina noticed that Dante's door was ajar and an angry voice was coming from his apartment. Reaching into her bag for her gun, she tiptoed to his door and edged forward until she could see into the living room.

Dante was on the floor, his head bleeding. As she watched, a man kicked him in the abs, hard enough that Fina winced in sympathy. There was another guy close to the door with his back to Fina. He was actually the larger of the two, but he stood like a statue, his hands clasped in front of him.

Fina inhaled deeply and took a step into the room. She reached up and cracked her gun against the back of the man's skull. He cried out and slumped onto the floor.

The other man stared at Fina in shock, and she leveled her gun at him as he made a motion toward his waistband.

"Don't even think about it. Ask Dante. I'm itching to blow off someone's balls."

The smaller guy slowly raised his hands. Dante's eyes danced around the room as if he couldn't make sense of the scene before him.

"Step away from him," she instructed, and nudged the man on the floor with her shoe. He was motionless.

"Is this your bitch, Dante?" the man asked.

Fina snorted. "Ahh, excuse me. Other way around." Fina walked forward and put herself between Dante and the man. "I'm sure you have legitimate business with Dante, but I need him right now. So." Fina nodded toward the door. "Off you go."

The man looked at Dante and hurled a globule of spit onto his face. "This isn't over."

"It never is," Fina commented.

The man sneered at Fina and nudged his friend with the toe of his boot. The big man groaned and moved slightly.

Fina sighed. "Go, before I do something crazy like call the cops."

He struggled to pull his sidekick to his feet. Then he threw the larger man's arm over his shoulder, and they limped out into the hallway.

Fina closed the door behind them and locked it. She put her gun in her waistband and went back over to Dante. "Come on. Can you sit up?" she asked. She dragged him over to the couch. She tried to push him up onto the cushions, but he kept sliding back toward the floor. "A little help, maybe?" He groaned, but didn't move.

He was too heavy, so Fina gave up. Dante grunted and leaned his back against the couch. Fina went into the kitchen and got a roll of paper towels, a bag of frozen chicken wings, a glass, and a bottle of whiskey.

Dante gazed at her when she came back into the room. She sat down next to him on the floor and ripped off a wad of paper towels, which she blotted on his head wound.

"Put this on your eye," she said, and handed him the bag of chicken wings. His knuckles were cut and bloody. Fina unscrewed the whiskey bottle and poured a couple fingers' worth into the glass. She helped Dante bring the glass up to his mouth and steadied it while he took a sip. He winced, probably from the whiskey seeping into his split lip, but after a moment, his body visibly relaxed.

"What did you do to piss them off?" Fina asked.

Dante spit out some blood directly onto the floor, and Fina grimaced. It wasn't the blood, but the fact that he used the living room floor like a gutter. Fina's standards weren't high, but she had some.

"Little bit of a power struggle going on," Dante said, and he shifted on the floor. Fina tore off more paper towels and added them to the bloodied stack on his head.

"Good thing I showed up," she said, and took a swig from the bottle.

"I was fine," he grunted.

"You're such a fucking liar. You were on the floor in the fetal position. I'm not going to tell anyone, Dante, but at least show a little bit of appreciation."

"Whatever. I could have handled it."

Fina refilled his glass and helped him drink more of the amber-colored liquid. She felt a momentary twinge of pity for Dante. Whatever obstacles she had to face as a woman in this business, people rarely overestimated her. She always had the advantage of surprise. A young thug like Dante had a lot to live up to.

"Why are you here?" he asked her, and he started to push off the floor with his legs. He grimaced in pain as Fina helped him sit on the couch.

"I had a chat with the police. You told them that Brianna and I had a fight?"

"What would you call it?"

"A discussion, and you know I didn't have anything to do with her murder. I wouldn't do that."

"The last time you were here you broke in and shot my pillow. You've threatened to blow off my balls, and you just laid out a guy who's six feet three and 230 pounds. I think you're bat shit crazy."

"Well . . . thank you. But I don't do things unless I have a good reason, and I didn't have any reason to kill Brianna. In fact, she was a lot more useful to me alive than dead." Fina grabbed the bag of chicken wings, rotated it, and placed it back against his face.

"So what do you want?" Dante asked.

"I want to know who Brianna worked for, and"—she gestured with a bloody paper towel—"I think you owe me big-time."

"You think? You made me look like a pussy in front of those guys."

"I made you look like a player in front of those guys. You don't seem so small-time when you have multiple people gunning for you. You need to get a better grip on the PR angle of this business," Fina said. "So find out the name for me. ASAP, by the way."

"Or else?"

"Oh, Dante, let's not go there."

Fina stood up and walked toward the door. "Where's your phone?"

He looked around the room and gestured weakly toward the TV. Fina picked it up and handed it to him. "You must have some intellectually challenged girl on your speed dial who would enjoy playing nurse. Am I right?"

Dante pressed some buttons with his thumb. Fina put her hand on the doorknob and looked at him. "And remember, if my niece shows up at Crystal, call me."

"I did call you, remember? How about some credit for that?"

"Sometimes, doing the right thing is its own reward, Dante."

Fina turned the knob and slipped her other hand into her bag. She gripped her gun all the way to her car, in case Dante's visitors were hanging around. Once she was safely locked in her car, Fina released her hand from the grip and relaxed her muscles.

When did she become such a softie?

19

~~~~~~~~~

Bev's young recruit stopped by the Back Bay office mid-morning to report on her date the night before. Not all of the details, of course. Bev didn't need a blow-by-blow, so to speak, but she did want to know which services were performed and if the gentleman had been pleased. She'd already called him and gotten positive feedback, but she wanted to hear it from the girl's perspective.

The young lady sat on one of the yellow houndstooth-covered chairs and fiddled with her hands in her lap. She wasn't nervous so much as antsy, a response that was familiar to Bev. Girls generally had one of two reactions to their first dates: Either they were repulsed by the whole affair and swore never to do it again, or they were secretly pleased and not a little overwhelmed by the rush of power they got from the experience. This girl was in the latter category. It always pleased Bev when a girl realized that she could harness her natural talents to make a generous sum of money. She didn't need to type a man's memos or spend years in school to succeed. She was her own greatest asset. She just needed an open mind and a sense of adventure.

Bev didn't want to spook her; she'd give her a couple of days before sending her on another date. She presented the few days' break as an opportunity for the girl to be sure that it was really something she wanted to pursue. Bev was only looking out for her, after all.

Once they'd taken care of business, Bev and the girl chatted about the weather and a couple of shops on New-bury Street. She walked her to the door after a few minutes and instructed her to check in later in the week for her next assignment. Bev closed the door behind her and walked back to her desk.

This was getting fun.

There wasn't exactly a spring in Connor's step, that would be an overstatement, but he felt a little lighter today. Some of the change could be attributed to his new lawyer. She was like a junkyard dog, and for the first time in a long time, Connor felt that someone was really fighting for him. Before the whole mess, he would have been put off by someone like her—aggressive and abrasive—but he finally understood. Those kinds of people were every-where, and if you weren't one of them, you better have one in your corner.

In the midst of the trial, one of his colleagues had urged him not to become jaded and cynical, but that was impossible. He used to give that kind of advice, but had come to the conclusion that the people who gave that kind of advice hadn't suffered much.

He turned the corner and approached the steps leading to his mother's office. There was another reason for his improved mood, and he was turning it over in his head when a young woman—a girl, really—came out the door of Bev's building. She passed Connor on the stairs, and he gave her a friendly nod. A small smile flashed across her face, and he watched her walk away. She was very pretty—long, blond hair; clear skin; slim. But she looked young. Very young.

He knocked on the door to his mother's office and waited. Connor knew Bev had two offices, but they had an unspoken agreement that he would only visit the Back Bay location. He didn't know exactly what went on at the other office. He just knew that he didn't want to know.

Footsteps echoed on the wood floor, and Connor heard the locks scrape on the other side of the door. Bev opened the door and beamed at her son.

"Well, aren't you a sight for sore eyes! I wasn't expecting you, darling." She ushered him into the room and kissed his cheek.

"Is it a bad time?" he asked and let her smooth the collar of his shirt.

"No such thing when it comes to you."

Bev led him to the living room, and the two of them sat on the couch. Bev was wearing a sheath dress topped by a short-sleeved jacket. A chunky necklace encircled her neck, and her hair was perfect, as always.

Connor fiddled with his watch. "Was that one of your employees who just left?" He looked at his mother.

"I don't know," Bev said. She smoothed her dress over her lap.

"Pretty, blond?" Connor prompted.

"Oh, yes. Her. She's very nice."

"She looks very young," Connor said. He looked around the room to avoid her gaze. He rarely questioned his mother about her work, or anything for that matter.

"Sweetheart, you don't need to worry. I've got things under control."

"I know that with Dad's situation you have to manage everything on your own." Connor swallowed. "And I know that you're more than capable. I just worry that you don't have the sounding board that you've always had." Connor glanced at his mother and looked away. He didn't want to be that sounding board, but as a good son, he felt he should make a tacit offer to step into the void. He hoped that his mother wouldn't take him up on it.

"I do miss having your father as my partner, but I have a new partner, and we're managing fine. Obviously, it's not the same, but it's just fine. And it's not your job to step into your daddy's shoes," Bev said, and squeezed Connor's hands.

His shoulders relaxed slightly. "I love you, Mom. I just want to help."

"And I love you, but I don't imagine that's what you came to see me about."

"You're right. Actually, I wanted to see if you were available for lunch."

Bev smiled. "I would love to have lunch with you. Are we celebrating something?"

"Nothing in particular. I just feel pretty good today and thought we should take advantage of that."

"That's reason enough for me. Let me powder my nose before we go." Bev stood and took her purse into the bathroom. Connor sat on the couch and thumbed through an issue of *Southern Living*. He'd been raised in the South, but never felt the loyalty to the region that his parents seemed to. He knew there were many wonderful aspects of Southern culture, but mint juleps and pecan pie never seemed like a fair trade for the whole slavery thing.

"Your good mood wouldn't have anything to do with a recent news event, would it?" Bev asked when she came into the room. She was carrying a large quilted leather bag in one hand.

Connor put down the magazine and stood up. "I'm not pleased that a woman was murdered."

"Well, of course not, sugar, but she was his victim just like you were."

"I loathe the man, but I'm not convinced that Rand Ludlow killed his wife."

"Does it matter?"

"Doesn't it?" They stood facing each other.

"It's okay to want someone to pay for his sins, Connor, even if the punishment doesn't fit the crime. That man is a parasite, and he should be locked up before he can hurt anyone else."

"But if he didn't do it, that means someone else will go unpunished," Connor said. He studied his mother's face. As far as he knew, she hadn't had any plastic surgery, but she looked young for her age. She had some fine lines, but nothing sagged or wrinkled.

"Maybe. Maybe not." Bev walked over to Connor, put down her bag, and grasped his shoulders. "You are a good man. Just because you're glad to see someone else suffer doesn't change that."

"Uh-huh."

"It's a natural reaction."

"I shouldn't feel glad that someone else is suffering." Connor looked at his shoes.

"Oh, my sweet, sweet boy," Bev said, and gripped his chin in her hand. "Wherever did you come from?"

Bev picked up her bag and walked to the door. Connor followed her out. She locked the door behind them.

Connor watched his mother as she started down the hallway toward the front door. She seemed pleased enough for the both of them.

Fina managed to convince Haley to have lunch with her at a sushi restaurant in the mall on Route 9.

"I don't want to talk about feelings, Aunt Fina," Haley said over the phone.

"Fine. I have something to tell you, and then we can go to Bloomie's and buy some shoes. On Pap. Do you need me to pick you up?"

"Nah. Chloe will give me a ride."

Fina got to the restaurant first and was led to a booth in the back. The place had great sushi, but the seating left a lot to be desired. The booths were wooden and straight-backed. The only padding was provided by thin cushions that seemed to deflate even under an average-size person's weight. The seating wasn't comfortable under any circumstances, but particularly not if you were nursing aches and pains, like Fina. Once the hostess had walked away,

Fina reached around to the booth behind her and snagged the cushions from it. She put two more under her butt and placed the other two on Haley's side of the booth.

Fina was on the brink of ordering when Haley arrived, almost twenty minutes late. She tossed her purse onto the seat and slid into the booth. She eyed the extra cushions.

"Trust me. You're going to need them," Fina said. Haley stacked them up and sat on top of them.

Fina was irritated that Haley was late, but the last thing the girl needed was a lecture. It did make Fina wonder how parents decide which battles to choose with their kids. Elaine came to mind. She had no problem berating her children for the most inconsequential infractions, but didn't seem particularly concerned with their development as decent human beings. Maybe because she wasn't one.

"You look nice," Fina said to Haley after the waitress had taken their order. Haley's hair was shiny and smooth, her face graced with a touch of makeup.

"Thanks." She unfolded the paper napkin under her chopsticks and placed it in her lap.

"Hey, I stopped by last night, and your door was locked," Fina said.

"Oh. Was it?"

"Do you always lock your door at night?"

Haley shrugged. She ripped off the corner of her napkin and rolled the fragment between two fingers. "I guess."

"What if there's a fire or something?"

"Who are you, Smokey the Bear? It's fine."

"Okay, okay. Just asking. So, is there anything you need right now?" Fina asked.

Haley tapped her straw on the table to free it from the paper wrapping. "I thought we weren't going to talk about feelings."

"I'm not asking about your feelings. Is there anything practical that you need that your mom would have taken care of?"

Younger kids were easier. They couldn't grasp the finality of a grown-up's death, and those left behind could throw themselves into the daily routines that, on the surface, kept life moving forward. Not that you could replace a parent just by filling sippy cups and washing between dirty toes, but it gave you a place to start, a means of expressing love and concern. What did you do with a teenager? How did you fill a void that was constantly shifting shape?

Haley gazed at Fina. Her eyes welled up with tears. "Aunt Patty checks with me every day. You don't have to go all maternal on me, or your version of maternal." She fiddled with her napkin some more.

"I'm here. Just remember that."

"I will."

The waitress arrived with a bowl of edamame and a small plate of vegetable tempura. Haley reached for a soybean, and Fina dunked a fried broccoli floret in the dipping sauce.

"I have something to tell you," Fina said after she'd chewed and swallowed the vegetable.

Haley looked at her.

"It's about your friend, Brianna."

"What about her?"

"Have you talked to her recently?"

Haley shook her head and brushed salt off her fingers.

"Haley," Fina said, adjusting her butt on the stacked cushions, "I don't know how to tell you this, but Brianna is dead."

Haley looked down at her lap and carefully tore off a small strip of napkin. "Does . . . ?" She trailed off.

"What?"

Haley took a deep breath. "What happened?"

"She was killed."

"You mean, someone murdered her?"

"It looks that way."

Tears started streaming down Haley's cheeks. Her chin became slick from their wetness, and Fina reached into the booth behind them and grabbed a clean napkin. She handed it to Haley, who pressed it against her face.

The waitress came to the table with a plate of sushi for Haley and shrimp tempura for Fina. The Japanese woman glanced from Fina to Haley, whose face was still in the napkin.

"You need something else?" She held her tray at her side and smiled weakly.

"No, thank you," Fina said. "We're good."

The waitress bowed slightly and walked away.

"Haley? Are you breathing under there?"

"Yes" was the muffled response. After a minute, she pulled the napkin away from her face and put it on the table.

"I don't understand," Haley said.

"Which part?" Fina asked.

"How did all of this happen?"

"I don't know," Fina said. "Do you mind if I eat? It's not that I don't feel your pain, but I'm starving."

"Go ahead," Haley said. She dropped her hands into her lap and picked at her napkin. "What happened to Brianna?"

"She was found in an alley near Crystal. She was beaten."

Haley nodded slowly, and a tear rolled down her cheek. Fina bit into a large tempura-battered shrimp.

"I wanted to tell you because I know you were friends, and—"

"It's not like you approved." The teenage edge had crept back into Haley's voice.

"No, I didn't, but I certainly didn't wish her any harm, and I hate that you have to deal with any more grief."

"Did you tell Dad?"

"No. Uncle Scotty knows." Haley look annoyed. "I had to tell him, Hale."

"Why?"

"Because when Brianna was found, she had my business card in her pocket."

"So?"

"So that raises a red flag. The police wanted to talk with me, and Uncle Scotty sat in for the interview."

Haley's features sagged. "They think you killed her?"

"Not really. We're not very popular with the cops right now or very popular at all, depending on your point of view." Fina had another bite of tempura and washed it down with a sip of diet soda. "At the risk of sounding like a responsible adult, you really should eat something."

Haley looked at the food and wrinkled her nose in disgust. "I can't eat it."

"Okay. But eat something later. You're almost too thin as it is."

"Is there going to be a funeral?" Haley asked.

"I imagine. Do you want me to find out? I can ask Cristian."

"Is he the hot cop?"

"He is."

Haley wrapped a shred of napkin around her finger. "How can you date a cop?"

"I'm not sure you'd call it dating."

"You just fuck him?"

Fina shrugged. She knew Haley was trying to provoke her, but she chose not to bite. "Sometimes. We're friends. We like spending time together."

After ten more minutes of eating and intermittent conversation, the waitress brought over the check and left it on the table with two hard candies wrapped in wax paper that looked like strawberries.

"Have you talked to your dad since he got home?" Fina asked.

"Home from jail? Not really."

"Don't worry about him."

"I'm not," Haley said.

Fina frowned. "Not at all?"

"Pap isn't going to let Dad go to jail. That just isn't going to happen."

Fina placed some money in the check folio and wiped her hands on the paper napkin.

"Bloomie's?" Haley asked as she got up from the booth.

"Lead the way." Fina watched Haley walk toward the front of the restaurant. She was glad that Haley wasn't losing sleep over Rand's arrest, but there was something discomfiting about her conviction that Rand was completely above the law.

Fina stood and, as she walked out, glanced at her niece's side of the table. Her napkin was a pile of white shreds on the bench. It looked like a snow squall had touched down at that very spot.

Fina drove back to Nanny's and pulled into the underground parking garage. The car locked with a tweet, and she walked to the elevator, her bag slung over her shoulder. When she was halfway across the garage, a sound emanated from behind her. Fina stopped and turned around slowly. She didn't see anyone, but she slipped her hand into her bag and rested it on her gun. She waited a moment and then walked quickly to the elevators.

A rush of sound—scrapes and scuffles—came from behind her, and before Fina could get her gun out, she was on the ground with her face digging into the concrete floor of the garage. One man kneeled on her back, and another grabbed her left arm and yanked it behind her. He started to twist her wrist. Hot, searing pain tore through it. Fina listened to the men's labored breathing, and when the pain got to be too much, she yelled at the top of her lungs. The man wrenched her arm to produce a succinct *pop*.

Then, just as quickly as they'd appeared, the two men disappeared and left Fina lying on the ground. She rolled over into a fetal position and cried out when she pulled her wrist toward her torso. If she held still, it didn't hurt, but a millimeter the wrong way and she was in agony.

Squealing tires echoed through the garage, and Fina dragged herself out of the line of traffic. She leaned against the bumper of a Mercedes and brushed dirt off her cheeks. She'd been there for five minutes when the elevator doors opened and a man in a suit spotted her on the ground. The humiliation gave her just enough energy to pull herself up by the bumper and hobble up to Nanny's.

"It's broken," Milloy said as he laid her wrist gently on her lap.

"According to your X-ray vision?"

"You need an X-ray, and you probably need a cast."

"I don't have time to get an X-ray, and I'm definitely not getting a cast."

"I'm sure I'll regret pointing this out to you," Milloy said, "but a cast will actually enable you to move around and not have a lot of pain. You'll be able to go about your business."

"In that case . . ." Fina reached for her phone and pressed the button for Scotty.

She'd called Milloy when she got up to the apartment—after she'd washed her face and swallowed two pain pills left over from a previous misadventure. He'd swung by after a nearby massage appointment and confirmed what Fina suspected; that *pop* she'd heard had been her bone.

"I need an orthopedist," Fina told Scotty when he came on the line. He didn't ask any questions—one of the things she loved about him—and gave her a number and said his assistant would call ahead. Lots of doctors hated the Ludlows, but there was also a small contingency who worked for them as expert witnesses. Fina was spoiled by easy access to excellent medical care.

A knock on the door prompted Fina and Milloy to go still. Fina reached into her bag and handed her gun to Milloy, who took it to the front door and grasped it as he looked through the peephole. His posture relaxed, and he unlocked the door and admitted Hal. Fina's finance man looked at the gun, and his eyes darted to Fina.

"Oh, geez. This looks like a bad time."

"It's fine, Hal. Come in. I only have a few minutes, though," Fina said, and started to beckon him into the living room. She winced when a sharp pain shot through her wrist, reminding her that her left hand was essentially useless.

"What happened?" Hal asked, tentatively walking into the room. He was wearing black pants and a short-sleeved button-down in a shiny, pale green fabric. The shirt couldn't have been helping regulate his body temperature. His face was flushed and beaded with sweat.

"I was jumped. I'll be fine, but I have to go for an X-ray. What have you got for me?"

"I looked into that business in Quincy, Ridleys."

"And?"

Milloy emerged from the kitchen. He handed a glass of water to Hal and a diet soda to Fina. She struggled to pop the tab with one hand. Finally, Milloy took it from her and opened the pop-top in one fluid motion. He handed it back to Fina and sat down next to her on the couch. Hal gazed at him with admiration.

"It's a paving company. They lease out equipment for paving jobs and also do some jobs themselves."

"Is it legitimate?"

"As far as I can tell. It's a small operation. About twenty employees. I'll need to dig deeper, but it's a start."

"Any names?" Fina asked. She relaxed back into the blue velvet couch. The pills were kicking in, and she was starting to feel mellow.

"Ronald Costas is the name on the tax forms."

Fina looked at Milloy. "Does that name mean anything to you?"

Milloy shook his head. "Nope. Costas is a pretty common name around here."

"I feel like I've heard it before," Fina said, and sipped her drink.

"Maybe you're thinking of that local DJ?" Hal offered.

"I don't think so," Fina said. They were quiet for a moment. "It'll come to me. Has Emma sent you those names yet?"

Once Emma had completed the dump of Donald Seymour's phone directory, she was supposed to send the list to Hal. He'd check if the names rang any financial bells while she continued with general background checks.

"Yes, and I'm on it." Hal drained his glass of water and struggled to get out of Nanny's chair. Milloy stood up to walk him to the door. "Take care of yourself, Fina," Hal said.

Fina smiled at him. "Don't worry about me, Hal. I'm tough."

"I know, but nobody is indestructible," he said, and left.

Milloy came back to the couch. "I better call you a cab. I can't drive you; I've got an appointment."

"I can drive myself." Fina put her right hand behind her and pushed herself off the couch.

Milloy stared at her and shook his head.

"I need my car, Milloy, and once I get this thing"—she held up her left wrist—"put into something, I'll be able to drive."

"In the meantime, you can't move your wrist, and you've probably got enough pain meds on board to knock out Secretariat."

"I'll be fine."

"I'm not worried about you. It's the general public who's screwed."

"I'm onto something. This is not the moment to back off."

Milloy stood up and followed in her path as she slowly gathered her belongings and slipped on her shoes.

"At least let me walk you down to the garage."

"Of course." She beamed at him. "See how reasonable I can be?"

20

It took three hours to get her wrist examined, x-rayed, and encased in a plaster cast. Fina opted for black, although, had she been less interested in blending in, she could have chosen lime green, hot pink, or traffic-cone orange.

The drive from the doctor's office was infinitely easier than the drive there. She still didn't have great range of motion, but the cast prohibited her from making any moves that would be excruciating. Her standards were slipping at a breathtaking pace.

She pulled into a parking lot and dialed Cristian's number. It went straight to voice mail, so she left a message. She was contemplating her next move when he called back and agreed to meet her at a martini bar on Route 9. There was little chance they would bump into his colleagues there, and Fina needed a drink.

The martini bar looked like it belonged on a cruise ship.

The pendant lights hanging from the ceiling were Middle America's idea of modern—funky shapes in bold colors—and the furniture was clunky and stodgy despite the leather and glass finishes. The display of bottles behind the bar slowly changed colors, like a light show for those slow on the uptake.

Fina was halfway through her drink when Cristian pushed through the glass front door. The attractive hostess greeted him, and Fina watched the young woman watch Cristian.

At the bar, he pushed out a stool and climbed up next to Fina. He stared at her arm.

"What happened this time?"

"I was jumped in my parking garage."

"At the condo?"

"Yup." Fina reached for the toothpick in her drink and pulled the olive off with her teeth.

"Is it broken?"

"Yup."

The bartender, a handsome twentysomething, came over and took Cristian's order for a soda. He walked away, and Cristian swiveled in his seat.

"Did you get a good look at him?"

"Them. This wouldn't have happened if there were just one of them. And no, I didn't get a good look. My face was pressed into the pavement." She turned so he could see the fresh scratches on her cheek. "But enough about me. Did you find Bob Webber?"

"You mean Houdini? Nope."

The bartender brought over Cristian's drink and deposited a bowl of mixed nuts next to it.

"Where the hell is he?" Fina wondered aloud.

"He's off the radar."

"I'll talk to my contact."

"I wouldn't be too optimistic if I were you."

"No chance of that."

"Obviously the guy doesn't want to be found."

Fina pushed the menu toward Cristian, and after conferring for a moment, she flagged down the bartender and ordered Kobe beef sliders and some tuna tartare.

"So these guys who jumped you; are they connected to the one who ran you off the road?" Cristian asked. "I thought you made that guy."

"I did—Joe Winthrop—and I'm keeping an eye on him, although I still can't figure out who he's working for. I'm guessing that the boss isn't happy that I'm still poking around. Hence the friendly reminder."

"Another?" the bartender asked when he meandered over and picked up Fina's empty glass.

"I better not, just some water. I'm on a lot of meds," she said, and grinned at Cristian.

"Terrific," Cristian said.

"Joe, the one who ran me off the road, made a visit to a paving company in Quincy, a place called Ridleys. The name on the tax records is Ronald Costas. I don't have a lead on him yet, though."

"Is this your way of asking if I know him?"

"Yes."

"Never heard of Costas or Ridleys. What makes you think it has something to do with you?"

"It's the only place he's been since I made contact with him, other than the grocery store and Best Buy. I don't think he'd venture out unless it was important."

A waitress arrived with two small platters bearing the sliders and the tuna. Fina unwrapped some chopsticks and took a bite of tuna while Cristian popped a slider in his mouth. He chewed thoughtfully.

"I'm not tasting the sake that's rubbed into the cows' hides."

"I think that might be a myth." Fina sipped her water. "Look, somehow Joe Winthrop and Ronald Costas are tied to Melanie's death."

"That's a bit of a leap."

"Cristian, it's the only thing I'm investigating now. Why else would somebody be gunning for me?"

"Because you can be seriously annoying?"

"Hey! I'm giving you leads. Don't ignore them just because you're perturbed with the source."

"I'm not perturbed."

Fina raised her eyebrow and picked up one of the sliders. She took a bite and wiped her mouth with her napkin. "What's happening with the Brianna situation?"

"Still waiting to hear from the lab."

"Was she raped?"

"There were signs of sex, maybe a little rough, but it's not clear if it was consensual."

"Have you figured out who she worked for?"

"We've got it narrowed down."

"Any chance you'll tell me who the candidates are? Remember, I asked *before* she was murdered."

"So what? You get dibs on the info? It's an official police investigation now. Maybe I'll tell you once we figure it out." Cristian sipped his soda.

"I told Haley she was dead," Fina said.

"How'd that go?"

"As well as you might expect. One minute she seems pretty normal, and the next she has a breakdown."

"She's probably in shock. Her mother was murdered. Her father has been arrested. Her friend has been murdered." Cristian used his chopsticks to grab some tuna. "You need to keep a close eye on her."

"I'm trying, but it's not easy. I don't know how much to push her. When I try to talk about stuff with her, she just stonewalls me or bursts into tears and then stonewalls." Fina turned toward him. "Can you believe it? I'm the touchy-feely one in the relationship. What's happening to me?"

"You need to get her a therapist—not that your efforts aren't admirable." He grinned.

"I'm going to try, but that's going to take a major campaign. Carl and Elaine and Rand aren't big on talking about one's feelings within the family, let alone with strangers."

"Yeah, and your family's the picture of mental health." Cristian sipped his drink. "Do you think your parents would be different if your sister were around?'

Fina had told both Milloy and Cristian about Josie. Initially, revealing the family history had made her uneasy, but over time, she discovered there was something comforting about sharing the secret. It was like a cipher for her family; she didn't have to repeatedly explain the Ludlow pathology.

"Maybe. I think they gave up in a way. Their hearts were broken and defective." She shrugged. "We grew up thinking that was normal."

Cristian pushed the slider plate in front of her. "You want the last one?"

"No, thanks. Knock yourself out."

Cristian popped the tiny burger in his mouth and chewed. "Speaking of the Ludlows, you're going to have to decide whose side you're on," he said, and had another sip of soda.

"Meaning?"

"Do you want the truth or do you want to protect your brother at any cost?"

"I want the truth." Fina looked into her glass. "But I'm not going to pretend it's going to be easy."

"I know it won't. I just wonder how strong your resolve is."

"Cristian." Fina turned on her stool to face him. "Melanie was my sister-in-law. She was Haley's mother. I'm not going to protect whoever killed her."

Cristian put his hands up in a defensive gesture. "Just asking."

"And now, you can report back to Pitney."

"Pitney's not asking. I just want to know if I'm going to have to arrest you in the near future."

"Not for conspiracy or obstructing justice. I can't speak for other potential charges."

Cristian's phone vibrated, and he pulled it out of his pocket. He looked at a text, and his eyebrows crept up his face. He typed a hurried response and put the phone back into his pocket. "Gotta go." He reached for his wallet, but Fina stopped him with her good hand.

"It's on me. It's the least I can do."

"Thanks." He squeezed her shoulder. "Try to be

careful. I don't want our next rendezvous to be in the morgue."

"Ever the romantic," Fina said, and she grabbed a slice of tuna. "Let me know what that text is about when you have a chance, okay?"

Cristian rolled his eyes and left. Fina chewed the tuna and adjusted her injured wrist on the bar. She was transitioning out of the temporary relief provided by the cast to the knowledge that her mobility was seriously compromised.

This sucked.

Bev didn't like her lawyer.

His name was Lawrence Serensen. He was in his midthirties and slicker than an oil spill. Unfortunately, she didn't have many options from which to choose. There were plenty of lawyers who were willing to overlook her business specialties, but few of them were actually good lawyers. It was nearly impossible to find someone with the right combination of loose morals, Mensa-level intellect, and the instincts of a snake.

Bev also didn't like being summoned, especially on a Sunday, but Lawrence insisted that cooperating with the police was in her best interest. They wanted to talk to her about Brianna, though they wouldn't say what about her they wanted to discuss. Bev had been worried about the girl, but now she wondered if Brianna was just ducking her calls after having cooperated in some capacity with the police. It was hard to imagine; her girls knew the consequences of disloyalty were significant.

Bev waited at the elevator bank of Lawrence's building, a building that was only a block away from the skyscraper that housed Connor's new attorney. They all huddled together, didn't they? Like a pack of wolves. Bev got on and pressed the button for the twenty-third floor. She took a deep breath and watched the numbers tick up in the digital display.

The doors spread open to a carpeted hallway dominated by a crystal chandelier and a large flower arrangement on a marble console table. Bev checked in and followed the receptionist up a flight of stairs next to a span of two-story windows overlooking the harbor. She was led into a conference room a few doors down that shared the same magnificent view as the staircase.

"I'll let Mr. Serensen know that you're all here," the young woman said, and left. There were four people waiting, and they only reinforced Bev's notion that the Boston Police Department was a collection of odd ducks. Of the three men, two were white and in their forties or fifties. They wore suits that looked poorly cut, the fabrics boasting a slight sheen. The older man sat, and the younger leaned against the windows. The third man was extremely handsome; Hispanic, Bev guessed. He wore jeans and a dress shirt with a tie and blazer. Next to him, a woman talked on a cell phone.

Bev sat down at the end of the large, polished table and studied the woman. Her hair was curly and unruly, springing from her scalp like dozens of little Slinkys. She was wearing a bright red pantsuit that did nothing for her complexion. It wasn't a good red; more like ketchup that had sat on a plate too long and congealed. Under the suit, her blouse was a patterned affair of red, yellow, and purple, and she had large bracelets of the same colors stacked on her wrist. The woman was an eyesore.

"Great. You're all here," Lawrence said as he breezed into the room, his assistant in his wake. "Anybody want anything else to eat or drink?"

There was a tray on the sideboard that held coffee, tea, and water. Two large platters held fruit and a variety of pastries and baked goods. The older cop walked over and grabbed a Danish and a cup of coffee, which he brought back to the table. The woman put her phone in her voluminous bag and straightened up in her chair.

"Bev? Can I get you anything?" Lawrence asked.

Bev cringed. If she'd told him once, she'd told him a hundred times: She was to be called Mrs. Duprey. He was young enough to be her child, for goodness' sakes, and that kind of familiarity only invited more of the same from others.

"No, Mr. Serensen. I'm just fine."

The assistant fluttered off and pulled the door closed behind her. Lawrence took a seat next to Bev. He opened an expensive leather folio and clicked a pen to expose the ballpoint.

"We're here because the police would like to ask you a few questions about Jennifer Billingsworth, aka Brianna," Lawrence said to Bev.

"I'm Lieutenant Pitney," the woman said. "This is Detective Menendez"—she gestured to the Hispanic man—"and Detectives Stevens and Rawlins."

"It's nice to meet you," Bev said.

"Can you tell us about the nature of your relationship with Ms. Billingsworth?" the lieutenant asked.

Bev looked at Lawrence, who nodded slightly. "She's my employee."

"And what does she do for you?"

"Mrs. Duprey is the owner of a service that provides companionship," Lawrence interjected, "which I might remind you is completely legal in the city of Boston."

"Right. Companionship," Pitney said, and the other cops chuckled.

Bev was silent. There was plenty she wanted to say, but she was well schooled in the practice of keeping one's mouth shut in the presence of the police.

"So Ms. Billingsworth works as a companion?" Detective Menendez asked.

"Yes," Bev answered.

"When was the last time you spoke with her?" Pitney said.

"She called me on Thursday. We had a lunch date for the next day, but she never showed. I haven't spoken with her since that phone call."

"Do you have any idea why she missed your lunch?" Pitney asked. She wrote something in the small notebook in front of her.

"I haven't the faintest."

"Did you make any attempts to contact her?"

"Of course. I spoke with her roommate and left a number of messages on her cell phone, but she hasn't responded." Bev glanced at Lawrence. He was clicking his pen. The sound was irritating.

"Are you concerned by her absence?" Pitney asked.

Bev considered the question. "It's unlike her. Brianna is very responsible."

"Did she have a date the night before your lunch or the night of your lunch?" the handsome detective asked.

"Not to my knowledge."

"Could she be doing business on the side?"

Bev smiled. "I doubt it. My business caters to successful men who meet very particular criteria. We're very selective. Why would she subject herself to company of a lesser caliber?"

Pitney reached down into her bag and pulled out a manila folder. She opened it and pushed a photo down the table. It slid across the polished surface. Lawrence took it, and Bev glanced at it before looking away in horror.

"Is that Brianna, Mrs. Duprey?" Pitney asked.

Bev closed her eyes and took a deep breath. "Yes. That's Brianna. What happened to her?"

"She was murdered," Menendez said.

Lawrence tipped the photo in Bev's direction to offer her another look, but she shook her head. He pushed it back down the table toward Pitney.

"Look," Lawrence said. "Brianna worked for Mrs. Duprey, but she didn't even know she was dead. Is there anything else?"

"Was that typical?" Pitney asked. "Having lunch with your employees?" She slipped the photo back into the folder.

"I'm sorry?" Bev asked.

"You said that Brianna called you and set up a lunch date. Do you do that often with your escorts?"

Bev stared at her. "Occasionally I share a meal with one or more of my employees. Don't you have lunch with your 'escorts' on occasion?" Bev asked, looking at the men.

Pitney smirked. "So it was just routine business? Brianna didn't call you for any particular reason?"

"None that she shared with me. I assumed she just wanted to check in with me." Bev touched her necklace. "I know you have tremendous disdain for my business, Lieutenant, but working for me is considered a plum assignment. Most of my employees strive to maintain a positive working relationship."

Click. Click. Click. Bev glared at Lawrence. That infernal pen clicking was intolerable.

"Actually, it's the illegality of it that I have a problem with. You act like you're hosting quilting bees when what you're really doing is breaking the law and exploiting young women."

Bev scoffed. "Exploitation? Please. What would you have them do? Work at minimum wage jobs that don't even cover the rent? It's always the people who have better opportunities who disparage the choices of women who struggle to make ends meet. How nice of you to be outraged on their behalf."

Pitney's eyes widened. "Wow. The compartments in your head must be more fortified than Fort Knox." She leaned forward. "Have you actually convinced yourself that your girls enjoy their work? They're being humiliated and degraded so you can make money. Does it ever occur to you, when one of your girls has finished giving a blow job to some man old enough to be her grandfather, that she actually *is* someone's granddaughter?"

"Ladies." Lawrence held his hands up to stop the verbal collision, and Detective Menendez put his hand on the back of Lieutenant Pitney's chair.

"It's fine, Mr. Serensen," Bev said, and put her perfectly manicured hand on the sleeve of his dark suit. "I'm used to this. It's unattractive women who have the most difficulty with my work." The male cops glanced at one another. "I just chalk it up to jealousy." Bev smoothed her skirt with her hand and smiled at Pitney.

Pitney pushed back her chair and grabbed her bag. "You can expect warrants for your office and books."

"On what grounds?" Lawrence asked.

"Our victim was an escort with Mrs. Duprey's business, which means there's a roster of men who are potential suspects. I need their names."

Bev leaned over and whispered in Lawrence's ear. He scribbled something on his pad. "Mrs. Duprey is happy to provide a list of Brianna's contacts."

Pitney smiled. "But she's so busy being a beacon of feminism and leadership, I can't imagine she has the time to provide me with information."

"My client makes a good faith offer and you reject it? That doesn't look good."

"We'll be in touch," Pitney said, and walked out with the others trailing behind.

Lawrence flipped his folio shut and slipped the pen into his breast pocket. "Are your books in order?" he asked Bev once he'd glanced at the door to make sure they were alone.

"Of course, Mr. Serensen. I will be happy to send the relevant set of books to you." Bev stood and walked to the door. "I trust you can contain this? I don't want my other endeavors to be jeopardized."

"That's what you pay me for," Lawrence said. "Can I walk you out?"

"No, thank you. I know the way."

Bev walked down the stairs and asked the receptionist for directions to the ladies' room. The space was as elegant as the rest of the office suite: marble, oversize wooden stall doors, and brass fixtures. Bev went into the handicapped stall, hung her purse on the hook, and stared into the mirror. She stood there for a moment, then reached into her bag for her lipstick and applied a fresh coat.

Everything was fine.

Fina eventually paid her tab and drove home. She walked through the parking garage with her gun firmly in hand and made it upstairs to Nanny's without any problems. The doctor had given her a bottle of pain pills, which she dipped into and promptly fell asleep on the couch in front of a Red Sox game. The phone woke her up a couple of hours later.

"I've got someone for you to meet," Dante yelled. Fina could hear loud music in the background.

"Who?"

"Someone who's gonna answer your questions about Brianna."

"Fine, but it's going to have to wait for the morning. Tell her—it's a her, I'm guessing—to meet me at the Elm Street Café at nine A.M."

"Why don't you just come down to the club right now?"

"I can't. Tell her to meet me tomorrow." Fina hung up. She turned off the TV and stumbled into the bedroom. When taking off her clothes proved too difficult, she collapsed onto the bed fully clothed and was out in a matter of minutes.

"I didn't expect to hear from you," Pitney said the next day as she sat down at a café table.

"Well, it occurred to me that despite our differences, I could be helpful." Bev picked up her teacup and sipped from it. The tea shop was around the corner from her Back Bay office, and Bev found the ambience soothing. Students rarely patronized the place, and the unemployed didn't lay claim to the limited tables with their laptops and bottomless cups of coffee.

"I can't imagine your lawyer approves," Pitney said as she waved over the waitress. She ordered a black coffee and a cranberry scone.

"Don't worry about Mr. Serensen. I can take care of him."

Pitney shrugged. "What's so important?"

"I'm genuinely upset about Brianna's death. She was a promising young woman. Did you know she was studying sociology?"

Pitney looked around the café. "Did you really summon me here to discuss her résumé?"

"Are you incapable of polite conversation, Lieutenant?"

"I don't have time for polite conversation, ma'am. Unlike everyone else who pretends their work requires a sense of urgency, mine actually does. If you have information, give it to me. If you don't, I'll take my scone to go."

The scone and coffee arrived at that moment. Bev and Pitney waited for the waitress to leave.

"My information is not directly related to Brianna's death." Bev paused. "Well, at least, I don't think it is, but I'll let you be the judge."

Pitney bit into the scone, and a plump cranberry dropped onto her plate. She picked it up between two hot pink–painted nails and popped it in her mouth.

Bev rotated her teacup in its saucer. "I want Brianna's killer to be found, but I'd like to minimize the disruption to my business."

"Uh-huh," Pitney said, and blew on the surface of her coffee.

"If I provide information, perhaps you would take that into account."

Pitney looked at her.

"I have a client who I think might be of interest to you," Bev said.

"Why's that? I'm typically not very interested in johns."

"Well, this one is a suspect in a high-profile murder case." Bev picked up her tea. She sipped delicately as Pitney leaned forward in her seat.

"I'm listening."

"And you'll minimize the disruption to my business?"

"I will do what I can if the information is as good as you seem to think it is."

Bev sat up in her seat. "Good. Rand Ludlow is a frequent customer of my escort business. He has a favorite girl who he sees on a somewhat regular basis. Perhaps his wife was displeased with the arrangement."

Pitney's eyes sparkled. "Rand Ludlow used hookers?"

Bev curled her lip in distaste. "Escorts. He hired escorts."

"Let me make sure I understand you: He hired escorts for sex?"

Bev was silent. Behind the counter, a young man had his hand propped on his chin, his nose in a book.

Pitney broke into a big smile. "That little bastard."

"I beg your pardon?" Bev asked.

"Sorry. Didn't mean to upset your delicate sensibilities." Pitney tore off a large segment of scone and put it in her mouth. "Aren't you running the risk of bad publicity by telling me this? If one of your clients is outed, the others are going to run scared."

"This isn't proof of anything, Lieutenant. It's leverage. I expect you to use it discreetly. Don't make me regret sharing it with you."

Pitney smiled slyly. "Are you threatening me?" she asked over her coffee cup.

"Of course not, dear," Bev said. She stood up, ran a hand through her hair, and fingered an earring. "That would be unsavory."

Fina showered with her arm sticking out of the curtain. She didn't wash her hair or shave her legs, and she couldn't swear that she'd adequately cleaned all the nooks and crannies. Oh well. Maybe Milloy or Cristian would do the honors.

She got to the café at nine fifteen A.M. and left her car parked in a loading zone around the corner. Inside, she scanned the room; there were a few young women seated alone. One was texting, another was typing on her computer, and the third had a copy of the *Herald* spread open on the table in front of her. Fina stood by the front door and watched the three women, hoping that one would seek her out. After exchanging a few glances with the texting woman, Fina wound her way through the tables and stopped next to her.

"Are you Dante's friend?" Fina asked her.

"You're late," the young woman said, and continued typing on the tiny keyboard.

"I'm really sorry. I just got this." Fina held up her cast. "I'm still not used to it. It's taking me a lot longer to do regular stuff."

"Hmph." The young woman put down her phone and gestured toward the chair across from her. "You're here now."

"Can I get you a refill or something to eat?" Fina asked, and sat down.

"No, thanks."

Fina motioned for a waitress and ordered a latte and a chocolate croissant. She took an inventory of the young woman seated across from her. She was in her early twenties and black. She wasn't thin or fat, but somewhere comfortably in the middle. Her curves looked solid, and her skin glowed. She looked healthy and strong, like she could chop wood or change a tire. Her lips shone with gloss, and her face was framed by tight curls.

"I'm Fina, by the way." Fina put out her hand, and the woman shook it.

"Olivia."

The waitress set down her latte and croissant. Fina poured a pack of sugar into the mug and stirred it.

"So, Brianna. What can you tell me about her?" Fina asked.

"Back up a second." Olivia held up her hand. "The only reason I agreed to talk to you is because Brianna was my friend. I want to know who did this to her, but I don't want to get involved."

"Understood. I assume you've spoken with the police."

Olivia drank her coffee. "The police don't need to hear what I have to say."

"Oookay." Fina took a small sip of her coffee, carefully testing the temperature. "I'm just trying to figure out who Brianna worked for and how it might tie into another case I'm working on. Obviously, I'll help Brianna's case if I can."

Olivia's phone dinged, and she glanced at the display. She put it back down on the table and looked at Fina.

"Our boss was a bitch."

"Your boss? So you're an escort also?"

Olivia straightened up abruptly. "Hell, no. What do you take me for?"

"Easy, killer." Fina grinned. "It's a reasonable assumption."

Olivia scowled. "Maybe it's reasonable, but it's completely inaccurate."

"So what did you do for the boss?" Fina shifted in her

seat. Her limited patience was even more limited than usual. The soreness of her arm, coupled with the inconvenience of the cast and her general frustration with the case, was making her irritable.

"I was a booker. I worked the phones—vetted potential clients and set up the appointments for the girls. It sounds easy, but it isn't. You have to be very careful what you say on the phone."

"I bet."

"You can't be explicit about the services, and you can't piss off the clients. It's a whole new level of customer service."

"So you would book Brianna on jobs?"

"And the other girls. But I really liked Brianna. She was cool. We hung out sometimes away from the office."

"Was anything different about her recently? Did she seem upset about anything?"

"Not really. She mentioned that someone was hassling her a bit, but she didn't say more than that."

"Was it a client?"

Olivia shrugged. "I don't know. She didn't seem threatened exactly, more like annoyed."

Fina bit into the croissant. She might have been the irritant in Brianna's life. "Why do you hate your boss so much? And what's her name?"

Olivia leaned forward with her elbows on the table. "Her name is Bev Duprey."

"Tell me about her."

"She's old, you know, sixty." Fina swallowed some coffee and marveled at the time horizon of twentysomethings. "She's rich and very proper. From the South, originally." Olivia arched one of her eyebrows to stress the information, but Fina wasn't sure what message she was meant to extrapolate from the gesture. That Bev was like a Civil War–era plantation owner?

"Bev fired you?"

"I quit."

"Why?"

"Because Mrs. Duprey is a racist bitch."

Fina bit off an edge of flaky dough, and a crumb disappeared down her arm. She shook her cast toward the floor to try to dislodge the tidbit. "What did she do specifically?"

"I started working for her after I spent a year in a corporate job. I had to do all kinds of shit to fit in there: wear certain clothes, keep my nails a particular length, and straighten my hair. It makes white people nervous if your hair looks too natural. Makes them worry you're going to break into some kind of tribal dance."

Fina snorted. "I hate the corporate world."

"So, I got the job with Mrs. Duprey, and after I'd proven myself, I decided to give the relaxer a break and go au naturel."

"I think your hair's gorgeous."

Olivia pulled on a curl. "So do I, but she didn't. She called me in and told me that I wasn't meeting the personal appearance standards of the company. I might understand if I were seeing clients—we're talking about a lot of old white guys, after all—but I never saw clients. I didn't see anybody but Mrs. Duprey and the other girls in the office. It's not like it was dirty. She's racist, and the worst kind, too. She pretends to be genteel and so well mannered."

"So, you don't only want to find Brianna's killer," Fina

said, and popped the last bite of croissant into her mouth. "You'd like to screw over your old boss if possible."

Olivia shrugged, and a sly smile crept across her face. "I'm very efficient. I like to kill two birds with one stone."

"You're my kind of woman, Olivia. Where can I find Mrs. Duprey? Did you guys really call her that?"

"Oh yes, ma'am," Olivia said in an exaggerated tone. "I told you, she's all about the facade. She's always trying to catch flies with honey."

Olivia gave Fina the address of an office in Back Bay and a description of Bev, and the two women gathered their bags and walked out to the sidewalk. Not even ten A.M., and Fina could already feel the sweat beading on her brow.

"Where are you working now?" she asked Olivia.

The young woman frowned. "I'm looking. There's not much out there."

"Write down this number," Fina said, and dictated the number for Matthew's office. "Tell the assistant that Fina wants Matthew to see if there's a spot for you."

"What about my work history?" Olivia asked.

"Don't worry about that." Fina waved her hand in the air. "They're ambulance chasers; they're the definition of sleaze."

"Is he going to try to make me change my hair?"

Fina guffawed. "Hardly, but if he does, tell him to take it up with me."

"Thanks," Olivia said, and put her phone into her purse. "You're much nicer than Dante made you sound."

Fina gently flexed the fingers protruding from her cast. "Dante's afraid I'm going to shoot off his balls. I would

expect him to have some reservations about our relationship."

She watched Olivia walk down the street and disappear
into a T station.

Fina was sweaty and sore and grouchy, but she had a
name.

Finally, she had a name.

21

~~~~~~~~~~

Fina went to Rand's house next, where she found Scotty's kids yelling and splashing in the backyard pool. She waved at them and said hello to the teenage girl who was acting as lifeguard. Inside the house, Patty was dumping a bag of tortilla chips into a bowl and grabbing juice boxes from the fridge.

"Who's the lifeguard?" Fina asked, grabbing a handful of chips.

"Our neighbor. Helps me out when I need an extra pair of hands." Scotty and Patty could afford a platoon of nannies and au pairs, but Patty had never warmed to the idea of having a stranger in the house. "She wants to work in education," Patty continued, "hence her willingness to babysit." The sons and daughters in the Ludlow social circle weren't interested in summer and weekend jobs; they were too busy interning at million-dollar hedge funds or the mayor's office. Babysitting was a quaint concept left to those with futures in poorly paid yet essential professions.

"Why aren't you at your pool or the club?" Fina asked.

"I thought there was a better chance of crossing paths with Haley on her own turf. Also, Rand is doing some work from home, so your parents and Matthew will probably stop by at some point. Give the kids a chance to see them."

"No need for me to linger, then."

"Fina," Patty said sternly, and folded down the top of the chip bag.

"I'm kidding . . . kind of."

Haley and Rand walked into the room together, but were quiet. Fina couldn't tell if the silence was on purpose or if they'd reached a natural pause in their conversation.

"What happened to your hand?" Patty asked.

Fina held up the cast. "I broke my wrist," she said. She glanced in Haley's direction. "No biggie."

Haley opened the fridge door and perused the options.

"There's nothing to eat," she proclaimed and swung the door shut.

"There's tortilla chips and salsa, and I got some of that hummus you like," Patty said, and she put the drinks and snacks on a tray.

Haley didn't respond. Rand stood next to her and grabbed a chip from the bowl.

"I can't have this crap in the house, Patty. I'm going to get fat."

"Mom always had it, and you didn't complain," Haley said.

Rand ignored her and brushed the salt off his hands.

"Haley needs a check for the country club overnight," Patty told Rand. "And you need to sign the permission slip."

Fina leaned back against the island and watched her brother and sister-in-law work out the details of Haley's upcoming weekend away. Haley stood next to her father. She was wearing a tank top that exposed her bra straps and a pair of sweat shorts that had a logo emblazoned across the ass. Her hair was loose down her back, and after a moment, Rand reached out and ran a hand down it. It was the sort of long, silky mane that women paid good money for, but rarely achieved. He did it a second time. Haley closed her eyes, and a grimace washed over her face. She stomped out of the kitchen.

Patty stopped talking midsentence, and the three adults looked toward the door through which Haley had disappeared.

"What now?" Rand exclaimed. He ran his fingers through his own hair. "Christ! I can't do anything right."

"Exactly. Stop trying. She's a teenager," Patty said. "I'm heading out back." She picked up the tray and left the kitchen.

Rand reached into one of the cabinets and pulled out a glass. He filled it with water from the fridge dispenser and gulped half of it down in a few swallows. "Do you have anything good to tell me?"

"I got a name that might be helpful. I'm going to set up a meeting."

"Who is it?"

Fina rested her cast on the counter. "That doesn't

matter right now, but it's a lead related to the hooker who was killed. The hooker they questioned me about. I assume you heard about that."

Rand nodded. "What does that have to do with Melanie?"

"That's what I'm figuring out."

"Sounds like a dead end to me." Rand finished the water.

"It may be, but I have to follow every potential lead, even the long shots."

"It just seems like maybe you could spend your time more productively."

Fina snorted.

"What?"

"So says the man who visits hookers in his free time."

Rand glared at her, but she pointed at him with her cast before he could speak. "And I got this broken wrist because of your shit, so spare me the performance review. I'm not in the mood." Fina grabbed her bag and started toward the door.

"Always a pleasure, little sister," Rand said, and put his glass in the sink.

Fina stomped out, not unlike (she realized) her niece had just moments before.

Bev fiddled with the satin ribbon that marked the place in her day planner. She'd been put on hold. It infuriated her.

"Rebecca? It's Mrs. Duprey," she said when the young woman came on the line. "Why was I put on hold?"

"I'm so sorry, Mrs. Duprey." The young woman didn't

stammer exactly, but stumbled over the apology. "We're a little shorthanded at the moment."

"Why is that? Who didn't show up?"

"Danielle, but she's on her way. I think she had car trouble."

"Ask her to call me after she completes her shift."

"Yes, ma'am. How can I help you?"

Bev stood up from the table with her cell at her ear and pulled a small pair of scissors from one of the kitchen drawers. She returned to the table and snipped off the fraying end of the ribbon. "Who's unmatched for tonight?"

Rebecca took a moment and then read Bev a list of names. Some clients requested a specific girl or type, but some liked to sample a little of everything, like dipping into a box of high-end chocolates.

"I'd like to match client number oh-eight-oh-seven with Katelyn. She's on tonight, isn't she?"

"Yes, ma'am."

"Good, but let me call her, Rebecca. We have something else to discuss."

"Of course, Mrs. Duprey." If the other girls noticed her heightened interest in Katelyn, they kept it to themselves.

"Thank you, dear." Bev ended the call and remained seated at the table. She gazed out the window to the garden in the backyard, which her neighbors had reclaimed from the wilds. Technically, it was a community space, but she was happy to have them exercise their green thumbs if it improved her view. She certainly didn't have time for anything as quaint as gardening. Even if she had the time, Bev wasn't one for hobbies. When Chester was in good health, they hadn't pursued leisure activities. Their businesses were all-consuming, and what was more satisfying than making lots of money? Bev would work until the day she died.

The TV was blaring in the living room, and Bev took a deep breath and pushed through the door leading from the kitchen. Chester was lying in his usual position, and the nurse was seated in the recliner next to him. It was an ugly chair, but once Bev started spending all her nights at his side, she broke down and bought the hideous yet surprisingly comfortable piece of furniture. Now they were like every couple their age in the middle of the country, spending their evenings with their eyes glued to the TV. How had it come to this?

The nurse straightened up when Bev entered and put the magazine she was reading on the side table.

"I'm on my way out," Bev told her. "Is there anything you need for Mr. Duprey?"

"We have everything we need, Mrs. Duprey."

"Good. You can reach me on my cell. I'll be back in a few hours." Bev leaned over the bed and kissed Chester's cheek. He smelled faintly of talcum powder, and she fought the thought that flooded into her brain: Her husband was an infant.

She hurried out of the condo and pulled the door closed. She leaned against it and gasped for breath. Some moments were unbearable.

Fina circled the block a couple of times and finally found a semilegal parking space across the street from the address

Olivia had provided. She was on Beacon, amongst the four-
and five-story brownstones that loomed over the street. Fina
rolled down her windows and turned off the car. The hot
breeze gently rustled the leaves and at least provided a
change from the relentless humidity.

She was thirsty, but hadn't picked up any liquid, not
knowing how long she was going to be doing surveillance.
Fina didn't yet have a plan for approaching Bev Duprey,
but sometimes, staking out someone's territory was
enough get her creative juices flowing.

She didn't even expect to have a sighting, but when a
sixtysomething woman climbed the steps of the address,
Fina was fairly certain she was looking at the madam of the
best little whorehouse in Boston. The woman was elegantly
dressed in a pale yellow skirt suit. Her hair was neatly coiffed,
but natural, as if she'd just come from the salon where a
stylist pulled and teased the pieces just so. Bev was slightly
overweight, a bit round and padded through the middle,
but her posture was outstanding. Someone had spent her
youth walking around with a phone book on her head.

Before confronting her, Fina needed more information.
She also needed some junk food and some pain pills, so
she headed to Nanny's.

The prospect of a cool shower was appealing, but exhausting, so Fina ran a cold facecloth over her skin in an effort
to clean off the day's first layer of sweat. She washed a
pain pill down with a diet soda and two of the four sec-
tions of a Sky Bar, vanilla nougat and caramel. Yum. That
left fudge and peanut for later.

In the living room, she flopped on the couch and picked up her phone. She left a message for Emma asking for info on Bev Duprey and was about to call Milloy when there was a knock on her door.

She peered through the peephole and saw Hal.

"I was about to call you," Fina said as she ushered him into the condo.

"I was in the neighborhood, so I thought I'd bring you the update in person."

"Great. You want water or a soda?"

"Just water," Hal said, and lowered himself into Nanny's side chair. "How's your wrist?" he hollered while she was in the kitchen.

"It's broken," Fina said, and walked back into the living room. She handed him a glass of water. "It's a pain in the ass, but no big deal."

Fina sat down and tried to figure out where to rest her casted wrist. It was heavier than her arm, and the plaster was obviously unyielding. You didn't really think about your limbs until you had to carry them around and they did nothing for you in return.

"So you have some info?"

"I finally have a name connected to Zyxco, Inc." Hal struggled to free a phone from his pocket and tapped on a few buttons. "I can't take complete credit for it. Emma narrowed down the list of names from the phone dump, so I was able to dig deeper into a focused group."

"And? The suspense is killing me, Hal."

"The owner of Zyxco, Inc. and hence, Mode Accessories, is . . . Chester Duprey."

Fina paused with her soda can in midair. "What?"

"Chester Duprey."

"Duprey?"

"Duprey."

"How is that spelled?" Fina took a swig and placed the can on the coffee table.

"*D-U-P-R-E-Y.*"

Fina stood up and paced the floor in front of the windows overlooking the harbor.

"Is there a problem?" Hal asked, concern etched on his face.

"Yeah. I think my head's going to explode."

"Ahhh," Hal murmured. "Not sure what to do about that."

Fina came back to the couch and sat down on the end closest to Hal. "Give me all the details on this guy," she said, and Hal took a deep breath. She held up her hand. "Wait. Not all the details. Give me a high-level, critical detail summary." Fina had worked with Hal long enough to know that he was a closeted Chatty Cathy. Wind him up, and he would go on forever.

"Chester Duprey is seventy-six years old, originally from Biloxi, Mississippi. He's owned a number of successful businesses, mostly in various parts of the South. Before coming to Boston, he was in Richmond, Virginia, for four years."

"How long has he been in Boston?"

Hal consulted his phone. "About five years."

"What else?"

"No trouble with the law, although he's been audited a couple of times. Gives a decent amount of money to charity. Lives on Beacon Hill."

"Family?"

"A wife and a son. Beverly and Connor."

Fina reached into her cast and tried to scratch an itch with her fingernail, but she couldn't reach it. She looked around the room for an implement. "I can't focus with this fucking cast!" she exclaimed and went to the kitchen. She returned a minute later with a tiny two-pronged lobster fork in her hand, which she proceeded to slip into her cast.

Hal crinkled his brow in anxiety, with maybe a dash of disgust thrown in. "Don't hurt yourself, Fina. Oh, I almost forgot. He's very ill. Chester Duprey."

"What's wrong with him?"

"He had a massive stroke and didn't regain much use of his body."

"Is his mind intact?"

"I don't know. It's costing them a fortune, though, taking care of him."

Fina altered her scratching pattern. "I cannot fucking believe this."

"Which part?"

"That Chester Duprey owns Mode Accessories."

"Do you know him?"

"No, but as of this morning, I know his wife."

Hal's face fell. "So this isn't news?"

"Hal, this is more than news. You made a connection for me that I didn't even know I was missing."

Hal beamed. "That's a relief." He finished his water and wiped his mouth with the back of his hand. Then he stared off into space for a moment. "I still don't know what Mode is a cover for, though."

"That's okay," Fina said, and tossed the lobster fork onto the coffee table. "I think I do."

"Why am I tagging along? Is she a big girl? Physically threatening?"

"No, but your presence does prompt people to be particularly candid. Mostly, I just need another set of ears."

Milloy rolled his eyes.

"Ears I can trust," Fina said. "Plus I just like having you around. You smell good."

"Thanks."

They pulled up to a four-story, white brick row house near Huntington. Unlike its richer counterparts on Beacon Street, the structure didn't boast a yard or an elaborate staircase. The windows were flush to the building, and the roofline was utilitarian, minus any detailed molding or decoration.

Fina leaned on the bell next to Olivia's name. "I don't know if she's holding back or if she just doesn't know stuff. I liked her this morning."

"But you're a fickle woman, Ludlow."

"Not fickle. Flexible. Open-minded. I'm willing to believe all kinds of shit if I can prove it."

"Who is it?" A young woman's voice carried through the speaker.

"It's Fina Ludlow, Olivia. I hate to bother you, but something's come up, and I really need to talk to you."

"I was on my way out."

"It won't take long, I promise."

Fina and Milloy waited for a moment in silence.

"Okay. Come up." The door buzzed, and Milloy pulled it open and followed Fina inside. They climbed the stairs to the fourth floor and knocked on the door of apartment 4C.

Olivia opened the door and spent an extra moment checking out Milloy.

"This is my friend Milloy," Fina said. "Milloy, this is Olivia."

They shook hands, and Olivia gestured toward a futon. The apartment was a studio with a small kitchen against one wall and a tiny bathroom off the main room. The table was covered with a white tablecloth, on which sat lots of shiny little pieces.

Fina walked over to take a closer look as Milloy sat down. "What's all this?"

"I make jewelry. Just a hobby."

Beads and charms and bits of silver cluttered the workspace along with pliers, wire cutters, and a small butane torch.

"Looks like a pretty serious hobby."

Olivia shrugged. "Less messy than painting, but challenging and a little dangerous."

"Oh God, don't tell her that," Milloy said, and rubbed his eyes. "Sounds right up her alley."

"What's up?" Olivia asked. "I really was on my way out." She was wearing tight jeans and a tank top that showcased her cleavage.

"What do you know about Bev Duprey's husband?" Fina asked.

"I know she has one, and he's sick."

"Was he ever involved in the business?"

Olivia shook her head. "Not when I was there. I think

he might have stopped by once or twice before he got sick. Why?"

"What other businesses does Bev run?"

Milloy watched the exchange with his arms spread across the back of the couch. Fina sat down next to him, but Olivia remained standing.

"The only business I know for sure is the one I worked at," she said, and glanced at Milloy.

"You can talk in front of him," Fina said, indicating Milloy. "He's cool."

"I already told you. I worked at the escort service—as a booker," she hastened to add while looking at Milloy. "That's it."

"But you just said it was the only business you knew for sure. What other businesses did you suspect Bev was running?"

Olivia walked over to the table and picked up a piece of silver. It was brushed, and tiny depressions had been hammered into its surface. She held it up. "I think it's going to be an earring."

"Olivia . . ." Fina said.

"Look, I hate that bitch, all right? But she's a scary bitch. If she finds out I've been ratting her out, she'll come after me."

"How would she know *you* ratted her out? I bet she's made her share of enemies over the years."

"She's powerful. She knows people." Olivia put the metal back on the table and sat down in a faded uphol-stered chair next to the couch.

"I won't let her hurt you," Fina said. "We won't."

Milloy raised his eyebrow at Fina, but she ignored him. "Tell me about the business in Framingham."

Olivia's eyes widened. "You know about Gratify?"

"Yes," Fina bluffed, "but I'd like to hear it from you."

Olivia took a deep breath. "Okay, the escort service is her pet project, almost like her charity. She pretends she's making men happy and empowering girls. Some ridiculous shit like that, but you can only grow it so big, right? You've got to keep it small to stay under the radar."

"Right . . ." Fina prodded. She had an inkling where this was going. Milloy glanced at her.

"Bev likes making money."

"So she's in porn?" Fina ventured.

Olivia nodded.

"But porn isn't illegal," Fina said.

"No, but there are laws that govern it, and she doesn't always obey them. And even if porn isn't illegal, it's low-class. She doesn't want to be associated with that."

"But why have the escort service if she can make more money with the porn?"

"I told you. She likes the escort service. If she had her way, she would only have Prestige, but times have changed. You have to keep up with technology to stay relevant."

"So what happens in Framingham?"

"Websites. Live chats. You know, where you log on and ask the girl to do stuff, and she follows your orders." She looked at Milloy.

"Don't look at me. I'm not into that garbage," he said.

"She's got a bunch of studios set up to look like bed-rooms. Sometimes there are half a dozen girls there, each in their own room. Doing shit so some chump in Kansas can jack off."

"Gross," Fina said, "but I still don't get the need for secrecy."

"It's the girls. Some of them are underage. Some of them are illegal. And it's not like the workplace is up to snuff. She doesn't want a visit from OSHA."

"So Bev uses her husband's larger corporation as an umbrella for her various activities? What about Mode Accessories?"

"Like I said, I don't know for sure, but I guess it's a front for the porn business."

"I don't get why she'd risk using underage girls. There are plenty of pretty girls who'll do the work."

"But they look old," Olivia said, and Fina looked mildly offended. "You know what I mean. They look like adults. They have to look young and perky. And a lot of the girls are runaways. Bev sucks them in and bleeds them dry."

"Does she use any of the same girls for both businesses? For porn and escorts?"

"Hell, no. It's like the difference between thoroughbreds and mutts. I'm not saying the porn girls aren't pretty, but they're not presentable in the way that the Prestige girls are. The Gratify girls are the feet paddling furiously beneath the surface, and the Prestige girls are the swans on top."

"I get it."

"And with the clients from the escort business? Bev would never risk using a girl who wasn't carefully selected. Those men are powerful. Discretion is one of the biggest selling points."

"What kind of men?" Milloy asked. He studied the stitching on the toss pillow next to him. Fina glanced at him.

"Powerful. Important. In the public eye."

"Is there another agency those men might use?"

Olivia shook her head. "Prestige is the top. If you can't get it there, you go to New York."

"Are there any underage girls at Prestige?" Milloy asked.

"I don't think so. Not because Bev has scruples, but she wouldn't trust them. She's got girls who look damn young, though."

"Is there a girl named Molly?" he asked. Fina closed her eyes and rubbed her temple with her free hand.

"Young, blond? Yeah. How do you know Molly? I thought it wasn't your thing?" Olivia asked with a smirk.

"I know her," Fina said. "Does she work for anyone other than Bev?"

"Not if Bev has anything to say about it. No freelancing allowed."

They were quiet for a moment.

"You good?" Milloy asked Fina.

She nodded. "I got what I need." She stood up and moved to the door. "Thanks, Olivia. I really appreciate your help. I'll keep you out of it. Did you call Matthew yet?"

"Left a message earlier today."

"Let me know if he doesn't call by tomorrow."

The trip downstairs was a quiet one, both Fina and Milloy caught up in their own thoughts.

In the car, he turned up the air conditioner and drove

past the Museum of Fine Arts. He wended his way through the Fens and found a place to pull over on Park Drive.

"So?" he asked once he'd put the car in park.

Fina took a deep breath. "So."

Milloy waited a moment. "Talk to me."

"So, the escort, Brianna, worked for the madam, Bev Duprey, who is also the madam for my brother's escort, Molly. Bev also runs a porn business in the MetroWest area, and my sister-in-law had Bev's number in her recipe box." Fina turned to look at him. "Any other fucked-up detail I'm forgetting?"

Milloy shook his head. "I can see why you wanted an extra pair of ears. I'm surprised blood isn't pouring out of yours."

"Oh, just wait. The night is but a pup."

Milloy dropped Fina at Nanny's, where she changed her clothes and went down to the workout room on the fourth floor. She jacked up the volume on MTV and the speed on the treadmill and ran until the sweat covered her skin in a glistening coat. Her injured wrist ached and itched, but she ignored it and just kept running. Another resident poked her head in at one point, perhaps to ask her to lower the volume, but beat a hasty retreat when she saw Fina running as if her life depended on it.

After an hour and ten minutes, she punched the buttons to slow down the treadmill and caught her breath as sweat stung her eyes. She hadn't figured anything out on the machine, but her twitchy energy had abated.

Upstairs, she itched inside her cast with the lobster fork

and gulped down a large glass of water. Her cast was starting to emit an aroma. Maybe Milloy had a saw that would
make quick work of the restraint.

Fina blotted her face and neck with paper towels,
refilled her glass, and took it into the living room, where
she stood at the windows overlooking the harbor. The
last vestiges of twilight reflected off the jets departing
Logan. A dinner cruise passed through the no-wake zone.

Fina finished her water and stripped off her clothes in
the bathroom. She showered, pulled on shorts and a
T-shirt, and wandered into the kitchen.

Her workout had resulted in a powerful hunger, so she
opened the cabinet and started rummaging. Fina got
groceries delivered every few weeks—not really groceries,
more like indestructible foodstuff—but her reserves were
getting low. In the far recesses of the freezer, she found
a half-empty carton of Karamel Sutra ice cream. She
grabbed a spoon and napkin and carried the pint and a
diet soda into the living room.

Her first spoonful was interrupted by a knock on the
door.

"It's Matthew," a voice called from the other side.

Fina let him in, lay down on the couch, and resumed
her meal. Matthew pushed her feet over and sat down.

"Why are you flushed?" he asked her.

"I just did a hard workout."

He looked at her wrist and shook his head. "I heard
about your little run-in. That thing is going to be a bio-
hazard in no time at all."

Fina held the pint of ice cream out to him. Matthew
shook his head.

"What brings you to my neck of the woods?" Fina asked.

Matthew's smile widened.

"Oh, right. Your friend with benefits lives down here. Doesn't she want you to make an honest woman of her?"

"Hardly. She's a partner at Stokes and Williams. She just wants a reliable roll in the hay and then some legal pillow talk after the fact. And she's trying to get me to jump ship to her firm."

"That's an interesting recruiting technique. Are you considering it?"

"What? Leaving the firm?"

"Yeah."

"Nah. I know you think it's an advertising ploy, but we do actually stick up for the little guy."

"I know you do. I investigate a lot of the cases, remember?" Fina didn't agree with everything that Ludlow and Associates did, but she knew that without them, a lot of grievously injured people would be truly screwed. What happens when you're a thirty-nine-year-old single mother of three and you get injured in a car accident that's the other guy's fault? One stroke of bad luck and the precarious dominoes of your life begin to fall: hospital bills, lost wages, day care costs. Lots of people were a paycheck away from disaster, and the Ludlows kept that disaster at bay. Sure, they made lots of money in the process, and punishment wasn't always meted out fairly, but Fina wasn't sure that negated the good they did. Ludlow and Associates operated in the gray.

"I'm not planning on going anywhere, but I didn't come over here for career counseling."

"Glad to hear it. Hey, did you hear from a woman named Olivia? About a job?"

"She's coming in next week for an interview. You think she's good?"

"I don't know what she'd be like as an assistant, but she's smart and sassy. I liked her."

Matthew rolled his eyes. "Great." He pulled his phone out of his pocket and tapped a few buttons. "So I've reviewed a chunk of files and pulled out names from those that were most lucrative."

"You mean those in which the defendant was essentially destroyed."

"You say *tomato*, I say *tomahto*." He handed her the phone. "It's just a portion of them, but I thought you'd want info as soon as I got it."

"Yes, thanks." Fina studied the screen. She felt a headache creeping across her brow, probably from her overexertion.

"Anything?" Matthew asked.

"Gimme a sec."

Fina scrolled down the list. "Holy fuck!" She sat up.

"What?" Matthew leaned over and grabbed the phone from her. "Which one? Holbrooke?"

"No."

"Duprey?"

"Yes! Yes, Duprey!"

"All right, calm the fuck down."

"What is that case?"

"I can only tell you what's on public record."

"Fine. Tell me."

"Give me a second to pull up some notes." Matthew

reached into his shiny leather briefcase and pulled out a slim laptop. He punched a couple of buttons and studied the screen.

Fina kicked him gently with her foot. "Hurry up."

"Don't you have any pills you can take, you know, to calm down?"

Fina let her head fall back and stared at the ceiling.

"Okay. Here it is. It was a med mal case. Big ruling in our client's favor: $8.9 million."

"So how does Duprey figure into the case?"

"He was one of the doctors."

"Okay. What were the specifics?"

Matthew looked at the screen. "Right. This makes sense. It's a cerebral palsy case. That explains the steep damages." Matthew looked at her. "You've worked one of those cases, right?"

"I've done some background work, but then it gets passed on to the expert witnesses."

"Right, well, in this case, a woman, Jackie Watson, went into the hospital, Cincinnati Unified—"

"That sounds like a chemical company or an airline."

"She went into Cincinnati Unified to deliver, no problems with her pregnancy, but one thing leads to another, and she ends up with a severely disabled baby, Amber Watson."

"Is that how you won in court? 'One thing leads to another'?"

"No, it was a little more complicated. One of the ob-gyns was Connor Duprey."

"Bev and Chester Duprey's son. So he was found responsible?"

"How do you know who his parents are?"

"Long story. So was he found responsible?"

"He, two other doctors, and Cincinnati Unified."

"Did he lose his license?"

"It was suspended. Can't practice medicine for the time being. His insurance is on the hook for a huge payout. The usual."

"Why such a huge payout?"

"The CP was severe. It costs a ton of money to care for a kid like that."

Fina scraped the bottom of the ice-cream carton. "Just to play devil's advocate for a minute, between the two of us, I thought there was no definitive evidence linking cerebral palsy with delivery."

"Fina . . ." Matthew smiled and wagged his finger at her.

"I'm just trying to understand the two sides so I can figure out if the Dupreys have any grounds for thinking this was a miscarriage of justice."

"It's hard to draw a straight line from a difficult or delayed birth to CP. Other factors may contribute to the development of CP, but the delivery can't be ruled out."

"So how'd you get so much cash?"

"Because we're highly skilled."

"Other than that."

"Juries don't like ambiguity or injustice. When they see a severely disabled child, they want someone held responsible."

"So you parade the kid in front of the jury and get the sympathy vote."

"I stand by my case."

"I'm sure you do."

Matthew closed the top of his laptop. "Nobody wins in those cases."

Fina looked confused. "Ah, don't you guys?"

Matthew shrugged. "Sure, but somebody's got to take care of Amber Watson. Her dad works at a factory, and Jackie's a stay-at-home mom. They've got three other kids. This way, she'll get the care she needs."

Fina grinned. "You're like a caped crusader."

Matthew rolled his eyes. "Does this info help?"

"Damn right it helps. I wish we'd figured it out sooner."

Matthew picked up his briefcase, and Fina walked him to the door. "What are you going to do with this?" he asked.

"I don't know. Maybe pay the doctor's mother a visit."

Matthew raised an eyebrow. "Good luck with that."

"She's a Southern woman. I'm sure our conversation will be extremely civil."

"She hasn't met you yet."

"Aww. That's so sweet."

Fina closed the door behind him and walked into the bedroom. She lay down on the bed and listened to the hum of the air-conditioning. Bev Duprey was going to lead her somewhere. She just didn't know where.

22

Sleep came in fits and starts.

Fina forced herself to stay in bed until seven A.M., but once up, spent the next two hours showering, eating, and pacing.

What kind of hours did madams keep? Fina didn't know, but given Bev's apparent adherence to social mores, she imagined that she kept typical business hours.

Fina couldn't deal with the idea of driving, so she hailed a cab outside her building and spent ten minutes listening to what she thought must be Somali pop music. At Bev's Back Bay office, she mounted the steps to the bank of buzzers outside the front door. Most of the names were on neatly typed slips of paper, but two were scrawled on scraps of paper shoved into the windowed slots. Fina pressed one of those buzzers and waited. She pressed it again, and after a moment, there was static and a harried voice.

"Hello?"

"Got a package."

"Ahh . . . I can't come down right now."

"Just buzz, and I'll leave it in the entry."

"I'm not supposed to do that."

"Fine. I'll leave a slip and you can pick it up between noon and three P.M. Our storage facility is next to North Station."

"What? But I . . . You know what? Just leave it."

"Whatever you want, ma'am."

The lock released, and Fina slipped into the entry hall. Olivia had told her that Bev's office was on the first floor. Hopefully, she was in. If not, Fina might indulge in a little B&E.

She walked quietly to Bev's door and stood listening for a moment. She could hear footsteps on the other side. Her knuckles rapped gently on the door, and she waited. The footsteps stilled, then moved in her direction.

"May I help you?" Bev asked when she opened the door. It was the woman whom Fina had seen the day before. Today, she was wearing a pink dress with a faint brocade pattern and large gold earrings in the shape of knots. Her makeup was just a tad heavy, but her skin was remarkably smooth. She smiled at Fina, revealing straight, white teeth.

"I think you can," Fina said, smiling back. "We have something to discuss, Mrs. Duprey."

A slight frown crept onto her face. "Since I don't know you, I don't see how that could be. What is your name, dear?"

"Fina Ludlow."

Bev's smile hardened. "The name's not familiar." She took a step back. "I'm quite sure we have nothing to discuss," Bev said, and started to shut the door.

Fina thrust her foot into the path of the door. "Really? The name's not familiar? What about Rand Ludlow? Or Carl Ludlow?"

Bev's lip curled.

"I know you're a busy woman, Mrs. Duprey." Fina grasped her hand around the door. "Let's just get this over with."

Bev glared at her. "I could call the police."

"Be my guest. They might be interested in what we have to discuss."

Bev stared at the floor for a moment and then let go of the door. Fina walked in and sat down on a yellow houndstooth chair in the living room. Bev sat down in the chair across from her.

"No offer of tea? I've heard so much about your good Southern manners," Fina said.

"And clearly you have no manners, but that shouldn't surprise me. I assume your upbringing was akin to being raised by a pack of wolves."

Fina snorted. "Pretty much."

Bev fiddled with a gold linked bracelet on her wrist. "Are you an ambulance chaser, too?"

"No. I'm a private investigator."

"But you work for your family?"

"For them and for others."

"Investigating innocent people, no doubt. What's so important that you had to force your way in?"

"Did my sister-in-law, Melanie Ludlow, contact you?"

Bev considered the question and then shrugged. "I can't recall."

"This isn't a Senate hearing."

"Well, what reason would your sister-in-law have for contacting me?"

"I understand the connection between you and my brother and father. I know that they won a huge settlement against your son in court."

Bev tilted her head. "Is that what you call it? 'Won a settlement'? A more accurate description would be that your family destroyed the lives of three outstanding doctors. Burned them to the ground."

"I'm not here to debate the merits of the case. I have nothing to do with that."

"Of course you don't. I'm sure you've never benefited from the spoils of your father's work."

"Unlike Connor, you mean. Isn't medical school awfully expensive?"

Bev brushed a lock of hair behind her ear.

"I know about the case, but I also know about our other connection; that you've supplied 'companionship' to my brother Rand," Fina said. "I've met some of your whores."

"They're not whores, Ms. Ludlow. They're escorts."

"They're young women who fuck men for money."

"You're the one who sounds like a common whore, what with that language. I can't imagine your mother is proud of you."

"God, I hope not."

Bev uncrossed and crossed her ankles. "I still don't understand why you're here."

"Back to my original question. Did my sister-in-law contact you, and if so, why?"

Bev was silent.

"How about an easier question: Did my brother find your service coincidentally, or did you seek him out?"

Bev smirked. "Your brother has expensive taste. It's only natural that he would seek out Prestige. We're the best."

"Right. And Brianna?"

Bev raised an eyebrow.

"Yeah, I know about Brianna. We met a couple of times."

"Did she tell you about me?"

"No. Actually, Brianna was very loyal. I certainly hope you didn't kill her over some presumed betrayal."

"That is a grotesque suggestion."

"Right. You don't think your little operation in Framingham is grotesque?"

Bev gripped her hands together. "As interesting as this conversation is, Ms. Ludlow, I am a busy woman. I don't think I can be of assistance to you."

Fina reached into her cast and scratched the area near her thumb. She got up and walked to the door. "If I find out that you had anything to do with my sister-in-law's death, I will dismantle your life and your business and your precious dignity, piece by piece."

Bev glared at her.

"It would be a mistake to doubt my resolve," Fina said.

"I don't doubt your resolve at all, Ms. Ludlow. Just the wisdom of your threat."

Fina opened the door and slammed it behind her.

Bev sneered. Christ, she hated these people.

Fina ran smack into a man standing outside Bev's door. He was about her age, with sandy hair and a slight build.

"Sorry," Fina said, and she started down the hall.

Connor watched her leave and thrust his hands into his pockets. He closed his eyes for a moment and then knocked on his mother's door.

There was a muffled sound on the other side, and then Bev threw the door open and scowled at him. When she realized it was her son, her features softened, and her hand pressed against her chest. Her color was off.

"Mom, what's wrong? What's going on?" Connor put his hand on her shoulder and guided her to one of the chairs in the sitting room. He gently pushed her into it and went to the kitchen for a glass of water. Bev smiled at him when he gave it to her. She took a long drink and set the glass down on the coffee table.

"Let me check your pulse." Connor sat in the chair next to her and took hold of her wrist.

"Connor! Don't be ridiculous. I'm fine," Bev said, and reclaimed her wrist.

"You're not fine. Obviously that woman upset you."

Bev took a deep breath. "You're right. She did, but I'm fine now. You just caught me at a bad moment."

"What was that about?"

"I don't really care to talk about it, dear."

"Does it have something to do with Dad?"

"Goodness, no. Nothing to do with your father. Really, you needn't worry."

Connor felt the heat rise under his collar. "Mom, I appreciate that you want to protect me, but I'm a grown man. I'm not as fragile as you think. You can trust me."

Bev grasped his hand. "I do trust you, Connor. I just don't want to burden you. You have enough to manage without . . . this." Bev waved her hand in the air as if pushing away an unpleasant scent.

"Stop treating me like a child," Connor said in exasperation. "Don't you understand how inept that makes me feel? On top of everything else?"

Bev flinched slightly. "Fine. If you must know, that woman was Fina Ludlow."

Connor tilted his head and looked at her.

"She was here regarding her sister-in-law Melanie," Bev said.

"Those Ludlows?" Connor asked.

"Yes, those Ludlows. Her brother is Rand Ludlow, and Carl Ludlow is her father."

"Why would she see you about her sister-in-law?"

"She's convinced herself that I know something about her death." Bev took a sip of water.

Connor studied the floor. He raised his eyes and looked at his mother. He felt a chill, and for just a moment saw what other people might see when they looked at Bev: her strength and unrelenting will.

He looked away.

"And that, of course, is absolute bull honkey, as your daddy would say." Bev released Connor's hand. She pushed his hair away from his eyes. "She can't face the fact that her brother is a murderer, so she's grasping at straws."

Bev gazed at the painting over the fireplace. "I pity her, actually. It must be awful contemplating that your loved one is a monster."

Fina walked to Ludlow and Associates and mulled over her visit to Bev Duprey. She hadn't uncovered any answers, but she'd put Bev on notice. Maybe she should tell Cristian and let the police deal with it.

Carl's gatekeeper ushered her into his office, where Carl and Scotty were staring down Pitney and Cristian.

"Your timing is impeccable," Pitney said, and smiled at Fina. The lieutenant was wearing a kelly green pantsuit that contrasted sharply with her orangey hair. All she needed was a pot of gold to complete the look.

Cristian looked at Fina. "How's your wrist?"

"Thank you for asking, Detective Menendez," Fina said, and looked pointedly at her father and brother. "It itches like a motherfucker."

"My daughter, the sailor," Carl said, glaring at her.

"We were just letting the boys know that we got some new information about Rand's leisure activities. Did you know your brother pays for it?"

Fina shrugged. "Go figure."

"I wonder how Melanie felt about that?" Pitney asked.

Fina shook her head and sighed. "Do you really think that Bev Duprey is a reliable source?"

Pitney and Cristian exchanged a look. "What do you know about Bev Duprey?" Pitney asked.

"Just, you know, stuff," Fina said as she walked over to the fridge. She reached in and pulled out a diet soda, which she handed to Scotty. "Do you mind?" She held up her cast. He popped open the can and handed it back to her. Fina took a sip.

Pitney stared at the ceiling. "I swear to God, if I find out you're obstructing this investigation—"

"Blah, blah, blah," Fina said. She sat down on the couch. "I'm not obstructing anything. When I have something to tell you, I'll be in touch." Fina took a sip of her drink. "I do have a question for you, though."

"What's that?"

"Why was my brother arrested for Melanie's murder when there's a plausible alternate theory of the crime? One that creates more than reasonable doubt. Perhaps there was a teensy rush to judgment."

Carl glared at her. He always got antsy when unexpected topics arose. Such a control freak.

Pitney rolled her eyes. "Please. Do tell."

"It just seems like $8.9 million dollars and a wrecked career are more motivation than adultery." Fina sat down on the couch.

"I wouldn't categorize sleeping with hookers as run-of-the-mill adultery."

Fina shrugged. "You're picky that way. Why don't you ask Bev Duprey why she's so pissed at my brother?"

Cristian's gaze moved between Fina, Carl, and Pitney.

"I don't have time for guessing games. Spit it out or come downtown and make yourself comfortable," Pitney said.

"Ludlow and Associates won an $8.9 million settlement against a hospital and a group of doctors in Cincinnati. One of those doctors was Connor Duprey."

Carl puffed up his chest. "If that isn't a goddamn motive, I don't know what is!"

Pitney put her hand up. "And Connor Duprey is . . . ?"

"Bev Duprey's only child. I think he's a real mama's boy." She sipped her soda and put her feet up on the coffee table. "Maybe I should join the police force," she mused.

Cristian coughed loudly. Pitney smacked her lips together and stormed out of the room with Cristian in her wake.

Scotty closed the door behind them.

"What the hell is going on?" Carl demanded. "You knew about this woman and you didn't tell me?"

"I only found out about her yesterday, but I met her for the first time this morning."

"And? You think there's something to your theory?" Scotty asked.

Fina sat forward on the couch. "I don't know, but Bev Duprey might turn out to be the best thing that ever happened to Rand." Carl and Scotty studied her. "But there's something else that's bugging me; why did Melanie have her number?"

"Melanie had the madam's number?" Scotty asked.

"What are you talking about, Fina?" Carl said.

"When I searched Rand's house after Melanie disappeared, I found a phone number tucked into her recipe box. It was the number for a business called Mode Accessories, which is actually a front for a porn business owned by Bev Duprey's husband, Chester. Did Melanie find out about the hookers? Did she try to contact Bev Duprey?"

"Christ," Scotty said, and ran his fingers through his hair.

"You think there was a confrontation?" Carl asked.

"I don't know, but there's some connection between Melanie and Bev. This woman has a sleazy, illegal business empire. She was Brianna's boss, the escort who was murdered. Sounds like a good murder suspect to me."

"Go do something with this," Carl ordered. "And I expect an update."

"Yes, Father," Fina said, and left.

Scotty followed her out, and they walked toward his office. Scotty's face looked drawn, and his pants seemed looser than usual.

"You don't look good," Fina said.

"I'm exhausted. I'm trying to juggle my regular workload with all this crap. I'm not sleeping well, either."

"That's no surprise." As they walked through the corridors, everyone they passed nodded or said hello to Scotty. Her brother generated positive feelings in the employees, unlike their father, who mostly generated fear.

"Patty bit my head off this morning."

"About anything in particular?"

"Not really. I think it's just the stress."

"And the extra kid she's taking care of. Not an easy kid, either."

"She knows Melanie would have done the same for her."

"Sure, but that doesn't make it any less work."

They arrived at the waiting area outside of Scotty's office. His secretary jumped up from behind her large, spotless desk and came around to greet him. She handed him a sheaf of pink phone messages that he quickly flicked through.

"Michelle," he said to his secretary, who'd returned to her spot behind her desk, "remind me why Jimmy Costas is calling me?"

"He wanted a referral, someone to represent him in a property dispute," Michelle responded without looking up from her computer.

Fina looked at Scotty. "Who's Jimmy Costas?" she asked. She followed him into his office.

Scotty plopped down in his chair and placed his palms on his desktop. He seemed to be trying to get his bearings. "Vanessa's brother. Don't you remember him from high school? He's the one who got on Dad's treadmill when he was trashed, turned the thing on, and split open his chin."

"Vanessa Lamont's brother."

"Right. Do you need something else, sis?" He looked at the phone. "I've got to make calls."

Fina rubbed her forehead with her good hand.

"Fina?"

"No. I don't need anything. I'm good." She left his office and pulled the door closed behind her. She wandered down the hallway for a moment before finding an empty conference room. She sat down and stared at the cast on her wrist.

Was Ronald Costas, the owner of Ridleys, related to Vanessa Costas Lamont? Costas was a common name, but she couldn't ignore the coincidence. But if they were related, what did that mean? What was Joe Winthrop's connection to Ronald Costas?

All this new information was like a tsunami. If Fina could keep her head above water, keep breathing, she might come out of it in one piece, albeit in an altered landscape. But at the moment, she couldn't make all the pieces fit together.

Work your leads. That was one of the tenets of PI work that Frank had taught her. Push and pull and massage and knead until something, anything, comes loose. She decided to check in with her various contacts and picked up the phone to call Dennis.

"What's Joe Winthrop up to at the moment?" she asked.

"This guy's going to a lot of trouble to stay off the radar," Dennis told her. "He's like a monk, stays in his room all the time."

"I assure you, the guy is nothing like a monk," Fina said.

"He doesn't seem to work. Either he's independently wealthy or a kept man."

"I vote for a kept man. Let me know if anything changes."

She left another message for Emma pressing for information about Bev and Chester Duprey. If she could get dirt about Bev's illegal activities, she might be able to leverage it against her, assuming the police didn't already know about her illegal activities and were just biding their time. She also asked Emma to check for a family connection between Ronald, Jimmy, and Vanessa Costas.

Her next call was to Matthew's office, and soon after his secretary brought down a dolly of files on the Duprey trial, including the trial transcript. The rest of the day was consumed by the tragic life of Amber Watson and the waves of misery prompted by her birth. For every expert there was a counterexpert; for every sad tale about Amber there was a glowing endorsement of the doctors' competency. The whole thing was a morass of suffering.

She packed up her things around seven P.M. and drove to Frank and Peg's. Dinner was long over, and Frank was in the front yard, grappling with a hosta plant.

"Want some help?" Fina asked. She walked across the yard and stood over Frank, who was crouched over a bed of loam.

"Nah," he said as he got up and wiped his hands on his pants. He was wearing a pair of khakis that were filthy with dirt and grass stains and an equally soiled white T-shirt. His hair was messy and wet with sweat. "I don't want you to get dirty."

"I don't mind."

"I think I'm done for the day." Frank waved toward the front stoop, and they walked over and sat down next to each other. A car came by, and the driver slowed and waved at Frank. No matter where they lived, Frank and Peg ended up being the de facto ambassadors of the neighborhood; they were friendly, took care of their property, looked out for their neighbors, and were calm in a crisis. But they weren't nosy or officious. The world would be a much better place if there were more Franks and Pegs in it.

He twisted on the stoop as if to stretch his back.

"I'm surprised Peg is letting you do this," Fina commented.

"Use it or lose it, Fina. That's the key to aging."

"Exactly my philosophy," Fina said, tapping her cast.

Frank grinned and shook his head. "Is that what you call that? What happened?"

"I got jumped in my garage."

"And you didn't call me right away because . . . ?"

"Because the damage was done, but that's why I'm here. I'm telling you now."

"Frank, do you want some lemonade?" Peg called through the screen door. "Oh, hi, hon. I didn't know you were here," Peg added when she opened the door. She was wearing a T-shirt and shorts, which showed off her trim figure. Peg's legs were strong, but not overly muscular; when you looked at her, it wasn't hard to see the twentysomething that Frank had fallen for decades before.

"I just stopped by to say hi."

"I'll get you both some lemonade."

Peg retreated into the house and came back a few minutes later with two plastic tumblers filled with ice and lemonade. She deposited the drinks and went back inside. Frank took a gulp and set his glass down on the step.

"Do you remember Jimmy or Ronald Costas?" Fina asked. "I think they're clients at the firm."

He was quiet for a moment and picked at some dirt under one of his fingernails. "Isn't Ronnie in construction? That seems to ring a bell. Is Jimmy his son?"

"Not sure. But Jimmy's sister is Vanessa Lamont."

Frank raised an eyebrow. "What's this all about?"

Fina sipped her lemonade. It was slightly tart and made her taste buds smart. "I've got a bunch of people, but I can't figure out exactly how they're connected or who's done what."

"And this ties in to Melanie?"

"It has to, right? There are too many weird coincidences."

"I'm not a fan of Mark Lamont's."

"I'm not exactly a fan, either, but he's a necessary evil. You know that."

A man and woman pushing a stroller the size of a small car walked by and greeted Frank. He waved and said hello in return.

"And your brother?" he asked.

"What about him?"

Frank turned to look at her. "Do you think he killed Melanie?"

Fina rubbed her eyes. "I don't think so."

"But you're not sure?"

"I don't have evidence proving he did or didn't."

"But what do you think? Is he capable of it?"

"I don't think so, but . . ." She held her hands open. "Christ, Frank. I don't know."

Frank patted her hand and left a sprinkling of soil on her skin. "What's done is done, kiddo."

"Yikes," Fina said, and took a big swallow of lemonade.

Her stomach grumbled as she pulled away from Frank and Peg's, so she punched the speed dial on her phone and waited a few rings for Cristian to answer.

"Wanna get some food?" Fina asked.

"I guess I have to eat," he said.

"Very nice. Way to make a girl feel special."

"You made us look like dolts this morning."

"You were trying to make us look like dolts," Fina said. "Turnabout is fair play."

"Fine. Meet me at the Mexican place on Mass Ave."

Fina dove into the basket of tortilla chips that the waitress placed on the table. She looked around at the other tables while she waited for Cristian. Most of them seemed to be occupied by students, some of whom had large instruments parked next to their chairs. The New England Conservatory of Music and Berklee College of Music were just around the corner, and Fina was always struck by the juxtaposition of bright young minds studying Beethoven and unwashed homeless people struggling in the twenty-first century.

Cristian pushed through the door and slid into the seat across from her. Fina ordered a diet soda and a chimichanga, and Cristian opted for a soda and a burrito with extra jalapeños.

"I didn't mean to make you personally look like a dolt," Fina said before popping a chip in her mouth. "I don't feel bad about Pitney, though."

"She's a good cop."

"I'm sure she is, but we're working at cross-purposes at the moment."

Cristian tapped his straw open on the table and took a sip of his drink. "How long have you known about Duprey?"

"I just found out."

"What are you going to do about it?"

"I don't have a plan at this point. We did talk, though."

"You and Bev Duprey?"

"Yup."

"I would have loved to have seen that."

"It wasn't as exciting as you might imagine. Pretty unsatisfying, actually."

"What did you find out?"

"She didn't have much to say. I did most of the talking."

Cristian fiddled with his watch. He had a nice coating of hair on his arm. Not so much that he looked like a gorilla, but enough that you knew he was a man.

"What's going on?" Fina asked.

"What do you mean?"

"You seem distracted."

He shrugged. "I'm good."

They sat for a few moments in silence, and Fina ate more of the chips. Cristian looked at the students.

"Couldn't you carry a really big gun in one of those cello cases?" Fina asked, gesturing toward a skinny young man a couple of tables away.

"I suppose, but not everyone is always thinking up inventive ways to conceal weapons."

"Any word on Bob Webber?"

Cristian shook his head. "He's a ghost."

"Something happened to him."

"You know that or you think that?"

"I think it, and you know you do, too. People don't just disappear willy-nilly."

Cristian shrugged. "People are flaky."

The waitress brought their plates.

"Could you cut a little bit of this for me?" Fina nudged her plate toward Cristian. "I'm always a little wary when the food is ready so quickly," she confided once the wait-ress was out of earshot.

"Frying doesn't require much time," he said as his knife cracked into her deep-fried burrito. He cut a dozen small pieces off it and pushed the plate back over to her.

"I suppose. Thanks."

They ate in silence. The cello player and his friends clamored by, and their table was quickly claimed by a group of young men engaged in a political argument.

"I can't take this," Fina said after a few minutes. She put down her fork and stared at Cristian. "What is going on? You're being quiet and weird."

Cristian picked at a piece of burrito with his fork. "I'm not sure what's going on."

"Oookay . . ."

"Pitney and I interviewed some of Brianna's friends."

Fina watched him. "And . . ."

"They weren't her friends, really. More like her colleagues." Cristian took a sip of his drink. "I saw Haley there."

Fina felt a chill settle over her. "What do you mean? Where was this?"

"At a club."

Fina sat back in her seat. "She goes to clubs all the time. I know it's illegal, and I try to discourage it, but I'm kind of fighting a losing battle."

Cristian shook his head. "I don't think it's just that."

"Cristian, I know she has sketchy friends. She was friends with Brianna, for Christ's sake."

"She was a part of the group, Fina. It seemed like she was one of them."

Fina felt her face flush. She didn't know what would happen if she spoke. She might scream or cry, or maybe no sound at all would come out. She took a few sips of her drink and waited for her heart rate to slow. Cristian poked at his burrito and stole glances at her.

"Are you saying she's working as a hooker?" Fina finally asked.

"I don't know. Maybe she's just hanging out with them, but I just got the feeling—"

"Were they all Bev Duprey's girls?"

"No. Some of them were Dante Trimonti's. A few, I don't know who they work for yet."

"So you're not sure?"

"I'm not one hundred percent sure, but I'm concerned enough that I thought I should tell you."

Fina's broken wrist started to itch. She reached into the cast with her finger and scratched it furiously. When she pulled it out, there was blood on her nail.

Cristian reached over and grabbed her hand. "Stop it. You're going to make it worse."

Fina leaned toward him and whispered, "How can anything get worse?"

"Do you have your phone?" Cristian asked.

"Yes. Why?"

"You need to call Milloy."

"You want me to call Milloy?"

"Yes."

"Why?"

"Because I'm afraid you're going to draw more blood— yours or more likely someone else's. Just call him and let him help you. I can't. You're veering into dangerous territory."

"I don't need a babysitter. I need to figure out what the fuck is going on."

"Call him, Fina."

Fina took a deep breath. "I'll be fine." Cristian glared at her. "Seriously, I'm completely capable of being calm and professional. I'm just going to take the information and investigate. I'll just do what I do best."

Cristian reached into his wallet and pulled out a twenty, which he tossed on the table. "I'd feel better if you'd call Milloy."

"And I'd feel better if there weren't a chance my fifteen-year-old niece is a hooker."

Cristian stood up. "I'm going to call you tomorrow, and you'd better pick up. If you don't, I'm going to call Milloy and then 911."

"That won't be necessary. I'll answer."

"Don't do anything rash."

"I won't. I promise."

Fina added some bills to the table and followed Cristian out. She walked in the direction of the Pru. When she looked back, Cristian was watching her. He looked worried.

As he should be.

She didn't call Milloy. Instead, she walked around Back Bay for an hour and found herself outside Bev Duprey's office. She cut through to the alley that ran along the back of the building; the lights were off in Bev's unit. A homeless man came shuffling down the cobblestone passage. He wanted to engage Fina in a discussion about the people with vacuums who were landing on the roof, but she wasn't in the mood.

Back on Beacon Street, she called Emma.

"I know, I know," Emma answered. "The Dupreys. I'm working on it."

"Glad to hear it, but I wasn't calling about that specifically. Do you have a home address for them?"

"Hold on a minute."

Fina waited. Unlike most people she called, there was rarely background noise when she talked to Emma on the phone. No blaring horns or loud music or silverware clanking around. It was as if Fina had called another decade altogether.

"Here it is: 22 Wickham Street, #4A."

"Is that the Flat of the Hill?"

"Yup. Do you need directions?"

"No. Thanks." Fina hung up and started walking northeast on Beacon Street. The temperature was actually bearable. It was on the cusp between warm and hot, but the humidity had dropped, and the walk didn't produce beads of sweat in the small of her back.

She dialed Mark Lamont's number and left a message that matched her brisk pace.

"Mark, it's Fina Ludlow. We've got to talk about Bob Webber and some other shit that's going on. He's disappeared. I know you're busy, but I really need to talk to you."

It took her fifteen minutes to reach 22 Wickham Street.

She sat down on the steps of the brownstone across the street and peered up at the fourth floor. Fina didn't have a plan. Her head was swimming with the flotsam and jetsam of the last twenty-four hours, but the thing that kept rising to the surface was Haley. She had to figure out if Haley was involved with Bev, and then she had to protect her.

A man walked toward her and stopped to enter the building in front of which Fina was sitting. He paused at the door.

"Can I help you with something?" he asked. It was a polite way of ascertaining why a stranger was staked out on his stoop.

"No, thanks. I'm leaving." Fina stood. "I was waiting for a friend, but I think we got our wires crossed." She shuffled down the stairs and headed in the direction of Charles Street.

The smart thing to do would be to hail a cab, but Fina felt like walking. And if someone hassled her, and she smashed his skull in with her cast . . .

She couldn't lie; the idea held some appeal.

23

The next morning, Fina wasn't concerned about waiting until Bev got to work. She wanted to beat her there.

Her alarm went off at six A.M., and after submerging herself in the tub with her cast hanging over the side, she dressed, scarfed down a peanut butter sandwich and a diet soda, and took a cab over to Beacon Street. She had the cabbie drop her a block away from Bev's office, and she paced on the corner, glancing at her watch as if waiting for a tardy car pool.

No one entered or left Bev's building, so Fina crossed the street and stood by the front door. A few minutes after seven A.M., a young man in khakis, a blue button-down shirt, and a striped tie came bounding out of the front door. Fina was ready with an excuse, but he was plugged into his music and paid her no attention.

Inside, she put her ear to Bev's door and listened for a

few moments. She didn't hear anything, so she knocked and waited. After a full minute had passed with no response, Fina reached into her bag and pulled out her lock picks. It took longer than Dante's—thanks to better locks and her plaster cast—but she gained access after five minutes and slowly opened the door.

The condo was empty. Fina went straight to the office, pulled on a pair of gloves as best she could, and began a thorough search—filing cabinets, desk drawers, the underside of furniture, even the air vents. She found what she expected to find: meticulous records for an above-board escort service. Most likely, Bev kept two sets of books; one for show and another that reflected the true nature of the business. The books Fina found detailed "client meetings" that identified the clients and escorts by numbers only. There were no references to sexual acts or anything else that could be used for either blackmail purposes or prosecution. And there was no reference to Haley or Rand.

The kitchen, bathroom, and living room resembled those of a high-end corporate housing unit: floral soaps and fluffy towels, an assortment of tea, and attractive yet durable dishware. The magazines in the living room were women's titles, including *Southern Living*, *Martha Stewart Living*, and *Good Housekeeping*.

Fina searched furiously for forty-five minutes and then filled a glass with water in the kitchen. She drank it down, washed the glass, wiped it clean with a dish towel, and sat down in the living room. She hated waiting, but she wanted Bev to take her seriously, and breaking in was an expeditious way to achieve that goal.

Fifteen minutes after sitting down and struggling to calm her racing mind, there was a sound at the door. It opened, and Bev walked in. She inhaled sharply when she saw Fina.

"What the hell are you doing here?" she spat.

"Sit down."

"I'll do no such thing. This is private property. I'm calling the police." Bev reached into her bag, and Fina reached into hers. Bev pulled out a phone and began dialing, and Fina pulled out her gun and laid it on the wide armrest of the club chair. Bev paused mid-dial.

"You're going to shoot me?"

"That's up to you. Sit down."

Bev looked annoyed, but she dropped her phone back into her bag and sat down in the other club chair. She fussed with the hem of her printed floral skirt. On top, she wore a white short-sleeved sweater set and a necklace of chunky whitish stones. The cut and fabrics had an understated elegance that must have been pricey.

Fina glared at Bev. "Are you using my niece as a hooker?" she asked.

Bev exhaled loudly. "I'm willing to have this ridiculous conversation with you, but I have an important business meeting in"—she looked at her gold watch—"five minutes. Why don't we discuss this later?"

"Answer my question."

"I don't even know who your niece is."

"I have it on good authority that she hangs out with your hookers."

Bev shook her head in disapproval.

Fina picked up the gun. "You know what? You don't

have to answer the question. All you have to know is that if you have any contact with her from this moment forward—"

There was a knock on the door and a voice called out: "Mrs. Duprey?"

Bev glanced at the door. Fina grasped the gun, stood up, and peered out the peephole.

She closed her eyes and rested her forehead on the door. "Oh, no," she moaned softly. She tucked the gun into her waistband at the small of her back and opened the door. She stood back and gestured for the visitor to come in.

Bev closed her eyes and took a deep breath. When she opened them, Haley was standing there, staring at the two women.

Fina opened and closed her fist a couple of times. She looked at Bev and then Haley.

"Have you been working for this woman?" she asked Haley.

"Oh my God! Are you kidding me?" Haley's arms fluttered at her sides, like a bird trapped in a room with lots of windows, but no means of escape.

"Cut the shit, Haley!" Fina yelled. "Tell me the truth."

The color was draining out of Haley's face, and her chin began to tremble.

Fina grasped her shoulders. "Just tell me the truth. It will be okay. Really, I'll take care of you, but you have to tell me the truth."

Tears rolled down Haley's cheeks. She glanced at Bev, who stared back at the girl.

"Yes," Haley whispered.

Fina hugged her and glared at Bev over her niece's

shoulder. After a moment, she released Haley and cupped her chin with one hand. "No more. You are never to see this woman again. If she approaches you or threatens you, tell me immediately. If I'm not available, tell Milloy."

"You told Milloy?!"

"No, and you don't have to tell Milloy anything specific to get his help. You just tell him that this woman"—she looked at Bev—"is bothering you. Okay?" Haley nodded. "Do you understand, Bev?" Fina asked. "You are not to contact her or threaten her."

Bev looked off to the side. She looked annoyed. "I wouldn't dream of bothering her."

"Good." Fina looked at Haley. "I want you to go to Aunt Patty's and spend the day there. If you want to stay in bed all day, fine. Tell her you don't feel well. Or spend time with your cousins. But I want you at Scotty and Patty's until I come find you. Tell your dad you want to be there." Fina steered her toward the door. She leaned toward her. "Can I trust you to do that?"

"Are you going to tell my dad about this?"

Fina raised her palms. "I have no idea, but I'm not going to do anything without talking to you first."

"I'll go to Aunt Patty's."

"Good. I'll see you later." Fina gently nudged her out the door and closed it behind her. She leaned against it and studied the ceiling. "I should kill you right now."

"That would be ill-advised."

"Oh, really? Why's that? Who's going to miss you? Your disgraced son or your bedridden husband?"

Bev leaned forward in her seat. "This is all your family's fault."

"So you go after an underage girl and kill her mother?"

"I had nothing to do with her mother's death."

Fina walked over and put her hands on the back of the empty chair. "Is that why Melanie contacted you? Because of Haley?"

Bev tucked a piece of hair behind her ear.

"That would make sense," Fina ventured. "Rand's activities would humiliate and piss her off, but it wouldn't necessarily set her on a rampage. But Haley would. If she thought you were hurting her daughter, she'd come after you."

Bev scoffed. "Really? She was such a dedicated mother? So concerned for her daughter's well-being?"

"Of course! She wouldn't want her working as a hooker!"

"Why do you think girls do this job, Ms. Ludlow?" Bev sneered.

"Because people like you prey on them."

"I know that's your theory, but even if that were true, I'm never the first to have hurt them."

"What the hell are you talking about?"

"I'm just saying that your sister-in-law wasn't exactly mother-of-the-year material."

"No, she wasn't, but neither are you, despite the sanctimonious bullshit you believe."

"You may question my actions, but I've never done anything to damage my child. Never."

"Every parent damages their child in some way. Why do you think there are so many shrinks in this town? You're deluded if you think otherwise."

Bev stood up and smoothed her skirt. "I will stay away

from Haley, but I strongly urge you to stay away from me and my family."

Fina was quiet for a moment, then shook her head slowly. "I don't know if I can do that."

"I have access to powerful resources—friends, business partners—and I promise you, they will not tolerate your interference."

"So, what? You're going to kick me up the food chain?"

"If necessary. Consider yourself warned: If you meddle with my interests, you'll be meddling with some very dangerous people."

Fina walked over to the door and opened it. "I look forward to it."

She walked out and slammed the door behind her.

That bitch could burn in hell.

Fina walked to the Public Garden, where she fit right in with the homeless people who were grimacing and talking to themselves. She sat down on a bench and forced herself to breathe deeply for a couple of minutes. Once she'd reclaimed a modicum of calm, she bought a diet soda and a pretzel the size of Big Bird's hand from a vendor. She returned to the bench and ate, washing down the jagged salt crystals with gulps of soda. When her phone rang, she glanced at the screen, swallowed a mouthful, and hit the answer button.

"I haven't killed anyone," she told Cristian. "That's what you want to know, right?"

"That's good news. What have you been up to?"

Fina was silent. There was a cluster of elderly people

doing tai chi on a patch of grass near the Swan Boats. With their achingly slow, synchronized movements, they looked like a flock of graceful, grounded birds.

"Fina?"

"Yeah?" Fina heard shuffling and banging in the background.

"We should meet."

Fina's stomach tightened. "Why? What now?"

"Nothing related to Haley, but we need to talk. Where are you?"

"The Public Garden."

"I don't suppose you want to swing by headquarters?"

"Ha. I don't think so."

"Well, I don't have a lot of time. You're going to have to meet me halfway."

"Fine. Meet me in the lobby of the Westin."

"I'll be there in half an hour."

"See ya." Fina dropped her phone into her bag and finished her soda. It wouldn't take her thirty minutes to walk to the hotel, but she threw out her soda can and napkins and moved in that direction anyway. She was in no mood for the crowds or tight sidewalks of Newbury Street, and instead opted for the less charming thoroughfare of Boylston.

Since leaving Bev's office, she'd struggled to ignore all thoughts of Haley, but blocking things out never worked for Fina. Other people, like her mother, just chose to see what they wanted to in the world, but Fina was missing the self-delusion gene. She didn't know how to block out the unsavory stuff, which might explain her line of work. If you couldn't put it out of your mind, you might as well jump into the fray.

Fina couldn't stop the maelstrom in her head, but she had to focus. She would keep Haley safe and deal with the fallout from her situation later. She would crush whoever had killed Melanie. She would destroy Bev Duprey. It was an exhausting to-do list.

In the hotel lobby, Fina found an empty seating area and sat down in a chair upholstered in beige microsuede that was too big for one person, but a touch too small for two. Fina felt like Goldilocks as she sank down into the seat. She watched the top of the escalator, and after a few minutes, Cristian's head appeared. He was wearing jeans, a fitted T-shirt, and a sport coat. The coat was a nod to looking professional, but more importantly, a means of concealing his gun. He wasn't undercover, but didn't need to advertise his profession, either.

Fina scooted over as he approached. "Here." She patted the empty foot of space on the seat. "Sit next to me."

Cristian shook his head and grinned. "I don't think we'd fit."

"Of course we would. We just have to suck it in. What's the point of these chairs otherwise?"

"You're getting loopy. Never a good sign." Cristian pulled a matching chair close to hers and sat down. "I'm guessing you made another visit to Bev Duprey."

"Are you asking me as Pitney's helper or my friend?"

Cristian shook his head in frustration. "Enough of that, Fina. I'm asking as someone who wants to solve this case and minimize the damage."

"Yes. I paid her a visit."

"And?"

"She's an uncooperative bitch."

"You're too close to this case."

Fina grimaced. "You think?"

"Did you get any information about Haley?"

Fina looked at him and then glanced away. She tugged on her lower lip with her free hand.

"Fuck," Cristian murmured, and ran his hand through his hair. "I was hoping I was wrong."

"So was I, and you cannot tell anyone about this." Fina gripped his knee. "I mean it. This could ruin her life. She has to be kept out of it. Okay?" Cristian didn't respond. "Okay?" Fina asked more urgently.

"I have to do my job."

"And your job, in this case, is to protect a fifteen-year-old girl."

"Christ, you make life complicated."

"Life is complicated; it has nothing to do with me."

Cristian's phone rang, and he glanced at it. The press of a button brought silence, and he slipped the device back into his pocket.

"So what's your news?" Fina asked.

"Bob Webber, the guy who claimed he saw Melanie? He turned up."

Fina watched an older man canoodling with his age-inappropriate wife. "What does he have to say for himself?"

"Nothing. He's dead."

Fina's gaze snapped to Cristian. "What? Where'd you find him?"

"An abandoned construction site in Norwood."

"Seriously?"

Cristian didn't bother answering.

"What happened?"

"No idea. You have any theories you'd like to share?"

Fina studied the couple again. The man was reaching into his wallet and pulled out a stack of bills, which he placed in the woman's hand. She stood on tiptoe and kissed him on the lips. His wrinkled skin looked like a time-lapse photo of her smooth, taut complexion.

Cristian stood up abruptly. "Look, if you're gonna hold out on me, then I need to spend my time finding out what you won't tell me."

"Cristian, I'm not trying to stonewall you. I'm thinking."

"Who put you in touch with Bob Webber?"

Fina looked at him. "I can't say just yet."

"You're drifting into obstruction."

"I know, and I'm sorry about that. I need twenty-four hours."

"For what?"

"To figure some stuff out."

"Do you ever think what would happen if everybody were above the law?"

Fina peered at him. "What? No, not really."

"The only reason your approach works is because most people operate ethically and within the bounds of a civilized society."

Fina stood up. "Agreed. What exactly is your point?"

"That you would hate living in a world of Fina Ludlows," Cristian said.

"I *do* live in a world of Fina Ludlows; why do you think I'm like this? Anyway, I can't deal with a theoretical discussion right now. You can lecture me later."

"Fine. You know where to find me when you're ready to talk."

"Cristian," Fina implored, "don't leave pissed. Come on."

He waved his hand over his shoulder as he walked away.

Fina reached into her bag and pulled out her phone. She called Emma and fought the urge to hurl her phone across the lobby when she got her flat, monotone voice mail. Fina told her she needed the Costas information ASAP, then clicked over to a call from Patty.

"What's going on with Haley?" her sister-in-law asked.

"What do you mean?"

"She's acting weird. She showed up and said she's supposed to stay with me until you say otherwise."

"Those were her marching orders. Sorry. I should have asked you first, but it was kind of an emergency."

"I don't mind, but I'm not sure what to do with her. We're at the club, and she's just sitting here on a chaise, staring off into space."

Fina looked at her watch. "I'll stop by for lunch and check on her."

"Fina, what's going on?"

"I can't talk about it, Patty. It wouldn't be an exaggeration, though, to say that you're playing a critical role in her well-being right now. I really need your help."

"And you have it, but you're going to have to fill me in at some point."

"I will. I promise."

"Does Scotty know what's going on?"

"No!" Fina said vehemently. "And I don't want him to, not yet. Nobody knows."

"This sounds very unwise."

"It may be, but it's the best I can do."

The call ended, and Fina's gaze skipped across the lobby. She wanted to rent a room, take the elevator upstairs, and collapse on a big, freshly laundered bed.

Instead, she walked to the escalator and stepped on for the ride down.

Fina pulled into a parking space at the club and reached for her phone. She tapped her finger lightly on the screen while trying to make up her mind. After a moment, she dialed and got Mark Lamont's voice mail.

"Mark, hi. It's Fina Ludlow again. We need to talk. It's important. Urgent, actually. Call me as soon as you can. Thanks."

Mark's lack of communication was starting to piss her off. She knew she was poking a snake with a stick, but the snake was in her way.

At the pool, Patty was reading on a chaise, while the boys tried to drown one another and Haley sunned herself. She looked momentarily stricken when Fina showed up, but resumed her tanning position when it became clear that her aunt wasn't going to mention their earlier meeting.

"You want some lunch?" Patty asked as she gathered the boys out of the pool.

"How about a burger and some fries? Thanks. I just need to check my messages."

Her nephew Chandler stood next to her, dripping water on her shoes.

"Does it smell yet?" He gestured at her cast.

Fina gave him a searching look. "Does that really happen?"

"It does when you shove a piece of cheese down it," Patty offered as she burrowed in her bag for hats for the boys.

"Note to self: Don't keep cheese in cast," Fina said. Chandler beamed.

Haley threw on a T-shirt and followed Patty and the boys over to an empty table. Fina sat down on the chaise and checked her messages.

She was staring into space when Dr. Murray interrupted her reverie.

"You never look like you're relaxing when I see you here, Fina. In fact, you look tense."

Dr. Murray was wearing swim trunks and a golf shirt. In one hand, he carried a navy blue canvas bag, and in the other, a biography of Mark Twain.

"It's that obvious?"

"To the trained eye," Dr. Murray said and smiled.

"Has your daughter had her baby yet?"

"No, although she'd like to. She's entered the home stretch and just can't get comfortable."

"Does she know what she's having?"

"A girl."

"Nice." Fina stood up so she could be eye level with Dr. Murray. "Can I ask you a question?"

"Sure."

"It's of a professional nature."

Dr. Murray nodded.

"What makes one teenage girl toe the line and another

get into trouble? Aside from the obvious: personality, parenting, that kind of thing."

Dr. Murray shrugged his shoulders. "Well, the obvious accounts for a lot. If we could identify the less obvious factors, maybe we could do a better job of steering kids away from trouble."

"Right, of course. I was just thinking about the extreme end of the spectrum: excessive drugs and drinking, risky sexual behavior."

"There are the usual things, like a genetic predisposition to addiction, a need for attention, thrill-seeking, lack of self-esteem."

"And girls who work in the sex industry?"

Dr. Murray glanced around. "Are you sure you wouldn't prefer to speak with me in my office about this?"

"I don't have time, but please, bill me."

"I'm not worried about my fee. I'm worried about giving you incomplete or misguided information."

"I'm not going to sue you. I promise."

He chewed on the inside of his lip for a moment. "Well, young women who work in the sex industry—and keep in mind this isn't my specialty—generally suffer from all the issues I mentioned, but there's another similarity in their experiences."

"Which is?"

"Childhood abuse. Specifically, sexual abuse."

Fina reached into her cast and scratched the area around her thumb. She was intent on the task as she waited for the lump in her throat to subside. Dr. Murray stood quietly. Fina looked over at the door leading to the kitchen. The waitstaff hustled in and out in their white polo shirts and khaki shorts, rushing to bring chicken fingers and fries to those to the manor born.

"But wouldn't there be a lot more hookers if every abuse victim became one?"

"Ah, but I'm not suggesting that every abuse victim works in the sex trade. I'm suggesting, as the research has indicated, that of the women working in the sex trade, a high percentage of them were victims of childhood abuse—sexual abuse."

"I understand."

Dr. Murray followed Fina's gaze across the pool to the eating area. "The most critical thing for any abuse victim is to get counseling. Good counseling. It can make a significant difference."

Fina nodded slowly.

"If you ever find yourself in need of such a resource, I would be happy to provide a referral."

"I appreciate that," Fina said. She waved at Patty, who was trying to get her attention. "Hope that baby comes soon."

Dr. Murray patted her shoulder. "Me too. I can't wait to meet her."

Fina joined the group at the table and tried not to stare at Haley throughout lunch. The boys provided a welcome distraction, and Patty maintained a running commentary about a potential kitchen renovation. She glanced nervously at Fina, who ate her burger and fries seemingly in a trance. After everyone had finished, Fina grabbed a can of diet soda for the road and followed them back to their chairs.

"Are you doing okay?" Fina asked Haley as her niece settled back into her chaise.

Haley's eyes looked blank. "Yeah."

Fina leaned down and gave her a hug. "You're safe now. From everything," she whispered in Haley's ear.

Haley's eyes watered. Fina gave Patty a quick squeeze, waved to the boys, and hit the road.

24

Fina pulled up to Risa's house wondering how she got there, but at the same time, not surprised that she had. Sometimes she had to trust that her unconscious mind had a better grip than her conscious mind.

Risa's lawn was lush and green despite the heat, as were those of the neighbors. Come five A.M., the street probably twinkled with the mist of inground sprinkler systems.

Fina climbed the steps and knocked. After a minute, Risa appeared in the front hallway and opened the door.

"I'm surprised to see you," she told Fina, and gave her a hug.

"Really?"

"Since your brother's arrest, I assumed that we were on opposite sides."

"It's a little more complicated than that. Do you have a few minutes?"

Risa opened the door wider, and Fina followed her to the kitchen. The air in the house was cool and fragrant.

"It feels good in here," Fina said.

"Central AC. We put it in when we did the renovation. It's a godsend, especially during these freak heat spells."

Fina sat down at the kitchen island and watched Risa wash her hands in the large farmhouse-style sink.

"I just tried a new recipe," Risa said. "Want some pie?"

"Always. What kind?"

"I have apricot raspberry and banoffee, which is bananas and toffee. I'm trying to decide which to serve at a luncheon. The apricot raspberry is lighter, more seasonal, but the ladies do love their sweets."

"Sounds delicious."

"I'll give you a little of both."

Risa reached into a cabinet and pulled out two dessert plates onto which she doled out wedges from both pies and scoops of ice cream. "Raspberry iced tea?" She held up a glass in Fina's direction.

"Yes, thanks."

The ice cream pooled into the side of the apricot raspberry slice, and Fina broke through the sugared crust with her fork. She washed down the bite with tea, and then scooped up a forkful of whipped cream, bananas, and toffee. Risa took the seat next to her and broke off a piece of crust from her slice of fruit pie. They ate in silence.

"That toffee is sweet," Risa said after a couple of minutes.

"Sweet, but delicious. It gets my vote. The apricot raspberry is yummy, too, but I always feel like a fruit dessert is a bait and switch."

Risa considered the opinion and then ate another bite of the apricot raspberry. She set down her fork. "So."

"So," Fina said.

"So Rand was arrested."

"He was. I still don't think he did it. In fact, I'm gathering evidence that he didn't."

Risa raised an eyebrow.

"But I'm not here about that, actually." Fina speared a banana slice and dredged it through the toffee. "Did you have any sense of the family dynamics with the three of them? Melanie, Rand, and Haley?"

"Why don't you ask them? Rand and Haley, I mean."

Fina studied the ice in her drink. "I'm asking lots of questions, but I'm interested in another perspective. You spent time with all of them, and you always have an opinion."

Risa smirked. "Yes, I suppose I do. Well." She popped a wedge of apricot into her mouth and dabbed her mouth with her napkin. "I think they were functionally dysfunctional."

"Which means?"

"Which means from the outside they looked highly functional, and they did function—everybody went to work and school and had a social life, et cetera—but the way they interacted wasn't especially healthy. Not that I'm an expert."

"No, but you and Marty seem happy, and your kids aren't train wrecks."

"This is true. Everything with those three was always an extreme; either they were fighting or buying diamonds or grounding Haley or letting her run wild. A couple more kids would have helped. Spread out the drama."

"Or increased it," Fina commented. "Had it been worse recently?"

"Haley seemed more distant." Risa thought for a moment. "Distant from Melanie and pissed at Rand."

Fina drained her glass of iced tea and pressed her fingertip on a flake of crust on her plate.

"But," Risa said, sighing, "she's also his little girl."

Fina shuddered. Risa tipped her head in a questioning way. "Just got a chill from the AC," Fina said.

"You done?" Risa asked. She took Fina's plate and glass and rinsed them in the sink with her own. "If I've learned anything as I've gotten older, it's that you never know what's going on in someone else's marriage or family."

"Right."

"And what may seem dysfunctional to one person may be standard operating procedure to another."

"But they didn't seem happy to you?"

"Who knows? It wouldn't make me happy, that's for sure. Marty may seem like a big bore to the rest of the world, but there's a lot to be said for dependability."

Marty did seem like a boring, albeit good, guy. Maybe as Fina aged, a man like that would appeal to her. Probably not.

"Thanks for talking to me and for the pie. I'll be in touch."

Risa followed Fina to the front door and leaned her hip against the frame.

"Be careful, Fina."

"I am," she tossed over her shoulder as she walked down the stairs.

"I don't mean your physical safety. I mean be careful poking around. You might not like what you stir up."

"I rarely do, Risa."

Fina got back in her car and took a swig of diet soda from the can in the cup holder. The toffee had left a sweet film on her tongue. The drink was tepid, but it washed the cloying flavor out of her mouth.

She was getting fatter and unhappier as the day progressed.

Milloy met her back at Nanny's, and she told him everything she'd learned in the last twenty-four hours, with the exception of her suspicions about her brother. She couldn't say that out loud. Not yet.

He reached over and took her hand. "I don't know what to say."

"About which part?"

"Haley, specifically. I can't believe she's been working for Bev."

"Do you realize how fucked up that is? She should still be a virgin!"

Milloy looked bemused. "Were you at fifteen?"

"This isn't about me, and I certainly wasn't trading sex for money."

"What are you going to do about it?"

"I don't know what I'm going to do. I think—" The phone interrupted her. "What's up, Emma?" she asked.

Milloy grabbed the *Globe* that was sitting on the coffee table and glanced at the sports section while Fina caught up with Emma. The Sox were well into their June swoon. Milloy liked attending the occasional game at Fenway, but couldn't commit to 162 games of ardent devotion. All those guys who were sports fans and claimed they weren't ready to commit to a woman were full of it. They didn't have commitment issues, they had woman issues.

Fina hung up and looked at Milloy.

"Emma says that the Ronald Costas who owns Ridleys is Vanessa Lamont's father."

Milloy tossed the paper onto the coffee table. "I don't understand. What beef does Lamont have with you?"

"I have no idea." Fina stood and wandered over to the window. There were clouds gathering in the west, suggesting a thunderstorm might develop. Sometimes, a storm would break the heat, but recently, it had merely been an emphatic reminder of the humidity that cloaked the city.

"This is just getting worse," Fina said, leaning her shoulder against the window frame. "I can't believe that Mark is involved somehow."

"He is a criminal."

"I know he's a criminal, but I don't expect him to commit felonies against me and my family! I thought we were on the same side."

"Mark Lamont is on Mark Lamont's side."

"What the fuck is he thinking, running me off the road?"

"You need to put an end to it."

"I know."

Fina called Dennis and warned him that Joe Winthrop would make a move soon. Dennis had to attend to a family matter, so he'd enlisted Frank as his replacement. Fina was torn; there was no better backup than Frank, but she'd never forgive herself if anything happened to him. She pushed the thought aside and left a third message for Mark Lamont.

"Mark, I've got some information, and I think I'm just going to hand it over to the cops; I'm not getting anywhere with it. Maybe I'll stop by the new house, see if you're around," she said before ending the call.

"You think he's going to bite?" Milloy asked as Fina sank down next to him on the couch.

"Probably. He's going to lose patience with me eventually."

"With you?" Milloy shook his head and massaged her neck. "Who could ever lose patience with you?"

At eight thirty P.M., Joe Winthrop was still holed up in his apartment. Milloy had left hours earlier to rub down some privileged women on Beacon Hill, and Fina had spent the ensuing hours pacing and annoying her various contacts.

The time had come to act.

She took the elevator down to the garage, wrapped her good hand around her gun as was her standard procedure these days, and got in her car. She didn't have a plan, as usual, but she was sitting on enough anger and bewilderment to fuel any ideas that might spring to mind.

Speeding west on the Pike, she decided to make good on her promise to pay Mark a visit. He could ignore her phone calls, but that wouldn't make her go away.

When she pulled up to the new house on Forest Road, the driveway was occupied by a dumpster and stacks of building supplies. Fina peeked in the front window, but didn't see any furniture visible. As she walked around the back of the house, she noticed light coming from the lower floor. She knocked gently on the sliding glass door, and tried to open it when there was no response.

It was unlocked. Fina slowly slid it open and stepped into the space. This was the family room she had toured a couple of weeks earlier, and progress had been made in the construction. Small spotlights threw circles of light onto a blank wall. The floor was covered in a deep pile rug, and speaker wires hung from a number of locations around the room. A large blank space over the fireplace also spouted wires, and Fina guessed it was all part of the flat-screen/surround sound entertainment system. She seemed to remember that there was a separate screening room a few doors down, but you could never have too many screens, right?

Fina tiptoed past the kitchen, changing room, hair salon, and then slowly approached a door from which more light emanated.

"Mark?" she called softly.

No response.

She peeked around the door frame. The room was empty save for two washer and dryer sets boasting shiny silver fronts and digital readouts. She stepped across the hall to the exercise room and took stock of the equipment reflected in the mirrors. There was a treadmill and elliptical machine, a large multipurpose weight machine, and rows of neatly stacked free weights.

Fina's phone rang, and she hurried to silence it. She was slipping it back into her bag when a movement caught her eye in the mirror. She started to turn, but before she could, something brushed against her face and then tightened around her neck. In the faint light spilling in from the laundry room, Fina could see a man behind her, but she couldn't see his face. There wasn't enough light, and her vision quickly became blurred and jumpy from the lack of air.

She couldn't breathe. She clawed at her throat, but whatever he was using dug deeply into her flesh, and she couldn't get purchase on it. Fina kicked her feet back, but failed to make contact. Without letting up on the tension, the man pushed his leg into the back of her knees, forcing Fina onto the weight bench, and pressed down on her with his body weight. The odds were not in her favor.

She might have a shot—one shot—at breaking free. She let go of her neck with her casted hand and swung her arm backward into his kidney. He grunted and flinched. Fina stuck the fingers of her good hand between the ligature and her neck. She summoned all her strength and struck him once more in the kidney. In the split second when he eased the tension, Fina shoved her cast between the ligature and her neck. Its rough surface scraped her face, and the cast itself was jammed up against her chin, but the shape of the cast provided a small pocket of air between her neck and the implement.

Fina breathed deeply, and oxygen and anger flooded her system. She rocked forward on the weight bench, and her assailant banged his head against the bank of plated weights. He yelped in pain, and she reached behind her and insinuated her hand between the two of them. She reached for his balls and dug her fingernails in, as if trying to pop a balloon. He howled and reared up off of her. Fina rolled off the weight bench and scrambled toward the rack of free weights. She grabbed a ten-pound hand

weight and swung it wildly toward him. When it made
contact with his mouth, a crunching, crackling noise was
punctuated by spurting blood. He looked stunned, then
lunged toward her, but Fina already had her gun in hand.

"I'll shoot you," she told the heavyset, bleeding man.

"Fuck you," he garbled, and spit shards of teeth out on
the cushioned gym floor. The resistance band he'd used to
strangle her lay at his feet, like a bright green party streamer.

Fina studied him. "You're the dick who broke my wrist."

His lip curled up in a sneer, and he lunged at Fina.

She pulled the trigger.

"I wouldn't dream of doing this under normal circumstances," Bev said, "but I find myself in a rather unusual
situation." She sat across from a man in his early sixties.
He was trim, with gray hair and wire-framed glasses.

"I'm surprised to see you here, at my office," the man
admitted. He stole a glance at the family photo on his desk.
It had been taken on his fortieth-wedding-anniversary
cruise in Greece. His wife and kids were beaming at the
camera.

Bev plastered a smile onto her face and worked to slow
her breathing. "As I said, I'm here as a last resort, and I
did come after regular business hours."

The man considered her for a moment. He consulted
a file folder open before him on his desk. "You said that
before all this business he had a good record?"

"Exemplary. You couldn't ask for a more caring or
conscientious physician."

"But his license was suspended?"

"Yes, but not revoked." Bev mentioned the name of the attorney whom she was paying a king's ransom to get Connor back in the American Medical Association's good graces.

The man took a deep breath. "I can't make you any promises, but I'll see what I can do. We always need ob-gyns in the field." He stood up and walked around the desk, anxious for the meeting to end.

Bev grasped his hand. "You don't know how grateful I am," she said.

He held the door open for her. "And Bev? It's best that you don't come to my office again."

"Of course." She looked down at her pumps. "When it comes to our children, we'll do just anything, won't we?" She met his gaze.

"I suppose," he said, and waited for her to leave.

Bev started down the hallway and heard the door close behind her.

Groveling was not her strong suit.

Fina parked a few streets away from Mark's unfinished house. She pulled down the visor mirror and looked at her reflection. There were ligature marks around her neck from the resistance band, and her left eye was speckled with tiny broken blood vessels. Fina reached back, pulled out her hair elastic, and let her ponytail fall loose around her face. Her phone rang.

"Where are you?" Frank asked. "Your guy's on the move."

"Where's he headed?"

"West on the Pike."

"Toward Wellesley?"

"Yup."

"That's where I am. Let me know where he ends up, and I'll meet you there."

Fina sat with the phone in her lap. She flipped the visor back up and reached for a half-full bottle of water in her cup holder. The water tasted musty, and swallowing made her neck ache, but she drained it anyway. She threw the empty bottle in the backseat and rooted around on the car floor. She kept extra clothes in her car in case she needed to blend in or stand out. A blue Patriots hat would provide some coverage for her face, but high heels, a little black dress, and a blond wig weren't going to gild this lily.

Fina drove toward the junction of Route 9 and Washington Street. She pulled into a small shopping plaza and claimed an empty space. What might have been the last pay phone in America sat on the sidewalk. Fina got out of the car and dialed 911. She requested an ambulance be sent to Mark's house, but hung up before the dispatcher could get any details.

As she approached her car, she noticed a Brigham's sign glowing in the dark, and Fina looked through the front window to see a lone employee leaning on the counter, staring into space. She stepped into the over-air-conditioned shop and asked the clerk for a coffee frappe. He was a teenager, pimply and bored. He stared at her, his eyes like saucers, and then scurried off to fill her order. Goddamnit. She was scaring children.

Fina fiddled with her phone and listened to the whirring of the blender in the background. After a few minutes, the

kid placed a sweating plastic cup in front of her and rang
up the shake. She told him to keep the change before grabbing a straw and a spoon and taking the drink to her car.

After lowering herself into the car seat, she popped off
the plastic top and dipped into the cup with her spoon.
Her hand shook lightly. Probably low blood sugar, not
the attempted strangulation or gunplay she'd just experienced. She slipped the icy mixture into her mouth and
held it on her tongue.

The phone rang, and Fina jumped, causing the frappe
to slop over the edge of the cup. She tucked it into the
drink holder and sucked the excess off her hand. A bead
of liquid dribbled down into her cast.

"Yes?" she answered.

"He's just stopped in a parking lot in Framingham."

"What's he doing?"

"Nothing. Waiting, probably, to meet someone."

"Can you give me the exact location?"

Frank gave her the details, and Fina felt the hairs rise
on the back of her neck. She hung up the phone and stared
at the illuminated dials on the dashboard.

All this time, she'd been led astray. What was wrong
with her? She was always willing to believe the worst of
people; why had her intuition failed her this time?

Fina jumped on Route 9 heading west. She obeyed the
speed limit, not wanting to be questioned by a cop in her
present condition, and eleven minutes later pulled into
the office park a few cars away from Frank. Fina grabbed
her frappe and climbed into Frank's passenger seat.

He did a double take when he saw her. "Christ, Fina!
Are you okay?"

"Never better. Do you think he knows he was followed?"

"I don't think so. He's not the sharpest knife in the drawer." Frank's face was pinched with concern. "You need to go to the hospital."

"I will, but not quite yet."

"Fina!"

"Frank," Fina pleaded. "I'm so close. I've got to do this. I've got to finish what I started."

Frank shook his head. They sat in silence and watched Joe's car. Fina fussed with her sticky hands, and Frank produced a pack of baby wipes. She was shoving a used wipe into a small trash bag when Joe got out of his car, looked around, and started walking down the aisle. He stopped after a few cars, looked around again, and climbed into a black Lexus sedan with the license plate MONT3.

"Fuck," Fina groaned. "Fuck. Fuck. Fuck."

Frank watched her. Fina took a deep breath. "I'm going to go have a little chat."

"What do you want me to do?"

"Once I get in the car, I want you to call Cristian." Frank had met Cristian on a few occasions and heartily approved. Fina gave him the number. She told him her message.

"And then?"

"Keep an eye on us. Call an ambulance if I end up bleeding."

"You're not helping my blood pressure. What if someone else ends up bleeding?"

"You can call it a night, I suppose." Fina leaned over and gave him a kiss on the cheek. "Cheer up. It'll all be over soon."

Fina climbed out of the car and pulled the cap down on her head. She approached the Lexus from the side and pretended to tie her shoe so she could get a look at the driver. His face was illuminated by the neon of the Zyxco, Inc. sign. She carefully pulled out her gun and crept up on the passenger side of the car. When she reached the door, she tapped on the glass with the gun and tried the door handle.

A strong blast of cold air tumbled out when she opened the door. Fina bent down and pressed the gun into the side of Joe Winthrop's head.

"Get out," she said.

"What?! I don't—"

"Get out of the car or I'll shoot you."

Joe looked at the driver and then scrambled out. Fina slipped into his spot and turned in the seat. She trained the gun on the driver's head.

"Mark Lamont. Why haven't you returned my phone calls?"

25

Mark reached for the travel mug in his beverage holder and took a slow sip. He put the cup back and stared out the windshield.

"Put the gun away, Fina."

"I'd love to, but I kinda feel like I need it."

"You don't."

"Really? I needed it with your goon back at the new house."

Mark glanced at her. "I hope you didn't do anything stupid."

"For such a smart businessman, your hired help sucks. What a bunch of inept losers." Mark didn't respond. Fina kept the gun in her hand, but rested it on her thigh. "I thought we were on the same side."

Mark was silent.

"I was going to ask why you've been gunning for me, but I think I know the answer."

"You're not good at minding your own business, are you?" Mark asked.

"I have been minding my own business, but it keeps overlapping with your business. I've been investigating Melanie's murder, and for some reason, you found that threatening."

Mark's eyes bored into her. "You need to let this go."

Fina shifted away from him in her seat. "I can't. Bob Webber's sighting of Melanie in the North End was fiction, right? Is that why you killed him? You were afraid I'd find out the truth?"

"Let it go, Fina."

"You'd love that," Fina sneered.

"In our world"—he put his hands up in a helpless gesture—"people get hurt. You know that."

"Not my people!"

Mark adjusted the air-conditioning. "I have a lot of resources at my disposal. Don't play chicken with me."

Fina studied him for a moment. "Did Melanie find out that you were doing business with Bev Duprey?"

Mark stared out the windshield.

"Did she threaten to expose you?"

"The women in your family have big mouths. She should have shut up, just like you should now."

"You could have let her walk away."

Mark snorted.

"You could have called Rand. He would have dealt with her," Fina said.

Mark sipped his coffee. "Not this time."

"He would have," she insisted.

Fina watched Mark. There was no tremble in his grip, no unsteadiness in his voice. She wished her own pulse weren't racing, but maybe that was a sign of humanity, not weakness.

Fina took a deep breath, and something shifted in her brain. "Haley. Bev told Melanie about Haley. And then Melanie found out that you were one of Haley's pimps, if only in name. She must have gone ape shit." A bitter taste rose in Fina's throat. "You're right. Rand would have destroyed you."

Mark looked at her and raised his shoulders in a tiny shrug.

"How could you be so fucking stupid?" Fina exclaimed. "Didn't you know that Bev was tied up with my brother?"

"I didn't give a shit that your brother couldn't keep his dick in his pants! It was a business deal."

"So the whole Haley part was a surprise?" She waved the gun in his face.

"Like I said, Fina, our world is small."

"Not that small. Bev went after Rand on purpose."

"Why would she give a shit about Rand?"

"Don't you vet your business partners?!" Fina shouted. "Rand sued her son. He wrecked her son's life, and she wanted payback. And you helped her by killing his wife."

Mark glanced at his watch. "You need to forget this conversation."

"Right." Fina leaned toward him. She caught a whiff of sweat. "Just wait 'til someone hurts your kid."

Mark grabbed Fina around the neck and squeezed.

Her already tender flesh screamed in pain. Fina banged the butt of the gun down on his forehead and watched a gash unzip across his skin. Blood poured out. Mark swore and released his grip. Fina opened the door and jumped out of the car.

"I'll kill you, too, bitch," Mark said.

Fina ducked her head back into the car. "Yeah, good luck with that." She slammed the door and watched him peel out of the parking lot. Frank pulled out of his parking space and drove up next to her. The passenger-side window lowered silently.

"Time for the hospital?"

"Almost."

Frank sighed. "Do you need me to stay on him?"

"Nope. Did you reach Cristian?"

"Yes. It's nice to know I'm not the only one who finds you maddening."

A smile flitted across Fina's face, and she walked to her car.

Cristian climbed into her car in a Dunkin' Donuts parking lot in Newton. He took one look at her and pulled her toward him into a hug.

"Ow," Fina said.

"Sorry," Cristian said into her neck.

Fina slowly loosened his hands from her and gently pushed him back into his seat. "It's not that I don't appreciate the sentiment, but I'm feeling a little fragile right now."

"Let me see your face."

"Cristian, I'm fine. Seriously." She batted his hand away. "You're acting like a mom. Not my mom, but some-one's mom."

Cristian exhaled loudly. "You're going to have to come down to the station. Pitney is ape shit."

"Because I'm a better detective than she is?"

"Because you shot a guy and didn't report it."

"I did report it. Just not right away. Is she really going to argue with self-defense?" Fina gestured to her face.

"No, but things will go easier if you don't make her wait around." Cristian looked at the Brigham's cup in the drink holder. "Did you get the frappe before or after you shot him?"

"I have to keep my strength up," Fina responded defen-sively. "You don't know the kind of night I've had."

Cristian tipped his head back against the headrest. "Christ Almighty."

"How about in the morning?" Fina asked. "Will that satisfy Pitney?"

"That's pushing it."

"I know, but I need to do a couple of things."

Cristian pulled out his phone and dialed. Fina couldn't make out the specifics of the conversation, but she could hear Pitney having an apoplexy on the other end. After a moment of back-and-forth, Fina grabbed the phone from Cristian.

"I'll be in tomorrow morning," she told Pitney.

"You need to come in now or I'm sending a black-and-white for you and disciplining Menendez."

"Fine. I'll come in now. I'll have Scotty meet me there. I'm sure he's already prepared the paperwork for the suit."

"What suit?"

"Harassment for starters. You arrested the wrong man for Melanie's murder."

"There's no proof of that."

"What does proof have to do with anything!?" Fina hollered into the phone.

Pitney was silent. "If you aren't here by six A.M., hell is going to rain down on you."

"Let's say eight A.M., and you've got yourself a date." Fina hung up and handed the phone back to Cristian. "Eight A.M." She gave him a weak smile. "Guess I'll see you then."

"We'll be there all night. In case you change your mind."

"That is a woman's prerogative."

"What are you going to do now?" Cristian asked. "You're not going to shoot anyone else, are you?"

"Family business."

Cristian shook his head. "That's no guarantee that gunplay won't be involved."

A thin young woman with long, dark hair and big boobs walked in front of the car and pulled open the door to Dunkin' Donuts. "Any word on Brianna?" Fina asked.

"We found some tweaker walking around with her underpants and cell phone."

"Ta da! I didn't kill her!"

"We never thought you did."

"I know, sweetie. It's so hard to keep track of what's true and what's leverage, isn't it?"

Fina took hold of his face with both hands and gave him a soft kiss on the lips. "Off you go."

Cristian returned the kiss and then climbed out of the car.

Fina knocked on the door and let herself in to Scotty and Patty's house. Voices from a TV drifted down the hallway, and Fina followed them to the great room attached to the kitchen.

"Hey," Fina said.

Scotty and Patty were sitting on the couch, her feet in his lap and a glass of wine in her hand.

"Hey," Scotty replied, his eyes glued to the screen.

Patty smiled at her, and then her face sagged. "Now what?"

Scotty looked at his sister. "Jesus H. Christ." He prodded Patty's feet off his lap and hopped up. Fina walked toward him, and he put his hands on her shoulders while examining her face and neck.

"I'm fine."

Patty reached for the wine bottle on the coffee table and poured a generous amount into her glass. "You could have a pickax coming out of your torso and you'd say you were fine." She handed her glass over the back of the couch to Fina, who took a long slug of the cold chardonnay.

"We need to talk," Fina said to Scotty. "Attorney client talk."

Scotty gave her injuries another look. "What's the other guy look like?"

"He's shot."

Patty snorted. "And Elaine still thinks you're going to

settle down and be a soccer mom? I love it." She stood up and left the room.

Fina sank into the deep sectional and filled Scotty in on her latest exploits. He took notes and made a couple of phone calls. She took a trip to the powder room at one point and examined her face in the full-size mirror. The bruises from the car accident had faded, but the scratches on her face from her cast were weeping a mix of pus and blood. She considered her reflection for a moment. This degree of personal injury would only get more taxing as she aged, and more importantly, it would start to take a toll on her looks. Twenty more years of this and she'd look like a semi had run over her face.

"Is Haley still here?" she asked Scotty when she returned to the kitchen.

"In the guest room at the top of the stairs. She was watching TV. You gonna tell me why you want her with us?"

"Not yet."

Scotty jotted a few more notes on a yellow legal pad. "All right. I have what I need. What time should I meet you down there?"

Fina was silent for a moment. "Nine. I'm meeting Pitney at nine." She stared at Scotty, who was bent over his pad.

"Nine it is."

"I'm going to pop upstairs and see if Haley's awake."

"See you in the morning," Scotty called after her.

At the top of the stairs, Fina poked her head into the darkened guest room. The only light was provided by a large, flat-screen TV. Haley looked small in the queen-size bed. She was lying on her side, her body in a fetal position pointed toward the TV and the foot of the bed. A puffy down duvet was grasped in her hands. She blinked and looked up at Fina.

"Did I wake you?" Fina asked as she came into the room. She sat down on the bed near her niece's head.

"No."

Fina looked at the screen. A Hollywood has-been was sitting in group therapy, crying about his beloved Labradoodle that died in a Malibu fire. Fina looked down at Haley and watched the sweeping motion made by her eyelashes when she blinked. Haley had been one of those babies with long, lush eyelashes—the kind that generally disappear once infants become toddlers. Hers hadn't. They were a reminder of the soft, sweet-smelling baby she'd been.

"Hale," Fina said. "I need to ask you something."

"What?" Haley asked and looked at her.

"It's about your dad."

Haley's gaze floated back to the TV.

"I'm not sure how to ask," Fina said.

"Don't," Haley implored in a whisper.

Fina put her hand over her niece's, the one squeezing the duvet. "I have to." Fina took a deep breath. "Did he hurt you?"

Haley stared at the screen. She pulled herself in closer, shrinking her body into a small ball. They were silent for a moment. Then Fina watched a tear shimmer on Haley's lash.

Fina slid off the bed so she was eye level with Haley.

"I will never let him touch you again." She squeezed Haley's hand and then released it.

Outside the room, she collided with Patty, who was now wearing a robe, her hair wrapped on top of her head in a towel turban.

Patty glanced over Fina's shoulder toward the guest room. "She okay?"

"She's upset. She could use a little mothering." Fina walked to the stairs. "Apparently, she hasn't had any for the past fifteen years."

"Fina?" Patty asked, watching her scurry down the stairs. "What's going—?"

The slammed front door was the only answer she got.

Fina made the short drive to Rand's house and pulled into his driveway. She turned off the ignition and sat for a few minutes as the cool air in the car lost its chill. She rested her head on the steering wheel and tried to swallow the bile that was rising in her throat. As a rule, she didn't shy away from confrontation, but she was dreading this conversation.

She climbed out of the car and bypassed the front door. Instead, she followed the intricate pattern of slate pavers around the side of the house. Fina stepped from the shrouded path into the vast backyard. The perimeter was lit by small, unobtrusive lights, and the only sound was the slight rustle of wind in the trees. At the side of the pool, she stopped for a moment, bent down, and trailed her fingers through the illuminated water.

The house was dark except for one large square of light that emanated from Rand's office. Fina could see him sitting behind his desk, studying something on his computer screen.

The French doors·off the family room were open, so she slipped into the house and padded down the hallway to his office. She rested her head against the heavy wooden door frame and studied her brother. After a few seconds, he looked up and flinched.

"Jesus Christ. How long have you been there?" Rand made some rapid clicks with the mouse.

"You're awfully jumpy."

"You look like shit." He tipped back in his chair. "What's going on with you and Haley?"

"What do you mean?"

"She didn't want to come home tonight. She said that you thought it was a good idea for her to stay with Scotty and Patty."

"I do think it's a good idea." Fina sat down in the chair across from him with her back rigid. Just beneath the surface of her skin, her pulse was racing.

"Why? She needs her father right now."

Fina glared at him. "No she doesn't."

"I know you're pissed at me about the hooker thing, but you need to back off."

"Just let me help her, Rand. Stay out of it."

"I'm not going to stay out of it! She's my kid!"

Rand got up from his seat and poured two glasses of scotch at the wet bar. "Here." He handed a glass to Fina and sat back down at his desk. "Your heart's in the right place—you think she needs a mom since Melanie died, or maybe your biological clock is ticking—but you're interfering. Just back off and let me do the parenting."

A wave of nausea washed over Fina. For a moment, she thought she might vomit on the expensive Oriental rug. She closed her eyes and swallowed.

Fina took a long sip of her drink. She stared at her brother. "This is your last chance to stop this conversation."

"What are you talking about?"

Fina slammed her glass down on the desk. "I know, Rand. I know! I know what you did to her!"

"Know what?"

Fina's eyes widened, and she struggled to say something. "Have you actually convinced yourself it never happened?"

Rand rocked his glass back and forth, the amber liquid running up the side and then sliding back down. His jaw was set in a way that was familiar to Fina. All of the men in her family clenched their jaws when they'd had enough.

"You're . . ." Fina struggled to find the right words.

Rand held his hands up in a motion of surrender. "Look, there's been some misunderstanding. What did Haley say? You should know by now that she lies when it suits her."

A half-strangled noise escaped Fina's mouth. "She didn't tell me anything. I figured it out on my own. You molest her and then claim she's lying? You're poisonous."

Rand swallowed the remainder of his drink, got up, and grabbed the bottle from the bar. He sat back down and refilled his glass. Another sip, and then he tilted his head and examined his sister.

"What did you and Melanie fight about at Grahamson?" Fina asked. "Your relationship with Haley and her new line of work?"

Rand peered at her. "Our fight had nothing to do with Haley."

"So it was just about your extracurricular activities? Melanie did some digging that led her to Prestige?"

Rand blinked. "What are you talking about, 'Haley's line of work'?"

"Melanie went to see Bev Duprey because of you. She ended up getting killed because of you."

"Whatever happened to Melanie wasn't my fault."

Fina searched his face.

"I want to know about this Haley thing," Rand pushed.

Fina shook her head in disgust. "No. You don't get to know anything anymore. Stay away from her," Fina said. "If you don't, I'm going to let Dad in on your little secret."

Rand laughed sharply, like a seal barking. "Listen to yourself: 'I'm going to tell Dad.' You sound like a five-year-old. Dad's not going to believe your garbage, and there isn't any proof because it isn't true. Haley has always been difficult, and even more so since Melanie's death."

"Her murder," Fina insisted. "Melanie was murdered."

"And your only job was to get me off on the murder charge."

"Actually, my job was to find out who killed your wife, not that you give a shit."

"I loved Melanie once, and you don't know shit when it comes to my marriage or my family life. You can't keep a man, let alone be married and have a child."

She chose not to rise to his bait. Instead, Fina studied the pattern beneath her feet. Some woman, somewhere in Iran, had toiled for hours on the square foot beneath her shoe.

Rand stared at her. "Have you gotten me off the murder charge?"

Fina shook her head slowly and tried to process her brother's narcissism. "I think that charge—the murder charge—will be dropped."

"What do you mean, 'that charge'?"

"I don't know about the others."

Rand's faced tightened; she would have missed it if she weren't familiar with the planes of his face. "There are no other charges, Fina."

"Not yet."

Rand stared at her. He reached for his drink and finished it in one large swallow. "What are you talking about?"

Fina stood up. She leaned over his desk, her face just inches from Rand's. The smell of scotch hung between them. "I'm done covering your ass."

Fina started for the door.

"We're not done," Rand said, and rose up out of his chair.

"Maybe you'll end up in Walpole. You could be somebody's girlfriend—find out how your daughter felt," Fina said as she started to cross the threshold.

In two quick steps, Rand was across the room. He grabbed Fina's arm and shoved her into the door frame. "Shut your fucking mouth."

Fina pushed him away and punched him in the nose.

Rand cried out in pain and covered his face with his hands. Blood spurted from between his fingers, and he fell to the floor. She kicked him in the ribs, but he grabbed her ankle and dug his nails into her flesh. Fina reached into her waistband and pulled out her gun. She knelt down next to him and aimed it at his head. "I've shot one person tonight. You wanna make it two?"

Rand released her ankle and curled into the fetal position. He moaned and spat out a globule of blood and saliva. "You're supposed to protect the family!"

Fina stood up and kicked him in the balls. He mewled like a kitten.

"I *am* protecting the family, asshole. I'm protecting your daughter."

She left him bleeding on the rug.

Fina couldn't stomach the idea of going home to Nanny's, the wall of family photos peering down at her. Instead, she drove to Frank and Peg's house. She made her way down the bulkhead stairs and dropped down onto the edge of the bed in the basement bedroom. Thankfully, Fina had thought to stash the pain pills from the orthopedist in her bag, but she didn't want to take them on an empty stomach. She tiptoed upstairs and slipped into the kitchen.

A small light shone over the stove, and Peg was sitting at the table, her hands wrapped around a mug. Peg suffered from insomnia, and although Fina wasn't surprised to find her there sipping a cup of warm milk, she wasn't in the mood for conversation. But before she could retreat, Peg looked up, and their eyes met.

"Come sit down," Peg said. Then she got up from the table and left the room. Fina sat, and a few minutes later, Peg came back with a doctor's bag.

She didn't say anything as she tended to Fina's wounds. Peg had a deft, gentle touch, but she didn't stop when Fina flinched or voiced her pain. She and Fina were alike in many ways; they both got the job done even when it was nasty.

"This is just a stopgap," Peg told her as she threw out the soiled gauze. "You need to go to the hospital."

"I know." Fina watched as Peg poured another mug of milk and stuck it in the microwave. It dinged after a minute, and she placed it in front of Fina. "Did you wake up Frank?" Fina asked.

"No. He already knows you're hurt. One of us should get some sleep." She watched Fina, but her expression softened when she noticed Fina's eyes were welling up.

"What is it, sweetie?" she asked, and took her hand between her own.

Fina shook her head, but didn't speak. To do so would dislodge the lump in her throat and let loose a deluge. She quickly brushed off the tears that rolled down her cheeks. Peg pushed back her chair and wrapped her arms around her. She squeezed her, and Fina relaxed her muscles and sank into the embrace.

Fina woke up a few hours later in the basement bedroom and glanced at the clock. It was three A.M. She rolled onto

her back and stared at the ceiling. Five hours until she
was due at the police station.

People always talk about the wisdom of taking the time
to make a thoughtful decision, that well thought out courses
of action are generally the best, but Fina disagreed. If you
thought too carefully about doing something, you could
always find a reason not to. If you looked at the consequences, you'd be crazy to go through with it, but you'd
also be wrong not to.

Sleep eluded her, so she got up and ran a bath and
slipped into the steaming water. The walls of the bathroom were decorated with framed landscape photos that
Frank and Peg's oldest son had taken in Alaska. He'd
spent a semester at the University of Alaska Fairbanks and
was seduced by the breathtaking beauty and adventures
offered by the forty-ninth state. Fina knew that Frank and
Peg missed him terribly, but she also realized that his
absence cleared the way for her presence in their lives.

When she stepped out of the tub, her skin was red and
hot. She struggled to put her wet hair into a bun and then
pulled on her clothes. In the mirror, her bare face gazed
back at her. Her neck looked worse this morning; deep
purple bruises circled her flesh, and the burst blood vessels
in her eye were less discrete and blotchier than they'd
been the night before. She rummaged in the medicine
cabinet for a toothbrush and toothpaste. There was something amazingly restorative about brushing one's teeth.

"Fina," she heard Frank say when she opened the bathroom door and flicked off the light.

"Hi. Did I wake you?" she asked. He was sitting on
the end of the bed in sweatpants and a Bruins T-shirt.

Frank shrugged. "Something did. You headed to the hospital?"

"The police, then the hospital."

Frank nodded. "What's going on?"

Fina sank down next to him. She leaned forward with her elbows on her knees. "I . . . I'm . . ." She was silent.

"Wow. If you're speechless, it must be pretty awful."

"It is. Rand didn't kill Melanie, but he's done some terrible things." Fina didn't look at him. "I don't know what to do."

"Well, what are your options?"

"They all suck. That's the problem. If I give the police information, my father will go crazy, but if I don't, then someone else is going to get hurt—badly. And I actually like to cooperate with the cops when possible. I don't obstruct them just for the fun of it."

"So what if your father goes crazy?"

Fina gave him a pleading look. "Frank, come on. You know what. Family loyalty is everything to him, and he has a hand in every part of my life—work, my brothers, my niece and nephews."

"Maybe he shouldn't."

Fina was growing irritated. "Fine, but that's an issue for another day. I have to figure out what to do now."

Frank thought for a moment. "You can't control your father, but at the end of the day, you still have to live with yourself. You're fierce when it comes to protecting people, whether they're related to you or not." He gently tapped her cast. "That's what gets you into so much trouble. It's also one of the wonderful things about you."

"So you think I should tell the cops about Rand?"

"I think you should do whatever you think is right without worrying about damage control. Let the chips fall where they may. I know that's anathema to you Ludlows, but you're more than just a Ludlow. Sometimes you forget that."

They sat silently, the only sound a pipe humming in the ceiling.

"Do you have a thumb drive I can borrow? And your computer?" Fina asked.

"In the den."

Fina followed him upstairs, sat down in front of Frank's computer, and logged on to her laptop. She downloaded some documents onto the thumb drive, which she dropped into her bag next to a manila folder.

"You want me to go with you?" Frank asked.

"No, thanks. Milloy will do the honors."

26

~~~~~~~~

Frank went back to bed, and she speed-dialed Milloy.

"Really?" Milloy answered. "It's four A.M."

"I know, but it's important."

"What is it?"

"Can you meet me at police headquarters?"

"Because . . ."

"Because I could use a little moral support."

"Fine. I'll meet you there in half an hour."

On the steps of the station, Milloy's reaction to her appearance confirmed her assessment.

"You look like someone ran over you," he said, looking at her wide-eyed.

"I know. What can I say? I've had a busy twelve hours."

"How about a doctor after this?"

"How about this, my dad's office, a doctor, and then your place? I want to lie in bed and watch that show—you know the one, where they bring the baby home? The one where they realize they're in deep shit." Fina blinked and looked at Milloy. "Imagine that. I have a plan."

"You really are unwell."

Inside the station, Fina asked for Pitney and Menendez, and she and Milloy took a seat on a hard wooden bench to wait. The seating sent a clear message: *State your business and move along. Nothing to see here, folks.*

Fina was dozing on Milloy's shoulder when Cristian emerged from a locked area behind the front desk half an hour later and beckoned for them to follow him to a bank of elevators. If Fina had had the energy or the inclination, it might have been an awkward ride, but she didn't have either, and Cristian and Milloy seemed to be taking each other at face value; a cop and a member of the public, nothing more.

Pitney was waiting for them in an interview room. She was wearing purple trousers and a short-sleeve top with a starburst pattern. Her gun and badge were attached to her hip, and large gold hoops peeked out of her hair. Fina couldn't tell if her wan complexion was due to a lack of sleep or the unflattering glow of the fluorescent lights.

"How about you gentlemen leave us alone?" Pitney suggested.

Both Cristian and Milloy looked to Fina to gauge her comfort with the suggestion.

"That's fine," she said, and sat down across from Pitney.

"Do you want a soda?" Cristian asked before leaving.

"If you don't mind."

Cristian pulled the door closed, and the two women looked at each other.

"You look like I feel," Pitney said.

"You must feel like shit then. I do."

"You're early. When's your brother getting here?" Pitney asked.

"I told him to come in at nine A.M."

Pitney raised an eyebrow.

"I'm not going to make a statement about the shooting right now, but obviously, it was self-defense." She pointed at her neck.

"It appears that way," Pitney said, nodding slowly. "He's going to live, by the way."

Fina shrugged. "Well, at least he'll look like shit for a while."

Pitney folded her arms across her ample chest. "So why are you here so early without counsel?"

Fina reached into her bag, pulled out the folder and the thumb drive, and placed them on the table. "I know you think that all I do is obstruct and withhold." She slid the items toward Pitney.

"What's this?" Pitney asked.

"It's information that might interest you about Bev and Chester Duprey's criminal operations."

Pitney raised an eyebrow. "*Operations* would suggest more than just the escorts."

"How about online porn, underage girls, money laundering?"

Pitney began to flip through the file.

"I think if you dig enough, you should be able to connect Mark Lamont to Bev. I don't have any direct proof that he killed Melanie, but you can get him on something with this stuff. At the very least, you could nail him for coming after me."

There was a knock at the door, and Cristian reached into the room and handed Fina a cold can of diet soda. He backed out and closed the door. Fina held the can against her chest with her cast and tried to open it with her good hand. After a moment's struggle, Pitney looked up from the file and took hold of the can. She popped it open and gave it back to Fina.

"Why are you doing this? Giving me this stuff?" the lieutenant asked, her face screwed in concentration.

Fina took a long drink. "Mark Lamont and Bev Duprey should go to prison."

"But I can't necessarily keep Rand out of this," Pitney said.

Fina looked down at the table. She looked up at Pitney. "I can live with that."

"You can?"

"I've told you all along that despite my family's history of circling the wagons, I wasn't going to let my brother get away with murder."

Pitney peered at her. "But you're telling me he didn't murder his wife. I'd love to nail him for it, but if he didn't do it—"

"I don't think he should get a free pass. I've said that all along." Fina slumped in her seat. She was exhausted and feeling prickly. "Frankly, it's going to piss me off if you can't acknowledge that I've been true to my word."

Pitney put her hands up. "I can concede that, I just don't get it. I would have thought you'd be okay letting the prostitution slide."

Fina took another drink. "I would have been."

Pitney studied her for a moment. "So what aren't you telling me? What *can't* you let slide?"

Fina smiled. "I'm not telling you what I'm not telling you. Take the information and do with it what you will. It's a big fucking mess, though," Fina said, gesturing to the file and the thumb drive.

Fina stood and put her bag over her shoulder. "There's one name I want you to keep out of all this," Fina said. She stared at Pitney. The lieutenant waited. "Haley Ludlow, my niece. She's a minor." She cradled the soda between her cast and her chest and grasped the doorknob with her good hand. "Can you do that?"

Pitney twisted in her seat to look at her. "We always try to protect minors."

"Good. That's all I care about."

"I thought family was the most important thing to you," Pitney said.

"Exactly," Fina said, and left the room.

Milloy was waiting for her in a chair near the elevators.

"How'd it go?" he asked.

"Fine." Fina sighed deeply. "An armed cop is nothing compared to my father."

Milloy dropped Fina at Ludlow and Associates, and she took the elevator to the forty-eighth floor. At six A.M., the office was stirring with the night shift paralegals and secretaries wrapping up their day and a fresh crew trickling in.

"Mr. Ludlow isn't in yet," the front desk receptionist informed her.

"I'll wait," Fina said as she started down the hallway, not waiting for permission.

Carl's door was locked, but Fina had learned to open it ages ago and could achieve access with a bobby pin, let alone a lock pick. Once inside, she pressed a button to lower the automated blinds, grabbed a blanket from the closet, and curled up on her father's couch. She didn't sleep—the chatter and phones in the background kept her buoyed on a sea of consciousness—but it felt good to close her eyes and lie on the couch, demanding nothing of her body.

"Why's it dark in here, Shari? I didn't put the blinds down," Carl said when he strode into the room an hour later.

"I don't know, Mr. Ludlow." She hurried in after him and punched the button for the blinds.

"It's me, Dad," Fina said, covering her eyes from the bright light that flooded the room.

"I thought my door was locked," Carl said to Shari.

"It was," she protested.

"It was," Fina agreed.

Carl looked ready to rebuke Fina, but paused after he studied her appearance. "Get me some breakfast, would you?" he asked his secretary. He shrugged off his suit jacket and handed it to her.

"Ms. Ludlow?" Shari looked at Fina.

"Whatever he's having, but the full-fat version, please."

Carl walked around his desk and laid his briefcase on it. He pulled out a few file folders, shut it, and placed it on the floor. He took his phone out of his jacket pocket and put it on his blotter.

"I assume you have something to tell me?" he asked after settling into his chair.

Fina got up slowly and shuffled over to his desk. She lowered herself into the chair across from him.

"Are those new?" He pointed at the bruises encircling her neck.

"Yes."

"What happened?"

"Mark Lamont sicced a goon on me." Carl cocked an eyebrow. "The guy tried to kill me," Fina continued.

"Unsuccessfully."

"Because I shot him."

"Is he dead?"

"No, but not for lack of trying on my part."

Carl squinted at her. "Why would Mark Lamont want to kill you?"

"Because he killed Melanie, or had her killed."

"What?" Carl leaned forward and squeezed his hands together.

"It's complicated, Dad, and I'm tired."

"I need to know what's going on."

Fina let her head loll back and stared at the ceiling. "You're not going to like it."

"I don't like most of what you tell me."

"And you're not going to believe it," Fina added.

Carl tapped out a staccato rhythm with his fingertips. "Try me."

"The reason Melanie was so upset the day she died

was that she found out Haley has been working for Bev Duprey."

"Who?"

"I told you about her the other day when Pitney was here. The woman with the porn business. Ludlow and Associates won a suit against her son. Is this ringing any bells?"

"Get to the point, Fina."

"Haley has been working for Bev Duprey."

"What kind of work?"

"She's been working as an escort."

Carl guffawed. "That's absurd."

Fina ignored him and kept talking. "Bev Duprey runs an escort agency, and she was pissed at Rand because he sued her son, a doctor, and ruined his life—" Carl started to protest. "According to her," Fina finished. "To get back at Rand, she positioned herself so he'd use her escort service, and she also lured Haley into working for her."

"Haley would never do something like that, Fina. It's totally fucked up. She'd have to be fucked up to do it."

Fina let the words hang in the air between them and looked at her father.

A gentle tap on the door announced Shari's return. She carried a tray into the office and placed it on Carl's desk. She pulled the door closed behind her as she left.

The tray was made of a lustrous dark wood and had a delicate white cloth protecting its surface. It held two toasted bagels, two small ramekins of cream cheese, capers, red onion, diced hard-boiled egg, and thinly sliced smoked salmon. There were also coffee, a bowl of mixed fruit, a carafe of orange juice, two mugs, and two glasses. Carl and Fina glanced at the food, then back at each other.

"Melanie found out, confronted Rand, and eventually ended up at Bev Duprey's office. They had a confrontation, and it would have ended there, but Melanie had the misfortune of bumping into Bev's business partner, Mark Lamont."

"So he killed her?" Carl said incredulously.

"I don't know exactly what happened, but I imagine she threatened to expose his business connections, maybe tell you."

"You have proof that Mark did this?"

"I can connect Mark to the attempts on my life, and I can connect him to Bev Duprey. And the eyewitness he fed me just turned up dead."

Carl poured some coffee into a mug and took a sip. "I don't believe this business about Haley, and even if I did, we need to keep her out of it."

Fina scooted forward on her seat. "Do you want proof? Do you want me to find some of her johns? Get you pictures?"

"You're talking about my granddaughter!" Carl yelled, and flinched as coffee slopped over the sides of his cup.

"And my niece! Aren't you at all interested in figuring out what the hell's been going on? Don't you wonder what her parents were doing when they were supposed to be raising her?"

"Enough. We need to get control of this. And we need to keep Rand out of it."

Fina exhaled loudly. "That isn't going to be possible." She inched back in her seat. Her father wasn't violent, but she felt better out of arm's reach. Trust Allah, but tie up your camel.

"Why not?" Carl sipped his coffee.

"Because the police have information about Bev Duprey's businesses, and it's bound to come out."

"What kind of information?"

"Dad, she's going to be busted, and it's going to be a circus."

"Fuck."

Fina took a deep breath. "And some of the information the cops have came from my investigation," she said. She struggled to maintain eye contact with her father.

"What?"

"They would have found it on their own eventually."

Carl tilted his head. "Are you saying that I paid for the evidence that's going to destroy your brother?"

"In a manner of speaking, yes, but he's not going to be destroyed."

Carl sprang up and came out from behind his desk. He didn't touch her, but got right in her face. The memory of Rand's hot scotch breath was replaced by her father's coffee-laden exhalations.

"You are a goddamn traitor," he seethed.

"And your son is a fucking pervert. While you've been busy building your empire, he's been molesting your granddaughter," Fina spat. "You better hope that doesn't come out."

Carl's features froze for a second. Fina watched his eyes scan from side to side.

Fina stood and poked her finger at his chest. "I will lie and cheat and commit all kinds of felonies, and I will look the other way when you and my brothers go after good people, but I will *not* stand by and let Haley be abused."

Carl stared at her. His face was flushed, and beads of sweat dotted his brow.

"You pretend whatever you want, believe whatever you need to," Fina said, "but he doesn't get to be her father, not anymore, and if you get in my way, you'll regret it."

"Don't threaten me, Josefina. I'm your father."

"Exactly. You of all people should know what I'm capable of," she said, and threw open the door.

"I just heard you were here," Scotty said, breaking off his conversation with Shari when Fina strode out of the office. "I thought we were going to meet at the police station." He looked at his sister and father, trying to determine what bomb had just detonated.

"Let's go now," Fina said. "I'm exhausted."

Carl looked at her and slammed his door shut. Shari fussed with the papers on her desk, and Fina walked down the hallway with Scotty trailing behind.

The three hours Fina spent being questioned about the shooting were the most pleasant she'd ever spent in the presence of cops (with the exception of Cristian, of course). Pitney was firm, but even, and the usual verbal barbs that marked the women's interactions were absent. Scotty threw searching looks in Fina's direction, but she ignored him and just answered the questions. It was only in the final moments of the interview that Pitney alluded to their earlier meeting. Fina supposed that Pitney had done her a favor; she was going to have to tell Scotty, and now she had a jumping-off point for the conversation.

Like any lawyer worth his fee, Scotty waited until they

had privacy before laying into her. They'd taken one of the chauffeured town cars to the police headquarters, and Scotty directed the driver to a nearby gas station mini-mart, where he ordered him to park the car and take a walk.

"What is wrong with you?" Scotty erupted as soon as the door slammed closed behind the driver. "You never, ever talk to the cops without counsel!"

"I know that."

"So . . . ?" Scotty threw his hands up in frustration.

"I knew you would try to stop me."

"Of course I would!" Scotty groaned and rubbed his face with his hands. Fina watched him. "What did you tell them?"

"I gave them information about the madam, Bev Duprey, and her businesses. She's connected to Mark Lamont, and she's been out to get Rand from the beginning."

"By supplying his hookers?"

"By employing Haley as an escort."

The color drained from Scotty's face. "What?" he whispered.

Fina told him about the Duprey lawsuit, her meetings with Bev, Cristian's tip about Haley, and Haley's arrival at Bev's office the day before.

"Are you sure?" he asked.

"I'm sure. Obviously, Haley doesn't want anybody to know about it."

"Obviously." Scotty sagged into the car's leather seat. "But why? I know she gets mixed up in the wrong stuff, but this is crazy."

"Which brings us to the next part. The worst part," Fina said. She turned in her seat to face him.

Scotty looked at her expectantly.

"Rand molested her."

Scotty's face became animated, but in slow motion. Fina saw disbelief and disgust mingle with confusion.

"You're wrong."

"I'm not," Fina insisted. "Ever wonder why she's so jumpy around him? Why she locks her bedroom door at night? Why she was so pissed at her mother?"

"Enough, Fina. I don't want to know!"

"You think I do?! You think it's been easy uncovering this piece of information? Contemplating it?"

"Who else have you told?"

"Just you and Dad."

Scotty looked aghast. "You told Dad?"

"I had to. I had to tell him that some of the evidence on Bev might be trouble for Rand."

"What's the point of getting Rand in trouble with the cops?"

Fina glared at him. "Aside from the fact that he should be punished by somebody for something, now he won't have any leverage for a claim on Haley. She'll be free of him, and people will think good riddance."

"We could have handled it—in the family," Scotty grumbled.

Fina shook her head vigorously. "No, we couldn't have."

"Well, you didn't give us the chance, did you?"

"What would have happened, Scotty? Really? Explain

to me what the consequences would have been within the family?"

Scotty started to stammer.

"Exactly. Dad doesn't believe it. I'm not sure you do, either. Dad won't tell Mom, who definitely wouldn't believe it. Everyone would expect Haley to sit across the Thanksgiving table from Rand, pretending that everything's fine. Don't you understand that that would fuck her up all over again? One of them was going to be compromised, and I wasn't going to let it be Haley."

Scotty rubbed his hands together. There were bags under his eyes. He cleared his throat in an effort to reclaim his voice. "So what's next?"

"If you and Patty can't take Haley, I will."

"Oh, Fina." Scotty snorted. "The kid's suffered enough already."

Fina put her head in her hands. "God, I was hoping you'd say that." She looked up at her brother. "I can't believe how much this sucks."

"No kidding."

"Do you want me to talk to Patty?"

"No, I'll do it. What about Matthew?"

"I'll talk to him."

"And Mom?" Scotty asked.

The siblings looked at each other.

"That's a shit storm I have no interest in unleashing," Fina said.

"Agreed." Scotty reached over and squeezed Fina's good hand. "Are you okay?"

Fina smiled weakly. "I'll be fine."

Scotty studied her for a moment, then opened his

door and summoned the driver. Fina reached over and shut the air-conditioning vent that was blowing frigid air on her.

She was already numb.

Milloy retrieved her from the hospital where she underwent a battery of tests, the results of which were carefully recorded in the police report. Fina wanted to banish the Ludlows from her mind, if only for a little while, so he took her back to his place. They ordered in Chinese—fried egg rolls, wontons stuffed with pork, crispy orange beef, greasy lo mein, and shrimp Rangoon. Fina ate until she was stuffed, took a long shower, and collapsed into Milloy's bed. It was only three P.M., but she fell into a deep sleep, only to awaken the next day having barely moved.

Milloy crept out for an early morning massage appointment, and Fina dozed for a couple more hours. She took a shower and rummaged around in his closet. She found a T-shirt dress she'd left on an earlier occasion that Milloy had thoughtfully laundered. In his kitchen, there was a plastic sleeve of powdered doughnuts and a single can of diet soda sitting in the fridge. He really was a peach.

The ripe aroma wafting from her cast hampered the enjoyment of her meal, so Fina called a cab and paid the orthopedist a visit.

Bev longed for the days when you could accompany travelers all the way to the gate. She supposed the restriction contributed to better security, but she wanted to walk her son right to the plane and watch it push back, confident that he was secure within its confines.

"Mom?" Connor interrupted her daydreaming. "Do you want anything?"

"No, dear." She was sitting in a row of chairs welded together, while Connor waited in line to buy a fruit smoothie from a cart in the middle of the ticketing area. She gazed at him admiringly as he placed his order. He was a handsome boy—smart, too. And he was kind and tried to help people. She and Chester had done a good job.

He dropped down into the seat next to her and sucked on his straw. Bev glanced at her watch.

"I've got a few minutes, Mom. There's a flight to New York every hour, anyway."

"I know, but you don't want to be late for your first training session. Remind me again of the schedule?"

Connor rolled his eyes and smiled at his mother. "I've already told you."

"Well, tell me again."

"I have two days of training in New York, then a week in Germany, and then I'll get my assignment." Connor sipped his smoothie and gazed at the passengers moving by at various speeds. "I hope it's somewhere in Africa. In some of those countries, one out of every eight babies dies before his or her first birthday."

Bev shuddered. "That's terrible, Connor."

"I know, but it means we could have a huge impact. We could really make a difference."

It was that glimmer of excitement, of hope, that would have to sustain Bev in the coming days. She supposed that her life was over in many respects, but she'd orchestrated a rebirth of sorts for Connor, and that was all that mattered.

He took a last sip of his drink and pitched it into a trash bin. "I guess I should head down," he told Bev.

"Of course." Bev stood and followed him toward security.

"Mom." Connor turned to her. "Are you sure you're okay? Is everything okay?"

Bev took his shoulders in her hands. "Connor, I want you to get on that plane and have the time of your life. You concentrate on being a doctor. Your daddy and I will be just fine."

Connor looked at her. He didn't completely believe his mother, but he wanted to, desperately. "You'd tell me if you needed me to stay?"

"Of course, sugar," Bev said, pulling him into a tight embrace. She inhaled deeply and tried to memorize his scent. She released him and tapped him gently on the cheek. "Now, scoot. Those babies need you."

Connor grinned. "Love you, Mom."

"You too, pumpkin."

Bev stood at the barrier and watched Connor snake his way through the line and the various pieces of equipment used to establish his level of threat to his fellow man. He turned when he was at the farthest reach of the hallway and waved to her. Bev stood on her tiptoes as she waved back, and then he disappeared from sight.

She hurried through the ticketing area and walked briskly on the moving sidewalk back to the parking garage. Once in her car, she glanced at the clock and gave herself ten minutes to weep.

After eleven minutes, Bev opened her phone and dialed a number. "Mr. Serensen," she said evenly, "I believe we have an appointment with the police."

Fina briefly considered getting a neon-colored cast this time; maybe the flashy color would temper her predilection for getting in trouble. But really, who was she kidding? She opted for black. The doctor didn't even bother giving her a lecture about taking better care of herself; he, like so many others in her life, had given up.

She took a cab to Cambridge and visited a liquor store in Central Square, where she bought a hundred-dollar bottle of Irish whiskey. Her purchase garnered the envious stare of the patron in line next to her, who clutched a bottle of malt liquor that he paid for with crumpled singles.

Outside in the heat, she grasped the brown paper bag around the neck of the bottle and walked the few blocks to Cristian's place. Fina didn't hurry. She meandered, and after a few moments, recognized what she was feeling. It was relief. The misery of the days before hadn't been abolished, but things made sense to her, even if she didn't understand them. She'd uncovered the who, what, where, and how of the past few weeks, if not the why. Fina knew better than most people that the mysteries we solve are far fewer than those we don't.

Cristian buzzed her up, and she joined him on the back porch, where he was nursing a beer.

"Here," she said as she handed him the paper bag. "A peace offering."

He took the bag. "I think you made that yesterday

morning at the station." He reached in and pulled out the bottle. He whistled. "Very nice. Thanks."

"You're welcome. I don't want you to think that I take you for granted."

Cristian put the whiskey on the kitchen counter and pulled a beer out of the fridge for her. He popped the top off and handed her the sweating bottle.

"How'd all that family business go?" he asked after taking a swig of his own beer.

"It went."

"Can't imagine they were happy you gave us those files."

"That's an understatement." Fina sipped her beer. "I asked Pitney to keep Haley out of it, whatever 'it' ends up being."

"She told me."

"It's important, Cristian. She's been through a lot. Worse than you can imagine."

Cristian gazed at her. "I'm a cop, remember? I can imagine." He moved his plastic chair closer to hers. "I'll do everything I can to protect her."

"Thanks."

"You're a good aunt."

"Thanks," Fina said, and she sipped her beer. "Thanks."

27

Fina took a week off to recuperate. She slept, ate, watched bad TV. She and Milloy spent a day on the North Shore eating fried clams and lounging under a lighthouse watching sailboats slice through the waves. She went to *Disney on Ice* with Cristian and Matteo and was aghast at the thought that she might have missed it. Matteo's genuine delight and the sight of women skating in hoopskirts were so captivating, she forgot her own troubles for a bit. After a few days, she felt sated and rested, like a regular human being. For the first time in weeks, she stopped accumulating injuries.

She tried to avoid the news, but snippets of information crept into her consciousness. Bev Duprey was arrested on various charges ranging from prostitution to money laundering. Mark was picked up on fraud charges related to his businesses and was under suspicion for Melanie's murder. His hired guns made court appearances for their attempts on Fina's life. Rand's name was floating around the stories, but for now, he didn't face any charges, just a cloud of suspicion and salacious gossip.

Fina visited Scotty and Patty's house each day to check on Haley. Scotty tried to engage Fina in discussions about the legal cases, but she brushed aside his attempts. She didn't want to devote any more psychic energy to it. She was willing to talk about Rand, since he was family, not business, but Scotty didn't mention their brother. Just as she suspected, it was a subject no one cared to discuss or even acknowledge.

Fina was starting to contemplate her future at the firm when Matthew left her a message requesting her presence at the club for lunch. After deleting the message, Fina breathed a sigh of relief. She didn't know if Rand would be there, but if she was being summoned to the club, she still had a spot in the family, even if she had mixed feelings about the position.

The next day, Fina and Milloy drove into the club parking lot. When Milloy reached for the door handle, she stopped him with her casted arm. "Not yet," she said.

He started the car again and fiddled with the radio. Fina depressed the button to roll down her window; she could hear laughter and shouting drifting out from the pool area. She looked at the other cars in the parking lot. Her father's car was parked a few spaces away, as were Matthew's and Patty's. She searched, but didn't see Rand's or Scotty's. Elaine's Mercedes sedan was in the row closest to the road, greedily taking one and a half parking spaces. How hard was it to park between the lines? Really?

Fina drummed her fingers on the armrest and contemplated getting out of the car. A breeze blew through the open windows, providing a moment of relief from the cloying humidity.

"Are you coming in?" Scotty appeared at her window.

"I didn't see your car." Fina craned her neck.

"Hey, Milloy," Scotty said, and bent down so he was eye level with his sister. "It's back there." He motioned toward the far end of the lot. "What are you waiting for?"

"I'm not sure. Am I really welcome?"

Scotty shrugged. "Dad is totally pissed, but that's no surprise." He tapped his fingers on the door frame.

"And Rand?"

"He's opted out of this gathering."

Fina nodded. "Haley's here though, right?"

"Yup."

Fina looked at Milloy. "You guys go ahead," Fina said. "I'll be right there."

Milloy raised his eyebrow in question, and Fina nodded. "Seriously, you can be the warm-up act."

He got out and left the car running.

"Don't wait too long or Mom will order you a salad," Scotty said, and the two men wandered away from the car.

Fina sat and listened to the pop station that Milloy had settled on. The repetitive bass line was irritating, so she reached over and turned off the radio.

"Fina?"

She looked out the window. "Dr. Murray. Hi."

He had on khakis and a button-down shirt. A large canvas bag brimming with towels was in his left hand,

and his right held a child's blow-up pool toy. "Everything okay?"

"Eh. You know."

Dr. Murray looked over at his family. "I'll catch up," he said to them, and watched them wander off in the direction of the pool.

"I don't want to keep you from your family."

"A few minutes won't make a difference. Anyway, you're saving me from the daily sunscreen debacle."

Fina smiled.

"Can I help in any way?" he asked.

"I'm just trying to screw up my courage." She wiped a strand of hair away from her damp face. "I think I'm in big trouble."

"Really?"

"Yup."

"I hope you don't mind my saying so, but in our short acquaintance, you haven't struck me as someone who worries terribly about getting into trouble."

Fina looked at him. His face was washed with a gentle smile.

"That is true. I don't have much trouble breaking the law. But it's my family this time, not the law."

"Ah. Families have laws, too, you know."

Fina didn't say anything.

"And people break them all the time," Dr. Murray said.

"Not in my family, they don't."

Dr. Murray considered her for a moment. "Are you sure about that?"

Fina stared out the windshield. A few cars down, two

kids were wrestling while their mother or nanny struggled to pull belongings out of the back of the luxury SUV. They were making a lot of noise, and from this distance, Fina couldn't tell if they were laughing or fighting.

She sat for a moment and tried to tune out her anxiety and aches and pains. Her stomach growled.

"I'm hungry," she observed after a minute, and closed her window. She reached for the keys, pulled them out of the ignition, and climbed out of the car.

"Here, let me take that." She offered a hand to Dr. Murray, and he passed her the blow-up toy, a flotation device fashioned in the shape of a frog.

They started toward the pool together.

~~~~~~~~~~

Turn the page for a sneak peek at
Ingrid Thoft's new novel

IDENTITY

Coming soon from Putnam

~~~~~~~~~~

Blood trickled out of her nostril onto her upper lip. It tasted metallic when the tip of her tongue instinctively swiped at it.

"Really?" Fina asked.

"Oh my God. I can't believe I just did that." Haley stood rooted to the floor, her gloved hands limp at her sides.

Fina freed her hand from the sweaty glove and grabbed a towel to blot her nose. "At least we know you can get in touch with your inner anger."

"Aunt Fina, I'm so sorry." Haley wrestled off her gloves and followed Fina over to a bench at the edge of the gym. "Should I get some ice or something?"

Fina gingerly palpated her nose with her fingertips. "It isn't broken."

Haley leaned back against the exposed brick wall. "I'm so sorry." Her niece looked genuinely distressed.

Fina swatted at her with the towel. "I'm fine. You think one errant punch is going to do me in?"

"I guess not."

"Hey, you've thrown your first punch and drawn blood. I'm proud of you, sweetie. You're a true Ludlow now."

Haley looked doubtful. "If you say so."

"How about a clean towel? That would help," Fina said.

Haley made a beeline for the desk near the front door of the small bare-bones gym. Fina didn't frequent the establishment, but it was in her neighborhood, and the signs for self-defense and kickboxing classes had piqued her curiosity. Her brothers had taught her to fight, and she didn't understand why it wasn't an equally valued skill set for girls and young women. Certainly it was more useful than sewing a button onto a shirt.

At the desk an older gentleman with cauliflower for ears handed Haley a fresh towel. Fina was dabbing at her nostril with it when her phone rang.

"Yes, Father?" she said when she answered.

"What are you doing?" Carl asked.

"Teaching your granddaughter essential life skills."

The line was silent for a moment. "I'm not sure I like the sound of that."

"Trust me, I'm doing you a favor."

"Well, wrap it up. I need you in the office."

"What's going on?"

The phone went dead.

Ahh. Another satisfying father-daughter interaction.

❊

Fina Ludlow was the private investigator at the family law firm. Ignoring her boss—her father, Carl—wasn't an option. She walked Haley to the T, then grabbed a quick shower at home, where she pulled on some jeans and a fitted T-shirt and put her hair in a bun. When actively working a case, Fina opted for sensible shoes, but not knowing the nature of the summons, she grabbed a pair of black strappy sandals. It was the end of August, and the Boston weather couldn't make up its mind: Summer? Fall? Summer? Fall? It had settled somewhere in between; cool breezes alternating with humid, still air.

Carl was sitting behind his desk when Fina arrived, a remote control pointed at the TV. A fifty-five-inch version of her father stared back at them, urging them to call the 800 number at the bottom of the screen.

"You make a habit of watching your own commercials?" Fina asked.

"I approve everything before it airs."

As a teenager, Fina had been embarrassed by the television ads hawking Carl's talents as a personal injury attorney. It was bad enough that her friends saw them between episodes of *21 Jump Street* and *Cheers*, but a family trip to San Diego revealed the true extent of her father's reach; his ads ran nationwide. People she'd never met had formed a likely negative opinion of her family. When Fina and her brothers complained about the notoriety, Carl reminded them that there would be no fancy trips or designer jeans without the ads, which was true, but Fina couldn't help but notice that her classmates got the same spoils from parents performing arthroscopic surgery and building skyscrapers downtown. Over the years, though, Fina grew to understand that the family firm had its redeeming qualities. They were the top dogs who represented the underdogs. Sometimes, Ludlow and Associates was the only option for poor souls down on their luck.

Carl gestured at his doppelgänger onscreen. "That tie is bothering me."

Fina shrugged. "Looks fine to me."

"Not that I should be taking style advice from you," Carl commented, hitting pause, freezing himself. "You couldn't bother to dress up a little?"

"For what? You wouldn't tell me what's going on."

"We have a potential client. She'll be here any minute."

"Who is it?"

"Renata Sanchez."

"Renata." She contemplated the name for a moment. "Renata from the Ramirez case?"

"That's the one."

Renata Sanchez had been a peripheral witness in a lawsuit a few years earlier. Fina had done some basic background on her and a phone interview, though they'd never met in person. She was the director of the Urban Housing Collaborative, an organization dedicated to addressing the housing challenges of the poor. She was a heroine or a pain in the ass, depending on whom you asked, and she didn't shy away from controversy.

Fina walked over to the bar tucked into the corner of the office. She pulled out a cold diet soda.

"That stuff is crap, you know," Carl commented.

"You think?" Fina asked, eyeballing the bottles of booze on the bar. Carl took good care of himself—his broad shoulders and flat stomach belied his age—but he had a selective memory when it came to his own vices.

Carl ignored her and clicked his mouse. Fina popped open the can and sat down across from him. She took a sip.

"So, tell me about Renata." Fina put her soda on the desk and rocked onto the back legs of the chair. The furniture in Carl's office was high-end and contemporary. Glass and leather dominated and symbolized his approach to the law: Carl was interested in breaking new ground, not upholding the traditions passed down through generations. The space was dotted with sports memorabilia and black-and-white photographs of Boston's twenty-first-century landscape. An antique map of Boston Harbor would never adorn these walls.

"You break it, you buy it," Carl said, gesturing at the precarious tilt of his daughter's chair.

Fina rolled her eyes. "The case?"

"It's a doozy." He brushed the lapel of his jacket. "She wants to sue the cryobank that provided the sperm for her kid."

"Why? Is there something wrong with the kid?"

"No. She thinks she and her daughter have a right to know the sperm donor's identity, despite signing off on an anonymous donation seventeen years ago."

Fina gently squeezed her nose. "There's no way she can win."

"Maybe not."

"So why are we even meeting with her?"

"I want to see how it plays out."

"Sounds like a waste of time to me." Fina dropped the front chair legs back to the floor.

"Let me worry about that." Carl narrowed his gaze. "Is that blood?"

"What?" Fina reached up to her nose and dabbed at a lone drop that had materialized. "Damn. I thought I stopped it." She rummaged in her bag for a tissue and blotted her nostril.

"Very classy," Carl remarked.

"Ms. Sanchez is here," Carl's assistant, Shari, said, poking her head into the office before Fina could respond.

Carl nodded and straightened his tie. Shari returned with a woman who couldn't have topped five feet two, her short stature only reinforced by her bottom-heavy physique. She had short wavy hair that was rich dark brown and skin the color of light brown sugar. Her pantsuit was black and looked inexpensive, but any lack of sartorial prowess was compensated for by her posture. She stood erect and looked Carl in the eye when he got up and shook her hand.

"Carl," she said.

"Renata. This is my daughter, Fina." Fina stood and offered her hand. Renata's grip was beyond firm, but short of crushing. It was clear this woman meant business.

Carl gestured to the empty seat next to Fina. "Please have a seat. Did Shari offer you something to drink?"

"Yes. She's bringing me coffee."

They sat, and Carl leaned back in his chair. "Fina is the firm's private investigator. As I mentioned on the phone, I think she could play a role in your case."

Renata placed a beat-up leather tote bag at her feet and

turned in her chair to face Fina. "I assume your father has given you the details?" She wore a thick gold ring on her right index finger. Her hands were small and doughy, almost like a child's.

Fina glanced at Carl. "Yes, but I'd like to hear it from you."

Renata pursed her lips in annoyance.

"I know it may seem like a waste of time," Fina said, "but there are things I'll hear in the telling that a third party just can't convey."

Renata placed her hands on the arms of the chair and crossed her legs. "Fine. I want to sue Heritage Cryobank."

"Okay." Fina took a sip of her drink. "And why do you want to do that?"

"To learn the identity of the sperm donor I used to conceive my eldest child."

"Why?" Fina asked after a moment.

Renata looked puzzled. "What do you mean *why?*"

Shari tapped on the door and entered bearing a tray. She set a small French press coffeepot and the necessary accoutrements on the corner of Carl's desk. She depressed the lever and then poured a cup for Renata before taking her leave. You'd think Carl were Queen Elizabeth II the way she backed out of the room.

"Why do you want to determine the donor's identity?" Fina asked. "Presumably you went into the arrangement satisfied that he would remain anonymous."

Renata stirred a spoonful of sugar into the hot liquid and added a liberal splash of cream. Fina waited as patiently as a Ludlow could and took comfort knowing that however eager she was to get things moving, her father was even more so.

"Things have changed."

"What things? Unfortunately, changing your mind isn't going to cut it in court."

"I signed those papers seventeen years ago. There was no other way for me to start a family, and I was naïve. I didn't think the identity of Rosie's father mattered, but it does. It's a fundamental human right to know where you come from."

"Not everyone would agree," Carl said.

Renata took a tentative sip and placed the china cup back onto its saucer. "Did you know that they recently outlawed anonymous sperm donations in British Columbia? They ruled that keeping that information secret is unconstitutional."

"So, what now?" Fina asked. "They're opening all those files for the world to see, despite the promise of confidentiality?"

Renata sniffed. "No, but they've acknowledged it's wrong."

"That's Canada." Carl looked unimpressed. "This is the United States."

"And there are lots of kids who don't know their biological parents because of adoption or abandonment or being the product of an affair," Fina noted. "Not knowing a parent's identity doesn't doom them for life."

"You've done research on the matter?" Renata asked testily.

"Anecdotal research," Fina said, and took a long drink, struggling to swallow her annoyance. "I interact with a diverse population in my line of work."

"If you're not interested in the case," Renata said, rotating the coffee cup on the saucer, "I'm sure I can find someone who is."

"That's not what we're saying," Carl assured her, "but as Fina said, changing your mind isn't the basis for setting new precedence."

Renata leaned forward in her chair. "Does a day go by that you two don't consider your blood connection?" Her stare volleyed between father and daughter.

Fina and Carl both squirmed.

"Our connection is hard to ignore," Fina said after an awkward pause.

"Exactly. Whatever the nature of your relationship, it's a vital part of your identities. I'm only asking that my daughter be given the same basic information. Times have changed. A piece of paper shouldn't stand in the way of progress."

Fina raised an eyebrow in her father's direction. Renata would have to be kept on a tight leash if they were going to take on her crusade.

"I've told Renata that the only legal precedence for breaking the contract is in the case of medical necessity," Carl said.

"Which doesn't exist in this case?"

"Correct," Carl said.

"But what if something were to happen to me?" Renata asked. "My daughter would be left with virtually no blood relatives. And what if she has a medical condition that we don't even know about? Medical testing has made leaps and bounds in the last two decades."

Fina touched her nose. "I don't know. It still sounds like a reach to me. Dad?"

"Renata, the chances of winning this case are practically nonexistent."

"That's what they said about the low-income housing the Collaborative built in Dorchester. They said it couldn't be done, that we would drown in red tape. One hundred and fifty families moved in last year."

"Be that as it may, we're not talking about politics," Carl said. "We're talking about the law. You could fight a long, public battle and still end up with nothing to show for it."

She straightened up in her chair. "That's a chance I'm willing to take."

Carl drummed his fingers on his leather blotter. "We can approach it from two angles," he said after a moment of contemplation. "We can research the feasibility of filing a suit against the cryobank on the basis that maintaining the donor's anonymity is a violation of Rosie's human rights, and in the meantime, Fina can figure out the donor's identity, which might give us leverage."

Fina looked at Renata. "Why don't I just try to find out his identity? It could be done under the radar with the same result as a messy lawsuit."

Renata waved Fina's suggestion away with a flick of her wrist. "It wouldn't be the same result. As I've said, this isn't just about my daughter's father; it's a human rights issue. All cryokids have a right to know."

"How does your daughter feel about this?" Fina asked, draining her drink.

Renata licked her lips before speaking. "She understands that I think it's important."

Fina tilted her head. "Okay, but what does *she* think?"

Renata fiddled with the ring on her finger. "She's fine with it."

"Renata, anything you say is protected by privilege, but I can't be effective if I'm operating in the dark." Fina looked at Carl. He nodded ever so slightly. "What does your daughter really think?"

Renata met Fina's gaze. "She's reluctant, but Rosie's always been very independent."

Fina gaped at her. "We can't take this on if Rosie isn't on board."

"Why not?" Renata said. "She's seventeen. She's a minor."

"Because it's unethical, and frankly, it's creepy."

"Excuse me?" Renata peered at her. "How is my fighting for her rights creepy?"

"Because you're talking about digging around in *her* life, into *her* personal information. She may be a minor, but she's old enough to decide if she wants to pursue this."

Carl held up his hand to silence the women. "Fina and I will discuss this further, Renata. Did you bring the documents I requested?"

Fina opened her mouth to speak, but Carl shot her a warning look.

Renata reached into her tote bag and pulled out a dog-eared manila folder. "Here are copies of the relevant paperwork. I have more in deep storage."

Fina took the file and mustered up a sour smile. "Great. Thanks."

Carl walked Renata out of his office. When he returned a moment later, Fina was flipping through the file.

"You're kidding, right? Even Mom wouldn't do something this insane." Fina and her mother, Elaine, had a contentious relationship that was fraught with resentments and grievances. Fina seemed to perpetually disappoint her mother, which tapped into her inner adolescent. Annoying Elaine had developed into a hobby of sorts.

"You heard her." Carl settled back into his leather chair. "It's a human rights issue."

"That's bullshit. There's no way the cryobank is going to give up the name, and Rosie will be in the news regardless. The PR is going to be a nightmare."

"That's not our problem."

Fina closed the file. "I don't like this."

Carl studied something on his computer screen. "I don't pay you to like things. You find out who this guy is, and I'll worry about the lawsuit."

"I don't know, Dad."

His gaze fell on her. "What? You're not interested in the work I'm giving you? You're done with the firm, too, not just the family?"

Fina felt the blood creep up her neck. She'd broken ranks with Carl during her last case, and he wasn't going to let her forget it. "I'm not done with the family or the firm. Stop being so dramatic."

He glared at her. "Then get on with it."

Fina slipped the folder into her bag and stood. "Why are you taking this on? There's no money to be made."

Carl shrugged. "I have a hunch. I think sperm banks are the next big thing. Just you wait."

Of course.

Carl smelled blood in the water and just had to swim closer.